C000062944

Chains
Across the
River

ADDITIONAL PRAISE FOR
CHAINS ACROSS THE RIVER

"A crowded tapestry of a novel, reconstructing a critical moment in American Revolutionary history."

—Marie Winn, author of *The Plug-in Drug, Red-tails in Love,* and
Central Park in the Dark

"*Chains Across the River* is a wonderful fabrication of the events surrounding Thomas Machin's life and his amazing feats of putting chains across the Hudson River to keep the British at bay. Bevis Longstreth expertly uses his vivid imagination to fill in details too rich for history to possibly tell. I recommend this book for anyone with an interest in our revolutionary war history who wonders what it might have been like to be a fly on the wall for these exploits."

—Paul Banks, Interpretive Program Assistant, Washington's
Headquarters State Historic Site, Newburgh, NY

"Through Bevis Longstreth's *Chains Across the River*, readers immediately find themselves immersed in the excitement, stress, panic, and jubilee that embodies the American Revolutionary period. Longstreth masterfully brings to life key individuals of the Revolution including, George Washington, Henry Knox, Tom Machin, George Clinton, and Israel Putnam, just to name a few. Detailed historical accounts, told through the experiences of Machin and others, transport the reader to the late 1700s—its sights, smells, and undercurrent of ever present tensions— in this page-turning novel with many chapters set in the famed (and feared) Hudson Highlands."

—Cassie Ward, Director, Putnam Historical Museum

"In his latest novel, *Chains Across the River*, Bevis Longstreth has introduced readers to an almost forgotten part of the American Revolution—the attempt to build a chain across the Hudson River to block the British fleet's access to the north. Thomas Machin, a British engineer who deserted from the British to join the Americans, was the man put in charge of the project and Longstreth has set him at the center of a fascinating tale of war, love and betrayal as America fought to be free."

—Susan Carey, Book Critic and Editor

"Who knew that the American Revolution was so full of engineering challenges? Bevis Longstreth's resourceful hero is a civil engineer and a man of many feats, the greatest of which is stretching chains across the Hudson to keep a British armada out. Longstreth's novel is as lively as it is instructive."

—Frances Taliaferro

"Historical fiction at its best. Rooted in a meticulously researched recounting of the Revolutionary War as it unfolded along the Hudson River, *Chains Across the River*, provides an intimate and compelling look at the lived experiences of both British Loyalists and American Revolutionaries living in towns along the river's banks.

The stakes were high with both sides deeming control of the river an essential determinant of the war's final victor. Desperate to stop the British onslaught, General Washington bet on the outlandish proposal of a British deserter turned engineer who proposed a massive chain stretched across the Hudson to block the British Navy from sending its formidable armada upstream to cut off East from West. But the river and the terrain along its banks were treacherous, posing immense challenges to the chain's builders and to those intent on foiling its deployment. Intrigue prevails and tension mounts as the British attack upstream only to retreat and gather a larger force the following Spring. Time is of the essence as neighbors plot to foil or aid the chain's chief builder's plans.

Artfully interweaving protagonists, places and proceedings, Bevis Longstreth immerses the reader in a gripping and enthralling saga about a little known yet decisive moment in American history."

—Gordon Berlin, Research Professor
Georgetown University Past President MDRC

Chains Across the River

A Novel of the American Revolution

Bevis Longstreth

**HONEYCOMB
PUBLISHERS**

New York, New York

Chains Across the River: A Novel of the American Revolution
Copyright © 2021 by Bevis Longstreth
Honeycomb Publishers

All rights reserved. No part of this book may be reproduced or transmitted
in any form without the written permission from the publisher.

First Edition 2021

Cover and interior paintings by Noah Saterstrom
Book jacket design and interior formatting by Golden Ratio Book Design

This is a work of fiction. All of the characters, organizations, and events
portrayed in this novel either are products of the author's imagination or are
used fictitiously.

ISBN: 978-0-578-75050-7

Printed in the United States of America

1

LONDON BOOK-STORE

"Two months and more we've been camped on the Common, do you realize that, Sam my friend." Private Tom Machin leaned across his cot and gave his bunkmate a poke. "When do we get to sleep under rafters and roof, I ask you, Sam Minnie?"

The sky was turning, brightening in the east, where the odors of salt, seaweed and rotting fish assured even the least geographically inclined redcoat of the ocean's presence.

"Like as not, another one for the dung heap of failed promises from the leaders of our woebegone 23rd."

"And what a giant pile it is. They keep one, though. Complain once, ten lashes with the cat. Twice and it's a hundred. 'Exponential', we engineers call it."

"Cut the scum, Tom, you're taking on airs again. You're a private, just like the rest of us."

"But I…"

Cut it, I say. Don't make a fart's sound in Hell that you was a vol… un… teer."

Benjamin Yeoman burst into the tent. "You won't believe this, Michael Kemp tried to desert last night. They caught him couple of hours ago. No hanging this time, the Sarge told me. Hangings are weakening the regiment. So, they will 'reduce' the punishment to 1,000 lashes, 250 a week. We parade to witness."

"So, after 1,000 lashes, rotten food and miserable shelter, the British soldier's expected to fight fiercely for King George—but against his own people?" Tom was whispering, his voice soaked in sarcasm.

"After so much of the cat, Mike won't walk much less fight. Cause more desertions," said Sam, whose brevity and exactitude of expression never ceased to amaze Private Machin, whose more formal education had imparted neither skill. "He's one of those soldiers snatched from the streets of London. Most likely to desert."

"You're right. It's the way they deal with us "lower sorts." And they're treating all of America the same: cow them into submission and obedience by oppressive laws, like the Townshend and Stamp, and now the Fishery Act."

"Doing what?" Though known for an ear to the ground, Ben hadn't heard about this.

"It forbids trade with Britain, Ireland and the West Indies. But there's more. Bans them from Newfoundland fisheries."

"Oh, no. That's beyond harsh, Tom. Brutal! Cruel, like taking the harp from the Irish. Newfoundland is their 'breadbasket', for Christ sake. They wouldn't do that. Where do you hear this stuff?"

"The London Book-Store," Tom said, flashing a knowing grin.

"I've seen it," Sam said. "Not far from here. Ben, I'll take you there if you like. Lots of military books. Our officers go there. Proprietor a big friendly type; uncommonly curious. Gossip seeps out."

"Fall in! Kit and weapon for one day's march. Carry haversacks, bread and cheese." The Sergeant's call knifed through the still of sunrise. Machin and his mates scrambled to parade. A bright waning moon was descending in the west. They were in one of 16 companies of foot—some 1200 redcoats in all—under the command of Earl Percy. They had been ordered to Lexington and Concord in support of 700 who had preceded them overnight, having been ferried across Boston Harbor, landed at Lechmere's Point and marched first to Lexington and then to Concord, there to seize military stores reported to have been assembled for the Provincial Congress.

Private Machin was in the lead company as they approached Lexington to the scrambled sound of church bells, drums and shooting. At the village green they met the redcoats who had gone before, now retreating in shocking disarray, many wounded among them, being assailed by Patriots on either side and behind. A real fire-fight, Machin realized, his first and different from those he had read about. Redcoats were packed together, straining to move as a giant turtle might when terrified, bending every muscle to move faster but limited by the weight and tightness of their cluster. The enemy was all but invisible, imagined mainly by the smoke and sound of its weapons, and the splattering impact of its bullets. Even for those capable of returning fire, few targets of opportunity were on offer from the Patriots.

The rescue column spread out, knelled and, more to scare than to harm the well-hidden Patriots, discharged their muskets. They then turned around to join the retreating redcoats as they continued their bedraggled quick-step to Boston. They were exhausted from the day's travail: a 20-mile march to Concord, ending in a brutal fire-fight as unexpected as it was bloody, and then the retreat to Lexington Green.

No redcoat could comprehend what had happened. All had been tumult and confusion. Where the sniveling cowards from the militia, where the rude rabble of Patriots guaranteed to run from a disciplined line of British regulars. Where that much ridiculed, motley crew of Yankee Doodles. That race of convicts, as the lexicographer Samuel Johnson labeled them, who ought to be thankful for anything we allow them, short of hanging?

In all, Private Machin learned upon reaching Charleston peninsula and the protective shield of the British fleet, the brutal running gun battle all the way to the Cambridge bridge resulted in 73 British killed, 174 wounded and 26 missing. He heard Patriot losses were far less. He saw the number of Patriots growing instead of shrinking along the path of retreat to Boston. A bloody mess for the British, boding ill for future days.

For Private Machin, with almost too much time to think during the retreat to Boston, he questioned his decision to volunteer. Instead of being discharged when the Yankee uprising was quickly quelled, Machin felt trapped in the jaws of a beastly war, exposed to personal dangers he reckoned not and forced to fight for the wrong side. He did not imagine himself a brave man. He had made a mistake and the pain of its consequences infected him, mind, body and soul.

Machin realized that the Yankees, attacked in their villages, would fight desperately. Loyalty to crown was swift to dissolve in the steadfast waters of loyalty to home. This insight was entirely new to Machin, and he thought, perhaps new to the entire British Army. It came on the wind of a simple question he asked himself: In their shoes, wouldn't he do the same?

* * * * *

It was April 20, 1775, the day after Lexington and Concord wrote their names in blood across the pages of history. Private Machin took Ben Yeoman to Henry Knox's bookstore next to the sign of the Three Kings in Cornhill. Knox had shrewdly named his shop the "London Book-Store," seeking to trade on the educated Bostonian's need to feel connected to the empire and its capital city. From the start, Knox enjoyed the patronage not only of Whigs and members of the Sons of Liberty, but Crown officials, American Tories and British officers. He had created, in fact, a lounge fashionable both morning and afternoon. Beyond a large inventory of books, the shop offered stationery, quills, flutes, reading glasses and a variety of specialty items intended to intrigue and delight the intellectual classes, whether British or Bostonian.

Tom introduced his mate to the large and rotund proprietor, who, naturally enough, appeared distracted by the buzz in his shop. He seemed to be trying to hear and even participate in each of several animated conversations among his patrons, all focused on Lex-Con, as it was called. However, when he learned that Tom and Ben had seen action in yesterday's battles, he brought his considerable powers of concentration to bear solely on them. Tom knew Knox had long been hostile to the British occupation, and the hostility was waxing. For his part, Ben had picked up from loose Regimental talk that

Knox was considered a rebel important enough to be watched and even prevented from leaving Boston without permission.

What Ben didn't know was that Knox had on a couple of occasions urged Tom to defect to the Yankee cause. Over many months, Knox had learned of Tom's training and experience as an engineer, and of his knowledge and interest in artillery. It was an interest they shared, one that created a bond beyond the technicalities they discussed.

* * * * *

They had reached across an ocean of differences to find friendship fast after Private Machin first entered the bookstore upon arriving in Boston from New York in 1774.

"You look wobbly from the passage, mate. What brings you here?"

"I'm Private Tom Machin, and you, I presume, are Mr. Knox. You got my arrival right. A rough landing."

"Indeed. Harbor salt still cakes your face."

Henry Knox could size up a stranger with uncommon insight and accuracy. Observing the redcoat before him, he saw a man uncomfortable in a private's uniform, indeed, any uniform, a man immodest in accomplishment but hesitant to show it. He was medium sized, standing straight as if to make himself taller, ruddy of complexion and well shaved except for the hair clusters emerging from nose and ears, indicating he didn't care or have time for, or access to, a mirror. His forehead was high and prominent, with sandy hair spilling down almost to his thin eyebrows. His eyes were deep-set and dark, without even the hint of a twinkle. He had an aquiline nose bigger than an artist seeking balance would have placed on his face, which was of modest size though sharply etched, featuring high cheek bones and a prominent chin. Knox figured him to be of Celtic stock with a minor strain from the days of Roman occupation. In all, Knox saw in Machin not a noticeably handsome man, but one of intelligence. A man of interest.

"What can I do for you?" Henry Knox put the question again, openly, flashing a broad smile from his remarkably large face.

"I must tell you, I believe you're the first redcoat from non-officer ranks to step foot in this place—my "temple" I like to call it. I place you from Suffolk or Staffordshire. Am I close? Tell me what did you do before being pressed into the British Army?"

"Mr. Knox, can we talk privately; that is, will you keep what I say to yourself? I mean can I trust you? I know that sounds stupid and naïve, but I…."

"I understand. You're seeking a friend outside the Army. Someone reliable. Someone with whom you can talk freely. You've found him."

The anxiety on Tom's face melted away.

"I volunteered. Leek, Staffordshire. February 17, 1773. Hard to forget that day. I'm an engineer by training and experienced in building things. I volunteered to get to America. Was told that, except for a tiny cabal of rebels, the Americans loved their King and country. There would be no real war, because the Americans wouldn't fight. We'd be discharged within a month or two of arrival. It all sounded reasonable. But I was naïve in more ways than one. I thought the Army would recognize my experience and position me to use my skills. Especially in artillery. No dice. Not a flicker of interest in who I was or where I'd been. And the Army is a one-way street. Walking in, so easy. Walking out, impossible. So, here I am, fighting in a quarrel I have no stomach for."

"Come over here. There's a bookshelf full of books I bet you'd like. All about artillery.

A few weeks passed before Private Machin returned to the London Bookstore. He arrived late in the day, just as Henry Knox was preparing to close.

"Greetings, Tom. I've been thinking of you and your story. Let's rehearse it again, if you don't mind. You said you joined the Army to get to America. You didn't tell me why?"

Private Machin was alone with Henry Knox. Henry had drawn a shade down to cover the glass door and placed a "Closed" sign on the doorknob. Tom sensed his new friend was about to launch an appeal of some kind, or disclose some mystery.

"I had finished my apprenticeship with James Brindley. He's an engineer; builds canals. I learned a lot from Brindley, though he was mostly illiterate. Odd that, because he was numerate, quick and certain with calculations. I learned more than engineering. Brindley hated the caste system of Britain. It gnawed like a worm in an apple. He had no way to defeat it. For him, every moment of every day mirrored the class structure, reminding him of a bone-deep resentment that he couldn't shake. Didn't *want* to shake. He fed off of it. Some of his hatred rubbed off. Caused me to think more and more about the ways in which so many among us had their personal freedoms taken away by their so-called 'betters.'

"My parents were long gone. I had no siblings. No savings. America offered escape from tight class distinctions, from being forever locked out of the better parts of society; exclusion made more painful by being allowed, as all those subject to the Crown were, to watch but not partake. Looking at Brindley, I could imagine myself growing old and angry. I imagined the liberty sought by the Americans meant freedom from the bondage of class. A land of opportunity, adventure. If Army serfdom was the cost of entry, I'd pay it."

A weighty man, well over 200 pounds, Henry rose from his desk and moved directly in front of Tom, towering over him. He placed his hands gently on Tom's shoulders.

"Would you pay it again, if you knew then what you know now? I don't hear loyalty to the Crown or to the cause that brings his Army here."

"I have complicated feelings. The life of a British private is much worse than I imagined. Especially since I had assumed my status as an engineer would be recognized and used. But I've never been a quitter." Tom glanced up at the huge figure above him, hoping to glean the reaction to his story. Henry's face revealed nothing.

Tom was practiced at making up stories that wandered from the path of truth, or sometimes completely contradicted it. The practice seemed embedded in him to such an extent that even being caught out in lies, often with harsh results, couldn't break him of the habit. And now he was making up a story for the bookstore owner. Quitting had been his plan from the outset. With war now a certainty, he would desert as soon as an opportunity appeared.

Brindley's influence was the fuse, but the match was struck by an Englishman named Thomas Paine. At Brinkley's suggestion, Tom had gone to Lewes, in the County of Sussex, to hear Paine speak. It was an unforgettable event. What Paine said that night at the White Hart Hotel stuck like glue in Tom's memory.

"My father was a Quaker, my mother was an Anglican and I'm a Deist, meaning I believe God was responsible for creating the world but maintains a strictly 'hands off' position to what goes on there.

"I've been a stay maker, a sailor and a school teacher. Now I'm a pamphleteer. I live in Lewes because of its notorious reputation for being pro-republican and anti-monarchy. I believe that ordinary people, like you and like me, can make sound judgments on major policy issues. When, in a gathering like this, I challenged the existence of a monarchy, a keen supporter of the King said 'without a monarchy, Sir, our Government could degenerate into democracy.' 'Precisely,' I replied.'

"There is a great distinction for which no truly natural or religious reason can be argued, and that is the distinction of men into Kings and subjects. Males and females are the distinctions of nature, good and bad the distinctions of heaven. But how a race of men came into the world so exalted above the rest, and distinguished like some new species, is worth inquiring into, and whether they are the means of happiness or of misery to mankind.

"As regards America, I'm embarking for that place very soon, and I urge all freedom-loving people to do likewise. For the urge for freedom is awakening there. Indeed, the cause of America is in great measure the cause of all mankind. Small islands, not capable of protecting themselves, are the proper objects for kingdoms to take under their care; but there is something absurd in supposing a continent to be perpetually governed by an island."

Paine's match burned swiftly. Tom Machin left the Hotel determined to join the army for service in America. It would be a one-way voyage. And his service to the Crown would be short-lived.

Henry persisted.

"When you shipped out, war against America was not even on your mind, much less the cause you signed on to fight. In fact, by continuing in the Army, you will be fighting to end the liberty you sought by coming here. This is more than a theoretical irony.

To avoid it, the only option I see is desertion. If you choose it, I will help."

"Do you think the Patriots can win?"

Henry smiled at the question, having faced it many times.

"I know liberty is worth fighting for. And fighting against it is hard to become impassioned about. The Patriots can win, and will unless they fold up their tents early. Our population is 2.5 million, doubling every 25 years or so. Much more than England's growth. Our lands are vast. If the colonists who turn into Patriots grow as they are, today, and remain firm in the face of Royal firepower, in time we will wear through their thin shell of determination."

"All you say makes sense. But, believe me, I'm no quitter. Let me think on it. I'll be back." More excited than he chose to reveal, Tom stood, shook the hand of Henry Knox and swiftly exited the bookstore. The idea of desertion had already grown in Tom's mind, but he feared getting caught more than waiting out the war. Had he known Henry would encourage him? Is this why he came to the bookstore so often? Just as one can sense when a woman is open to being kissed, so could Tom sense in Henry Knox an awareness of the debate he was conducting within his unsettled mind. He couldn't say exactly what Henry was thinking, but when his offer came, it pushed Tom beyond the restraining fears.

On the way back to barracks, Tom asked himself why he had lied to Henry Knox. There was no good answer. The practice was in his bloodstream, despite some memorably bad results. That very night that he had heard Thomas Paine speak, he had stopped in a tavern for dinner and a pint. There were other diners who had heard Paine. Tom began to boast of his close personal relationship with this leading citizen of Lewes. Noting rising interest among the diners, and unquestioning acceptance, Tom even claimed some of Paine's ideas were fashioned through discussions with him. Admiration grew in the eyes of the group around him, as word travelled the width and length of the tavern that this gentleman was intimate with Thomas Paine. As he was carrying on about his close friend Paine, the man himself appeared with a couple of friends, bent on dinner. The group surrounding Tom urged him to step forward and greet his close friend, the pamphleteer. Alarmed, he hung back, looking for a way to escape what loomed as a disaster. Insisting, they pushed him forward.

"And who might you be, Sir? I recall seeing you in the audience."

Tom introduced himself, amidst angry shrieks from the group he had deceived. Bedlam ensued, with Tom receiving a severe thrashing from this enraged hive of duped pubcrawlers. Limping his way home, he admonished himself severely for lying. Correctly analyzing his thirst for respect and admiration, he swore never to lie again.

2

BATTLE OF BREED'S HILL

It was the mildest spring in memory. On May 25, 1775 the *Cerberus* sailed into Boston Harbor to land three British major generals with orders to put down the rebellion with force. William Howe was the senior officer, well known for feats of bravery. Henry Clinton, a prickly and gifted tactician, and Tom Burgoyne, a massive egotist, the other two. They found Boston under siege by an army of Patriots numbering nearly 10,000 men, a rag-tag bunch untrained and unpracticed in the arts of war.

The Americans had overnight built a substantial redoubt on Breed's Hill, commanding the harbor. Howe elected immediately to assault Breed's Hill by direct attack, expecting to rout these raw troops, throw them into panic and drive them back to Cambridge, where the Patriot headquarters and supplies were lodged. Thus would Howe, in one crushing assault, end the rebellion.

Tom Machin fought in the Battle of Breed's Hill, but not in the front lines until the third assault, by which time the Patriots had run out of ammunition and were forced to withdraw from their positions. His initial task for the day was to load the side boxes on Howe's artillery with the balls necessary for their use. This ammunition had been unloaded from the *Cerberus* a day or two before the Battle and was now in barges. Upon examination of the balls they were directed to carry to the guns, Machin saw immediately that they were 12-pounders, useless for the six-pounders that comprised the whole of Howe's fieldpieces. The mistake was a common one, and for foot-soldiers easy to make, unless one were trained to notice such things. As engineers were. As Tom Machin was. He tried to tell the sergeant but the effort was limp and he was waved off. General Howe had taken six hours to ready his forces for what was to be a devastating strike, and now he was most demonstrably in a hurry. Machin could have tried harder, even insisting on disclosure, but without admitting it, he had already crossed the emotional border leading to desertion, Knox's reasoning playing over and over in his mind. Joining the others in silence, he did his share of the work, filling the guns' side boxes with ammunition useless to Howe's guns.

When ordered to commence firing in the softening up exercise that typically precedes an assault by foot, the British artillery got off a round or two and then went silent. Informed of the mistake, Howe didn't pause to order that the six-pounders be found and used to restock the side boxes. Blood up, Howe's confidence brooked no doubt. He knew how the charge would unfold, with or without the preliminaries of an artillery barrage. The advancing columns of redcoats would discharge their muskets, creating a frightening mix of smoke and noise. The 'Brown Bess', named for Queen Elizabeth I and of equal antiquity, was harmless over 125 yards, and could not be aimed with precision, since it lacked a rear sight. Howe knew the chief point of the Brown Bess was to frighten the enemy. Killing would be done with the bayonet, which the enemy would first see approaching them out of the billowing smoke, thrust forward by redcoats on the run, each yelling 'Hurrah' at the top of his lungs.

Alas for Howe, the hill was long and steep. The men had been forced by their leaders to carry, in addition to the 14 pound Brown Bess, up to 100 pounds of unnecessary baggage consisting of packs with personal effects, cleaning equipment, a blanket, a fifth part of a tent, a haversack filled with rations, a canteen, a cartridge box with sixty cartridges and a short sword.

To claim they actually ran up Breed's Hill would be gross exaggeration. Nor did the enemy allow them to advance during the interval between the orderly reloading and firing by column that the British Army required of its infantry. Every Patriot was loading and firing at will, as fast as he could, on his own, producing in aggregate a steady, continuous fire. Many were using "Yankee peas," the buckshot combined with balls in loading their muskets. The barrage was more than the redcoats could take. They retreated in great disorder, few having gotten close enough to threaten the Patriots with bayonets.

Of the 2,400 British engaged, 1054 had been shot, 226 fatally. American casualties totaled about 450, of whom 140 were killed. By the happenstance of orders, Private Machin escaped even a wounding. What he didn't escape, however, was sharp questioning about the 12-pounders he and his mates had stuffed in the side boxes of six pound guns. The questioning was conducted by a lieutenant and the sergeant who directed the men to the barge loaded with the wrong ammunition, and who had waved Private Machin away when he tried to call attention to the mistake. Tom wanted to blow the whistle on the sergeant, but knew he couldn't. His guilt in not intervening despite the sergeant's wave off, in knowing with certainty of the mistake and its consequences, in realizing that he had already decided on desertion, were together too fraught to allow him to attack the sergeant, whom he had grown to hate.

The men were blamed for negligence. The sergeant recommended 50 lashes. The lieutenant reduced it to 25. Fear of retribution froze every soldier's voice from asking the obvious question that each would have to ponder as the lash left blood and scars on their backs: why the sergeant had directed the men to the wrong barge, without even checking its contents. Fortunately, for Private Machin, since both sergeant and lieutenant were ignorant of his training and experience, they had no reason to raise the same question with him.

3

TOGETHER IN CAMBRIDGE

Henry Knox and his wife, Lucy, escaped from Boston to Cambridge just days after Private Machin had visited the bookstore to hear the bookstore owner's offer.

When Tom showed up after the Battle of Breed's Hill, a lobster-back recovering from the lashing and like many others, ready to desert, he found the bookstore in a stranger's hands. But that stranger said "Might you be Tom Machin?" All it took was a nod for the stranger to deliver a note marked "For Private Tom Machin—Personal." Tom found a neatly drawn map of the Harbor and detailed instructions as to how, if so inclined, Tom might on a moonless night escape to where Henry had hidden a canoe, on the shore across from the mouth of the Charles River, and then swiftly paddle the short distance to Cambridge. The canoe's location was clearly marked on the map. At the foot of the note, Henry had cautioned in solid lettering: YOU BEST DESTROY THIS NOTE!

When Tom looked up, the stranger said "Is all in order?"

Redcoats were deserting like rats from a sinking ship. Triple the rate before Breed's Hill. If Washington was running low on ammunition, Howe was running low on lashes. The treatment of captured deserters was an ugly business, one the men were forced to watch. Howe couldn't shake the conviction that anyone seeing the cruel and brutal spectacle would be deterred. Having never been subjected to the dehumanizing course of British Army life for the enlisted man, Howe could only imagine that one outcome. To be sure, deterrence was effective with some redcoats. But the lashings drove others to a more determined decision to desert.

Private Machin plotted to escape while on night duty as sentry on a fireboat in the harbor. To reach the fireboat, typically the sentry being replaced would row to shore, turning over the boat to his replacement, and then sleep for most of the four-hour stretch before having to return to duty. On the dark night Machin selected, he arrived at the fireboat in a canoe just before the sentry on duty shoved off in the boat customarily used to row to shore. "Why the canoe, Tom? Couldn't wait to relieve me?" The sentry shouted out these questions, hoping to be heard above the strong wind that was snapping the ship's stays like bands of rubber. He succeeded brilliantly, waking one of the ship's crew, who proved equally curious.

"Orders," replied Tom. "The regiment wants to experiment with canoes as a better means than bateaux for getting troops around the harbor. They're swift and quiet, once you master the balance. I was practically born in a canoe. Volunteered for the job."

"Maybe they're on to something, said the retiring sentry. "Appears to handle well."

Just then Tom moved to grab the painter with one hand and the ship's rope ladder with the other. Moving too fast in the dark, his reach for the ladder fell short, as his lunge forward caused the canoe to move back. With nothing to support that part of his body now extending beyond the gunwale, he fell into the water. The canoe capsized.

Both crewman and sentry bent double with laughter, stamping their feet in pleasure. "Born in a canoe?" asked the sentry. "Couldn't have stayed there very long," added the crewman.

By the time they had fished Tom and his pack and musket out of Boston Harbor and set the canoe to rights, the other three crew members were on deck. Mockery mixed with generosity, as the baiting was replaced by recognition that, despite it being the 27th of July, the blowing wind was making Private Machin shiver with cold.

Someone offered him a dry sweater, another a cup of rum. Tom noticed the vanishing trail of phosphorescent waters through which the replaced sentry had just rowed. He had almost four hours to get the crew settled back down so that he could paddle off, heading silently to the Charles. Asking for more rum, and urging the crew to drink with him, he regaled them with tales of Breed's Hill, starting with Howe's decision to ignore the artillery instead of fixing this commonplace error. The stupidity of officers holds eternal attraction for the enlisted. Tom had many examples to unspool. As the crew drank, Tom pretended, emptying his cup on the deck when, in the darkness, no one could see. An hour into this exercise, crewmembers started drifting off to their bunks. Before two hours had passed, they all were below deck, asleep.

Despite the accident, Tom did know canoeing. Kneeling 2/3rds back towards the stern, he paddled without sound, gracefully feathering the blade along the gunwale and using the j-stroke to thrust the craft forward in a straight line. The wind was his friend that night, blowing hard against his back out of the southwest. Once across the harbor and into the mouth of the Charles, he would be safe. A matter of minutes he thought.

Coming at him from the direction of Boston Neck was another canoe with two paddlers. As they drew close, he could recognize them as redcoats. The man in the bow shouted "North," demanding the second part to the night's password. Machin didn't have a clue. In desperation he shouted back "Wind." He saw from their faces that his long shot had fallen short. Their canoe came alongside. They asked what he was doing out in the harbor, alone. He said he had come from the fireboat, where he had been on sentry duty. "And where are you headed?"

Tom told them he was going to fetch the other sentry. "You think he's somewhere on the Charles?" the bowman said, obviously aware of the lie, for everyone knew the Charles was controlled by the Patriots. "You will come with us. Some explaining to do."

Gripping his paddle, Tom brought it up, then down hard on the bowman's head, blade first. There was a scream of pain. Putting his paddle aside, Tom reached the other canoe's gunwale and with both hands lifted the side of the canoe up with all his strength, standing for better leverage. The bowman, now only semi-conscious, fell from the canoe as it tipped, easing Tom's task of capsizing it. The redcoat in the stern fought to keep himself and his canoe upright. But he failed. With both redcoats in the water and their canoe turned over and half submerged, Tom took paddle in hand and pulled away toward the Charles.

Tom remembered the canoe Henry had hidden for him. Too late now to find it. No matter. He had somehow contrived to use a British canoe, which was carrying him to safety at last.

Private Machin's sweater spared him multiple explanations and possibly worse as he made his way toward Washington's headquarters in Harvard Yard. Dawn was awakening in the East as he sought the route from river to village square. A curious figure, perhaps, with duty trousers of uncertain origin, but not one passers-by found suspicious enough to question. Arriving at the entrance to the Yard, however, he was stopped by a sentry whose suspicions easily pierced the sweater, enabling him to imagine in full the uniform Tom still wore.

"Your name, rank, unit and business here in Cambridge. Be quick about it," barked the sentry.

"Tom Machin, formerly a Private in His Majesty's 23rd Regiment of Foot. A deserter hoping to join the Continental Army."

The sentry smirked.

"We get your kind every day. Deserter or spy? How to tell? Even if not a spy, how to know you'll fight for America, rather than just desert again after filling your belly with a few good meals and a hog's head of rum?"

Machin was exhausted. And ill equipped to countenance such a greeting. He had expected to be greeted with praise, asked for the story of his thrilling escape, told how grateful the Continental Army was to have him and, upon learning of his engineering skills, grow even more grateful. The sentry's cynicism and suspicion shocked him much more than the cold water of Boston Harbor had earlier that night.

"Here's how," Machin answered, his voice high-pitched and cracking in anger." "Because you hang spies. Because you hang deserters. Because I just risked my life because I want to fight for the same freedom you're fighting for."

The sentry flinched with surprise. He had rightly assumed that if Machin was a redcoat, he had to be from the lowest dregs of society: a thief, drunk or runaway impressed into service, or a criminal trading the miseries of life in the British Army for those of the British jail. Yet, here was something different, a voice sounding in education and eloquent anger.

"Hold on there, private. Do you have anyone who can vouch for you?"

"In fact, I do, a Boston bookshop proprietor named Henry Knox. But I don't know where he is. He closed his shop and left town some weeks ago, probably to join the Patriots."

"Ah, you claim to know Colonel Knox. Then you must know what command he was given."

"I regret to say I don't. I didn't even know of his commission."

"If you can't even identify the man you claim to know and came to see, I will have to lock you up."

Machin grew alarmed. There was no one to whom he could appeal. The sentry's suspicions, though irritating, were not irrational. And, then, perhaps out of desperation, it came to him. Henry Knox had lost the two small fingers on his left hand. A hunting accident. Would the sentry know? Knox was careful to wind a handkerchief around his maimed hand when out in public. But it was the only trick Tom had left and so he played it.

On hearing this bit of personal intelligence, known throughout the base, the sentry folded with grace, accepting Machin's claim. He then sent word to Colonel Knox, who at that moment was at breakfast with General Washington. The Colonel sent for Machin and met him in a room separate from where the General continued breakfast with staff.

They hugged, then talked, with verve and excitement, each recounting the separate but equally defining events that had occurred since they had been in the bookstore, events that were to change their lives.

"Tom, you're a deserter. A proud title, I declare. Wear it with pride. Now, let's have your story."

They sat over a pot of hot tea, while Tom rehearsed his decision to desert and all its ways and means.

"But enough about me. Henry, you look positively blooming. Marriage must go well. Your wife's name, Lucy if I recall rightly."

"Yes indeed, even at a distance. I had to take Lucy to Worcester, for safety. We write daily. She's a good woman, though born into a Tory family. Add to that, my new commission in the artillery. What a felicitous post! How lucky I am to have it fall into my lap. Nothing could I have wished for more. Nothing, that is, except some cannon. We are an artillery regiment in name only. Do you realize we lack not only gunpowder, but the normal accompaniment of guns, large and small? And think about this. In that pitiful condition, we have for many months maintained posts within musket shot of some twenty-odd British regiments. Add to that, the militia turning homeward as enlistments expire, having to be replaced by the new and untrained. It won't continue because it can't. One of these days Howe's going to discover we are naked. And act."

Knox saw confirmed in this deserter the abilities he had detected when Tom first appeared in his bookstore. He would take Machin under his wing, promising, in time, a commission in his regiment. After a thorough debriefing on British fortifications in Boston, troop morale and developments in small arms and artillery, Tom found various ways to start being useful. He helped with the forts at Roxbury, a feat of engineering praised by General Washington, and working through the summer, he helped with other fortifications designed to encircle the British Army in Boston.

Occasionally Colonel Knox would laugh with Tom Machin over the notion that he was head of an artillery regiment possessing no artillery. Something close to the Swiss Navy, Henry said. "Now, that's an oxymoron." But they both knew that unless something was done, the joke would turn bitter, even possibly fatal to the Patriot's cause.

The cannon of Fort Ticonderoga had been captured in mid-May by the already famous Benedict Arnold and the powerful and unpredictable Ethan Allen, who led a proud and unruly Vermont militia calling themselves the Green Mountain Boys. Surprising the British garrison, they subdued greater numbers while experiencing little resistance. Occurring around the time of Lexington-Concord and reported just afterwards, this escapade caused profound shock within British leadership, hanging upon the Generals like a disease. It alarmed the whole British Army, the news spreading like a malignant virus, even to lowly privates like Tom Machin.

"Have you thought of the guns taken at Ticonderoga?" Tom asked Colonel Knox one Autumn day, as leaves were falling in Cambridge. "There are plenty I understand, four to twenty-four pounders, mortars, howitzers and more. Why not bring them here?"

Henry Knox was an immense presence who could, without more than a hard glare or sly smile, crush an opponent's argument. To strangers he appeared by dress and shape as fastidious and fat, but those who knew him found a delightful sense of humor housed in his "stout" frame. He was a natty dresser and meticulously groomed. And he was tall, well over six feet, with a carriage suggesting even greater height. Quicker to smile and forgive than to find fault and blame, he was naturally gregarious, an irresistible companion for those lucky enough to claim him as a friend. And, by any measure, a commanding presence at table or parade.

Now he sat ramrod straight, a bemused expression crossing his large owl-like, cherubic face, with its double chin and sweet mouth.

"Can't be done. Rains alone would bog us down, not to mention the Berkshires. Do you know how heavy that caravan would be? Across mountains? Over 300 miles?"

Tom Machin wasn't inclined to argument for its own sake. Far from it. He sought to be an adviser valued for independent thinking.

"It could be done in winter. With sledges and teams of well-yoked oxen. The drag of sledges on hard packed ice and snow is different from moving by wheels on deeply gullied and often muddy trails. With luck on the weather, we could average 10 miles a day. The trip might fit neatly into January."

At heart Knox was an optimist. He combined a keen mind with energy and spirit, which now broke forth in a smile.

"You have a point, Tom. One I should have made. Growing up, the bookstore owner I worked for would take me ice boating in the winter. We also sailed in the summer. I know the difference in friction between water and ice, between the energy needed to move a sailboat across a lake in summer or move an iceboat across that lake in winter. You're onto something, my friend. I'll speak to the commanding general."

On hearing the idea, Washington responded enthusiastically. How could he do otherwise, knowing little about ice sailing but all too much about the preposterously weak position his Army was in. As he said in his orders to Colonel Knox, "the want of the cannon is so great that no trouble or expense must be spared to obtain them." A long shot, he told the Colonel, is better than no shot at all.

Immediately following their counsel, Washington wrote Major General Phillip Schuyler in Albany to give Knox every necessary assistance, and if he needed more money, to supply him with it. And he wrote to the Continental Congress, informing that slow-moving body of his decision.

It was mid-November when Colonel Knox, accompanied by his younger brother, William, and the soon to be commissioned Lieutenant Machin, set forth, heading for Worcester to see Lucy, and then on to New York, where he was to pick up necessities envisioned for the project before turning north to Ticonderoga and its hoard of cannon.

Lucy welcomed Henry and his companions to the house Henry had rented for her in Worcester with an unalloyed joy that to Tom Machin's British eyes exceeded all bounds. Unabashed in the company of this stranger, she smothered Henry in hugs and kisses out of character for the favorite daughter of Thomas Flucker, one of the richest merchants in Boston, a reserved Bostonian and a dedicated Tory who had been appointed the Royal Secretary of Massachusetts.

Henry gave as good as he got. And, so, they clung to each other, pressing close to feel the warmth of their bodies from head to foot, for a brief moment oblivious of both time and those witnessing this passionate reunion.

Lucy had met Henry in 1773 when she visited his bookstore. There she came to know Will too, because although his visits to the bookshop were few, hers became very frequent as her interest in Henry grew into courtship. Surprisingly, it consisted of her courting him. She quickly learned that Henry was one of ten sons sired by his father, of whom only four survived to adulthood. Two of those had gone to sea. When his father disappeared in the West Indies, Henry, then nine years old, left Boston Latin Grammar School to support his mother and young William, then three, finding employment in a bookstore.

Over dinner, Lucy sought intelligence from Tom about conditions in Boston. "My mother and my two sisters are still in Boston, but we don't exchange letters. At least not yet. I write but receive no response."

"But your father, isn't he an important Tory in Boston, with appointments by the Crown?" Tom said.

"Yes, yes, but he went to London last fall. He never approved of our marriage. At the start he thought of Henry as the orphaned son of a bankrupt mariner, as well as a tradesman with little formal education. And he suspected Henry of having sympathies toward the radical Whig movement. Not an easy time for us to fall deeply, hopelessly, in love. In the end, father gave his consent, but reluctantly, teeth clamped. He and mother refused to attend our wedding. And now silence." Wrought by her reunion with Henry, Lucy came close to tears thinking of her family.

Henry moved close to her, draping his long arm around her shoulders like a bear comforting her cubs.

"Lucy was part of a very close-knit family. Being apart with no solid prospect of seeing them again has been difficult."

Tears pent up through weeks alone cascaded down flushed cheeks. She convulsed, then sobbed as Henry wiped her cheeks with his handkerchief.

"What's worse, my brother is an officer in the British Army. Fighting against my beloved Henry. And against Will and Tom. All this reality makes life harsh. It's only through your letters, Henry, my dearest Companion, that I survive."

"Come now, friends. Time for a change of subject. Lucy, remember the fun you had as a child sledding down the hill above the Common, bouncing over curbs, flying into the Common, dodging trees to reach the bottom? Well, we are about to embark on a long sledding adventure, one to thrill any ten-year old."

"Not ten any more. But interested. Just how long?" she asked.

"We reckon about 300 miles. We have to build the sledges at Ticonderoga, load them up with the cannon, yoke the oxen and set off down Lake George."

"You should name the sleds. Name them for the women in your lives, the ones you've left behind, the ones you'll be wishing you could curl up with as you fight the snow and cold. They give sailing vessels women's names. Why not your sleds?" Lucy was pleased with her suggestion. Henry was pleased she had recovered her spark.

"Good idea, Lucy. Count on it. Some nautical types believe the practice of naming ships for women came about because women can be so unpredictable." Henry laughed. "But don't worry, our sleds will be manageable, and we will name them for those we love, solely because we love them."

Observing Lucy and Henry, so close across the dinner table, Tom sensed a change in their mien and he said, "Henry, if you are half as tired as I, you're thinking only of bed," Tom pronounced. "It's past time we retired. As you said, big day tomorrow."

"You're right, of course. Let's save some stories for breakfast. You and Will have the upstairs bedroom."

Before Will and Tom had reached the second floor, Henry had taken Lucy into her bedroom and closed the door.

"Alone, my Speria, my nymph of the evening. I've longed so often for this moment, imagined it in every detail; now that it's here, I want time to stop. We must seize these moments, savor them, imprint them on our memory."

"My Fidelio, my own Harry, my heart's fast-beating desire, how formal you sound; sit down, won't you, and remove those ugly boots. I'll be back in an instant."

Lucy disappeared in the small dressing room adjoining the bedroom on one side and the bathroom on the other. Henry undressed as quickly as he could. He was standing naked beside the bed when Lucy returned, wearing a light, translucent robe open slightly in the front. She had brought a towel. Looking at Henry's erection, unmistakable even in the shadows of a room lighted with but one candle, she raised her thumbs in approval and tossed him the towel. "You might want to drape it with a wrap till we warm up the bed. Going to be cold."

"Your boudoir humor hasn't suffered a bit from disuse. Should I blow out the candle?" Henry asked.

Lucy got into bed. "Not on your life, Harry. I don't want to take my eyes off you, if you please."

The bed warmed fast. Fast, too, was their love-making, which left Henry with *la petite mort* and Lucy feeling highly aroused. Although they still thought of themselves as newly-weds, having been together for less than a year when they separated, they had learned a lot about life in the bedroom. It happened that in that venue, Lucy led with a puckish sense of humor that belied her tender age and refined upbringing. She had been given a remarkably thorough education by her sister, Hannah, who never seemed to have time to account for her knowledge, which even the uninitiated would know could not have been found solely in books. Growing up, Lucy knew her sister traveled in a tight group of young sophisticates, known for fast living and ambition to push beyond the penumbra of acceptability in Boston's fashionable society.

All that Hannah had to say rang true. And so it proved to be when put to the test. The main lessons she taught Lucy were simple to state. First, men and women become physically aroused at very different rates, requiring of the man patience in practicing the arts of arousal for the woman and deferral of gratification for himself. Second, men and women may enjoy sex in very different ways, meaning that anything goes for each partner in promoting pleasure for the other, and what works for one won't necessarily work for another. Third, women enjoy sex just as much as men.

Lucy was conflicted, not wanting to disturb her husband, yet with growing urgency, needing him to bring her to the spot he had so quickly reached. She began slowly to undulate, causing the mattress to move up and down like waves across a lake. The effect on Henry, at first, was soporific. She turned to thrashing, with an occasional bump against her partner. This effort finally succeeded in waking him.

"Come to my Fidelio those thronging soft and delicate desires. He awakes to find his Speria in great need. Come patient one, do with your tongue what we trained it to do."

After their bedroom game was tied, they slept but not through the night. On awaking from time to time, the air felt damp and musty, suggestive of a bordello—appealingly so. Before sunrise, they had pleasured each other once more, variations on the unusual theme, developed by Lucy and accepted by Henry, of humorous, lusty, robust love in a world of make-believe.

Up early, Henry was all business the next day. Lucy marveled at the ease with which her husband could change "uniforms," without even the slightest pause to adjust. For her, the night's pleasures lingered with the brightening November day, warming her from inside out, a contrast, she realized, to the rays of the sun, warming the house from outside in.

4

FORT TICONDEROGA

Henry pushed his small unit to depart early. They rode hard to New York City, averaging 40 miles a day. Arriving November 25th, they arranged for necessaries to be shipped to Fort Ticonderoga, spent two days savoring the city and left again by horseback on the 28th, heading north. Henry wrote Lucy of his impressions. So taken with his description of the city's people, he couldn't resist reading the paragraph to Will and Tom.

"The people—why the people are magnificent; in their equipages, which are numerous; in their house furniture, which is fine; in their pride and conceit, which are inimitable; in their profaneness, which is intolerable; in the want of principle, which is prevalent; in their Toryism, which is insufferable, and for which they must repent in dust and ashes."

They nodded in approval.

"Hanging around that bookstore certainly gave you sparkle with the pen," Tom offered in admiration, jealously recalling that he had apprenticed to an illiterate engineer instead of having the educational advantages he assumed, wrongly, that Henry had enjoyed. "When we finish off the British, I expect you will write about it—extending your fame in another direction."

The trio reached Fort George at the foot of the lake on December 5th. The treasure they sought was on Lake Champlain just a short distance by land from the head of Lake George. Henry's plan, which he began to implement on the 6th, was to sort the weapons, load the most valuable ones on the two-masted, light-bottomed, shallow craft he had arranged through General Schuyler to be supplied and travel down the lake, which fortunately had not yet frozen over except along the edges.

Much of the Fort's artillery was too worn to be worth the upcoming struggle to bring to Cambridge. Henry selected 59 pieces, both brass and iron, ranging from mortars and howitzers to guns using cannon balls of from 4 to 24 lbs. They varied in weight from 100 to 5,500 pounds, totaling 119,900 pounds in all. Henry and his colleagues rummaged the Fort for flint, which Washington knew to be the best in the country, for use on muskets. He was rewarded with one barrel full. In addition, he took 23 boxes of lead.

The soldiers manning the Fort were few and appeared undernourished; they all lacked both strength and any sense of urgency—a sense that this was the race of their lives in a much bigger race for the country, the race that drove Henry, Tom and Will. Fortunately, there were others hired by Henry to make the whole trip. Numbering 300, they were a combination of soldiers and civilians, mostly teamsters. Without them, embarkation would never have occurred. It took until 3pm on December 9th to get everything aboard the scows and bateaux gathered at the Lake George landing.

Before shoving off, Henry gathered his little army in close so as to be heard against a frigid wind beginning to roar from the north.

"I know you are aware of the urgency of our mission. But before we start on what will challenge us in many ways until we reach General Washington's Camp in Cambridge, I wanted to remind you of the General's message to me. He said the want of these weapons is so great that no trouble or expense must be spared to bring them to him. We must all—every one of us—bend our utmost endeavors to complete this assignment at the earliest possible date. Nothing less than the survival of our Army is at stake. Let's have a cheer for the Continental Army and its Commanding General George Washington."

Henry was rewarded by the response, a loud shout heard by all despite the muffling effects of wind-blown snow, which had started to fall in tiny flakes as it always does in very cold conditions.

Jumping to his feet, Tom added: "And now, another cheer for the snow, without which our sledges would not budge."

Henry left Will in charge of the transport, going ahead with Tom in a faster vessel in order to collect and organize the oxen, horses and sledges for the longer leg of the trip. Before the vessel was out of sight, the scow Will commanded ran aground on a submerged rock. He had been under sail, and the north wind, snow laden, was driving the craft faster than Will thought possible. He had failed to post a lookout in the bow, not imagining this lake, known for its depth, could pose such a hazard far from shore. Henry was admiring the scow's speed just as it hit the rock. He saw it stop, masts rocking forward at a crazy angle, sails flapping, bow dipping to take in water, cargo shifting despite being well lashed down, and some of the crew, not being lashed at all, falling forward to slide hard against the sides of the scow or, in one case, overboard into the ice-cold lake. And then, as if to repeat the distress, the ugly sounds of what he had just seen reached his ears.

Growing up, Will had been an impatient and reckless child. Despite Henry's frequent coaching, or perhaps, Henry often thought, because of it, and the overall care Henry lavished on the only sibling he ever really knew, Will had matured with the reckless streak intact, dependent again and again on his older brother to clean up the messes his impatient and thoughtless behavior left behind.

While Henry and Tom watched from a distance, Will's teamsters battled the elements to free the scow. Finally, aided by a drop in the wind, they parted boat from rock. Continuing together into the night, the convoy reached Sabbath Day Point by 9 pm. A hunting party of Indians camped there were friendly and generous, sharing warmth from their fires and ample venison roasted in their manner.

Early next day the journey resumed. The temperature had dropped to 10 degrees F, and the wind had arisen again, sadly from the southwest, rendering sails and masts worse than useless. They rowed against the wind and waves building to white-caps, back-breaking work in which all pitched in to help make what meager progress was possible. Long, narrow and edged with mountains on either side, Lake George funneled the wind, concentrating its strength just as a narrowing river turned ripples into giant power waves. After struggling for four hours, they went ashore to build several large fires, thaw out and rest during a night in which the now bitterly cold wind continued to howl through the tall conifers that soared above them. Sleep was intermittent, as the fires had to be kept alive as shields to tame the elements.

Henry and Tom left at dawn with the advance party, reaching Fort George at the end of the lake after over six hours of pulling against a brutally strong and cold wind.

That night, with snow gathering force around their tent, Henry began composing letters to the Committees of Safety along his route, requesting help in supplying all that he and his colleagues could imagine needing. Food, of course, for men and beasts; shelter; clothing to back up what they had; shovels; block and tackle; ropes; sledges to replace those worn out or smashed; fresh oxen and horses.

Do you think they will have ammunition for all the different guns we are hauling?" Tom asked. "I know we lack the thirteen-inch shell used in the mortars. Perhaps we should write ahead."

"You're right. We have none, and it's highly unlikely, given where those mortars came from, that there are any at Camp. I'll write Colonel McDougall in New York to get a supply sent to Cambridge immediately, to be there when we arrive."

The next day brought delivery of 80 yoke of oxen, several span of horse, some cattle and 80 heavy duty sledges with steam-bent hickory runners sheathed in iron. And of equal importance, more than half a mile of three-inch rope for lashing. Squire Palmer of Stillwater had done the critical task Colonel Knox had assigned to him. Done it well and on time. A propitious sign, Tom thought.

Will arrived the next day, having driven his teamsters hard. The wind had lasted the whole trip, blowing strong, stronger and then strongest, since the first day, always from the southwest. To make matters worse, one of the bateaux swamped, sinking with heavy cannon aboard. Luckily, the water was shallow, the gunwales above water-level, making it possible to bail out the vessel and save its cargo. The experience, however, following the first mishap, put Will in a deep funk. As the difficult transfer of weapons from boat to sledge commenced, Will seemed lethargic and disinterested in what was happening around him, like a child thrown from his horse once too often to clamber back into the saddle.

Over dinner, Will's personal doubts bled into anxieties about the whole undertaking, and spilled out. "Henry, I fear we've misled General Washington. This project is impossible. Look how long it's taken already, and we are only 10% of the way. And that over water—the easiest surface. Carry 60 tons of iron across two mighty rivers and the mountains between. People would say we're insane. That's what the General should have told us, but he didn't. He needed to believe we could do it. And we let him. For God's sake and his, we must abandon this dream; it's doomed. We must awaken him to the hard truth."

Years of caring for one's younger brother while earning bread for one's family drives one to the adult side fast. Henry knew Will's personal fear of failure, now heightened by the two preventable accidents on Lake George, would be too powerful for his pride to contain.

"I get your concern, Will. I also know how exhausted you are. That long pull down the lake was brutal. Get some sleep. We'll weigh our prospects tomorrow."

Before going to bed, Henry and Tom discussed how best to bring Will back on board. Henry admitted to Tom his fear that, growing up, the unintended cost of his playing the adult was that Will felt free to play the child. It was a role he practiced until it became a deep-seated habit. They developed a plan.

Henry's team, to a man, was up before the sun. At breakfast, before a warming fire, Henry said "Tom, what brought you to Boston?"

"I needed a new beginning. Nothing to keep me in Britain. No family, few friends, no job. That's it, I guess. America offered a chance. In Britain, I had nothing left to lose."

"Where'd you grow up?" Henry asked.

"Outside London. In an orphanage. Like most, they treated us like little criminals, like failures, whose failing was to have become an orphan. We were beaten regularly. When, much later, I learned first-hand of the British Army's affection for the cat, and its use not just for punishment but as a pre-emptive deterrent and preferred tool to assure discipline, the similarity in thinking was overwhelming. As I joined the ranks of the 'lobsterbacks'—and they included virtually every enlisted soldier, for almost no one could escape some taste of the cat—the memory of being a child tied to a table and lashed became palpable. These cruelties, exercised by God-fearing people, brought me to conclude that either God was a devil in disguise, forcing people into evil ways, or there was no God to restrain people from evil ways that, just on account of being human, came naturally to some of them, some of the time. Whichever, I soon enough had reason to abandon religion. It was the repeated taste of prayers unanswered. That was that."

They had finished off the porridge. A few slabs of bacon were browning in a cast-iron pan, fat splatting out. They had cups with tea leaves, now filled with boiling water, warming their fingers as they waited to drink.

Will listened. "So Tom, with such a painful childhood, how could you enlist?"

"I had no money. Enlistment was the only way to get to America, my pre-paid ticket to that imagined land of opportunity. I had no notion of war breaking out. I believed my commitment would be brief. I'd serve it out; then seek a new life here."

"But you deserted," said Will. "Risked a hanging; odds high on getting caught."

"Lexington, Concord and Bunker Hill meant war. A war I couldn't fight for British values. Watching the Americans in battle, exposing their lives to preserve their liberties—it was literally breathtaking. Looking down at my red coat, I felt ashamed. I didn't belong. With a healthy nudge from Henry, I decided to take the risk of changing sides."

Henry said, "So, Tom, you're stake in this war is big. In British eyes, you're a traitor. We lose; you hang."

"By that theory, aren't we all at risk?" Tom said. "General Washington and all the rest of his merry Continentals. For in King George's mind we are all traitors to the Crown."

"I think we all know we've put our lives out there, on the line," said Henry, looking hard at Will. "The General knows it better than we. And he knows some other things. Like secrets can't be kept in war. Howe hasn't yet figured out that the Continentals camped in Boston's surrounding hills lack gunpowder and cannon. He hasn't yet heard Benjamin Franklin's plea that Washington furnish his Army with spears that extend beyond the British bayonet and bows and arrows, because they are as accurate as the musket and can be fired four times as fast. But when he does, he'll send his well-armed regiments—twenty of them—to kill or capture the whole of our Army; in that one swift stroke, he'll put an end to the revolution."

"More tea brother Will? The times are fraught. Having made our beds to lie down with General Washington, there's no turning back. No such thing as being just a tiny bit traitorous. Same as being a bit with child."

Tom said, "Which is another way of saying our mission to Cambridge won't fail because we can't let it fail. All our lives depend on it. Isn't that true Will?"

"Enough of this scholarly stuff," Will said. "No more metaphors. If we hope to make Cambridge in three weeks' time, we better stop the gab, finish loading those sledges and be off."

Smiling and back in the game, Will put down his tea and stood up.

5

EN ROUTE TO CAMBRIDGE

By Christmas Eve, they had reached Saratoga. The trio of leaders enjoyed a festive dinner with the McNeal family, then set off again, heading now into a waxing snow storm, snow falling fast and deep. Eight miles south of Saratoga they stopped for the night. Snow started tapering off, with two feet on the ground and the temperature plummeting.

Through the deep snow, they struggled on toward Albany. As they approached Half Moon Ferry, near the confluence of the Mohawk and Hudson Rivers, a thaw began, making travel through the snow more burdensome. Of much greater concern to Henry Knox, however, was the impact the thaw would have on the ice, for the train of sleds would have to cross both rivers before proceeding south of Albany to Kinderhook and then Claverack, where they would make a 90 degree turn east into the Berkshires. If the ice was insufficiently thick, they would simply have to wait. The weather turned even milder, the ice covering the Mohawk grew weak, and Henry began biting his nails down to the quick in frustration.

They made a hole in the middle of the Mohawk. The ice measured barely three inches. Even if they reduced the weight in the sleds, there was only so much they could do. The large cannon weighed some 5,000 pounds. Add to that a heavy sledge and a yoke of oxen, and it became obvious that three-inch ice wouldn't suffice.

We're stuck," Henry said. "Totally dependent on the wayward weather."

Tom's mind was churning, as it typically did when faced with seemingly hopeless dilemmas having to do with physical matters. From childhood, he had always believed if there was a way, he could find it, just by thinking. Sometimes this attitude paid off. Other times, it didn't. Henry called him a Brit with Yankee sensibilities.

Watching Tom's sudden focus on something unseen, Will couldn't avoid that useless feeling of being outside the action, wishing to be inside but having not a clue how to get there.

I can almost hear the gears up there grinding," Will said, pointing his finger at Tom's forehead.

Henry said "Out with it, Tom."

"We can speed up the thickening process as long as the temperature hangs around freezing, even if only at night, by punching holes in the ice from one side to the other, spaced, say, some 50 feet apart. We allow the water to pour out the holes, which it will do because of pressure, and freeze on top, thickening the ice."

Henry looked dubious.

"How could the freezing on top of the ice be faster than the freezing below?"

Tom smiled. "Counterintuitive to imagine ice as an insulator. But that's how it works. The river isn't as cold as the air. The layer of ice tends to protect the river from the colder air. The thicker the ice, the slower the freezing process below it. If we can get water on the surface, we can thicken the ice faster. Holes about two feet in diameter should work."

Henry grabbed Tom and gave him a hug.

"You're a genius! Let's lay out a route and give it a try. Will, explain the plan to the men. They should bring cutting tools."

After cutting the holes, they waited three days and nights for the water to freeze hard, aided by a change in the weather that brought first raw wind-swept cold dropping down to 10 degrees F, and then, on the third day, snow flurries. They knew heavy snow would be no friend, in adding weight without strength to the river's ice. Again, fortune turned their way. The heavy snowfall they knew was coming held off. At Henry's direction each sledge was pulled across using a long rope attached to a span of horses or yoke of oxen. A teamster carrying a sharp hatchet walked alongside, ready to cut the rope to save the horses if the sledge were to break through.

When the ice broke under the last sledge, making a crack that terrified the horses, the sledge was just 30 feet from the river's edge. The teamster did his duty with the rope, allowing the sledge and the 18 pounder slung on its back to plunge in the river, sinking to the bottom. Luck, however, stuck with them. The river where this accident occurred was not more than ten feet deep, enabling a rescue of the sledge by breaking the ice to create an open-water path to shore. Triple ropes and two teams of oxen worked to move the sledge and its cargo to shore.

They arrived in Albany on January 5th. One final crossing of the Hudson remained before they could turn east. They found lodging and a friendly dining room warmed by robust fires at each end in a tavern by the name of Albany Ale, situated on the side of a hill overlooking the majestic Hudson, close to the State House and General Schuyler's imposing estate.

Henry spent the evening writing to General Washington and to Lucy. Will and Tom talked, admitting to each other after a couple of mugs of mulled cider how envious they were of their leader for having such people to write. Each in his way was a lonely man, and being thrown together by Henry as part of his small leadership unit, they were able slowly, like flowers unfurling, to open up to one another. Difficult at first, by the time they reached Albany, their personal exchanges had become easy, wrapped in growing bonds of dependence and friendship. Considering the challenge of this trip, they agreed, how could it be otherwise.

"Here's a quandary for you, Will. We're praying for colder weather, to get us across the Hudson, and yet the colder weather plays havoc with our fingers. And once across, we still need very cold weather and a solid snow base covering the ground to make the sledges move easily, and this prayer, if answered, imperils our fingers further. But the matter of snow is tricky; we need snow but not too much of it. The danger is that with the cold weather will come huge snow falls."

Without much resistance, the waiter convinced them to order another round of mulled cider. Tom's pipe needed refueling. He hit it against his boot, inspected the residue to be sure there were no live coals, and refilled the bowl with the strong-smelling tobacco he kept in a water-proof pouch hanging from his neck.

Will, who didn't smoke, watched Tom perform this well-rehearsed ritual, repeated a few times a day.

"Better resupply here. Not likely to find tobacco for sale between Albany and Cambridge."

"You're right, Will. Foresighted, by God! You may not realize it, but you're becoming more like your brother every day. Looking ahead, thinking, planning. It's a pleasure to watch."

Will felt a strange surge of self-confidence. Attracting praise, or even approval, was not something familiar to Will, whose usual life experience was to be on the receiving end of criticism and abuse. Like alcohol to an alcoholic, a little bit of praise led him to want more, to ransack his brain looking for ways to get it. Tom was not trained in human intercourse, but his instincts, more often than not, were sound. Feeding Will's starved sense of value was a brilliant stroke, whether consciously rendered or not.

Tom pulled a map from a well-worn oilskin case. "Here's Albany. We cross the river and follow the Post Road south to Kinderhook and Claverack. From there, we turn east and things will get interesting as we conquer the ups and downs of the spine of the Berkshires through Great Barrington and on to Springfield, some 55 miles."

"I wish I shared your confident jollies. 60 tons we are moving on heavy, slippery sledges. I can just barely imagine how our teamsters, with the help of their whips and plenty of yelling, will get the guns up these mountains. It's the descents that worry me. The prospect of a runaway sledge is horrible to imagine with teamsters and animals below. Those sledges don't have brakes to offset very slippery runners. We're crazy if we think horses or oxen can restrain the sledges on steep downhills. How do we handle it?"

Will's voice boomed, making it seem to Tom that he was questioning the room, but his eyes focused on Tom alone, imploring him to invent a sufficient answer.

"Henry and I have talked about this many times. I had planned to use heavy ropes, wrapping them around the bigger trees, then having our teamsters slowly let the rope slip, allowing the sled to descend at our speed rather than gravity's. I did some calculations. The fact is, I couldn't get all the rope we needed by the time we had to leave. With the sledges carrying almost two tons of cannon, we'd have to use two strands. We might even need to use the block and tackle we brought. We will try to get more tomorrow, before we shove off. Again, Will, by anticipating the mountains you may have saved our bacon."

Tom was being sly with this compliment. He had enough rope to handle the job, but if more could not be found, it would just take much longer to descend.

They were about to retire for the night when Henry appeared, pleased at having finished his writing chores and ready for a nightcap. The waiter swiftly obliged with another round.

"Did you give the General an account?" Tom said, as Henry plunked his substantial frame down upon a chair surely challenged to support him. "Were you bubbling with optimism?"

"Of course not. I set a tone of cautious confidence, praising our team, including the uncomplaining beasts. And I asked him how goes our war for independence."

"Interesting turn of phrase, Henry," Tom said. "Hadn't noticed you referring to the war that way before. Are you really fighting for independence? That's an ambitious objective. In fact, it's the idea that prompted me to come here. But I understood that among most Americans, the belief was that the war started simply to force Parliament to acknowledge your liberties and redress your grievances."

Will was following the exchange closely. "Tom," he said, "being a traitor to the Crown, you can't get away with calling it Henry's war; it's your war too, and that's as sure a fact as I'm William Knox."

There were few patrons left and little warmth from the subdued embers slumbering in the fireplaces that bracketed the dining room of Albany Ale.

Henry said, "You're right. I was expressing a personal opinion, call it a hope. Mine is probably not the common opinion among the colonies. But it may evolve into that, unless the Crown and Parliament meet our demands. Is it likely they will submit? The most powerful nation on earth, widely believed to be, especially by themselves? They are more likely to convince themselves that they can weaken our will to resist, then humble and humiliate us in battle and, like shamed sheep, drive us back into the fold."

"I see your point. If we can resist long enough without total defeat, common opinion among our oppressed colonies will bend toward independence."

"A big if," Will added, sounding a blend of his customary fear and a new-found humor likely attributable to Tom's friendship and compliments.

By January 10th, they had reached the Berkshires, heading east along a timbering road too narrow and rock-strewn to be considered safe for the loaded sledges. It led 12 miles through a forbidding forest dense with tall pine, spruce and hemlock.

Though unaware, Henry Knox's little army, along with other Continentals under General Washington's command, would be powerfully affected by the publication on that day, in Philadelphia, of the pamphlet *Common Sense*, written by Thomas Paine, the very one whose lecture in Lewes Tom had attended. Paine was a bankrupt Quaker corset maker newly arrived from Great Britain, a sometime teacher, preacher, grocer and twice dismissed excise officer whose presence in Philadelphia had come about through his chance encounter with Benjamin Franklin in London.

Common Sense was the work of a genius that, in one form or another fell into the hands of almost every American who could read. If not precipitating the independence movement, the pamphlet was surely the propelling force that carried the movement forward to become the ultimate objective of military victory and independence.

The snow continued to fall, making travel hard and navigation almost impossible. At first, it was slushy, a mix with ice. Then, as the temperature dropped, it turned crusty, powdery and squeaky. They were pushing through snow two feet and more deep, with no footprints or other signs of life to lead them on. Blanford was the nearest settlement, a tiny group of five houses some ten or more miles ahead, through valleys and mountain passes unmarked on their maps. Henry was guided by a compass, pressed upon him by Lucy. It was a Flucker family heirloom, believed to embody luck as well as true north, and despite Henry's protestations, Lucy had insisted that he carry it.

By afternoon, they encountered a white-out, making it impossible to distinguish one object from another or, indeed, up from down. They couldn't see beyond the tips of their snowshoes. Nor could they hear each other, or even the crack of the whips unsuccessfully deployed to keep the teams of oxen and horses moving. The teamsters turned away from the whip to lead their teams by hand, wading through the deepening snow with snowshoes, taking turns breaking track. Henry had enjoined them to stick together, a caution vital to their survival in the enshrouding white oblivion.

The angry storm beat down on the travelers, showing no sign of let-up through the afternoon. The blowing snow stung their eyes like bits of glass. The wind made it feel colder. Only by removing their mittens and plunging their hands between their legs inside their pants, could some feeling be restored, and then only temporarily. The temperature dropped even further, worsening conditions that none among Henry's army could have imagined getting worse. Wind gusts strong enough to hurl a small dog battered them. They would have to stop in place, remaining unprotected overnight.

"A deathless cold," Henry exclaimed.

"Better a live donkey than a dead lion," Tom replied, shouting through the fast descending white darkness, though few could hear him. "Hunker down."

Henry ordered the train of sleds to draw up in circles where clearings could be found, with animals all facing in to the center, where fires were built from deadfalls not yet fallen, which were swiftly taken down by axe, cut up and split. The warming effects of swinging an axe in contrast to slogging along for hours beside the sledges turned those teamsters lucky enough to be chosen for wood gathering into a rambunctious group. Their feelings swiftly vanished as the storm continued past supper, past feeding and watering of the animals, past mostly futile efforts to sleep through the long night.

Dawn brought bright sunshine to cut through the bitter cold air that hung on them, still exhausted from the previous day's blizzard. The powdery snow squeaked under foot as the train of sledges began to move between what were known as the Spectacle Ponds and up a steep mountain pass, the highest point they would reach on the journey. The ascent was slow and taxing work, both for man and beast. Upon reaching the mountain's spine where it dipped slightly, an open saddle leading to the descending trail through dense forest, the teamsters were numb from the cold, with legs cramping from abuse the chief feeling left in their bodies. Even the animals complained with heaves and snorts bespeaking exhaustion. One teamster, sitting beneath a tall spruce to watch the slow oncoming train said loudly, but to no one in particular, "I'm so empty, so feeble, so beaten; it's impossible just now even to think of moving on."

When more than half of his small army had reached the top, Tom pulled Henry aside. "The troops are more than beat; to a man, reserves are exhausted; some, I fear, might be mulling mutinous thoughts. They need a rest, yes; but something more that you are very good at providing, Henry, and that's the will to endure, overcome and succeed. I don't need to tag you an aspirational leader. That you know. But perhaps not why. I know, because they've told me. It's because they want to be… you. That's it, my friend. Very simple."

"I'll see what I can do. Gather them around, when the last sled gets to the saddle."

Henry waited more than an hour for the last sled to arrive.

"Find a shaft of sun and rest awhile," Henry announced to the teamsters now crowding about. "Here's our situation. We are well over half way to Cambridge. About 175 miles under our belts, with 125 to go. That's good news. Better news is that we stand atop the highest point in this murderous forest, and we leave the mountains in

Springfield, only 25 miles east. Before that we'll come to Westfield, a village I expect to be both civilized and welcoming.

"It's worth a moment or two for each of us to remember, and reflect on, what we're doing in this mountain fastness, yoked to 60 ton and more of cannon. Each of us is part of a war to defend our properties, our families and our liberties from Great Britain. And ours is an essential part in that war when we recall that in Boston General Washington and his Continentals, without gunpowder or big guns, face well-armed regiments of British regulars. We must not falter. And I know we won't. And, before any among you is tempted to shake your head I'll tell you why.

"Each of you is a hero to the revolution. Whether you realize it or not, each of you was selected for this mission because somewhere, somehow known to the General, you exhibited heroic qualities. There are just five. Allow me to list them: optimism; patience; physical endurance; idealism; and courage. You may not recognize them in yourself, but the General saw them in you before we started, and I see them now. We are going to endure to deliver this cargo to the General. But now, for some nourishment, a ration of rum and an hour's rest."

With nostrils burning from the cold, but refreshed from biscuits, ham slices, rum and rest, and renewed in their sense of mission by Henry's talk, the men began the descent. The steepest and most dangerous part would be the first. Ropes were unwound and attached to the rear of each sledge before it began its downward journey. The other ends were wound one and a half times round as big a tree as could be found, no more than four feet high on the trunk. The teamsters would pay out the ropes as the sled descended at a pace controlled not by the horses or oxen yoked in front but by the men handling the ropes behind.

The first twenty sleds descended the length of the steepest grade without a hitch, the ropes being long enough to lower the sledges to a place where the safer pitch began. The twenty-first sledge carried the heaviest cannon, over two and a quarter tons packed into a weapon eleven feet long. Neither the teamsters nor their leaders had thought to adjust the technique as the trail got more packed and snow turned to ice from the heavy traffic. The force of gravity at play on the twenty-first sledge had little if any friction to diminish it. When the ropes snapped, one after another, the sledge had nothing save a pair of oxen to hold it back. They didn't, and couldn't, even if they had a mind to. Sensing a dramatic change in the sledge's weight, they started running. The teamsters yelled from their perch beside the tree wound tight with the ropes, now broken. They could see men below hurling themselves aside. The oxen couldn't escape their traces. The sledge crashed into them, knocking them down, then running them over before veering off the trail to be subdued by a virgin snowbank in the dark green forest. Assaulted by the sledge's sudden stop, the cannon's fastenings broke and the cannon flew onward, burying itself in deep snow. The oxen didn't fare so well. One was killed instantly by the sledge. The other was hurt enough to be put down, an act of mercy quickly performed with a musket.

Henry, who had been waiting at the bottom of the steep descent, rode back to supervise recovery of the cannon and repair of the sledge. Pointing to the oxen, he said to the group of teamsters gathered around him, "Nature's way of telling us we've failed. Let's give thanks there were no more than these poor beasts." Tom, standing nearby, was envious. Henry's way with words was a skill he lacked and one,

The oxen couldn't escape their traces.

he knew, was essential for command. It angered him; and awareness of being without obvious means to acquire this skill made him sad. At moments like this his state of mind was in turmoil: admiration for Henry's talents, which he assumed came naturally rather than through study and practice; anger at his own short-comings, which he considered beyond fixing; and deep sadness born of resignation. His mentor, James Brindley, had said Tom could be anything he wanted to be. At the time Tom believed him. Now, observing the remarkable Henry Knox, Tom rejected this possibility, accepting his flaws, both real and imagined. Yet, almost as an afterthought, he resolved to look for some counterweight to his shortcomings.

The recovery operation took the rest of that day and into the next. After repairing the sledge, they moved it into position below the cannon and, using thick boards to create an incline and two block and tackle roped to trees below to inch the cannon forward, six teamsters pulled it with agonizing slowness onto the sled. Spare oxen had joined Henry's army in Albany, a precaution that proved its value with this accident. Helping yoke two of them to the rejuvenated sledge, Tom realized with even deeper appreciation Henry's remarkable foresight.

The artillery train soon emerged from the mountains to follow a well-trod Indian trail east to Westfield. The village became a celebratory playground for Henry's army. The populace turned out to cheer the artillery train, exhibiting extremes of curiosity and hospitality. They fondled the big guns, measured the length of muzzles, pondered and even wagered on their weights, all the while plying "Henry's Heros," as the town's leading journalist described the cold, wet, ecstatic and exhausted teamsters, with hard cider and whiskey. One after another they staggered off to assigned billets and sleep.

Henry, not one prone to resist a party, responded to the residents' demand that a fat gun, nick-named "The Old Sow" because of it shape and size, be fired. Henry had his men put a charge, but not a precious cannonball, in the 24-pounder and light the fuse. The crowd cheered, but for many of Henry's men, the great boom brought to mind the hazards of a war they were returning to wage.

Arriving at Springfield, they were confronted by warming weather and melting snow that exposed the muddy ground beneath. The train slowed to a crawl and then stopped, awaiting the next freeze, which, fortunately, was not long in coming.

Having left the artillery in Framingham, Henry and his little army raced to Cambridge, eagerly anticipating a greeting they knew would include praise for their successful undertaking. They were not disappointed. In a gathering of Continental officers assembled by General Washington, he raised a glass to Henry, Tom and Will, and every teamster and soldier in the Ticonderoga artillery train: "You and your army of brave volunteers undertook a mission considered by many impossible and gallantly accomplished it. Thanks to you, we may now in earnest besiege the British in Boston."

Tom stepped forward.

"General, it is fitting for me, as one of those who so proudly followed Henry Knox, to praise his exceptional leadership. Without it, the job would not have been done. Indeed, Sir, without it the job would not have even been started."

Following this joyous reception, the General asked Henry to join his staff officers in a strategy planning session. Tom and Will repaired to a Cambridge pub, where they tried to imagine what was going on. Tom burned with disappointment. He had expected to be asked to attend with Henry. He felt left out and under-appreciated. And not just by the General. He had expected Henry to ask the General to include him. Henry's failure to do so, Tom took to be a slight. He was angry.

"Tom, it's hardly a time to be unhappy, but that's how you look. What's up?"

"Draw us two ales, if you will," Tom said to the waitress. "Just the normal let down after celebrating. Look, the issue that I'm sure the General has put on the table is when and how best to attack the British. Do you have any idea of numbers, Will?"

"In fact I do. At least, as of December. I had reviewed numbers for my brother. Here's what I remember. Inhabitants of Boston: 17,000, of whom at least 900 were declared Tories, including, by the way, Henry's in-laws. Most of the rest are Tory sympathizers. British regulars: 13,500. Against them, the General has about 14,000 Continentals, most of them raw recruits."

The pub was oddly configured, with an open fire pit in its center and tables spread around in circles. The welcoming fire was spitting and smoking as it consumed wet softwood logs. The tables were crowded with male patrons engaged in conversation, some open and conspicuous, others conspiratorial. Tobacco smoke hung thick above the tables, perfuming the warm air in a pungent mix that included wood smoke and the odors of humans robed for winter.

Will said "I hear the General's desperate to attack. Each time he brings up the idea, his generals urge caution. Now, with our guns, he's certain to snowplow through their caution."

"I agree. But I've been thinking about your claim that most of the Continentals are raw recruits. Tom Morgan's army, those dressed in deerskins and carrying Pennsylvania rifles instead of muskets, came to Boston as woodsmen experienced in Indian battles and experts with those long guns. At 200 yards they can reliably bring down a Redcoat officer, as they proved at Breed's Hill."

"Those rifles have some flaws, I've heard."

"The rifle Morgan uses is very accurate, due to the rifling in the barrel, but it's slow to load—takes a minute whereas a musket can be loaded and fired three to four times in a minute—and it carries no bayonet. Since the Redcoats use the musket more to create a ruckus of sound and smoke than to actually kill the enemy, and rely on the charge to bring them into close range where the bayonet is effective, they prefer that approach. So do some in our army, General Anthony Wayne for example. He is quoted as saying 'I don't like rifles. I would almost as soon face an enemy with a good musket and bayonet without ammunition—as with ammunition without a bayonet.' But Will, you understand I don't have a dog in this fight. I'm for artillery. And, now that it's here, I plan on helping put it to good use."

6

DORCHESTER HEIGHTS

Henry brought Lucy to Cambridge, where he had rented a small house on Brattle Street. On the evening of February 1, one of the General's couriers arrived at their door to deliver a message:

"The General and Mrs. Washington, present their Compliments, to Colo. Knox & Lady, begs the favor of their Company at dinner, on Friday half after 2 o'clock."

Surmising that the dinner was intended as a celebration of his long sleigh-ride, Henry found occasion to ask the General that the guest list be expanded to include Will and Tom.

After a moment's reflection, the General replied, "Why, of course. I should have thought to do that, myself."

The Washingtons resided in Vassall House, a Georgian mansion on the King's Highway, half a mile from Harvard's campus with a lovely view of the Charles. The mansion's larder was generously supplied with foodstuffs, wines and liquors captured from the British. The dinner proved a rousing success, with Henry and his colleagues regaling the General and his closest staff with tale after tale of mishap and hardship survived. With deliberate care, what reasonable men would consider heroic about the undertaking was suppressed by Henry, and by Tom and Will as well as they caught the drift of Henry's descriptions. Naturally, the less claimed by those who had prevailed, the more wonder and admiration filled the minds of their audience.

The table spilled over with Virginia hospitality: roasting pig, wild ducks, geese, turtle soup, plums, peaches and apples, limes to defeat scurvy and seemingly endless pitchers of cider, brandy, rum and Madeira wine. And for dessert, Martha's "great cake," as it was known.

There followed an eloquent toast by the General to Henry and his men. Aware of the many other times glasses had been raised since the day they returned, the General kept it short, beginning with expressions of gratitude to Lucy for permitting her husband leave to journey to Ticonderoga to fetch some guns and ending by observing that Henry's little army gave truth to the simple aphorism "By endurance, we conquer." Table pounding and huzzas filled the room as the General sat.

As the General spoke, Tom studied him closely, his first opportunity to do so. Tall, over six feet but so erect he seemed taller, he had slate-blue eyes and brown hair tied back in a queue. He radiated dignity with ease and a modest mien. And within, if searched for, tempered steel. Tom thought him sober, calm and brave. In all an inspiring leader.

Tom thought the cake uncommonly good, and unlike anything he'd tasted in England. On inquiring, he discovered it was rich, the product, as Martha disclosed, of 40 eggs, 4 pounds of butter, 4 pounds of powdered sugar, 5 pounds of fruit and half a pint of brandy.

Consuming her share of the great cake, Lucy considered the abundant fare being enjoyed at the General's table, in contrast with the sparse offerings in Boston, where the siege had choked off supplies except by sea. In her unrewarded efforts to contact her Loyalist family there, she had learned of the growing problems for many of near starvation and lack of heat. She also learned that for some few loyal to the Crown who were still in town, life continued in relative comfort, with an occasional splash of culture thrown in.

"Did you know," she announced, "that our sacred cradle of liberty, Faneuil Hall, has been converted by Billy Howe to an elegant playhouse for Shakespeare and home-spun farces? My sister, Sally, I learned from mutual friends, had a leading part in *Maid of the Oaks,* a satire written by one of Howe's Generals. A man named Burgoyne. Sounds French."

The gross disparities, both here and in Boston, were discomforting to Lucy, as was the fact that, in looking around the table, she could discern not even a tinge of distress among the diners.

James Warren, head of the Massachusetts Assembly and guest at the dinner, was noted for having surprisingly accurate sources of information about King George's Army. "I hadn't heard of your sister's starring role," he said to Lucy over dessert, "but I can tell you something of Billy Howe's Cleopatra, as she is known. A starring role, she plays, for our rebel cause. Inadvertently, as most believe, or deliberately, as a handful of highly suspicious sleuths with overflowing imaginations would have it."

Lucy replied. "You're such a tease, Sir, leading us on this way. Curiosity burns the table. Who is this Cleopatra?"

"Some of you know the story, but at the risk of boring them, I will answer you. General Billy, renowned for reckless bravery on the field of battle, indulges as well in an equally reckless taste for beautiful women, elegant dinners and long evenings at the faro table. Almost immediately upon his arrival in Boston harbor, he developed an irresistible itch for the company of Elizabeth Loring, wife of Loyalist Joshua Loring. Howe met his need with a creative trade: for plenty pounds sterling he hired Joshua to run the British commissary for rebel prisoners while Elizabeth, with little fuss, moved into his quarters."

Artemus Ward hadn't heard the story. "Might she be the explanation for Howe's failure over the entire summer to attack what he called our "rabble in arms"? In hindsight, it's such an astounding lost opportunity, one that even the smallest effort at intelligence could have revealed. Makes one veer off the trodden path for reasons."

"Quite right," said James. Take the Bible. Delilah, Judith and all those worthies. In the beginning… and evermore. Women beguiling men. But still. The case of Mrs. Loring and the smitten warrior Billy is unusual. A handful think she's one of our General's spies, faking her Loyalist roots and much else too." James turned an inquiring face to General Washington, whose soft eyes and unlined face of freckles and sun-beaten skin remained untouched at the suggestion, amiably non-committal.

"Others simply imagine she adds just enough extra attraction to Billy's warm bed to tip the scales in favor of postponing his next campaign to late spring instead of embarking in the bitter cold of winter."

General Greene added the fact that Billy and his brother, the Admiral, favored negotiation over war, having come across the Atlantic with the goal of achieving an early settlement. "Surely that line of thinking made procrastination in pursuit of rapture much easier."

"Rapture over rupture. I like it," the General said.

After-dinner conversation proceeded, as customary, in two locations, one occupied by the men and the other by the ladies. The General was given more to listening and questioning than to assertion and proclamation, especially when taking his ease with guests at home. He asked Tom why he had deserted to fight against those he sailed with to America.

"You've no doubt told your story a thousand times over, and I've heard some of it through others, but now I conjure you to let me hear it directly. For what you did was not without risk."

Tom at first was reluctant to respond, aware that he would be dominating the table for longer than he thought compatible with his station. Looking around the room, his shyness was eclipsed by the genuine interest he found.

"I can sum it up this way: In England I was trained as an engineer by a canal builder, one James Brindley, a remarkable man who believed passionately in what he called 'the aristocracy of talent and virtue, of wisdom and courage.' He saw his country governed by a different kind of aristocracy. One where power is derived from birth. He despised that system. Of course, it had wounded him more than once, as he came from simple, yeoman stock. Despite exceptional talent in engineering, he found his main chance in the profession limited by his origins. James urged me to flee the country to America. He saw it yet unstained by British rule, with a fair prospect of remaining so. I asked if he might join me. He declined, admitting to being too old for a new start. Frankly, the thought of going to a new land frightened me. Then, quite by accident, I attended a speech by Thomas Paine. He shredded the notion of monarchy. I resolved that night to follow James' advice."

The General was moved. "I hear that your man, Thomas Paine, landed in Philadelphia and is pregnant with a little book he's calling *Common Sense*. Perhaps you got a preview. Have you read Plato's *Republic*, Tom?"

Tom shook his head. In truth, he had hardly heard of Plato and only knew him to be, somehow, famed in antiquity.

"I'm much taken by the philosophy of your mentor, Tom. His definition of aristocracy hits at least two of Plato's four cardinal virtues, which were wisdom, courage, justice and moderation. So, you enlisted in the British Army to get here, and then, I imagine when hostilities commenced and you discovered you were fighting to support what your mentor had taught you to despise, you switched sides."

"Yes, that's it exactly. My regret is that James Brindley never knew of my defection. He died shortly after I sailed for America. Now, may I ask you a question?"

"Nodding, the General said: "Seems only fair, given my poking around your past."

"Well, Sir, it's simply this: how do you think we will fare in this conflict? Do you think the finger of Providence tilts the scales in our favor?"

"Ah, the ultimate question. One, as you can imagine, I've been asked before. I can't speak to the weight of that finger, whose existence is beyond my ken, but I know the 60 tons of cannon you fetched for me from Ticonderoga will move the scales, likely more than we can imagine. More, even, than an amulet. But, as I have written to my generals, tis not in we mortals to command success, but we'll do more. Yes, we'll do more because of our cause. And by our conduct, we'll earn and deserve success."

At the mention of his precious cargo and amulets, Henry spoke from a heart given more to honest praise than fulsome flattery.

"General, if I may say so, you are the palladium for this new-born country. Just consider, for example, the raw and rustic levies you must command and somehow, against the odds, shape into an army fit to oppose the British regulars."

"Well said, Henry," said Tom. "Friends, join Henry and me in raising a glass to the General."

There followed a tingling of crystal and hearty huzzas all around. The General, familiar with all that the Goddess Pallas stood for, flushed.

Recovering, the General said, "If wisdom be our theme, the question is what to do about Dorchester Heights. Since June, the Brits have kept Bunker Hill heavily armed but left the Heights unguarded. In fact, rumors have come to us that Howe wished we would take possession, as he could then 'sally forth' as he put it, concentrate his forces to dislodge us, and in that way put an end to this uprising—this ragamuffin revolt, as his brother the Admiral calls it. My aim has long been to attack him where he rests. We've had this debate before. You all know how disagreeable I find our inactive state. Since September I've wanted a speedy finish to this fight. I've argued that a well-aimed stroke might put an end to the war. But at every council, I've been talked out of attacking. What say you now?"

"How fast Howe forgets Breed's Hill," said Tom. "I fought there with the Brits. And I remember. We were lured up that hill by you rebels, and paid a pretty price. I recommend the General take the Heights to lure Howe out again." Others around the table concurred.

It being his strong opinion too, the General bowed to the unanimity among his dinner guests. "But the trick," he said, "is how to get up there and create the necessary defenses without being detected. The ground is hard-frozen, impenetrable as a rock. Even if we had the time, we couldn't dig trenches or throw up breastworks. Especially in the dark. In silence."

"Are the Heights within range of British artillery?" Tom asked.

"A mile and a half away, well within range of 12 or 18 pounders. Even the fleet could reach us," the General replied. "One thing is certain. We have to occupy the Heights over one night, or not at all. We want to bring on a rumpus with the redcoats, but not before we're ready to fight from the top."

Tom brimmed with optimism. "Couldn't we fashion timber frames here, and then move them to the summit with oxen, to be filled there with bales of hay and fascines of brushwood and branches?"

"Funny," Henry said. "Rufus Putnam talked to me just yesterday with the same thought. I was planning to see you about it tomorrow."

"Excellent! Tom, you should work with Colonel Putnam on the fortifications. Perhaps we could also carry up barrels, filled with earth and set in rows in front of these fortifications, ready to be rolled down on Howe's troops. Artemus, see if this is possible. If it is, see that the hoops are well-nailed to the staves." The General was plainly excited to be in the planning stage. His long arms extended like a bear's embrace, the General continued, speaking rapid-fire.

"Henry, we must plan night barrages from Roxbury and Cobble Hill to cover the noise of our working parties. We'll need to round up carts, wagons and all those well-rested oxen, the ones that pulled you across New England. Getting your guns up over 100 feet to the top should be child's play for the men and beasts who ferried them 300 miles."

The decision taken, intense planning began, looking to early March for the move on the Heights. Henry was charged with the bombardment of Boston, beginning at midnight, Saturday, March 2, from gun emplacements in Cambridge and Roxbury. The cannonade was heavy and loud beyond even Henry's imagining. The British response was even greater. Breath-taking. In addition to the Ticonderoga guns, Henry's works included a huge brass mortar taken by Captain Manly, a privateer, from an English ship he had captured on its way to Boston. Henry named it the *Congress*. As the bombardment began, Tom was trying to direct his complement of men in loading and firing the *Congress* and two other smaller mortars. The night was clear and lit by an almost full moon. Seeing

Henry nearby, he drew close and whispered, "I've never fired a mortar before. Nor have the men. I'm assuming it's the same as cannon. Don't mean to add to your worries. Just wanted you to know."

Henry pulled Tom close. "Neither have I. Tell anyone and I'll see you shot. Let's hope you're on the right track."

The mortar unit trained through the night, on the job. The *Congress* and two other mortars burst, casualties to the learning-by-doing process that characterized Washington's army. Tom's insistence that his men keep their distance from these weapons and take cover with each firing saved their lives.

The batteries resumed Sunday night and again on Monday night, each side raising the ante in terms of frequency and size of firepower. The roar pushed off the scale; sheets of fire filled the sky, seeming to vanish behind a moon ghostly white. Protected from detection by the roar, Washington's working parties and riflemen silently assaulted the Heights, followed by hundreds of carts and heavy wagons drawn by Henry's famed oxen and filled with Ticonderoga guns and the makings of two sturdy redoubts, to be swiftly assembled on site.

By dawn on the 5th, the General was beaming with satisfaction. Installations were complete and, as far as he could tell, so was the element of surprise. As expected, the occupation of the Heights triggered in Howe the impulse to attack. Now, he must have thought, *I have them where I want them. I can strike the decisive blow that will bring Washington to his knees.*

Howe's forces sallied forth, Breed's Hill a distant memory. The commander's pride and honor were on the line. It appeared to the Continentals that no reconnaissance had been undertaken. Henry and his artillerymen watched the embarkation of redcoats from various wharves in Boston, then saw them travel down the harbor to Castle Island, where they disembarked.

"My God, that's a crowd," Tom said. "It's a wonder those transports don't capsize with so many troops standing shoulder to shoulder like packed sardines."

"From the look of it, General Howe has thoroughly animated the troops. High spirits all round. He should remind them that today's the anniversary of the Boston Massacre—that's a nice touch," Henry said. "There won't be fighting today. Too late in the afternoon for them to parade, a few transports still headed to the Island, and the weather's changing."

Tom, too, had been noticing the weather, especially the wind, which had started to blow hard from the southeast. "You know what, Henry? The arm I broke long ago is pretty reliable in predicting in-coming storms. It's telling me a big one is on the way. Could soak those redcoats and dampen more than their powder."

"Yes, yes, their gunpowder. What a splendid act of Providence. Mum's the word, though. Providence hates being counted on. Runs away from humans arrogant enough to seek control."

That night the earlier warmth of an unusually balmy day changed to bitter wind-blown cold as a vicious storm of hail, snow and sleet crashed into Boston Harbor and blew across the well-anchored redoubts on the Heights. By dawn, the storm continued with heavy wind and cold driving rain. From the Heights, the Continentals soon recognized the beginnings of a British retreat. Howe had surrendered his pride to the forces of nature, redirecting his forces from an attack on the Heights to an evacuation of Boston. There would be no redux of Breed's Hill.

Loud huzzas from the Heights chased the soggy mass of British regulars as they lined up to re-board transports bound for Boston. Watching the departing army, Tom reflected on the certainty that, but for his desertion, he would be among those lobstercoats, feeling as he knew they must feel the humiliation of defeat for no better reason than the weather and Howe's hasty decision to bow to it without a test. The specific empathy he felt for his former mates in the army was at war with his general hatred of the British occupation, but Tom, like most thinking *sapiens*, could hold in harmony, at the same time, two or more contradictory ideas.

7

ELIZABETH VAN HORNE

Henry and Lucy invited Tom to dinner, to celebrate the victory of Dorchester Heights, a climactic triumph to be sure, but rather than one by force of arms, a matter of providence, as the General was heard to exclaim that night, standing tall above Boston with foresight sufficient to see through the tempest.

Thinking himself the only guest, Tom was surprised to be greeted at the door by Lucy and another young woman, introduced as Elizabeth Van Horne. She had come from Middlebrook, a village in New Jersey. He saw a thin young woman, graced with proper feminine curves, all in modest dimension. Slightly taller than Lucy and, in appearance, younger, to Tom's eyes, Elizabeth was an intriguing beauty. Long in the neck, she possessed an oval-shaped face sharply etched by a prominent forehead, high cheek bones, a distinct nose that belonged in this company, well-shaped lips, a dimpled chin and deep-set, rust-colored eyes that seemed too large for her face. Worn in a ponytail, her hair was long and black, a startling contrast to her ivory complexion.

The storm had blown out to sea, leaving a clear moon-lit night that was bitter cold. Lucy served hot mulled cider with hors d'oeuvres of seafood and fish. After stomach-warming toasts to the Heights, the rebel army, the oxen, the General and, finally, fortune's tempest, attention turned tipsy to Elizabeth, or Lisa, as she preferred to be known. Lucy explained that the Van Horne family, though settled in New Jersey, had spent time in Boston and were close friends of the Fluckers. The two Van Horne brothers, Tom and Phillip, had famously between them eight highly engaging daughters, three by Thomas and five by Phillip. The families lived together in a large mansion in Middlebrook. Lisa was the second girl born to Phillip.

"Allow me, if you will, to explain to Lieutenant Machin how I came to be under this solid and generous Knox roof." In Tom's ears, Lisa's voice sounded like music easy on the ears.

"Our home is known as Convivial Hall, well-named for it resembles a jolly hotel filled with officers, sometimes British, other times American, all of them there for amusement. The Van Hornes seem to have been born to entertain. My sisters and I, together with our three cousins, were encouraged by our elders to enjoy ourselves and have fun with our guests, equally from either side. My father taught us neutrality. He was practiced at this uncommon art. He encouraged us to develop charms that were apolitical. Generals came and went. Cornwallis, Sulllivan, Baron Steuben, many others. We were co-conspirators with our father in gathering information, and even wielding power and influence, through the softer arts.

"Until Anthony Wayne came one afternoon and stayed through the night, I had accepted father's claim that at least a third of Americans were neutral. Tony, whose attentions that evening changed my life irreversibly, insisted there was no such thing as a neutral resident of America. All would be judged, he said, one thing or the other. The key to citizenship, he argued, was to judge for oneself, to decide one's side before others decide it for you, and then to move off the sidelines and act. He saw this as the key to happiness too. He caused me to take the side I knew, deep inside, was where I belonged. He called upon me to come of age, and I responded. Soon after, I left Convivial Hall, without knowing for how long, with neither explanation nor goodbyes. I came to Cambridge and threw myself at the feet of Lucy and Henry."

Tom was surprised at this candid outpouring. Not just at the storyline, which was surprising enough. He felt moved by the storyteller. She spoke with earnestness, spooling the story with a soft voice impossible to doubt. But there was more than just her voice. Her words danced from a lithe frame that could have belonged to a trapeze artist. It moved in propulsive ways to augment or embellish her story. In all, it seemed an honest invitation to understand her in depth. No one had spoken this way before. It captured him.

"What will you do?" Tom asked, breaking a silence that endured long enough to feel awkward.

"I intend to help rid ourselves of the British. How, I don't yet know. Perhaps I could become a spy. The redcoats found me attractive. Lucy and Henry have promised to help me find useful employment. I'm older than I look."

* * * * *

Until summoned by General Washington to Fort Montgomery in July of 1776, Tom Machin remained in Cambridge, using his engineering skills in erecting fortifications to defend Boston and its harbor. He was also engaged in planning a canal to connect Cape Cod Bay with Buzzard's Bay, a project he was unable to complete before leaving New England for the Hudson Highlands. Henry had been ordered to New York on April 3, taking Lucy with him. The rental of their house in Cambridge was good through December, so they asked Lisa to sit the house for them until "things settled back to normal," as Henry liked to say, meaning, of course, a successful end to the fighting. Through March, Lisa and Tom had become increasingly friendly over meals at the Knoxes. The day after they departed for New York, Lisa sent word to Tom begging his company over dinner.

Upon entering the house that evening, Tom was aware of an unfamiliar fragrance in the air. "What's that smell?" he asked Lisa, when she appeared in a beautiful scarlet dress he'd never seen her wear before. Its bodice barely covered her breasts. A string of pearls hung from her long neck, curving in such harmony with the cut of the dress that one might conclude they were shaped by the same hand.

Looking hard at Lisa's cleavage, Tom said "I think I've located the source."

"Tell me you like it and I'll tell you its name," Lisa said, her voice a lilt.

"If I didn't like it, do you imagine I would call attention? It reminds me of frankincense. Am I on the right track?"

"It's called tuberose. A perfume from the creamy white lily by the same name. Make of it what you will."

She wore black gloves, extending almost to the elbow. He felt as if she were a river, and he a boat without oars or rudder.

"Take my hand. We will go in to dinner." The food was prepared and served by servants retained by the Knoxes. Madeira accompanied what was, for Tom, a forgettable meal. The unforgettable part was the conversation that ensued when Tom asked Lisa about her family, and what it was, exactly, that caused her to leave.

"Counting my three cousins, there were eight of us living in Convivial Hall under the guidance of my father, whose brother, Thomas, the father of those cousins, was dead. He turned our home into a court, where he could preside, entertaining guests of importance, be they British or American, it didn't matter as long as they could reward him for his generous hospitality. He molded the eight of us to be women of his court—in a word, courtesans."

"Meaning…"

"Father never came close to using the term "courtesan," which to some sounds dignified, even aristocratic, and to others just a fancy way of describing a high-priced prostitute. In fact, we were neither. We were, each of us, what we decided on occasion to be. Father would be shocked to hear me talk this way. And deny, deny, deny. But he knew exactly what he was doing. He knew it wasn't the cooking, or his personality, that brought the likes of Light Horse Harry Lee and Col. Stephen Moylan to Convivial. How it started, with my cousin Hannah or sister Mary, I know not. But Father encouraged them in exploring many forms of hospitality, asking only that we entertain. And he pushed the older two in bringing the younger girls into the game.

"But even to imagine yourselves as courtesans? You weren't paid?"

"Father would scream at the thought but, of course, there was payback. It went to him in myriad ways. Confidential information, for example. And, by the way, we enjoyed learning to entertain. To become good, really good at it. That's what the eight of us talked about. I see you blushing. The things we discussed, the merits of one trick over another; now that would be a debate to make you blush red to purple."

"You must have really hated the role your father cast you in to leave Convivial, cut off your family and all."

"Hold on. Lest you think me a prude, I must distinguish between, on the one hand, physical attractions and even love-making, to which I'm wholly in thrall, and on the other, serving both sides of this war by claiming neutrality, an idea I came to abhor."

"I'm beginning to understand."

"That's good, because I dressed this way, hair up, tuberose on, with the intention of seducing you right after dinner. Which, I confess, I've had an itch to do for weeks. Which, you will have noticed, is occurring right now. Come, we will go upstairs."

Entering the master bedroom, Tom said, "Lisa, how old are you? I recall you saying you were older than you look."

"17 going on 18. And you?"

"I'm in my twenties."

"That's not an answer. Why not tell me your age? Yes, and your birthday? Come on, out with it."

Tom didn't want Lisa to know how old he was. At 32, he worried she might find him too far down the path to be of interest. "Ok, I'm 25, born on January 20."

"Old enough to be experienced in bedroom matters. Right?"

"Depends what you mean. In Britain, I fooled around a bit, but...." He paused, tempted to claim prowess but aware how empty that claim would prove to be when exposed to one as practiced as Lisa.

"Look, now I'm going to disclose a secret I don't even like to admit to myself: I'm a virgin when it comes to making love to a woman who cares for me."

"I'm sure you're right about that! I think you mean you haven't slept with someone who didn't charge for the pleasure." Again, he blushed, this time more than the last. He began to think she was more than he could handle. That is, until he realized he had been hers to handle from the minute he crossed the threshold.

"Take off your clothes and lie on the bed. I'll be back in a minute." She disappeared into the bathroom. When she returned, still dressed as before, he, who had done as directed, said "Don't you want me to undress you?"

"Thanks, but I prefer to do it my way. I doubt you'll mind." Lisa began with her long gloves. And then the pearl necklace. She sang softly *L'homme arme*, and moved her body, sometimes with a swaying motion, sometimes in rotation, with an easy flow, as she continued to remove her clothes, piece by piece, watchful throughout for the expected stiffening of Tom's member, the particular response she sought from this audience of one. She got it before the second glove had been removed. From start to finish, Tom was overcome by Lisa's genuineness, her fidelity to the moment, her lack of embarrassment, awkwardness or shame, her so very natural pleasure in receiving and giving. And overall, her absolute control of every detail, her mastery of the process. A night to remember for a lifetime.

They lay beside one another in Knox's big soft bed, talking. Tom began quietly to laugh.

"What are you thinking?" Lisa asked.

"Someone said, when this war started, the world turned upside down. I'm laughing at myself for connecting that *bon mot* to my situation here, where things are also upside down: first make love; then fall in love. Crazy."

"If you fall in love so easily, I'm sure you'll find it as easy to fall out. But don't jump to conclusions. Wait till tomorrow. For me, I've never been in love in the sense that I think you mean it. I was raised to be in love with love itself and the men who attract me. Carnal love, the kind that may not last the night; different from the spiritual kind that, some believe, burns like an eternal flame through marriage and beyond."

"Which love weighs more on your personal scale?"

"I've only experienced one kind, so comparison's not possible. How about your scale?" Lisa had begun massaging Tom's chest and stomach, teasing his hair in ever-widening circles until she touched his member, then caressed it and felt it respond.

"My mind is clouded from passions spent and renewed. Readings would be unreliable."

"Not at all. Let's take another reading."

The next morning, over tea and muffins, Lisa, looking uncommonly embarrassed, said, "Tom, I realize, after these months of knowing you, I've never heard how you got here, or what you did before coming. Somehow, and it must be a credit to how comfortable you made me feel, I never sought background from Henry, and he never proffered it. So, talk to me while I boil a couple of eggs."

"My story's not particularly exciting. Grew up in Lewes, schooled in mathematics from childhood, entered artillery training during the Seven Years' War, saw some fighting in Europe, particularly in the Battle of Minden, continued with engineering education after that war, and worked on complex projects involving canals. I came to America in 1772 on assignment to examine a possible copper lode in New Jersey. False alarm. But the country appealed to me. I settled in Boston, where I was radicalized by young Patriots."

"How so?" She had placed on the table the soft-boiled eggs in neatly designed cups and now was leaning forward, intent on following every word of Tom's soft voice as he told his tale.

"Well, they gave me some Mohawk clothing, painted my face red with white stripes and took me along on that tea party you may have heard about. We tossed a lot of tea chests overboard that night."

"My God. You mean you were a member of the Boston Tea Party? That practically makes you a Founding Father. I'm so honored to… to have been tossing around with you in bed last night."

He scoffed at her mockery.

"I suppose you've heard the doggerel about the tea party."

Tom shook his head.

Father brought it home one day and couldn't stop reciting it.

"Rally, Mohawk, bring out your axes.

Tell King George we'll pay no taxes,

On his foreign tea."

Tom laughed.

"Then what? Were you at Concord and Lexington too?"

"No, but I did fight on Breed's Hill. We had only muskets, no artillery, and we ran plum out of ammunition and were forced to retreat when the Brits mounted a third assault. They were whipped, or would have been, if we hadn't run short. Leaving that redoubt was a bitter pill."

What was Tom thinking when he told Lisa this story? That was the question he put to himself throughout the day. Was it infatuation? Shame over his lowly means of reaching America's shores? Shame over deserting? He had again allowed his imagined belief in who he was, or wanted to be, to shred the truth. And to what purpose? Overnight he grew increasingly alarmed that his lies would be revealed.

The next day Tom wrote Henry. Having lied so completely to Lisa, he wanted to beg for a promise from his friend not to disclose the true story. Without telling Henry what he had told Lisa, he said he had told her a tale different from the one Henry knew. "No one except you and those at dinner that night with General Washington know my story. I beseech you, as my best of friends, and a most loyal one, to promise me, for life, you will hold my story private to yourself, telling no one."

Henry was perplexed and wrote Tom to that effect, concluding with the sought-for promise. "I will do as you wish. Not a problem. But why you wish this is beyond my ken. Deserting to the Patriotic cause is a credit to you, a brave, even noble, act, a mark of honor. Wouldn't the easier path be to correct the tale you told Lisa? When we next share a brew, you must explain yourself."

8

ORDERS FROM THE COMMANDING GENERAL

On July 21, General Washington issued orders to Tom: "You are without delay to proceed for Fort Montgomery, or Constitution in the High Lands on Hudson's River, and put yourself under command of Colo. James Clinton or the Commanding Officer there, to Act as Engineer in completing such Works as are already laid out, and such others as you, with the advice of Colo. Clinton may think Necessary—'tis expected and required of You—that you pay strict and close Attention to this Business—and drive on the Works with all possible Dispatch."

In a letter of the same date to Colonel Clinton, which Tom was directed to deliver, and which was open to be read by him, the General described Tom as "an ingenious Man," one who "has given great Satisfaction as an Engineer."

Tom's pride had never been reduced to a level one might call "modest," even though he had been subjected to horrendous abuse by a British Sergeant bent on stripping him of all dignity and self-respect. The General's compliments, however, took him to a new level of belief and self-confidence. He couldn't resist showing the letter to Lisa, in the course of telling her he had to sever their comfortable arrangements.

"'Ingenious' he calls you. I've got a bunch of nice words to describe you, but never would have thought that one up. Now 'great satisfaction' I do include in my litany of praise, but as a lover, not an engineer. I see you're pleased with yourself."

"Well, it's not too shabby, given the source. I mean it could be worse. Now, about leaving here, it's ...."

"Want me to go with you? No, don't answer that, 'cause I don't plan to. I may join you sometime, but for now we have to separate. In spite of what you call my 'coolness,' I'm likely to miss you more than you do me. I just won't let on that I do. You have a war to fight. I have only myself to think about."

As usual, he realized, she was already a couple of steps ahead of him, despite his having just surprised her with the news.

"I'd love to give you General Billy Howe to ponder. I wish you could just push Mrs. Loring aside and devote yourself to his undoing. Some say she's doing just that, but it's taking too long. With your surgical skills, you could operate with far greater swiftness."

"To be sure. And then we could retire to a beautiful farm in New Jersey. Nice dream. For now, we must write. You first, since I'll need your address, when you're settled." Lisa smiled, then grabbed him close, hugging tight.

"A soldier in wartime never settles. But write I will, wherever I touch down. I will leave tomorrow. Should be able to pull my things together by then. A better season to travel the Berkshires than on the Ticonderoga trip."

* * * * *

"Lieutenant Thomas Machin reporting to the Commanding Officer, as directed."

Tom was feeling good. His westward trip to the Hudson was trouble-free, a contrast from the winter journey in the opposite direction. He had elected to retrace his journey with Henry Knox through Springfield, Westfield, Great Barrington to Claverack, and then down along the east side of the Hudson to Anthony's Nose, where he was lucky to find a boat from the Fort with a soldier able to row him over to Fort Montgomery.

The Fort was located about 100 feet above the river, which at that point narrowed to a width of roughly 2,000 feet. To the south, the Fort was bounded by a small creek called Popolopen, flowing east into the Hudson. To the south of the creek was a point of land projecting farther into the river than the Fort, and somewhat higher in elevation, a mostly level spot of ground near an acre in size. It caught Tom's attention.

Alerted by the guard, Colonel James Clinton appeared before Tom, greeting him warmly. "We've been counting the days, Lieutenant, since the General told us of your posting. Welcome. Indeed, as you will discover, we need you badly. How did you fare from Cambridge?"

"It was a fine trip, retracing my steps on the Ticonderoga venture with Colonel Knox. It filled my head with memories, all happy ones. Funny, isn't it, how memory of the dreadful moments—and there were many of them—can be erased by the glory of completing the task. What a contrast in weather from January to July. I'm eager to be briefed and get to work. This landscape is extraordinary. Anthony's Nose is fit more for goats than men, although able climbers placed there with Pennsylvania rifles could do execution to enemy sailors. What a fine sight that would be."

"Nice point. A chaplain here a while back described the Highlands as 'majestic, solemn, wild and melancholy.'" His words stuck in my head. These hills, or mountains to some, are pre-Cambrian granite, and for ten miles or so rise high above the river, itself a glaciated sea-fiord tidal up to Albany.

"Here's the guard. He will take you to quarters. Get settled and then join me for dinner. There's much to discuss."

Over dinner, Colonel Clinton outlined the projects he planned for Lieutenant Machin. "Tom, our Commander-in-Chief, commends you highly. Am I correct in believing you were not drafted, but volunteered, to join Henry Knox on the Ticonderoga assignment? Many of us thought this an overly ambitious undertaking, one packed with danger and risk of failure. What motivated you?"

Tom nodded his head. "It was Henry's idea. So audacious. Coming from a Boston bookstore owner, just arrived in Cambridge, drenching wet behind the ears. And it's almost the first thing he says to the General. When Henry told me, I could hardly believe it. But then I remembered Henry's love of Homer and of Ancient Greece. He's a romantic. His idea was heroic, Homerian. Odysseus returning from Troy, Pheidippides running to Athens from the Plains of Marathon. He made the project irresistible. And, prosaically, Henry was in charge of a Continental Artillery that had no guns. Setting out, we could only imagine a triumphant ending as a long train of big guns wheeled into Cambridge."

"Looking back, how do you see it?"

Tom ran his hand through his hair a couple of times, a way he had to take time to think when caught out by a question. Finally, shaking his head, he said, "Besotted by revolutionary fervor, I guess. In hindsight, it seems a crazy thing to attempt, and, yet, after doing it, the trip seemed easy. One quickly forgets all that went wrong. Looking back, I can't recall anything as exciting since the night we tossed tea overboard."

"You were one of those Tea Party Indians? Amazing. Proud to know you, Tom. When did you arrive in America?"

Tom told the Colonel the same story he'd told Lisa. The lie took little time to travel around the Fort, with the same impact it had on Lisa. Telling this tale at the Fort, isolated so completely from his past, proved easy for Tom, whose mind was equipped to embrace as true what its better part knew to be a lie. A stranger to the Fort's men, he couldn't resist repeating the Tea Party fiction.

"Well, I'm not sure we can assign you challenges greater than the Ticonderoga frolic, but I'm going to try, since it's obvious you like them, and rise to the occasion. We need to lay out and build a Fort just to the south of Popolopen Creek, where the land is higher and extends out into the river more than here. It must be able to prevent the enemy from occupying the higher ground of the mountain to the west. Lord Sterling, who was sent in June to review fortifications in the Highlands, wants to make this companion fort a grand post, with a magazine of size. It would command passage of the river, protect the works here and afford cross-fire with our guns to deter hostile shipping."

"I know I'm speaking out before a careful walking tour of the area, but my impression from looking around as I arrived is that both Forts will be exposed on the west to attack by land."

"That's our Achilles Heel. But the passes through the Highlands are difficult. I think if we can station men in the right places, they can provide warning and engage the enemy with delaying tactics, but redoubts well-positioned at both Forts are essential. You will have an eye for siting. There's a hill behind this Fort that could serve."

"Are there more challenges on your list? I thought you were hinting."

"Yes, the next is how, beyond the batteries we mount here and at the southern fort, can we obstruct navigation on the river. I'm sure you know the British Navy commands the water, both around New York and to some as yet undetermined extent along the Hudson. They can transport their Army by water from place to place much faster than we can ours by land. General Washington and his Council of General Officers all agree that Continental success hinges on command of the river. Communication of every sort between Eastern and Western States is essential and depends in the largest way on free and easy access on and across the Hudson. Without it, the British could sever our forces, block transportation of troops and supplies, enfeeble us by cutting off our sources of flour, corn, cattle and horses, and then defeat us in detail. We know command of the river has been fundamental to British strategy from the beginning.

"Come over here, I've a table map showing the river to Albany. Its fleet can sail where they wish. Early on they saw the river offering the easiest route through New York across Lakes George and Champlain to Canada, as well as access to the Great Lakes via the Hudson's western tributary, the Mohawk."

Two negro servants appeared, one to remove the dinner plates, the other to serve tea and coffee accompanied by cornbread, still hot from the oven. When they left the room, the Colonel explained that they were slaves freed by wealthy Dutch patroons. Tom thought he sounded embarrassed.

"I don't disagree, but I see a huge challenge for the British Navy to actually control the whole of this river. Your map captures its length. And if they tried, I also believe it would weaken their ability to control much coast line. In saying this, of course, I am assuming the Tory sympathizers along the river are managed and our army controls both sides of the river with means to attack the British ships as opportunities arise."

"Valid point. But we just don't know. And we fear finding out. The British fleet—more than 120 vessels—is the largest armada ever assembled. Since May of last year, the Provincial Congress of New York has been set on achieving control of the Hudson. I was appointed to a committee of four to recommend fortifications along the Hudson; this Fort and the one at Constitution Island were two of our ideas.

"We have been directed to install a chain across the river here and to devise such additional means of obstruction as a clever engineer might dream up. Already under study are fire ships and rafts and *Chevaux-de-Frise*. The chain is your principal duty. But you must also undertake the armaments for our sister fort to the south. And, to pile on, you should be involved enough in the other projects to offer judgment. Alas for you, your reputation precedes you. Henry described a man decidedly inventive, especially under pressure."

Tom blushed.

"What about Constitution Island? I understood there was work going on there. Is it part of my job description?"

"Short answer: no. A better answer requires some history. Fort Constitution is sited a few miles upstream on a 160-acre island called Martelaer's Rock, opposite West Point. Its location is an orphan, as no one seems eager to claim its merits except a Connecticut surveyor, one Bernard Romans, whose vaulting ambition carried him to Philadelphia, where he successfully gained appointment as the engineering contractor to design and build what quickly became known as Fort Constitution. The origins of the siting decision predate Romans' engagement and are as murky as the waters of the marsh that comprises most of the island.

"The Fort suffers from three major defects: First, its guns are positioned at the bend in the river too far west to command the long reach of river to the south. An enemy vessel could turn the point without being seen, and in minutes with favorable wind and tide, slip past the Fort's guns. Second, the Fort is commanded by all the grounds about it and exposed to easy attack by land. Finally, the grounds on the west side of the river are some 500 feet higher than the Fort, rendering it vulnerable to fire from above, if the Enemy could occupy the high ground by landing troops unobserved by us or coming at us through forced march overland from the West.

"Romans' plans were monumental, in keeping with his ambition. Almost from the outset, he fought with New York officials. The project proceeded at the pace of a proverbial turtle. Finally, in late December, Romans was fired and in January the Continental Congress moved the chief site for defense of the Hudson here. Then, aware of so much lost time and expense, the growing British threat and the repeated bungling by the Commissioners for Fortifications, our Commander-in-Chief asserted sole direction of the river's fortifications, relieving the Commissioners of further service."

"Tell me how things stand with the chain idea?" Tom asked, thinking it past time to get to work.

"Sad to say, things are pretty much in a muddle. The obstruction project has seemed to rest entirely in the hands of a so-called "Secret Committee" of the New York Convention. And, yet, as I said, General Washington just asserted sole control. So, how efforts at obstruction proceed is cloudy. Getting clarity, clear lines of authority and the like, could be your first task. The Romans experiment cost us far too much time."

"I guess it's much quicker to appoint than to fire."

The Colonel nodded. "One hates firing because it reflects badly on those who made the appointment, who typically are the knowledgeable ones in position to fire. One delays the decision, trying to make it work. It seldom does."

Tom tried hard over the course of several weeks to determine where things stood with both the chain and the fire ship projects, looking for a point of entry where he might serve in either endeavor. He learned that General Washington had ordered the committee responsible for construction of Continental Frigates at riverside in Poughkeepsie to equip a number of fire ships. It turned out this job was taken over by the Secret Committee, which had undertaken to find ten vessels, preferably old ones not worth the effort to ready for battle, and outfit them with light wood, pine knots, pitch, tar, turpentine and grappling irons, as well as oars of 14 to 20 feet in length and many fire arrows. This project was put in the hands of a Captain John Hazelwood of Philadelphia, whom Tom greeted upon the Captain's layover at Fort Montgomery on his way to Poughkeepsie. Over dinner they found their engineering experiences a sturdy foundation for friendship.

"Well, I actually haven't been in this fire ship line of work long. I learned on the job, attacking the British on the lower Delaware. We ended up doing some serious damage. Lucky, yes, but intuition guided the execution."

"I see the concept: Sail or row the fire ship toward the enemy. When in range, shoot fire arrows into the enemy's sails, high enough to prevent the enemy from extinguishing the blaze. With the enemy distracted, drive the fire ship into the enemy vessel, attach her to the enemy with grappling irons, set the fire ship aflame very fast with a conflagration big enough to defeat any effort to suppress the flames, and escape in a long boat or by swimming. What could be easier?" Tom drained his glass of rum, and with a mischievous smile looked with all innocence at John, who fetched the bottle and added a shot's worth to Tom's glass and his own.

"Sadly, there are variables that bring luck into the picture—the tide, the wind, the moon, the element of surprise and finding your bearings in a night dark enough, with a wind loud enough, to cloak detection. Look, why don't you come with me to Poughkeepsie, learn how to outfit a ship for fire. I'm just going to do one, to demonstrate the kit. I'll make you an expert."

Colonel Clinton thought Captain Hazelwood's idea commendable.

Tied at the Poughkeepsie wharf, they found three vessels selected for incineration in the cause of liberty. John selected Polly, a sloop of about 100 tons. It was surprisingly snug and polished given its destiny.

A team of artificers suddenly materialized, sent by the Colonel to do Captain Hazelwood's bidding. Most of the supplies ordered by the Captain had been collected a week or so in advance. The critical ingredients, consisting of spirits of turpentine and saltpeter, were brought by John.

"Charging a fire ship is more easily done by young boys than old men like us. Setting fires comes naturally to them, and they're good at it, being robust and carefree. So, remember, give your inner child free reign.

"First we take the Faggots. And these have been selected well I see. Soft conifers filled with sap. We dip them in boiled turpentine. We pile them up in a first tier everywhere on deck from bow to cabin, being careful to leave easy passage for those aboard. The tiers must be constructed to give ample space for air to draft up the middle of each pile. Add bundles of straw, one foot long, dipped in the turpentine, to each pile. Then drip melted pitch to cover as much as possible of each pile. Do the same in the hold. Cut strips of canvas a foot in width and long enough to hang from the spars and rigging to the deck. Soak them in turpentine and tar. Finally, prepare a match with twisted yarn dipped in a mix of gunpowder and saltpeter, then soaked in turpentine and dried. Lay the match in branches of yarn leading into several piles; spool the main yarn back to the cabin where it can be lighted by the skipper, allowing time for him to escape into a whale boat lashed to the sloop through a door cut in the side of the vessel."

The artificers jumped into action, following John's instructions. Tom marveled at the completeness of the scheme. "It can't fail. Most impressive."

"Shouldn't fail. But a little luck still useful. The belt and suspenders idea."

"What if it rains or the waves cause the material to get wet?"

"Yes, a risk. I was coming to the roof of straw thatched over each pile and then soaked in turpentine and coated with hot tar. When hardened, this roof will assure dryness underneath."

"And shouldn't the piles be secured in place, against the enemy coming on board and tearing them apart?"

"Indeed, you're right. On the Delaware, we used a couple of chains crossed on top of each pile and then nailed securely into the deck. Forgot to mention that."

The Captain did everything swiftly, as if the whole war depended on it. Finishing his assignment, he bid all adieu, with an especially warm good-bye to Tom Machin, and began his journey by horse to Philadelphia. The other two vessels were quickly charged as the *Polly* had been, and then this little fleet sailed south with favorable wind and tide to Spuyten Duyvel. The idea was to have the vessels well-positioned to do damage to any of the British fleet bold enough to venture north from New York Harbor.

Very soon thereafter, word came to Fort Montgomery that the British Frigates, *Phoenix* with 44 guns and *Rose* with 24, accompanied by three smaller support ships, had been detached from the fleet and had sailed with impunity through cannon fire from Forts Washington and Lee on July 12th. They reached the Tappan Zee, the broadest part of the Hudson, some 30 miles above the city, where they began using cannon and shore parties to harass the patriotic farmers on both sides of the river.

Colonel Clinton summoned his officers to ponder this disturbing news.

"If these warships, with tenders, could pass so swiftly up the river without suffering serious damage from our shore batteries, why couldn't 30 or more ships of the line follow? Friends, don't we have a very serious problem on our hands?"

All those in the room had already been asking themselves the same question.

Tom said, "With transports, they could bring an army up and, controlling the land as well as the river, deny General Washington any escape route from the city."

"We must try the fire ships. If they work, the enemy might be intimidated enough to stay in New York Harbor for a while."

"What makes you think the General will need to escape?" quipped Captain John Lamb. "Perhaps he'll strike a knock-out blow when the enemy lands. The terrain is unfamiliar to them."

"Anything's possible," said the Colonel. "But given the massive forces aligned against him, I doubt our shrewd General would hazard a general engagement. That's precisely what Howe wants: a 'decisive action' he calls it, to quickly wind things up. Washington knows the key to this war is survival, living another day to fight. Again and again. To draw blood, without risking annihilation from vastly superior forces. This strategy tugs against the fighting instincts of warriors like General Washington. I've heard that at times it has even made him ashamed. Yet he knows it's the only way. Time is our friend. Delay is Howe's worst enemy."

In early August, orders came to deploy two fire ships against the British frigates, now anchored in deep water on the west side of the Hudson, opposite the mouth of Yonkers' Saw Mill River. Colonel Clinton, who had been charged with following their movements since early July, suspected that they had been warned of a possible engagement, and for that reason had moved to deeper waters. The Colonel, having been promoted to General, decided to travel to Yonkers to watch from the high ground there, as two of the fire ships were brought into action. He asked Tom to join him. Late on the moonless drizzly night of August 16th, the fire ships were towed out of Spuyten Duyvil Creek by three row galleys manned by Connecticut watermen instructed to be as silent as snakes. Favored by wind and tide, the pending conflagration moved north toward the British vessels, anchored four miles away.

Tom heard bells aboard the British vessels followed immediately by the cry of Sentinels passing the word, "All's well." Before anyone on shore could comment, the fire ships burst into flames. The scene suddenly changed, dark to light, murky outlines of vessels becoming brightly etched shapes, over which towered the cliffs of the Palisades. One fire ship appeared to be closing on the *Phoenix*; the other had already thrown grappling irons against one of the British tenders, the bomb ketch *Shuldham*. Confusion reigned on the decks of the British vessels. Cannons were fired. British seamen could be seen climbing to get out on yard-arms, hoping to drop to the deck of the fire ship and extinguish the blaze. After about ten minutes of chaos, the *Phoenix* parted from the fire ship and disappeared in the darkness, apparently having escaped the flames.

The bomb ketch had ignited swiftly after the other fire ship became attached. Tom could see men from the ketch leaping into the water. General Clinton pointed to a whale boat, loaded with men, moving away from the fire ship and ketch, pulling toward shore. The whale boat tied to the other fire ship was nowhere to be seen.

It wasn't until a report was received back at Fort Montgomery that Tom learned how things had turned out. The skipper and crew of the fire ship that attacked the bomb ketch escaped without loss. The ketch was destroyed and the British lost close to 70 men, as well as some women and children.

The other fire ship had reached the *Phoenix* too late for surprise. After some ferocious fighting, the *Phoenix* freed itself, slipped her cables, cut away all enflamed rigging and, towed by her long boats and helped by the tide, moved off into darkness, leaving the fire ship to be consumed by fire of its own making. The skipper and five of his crew drowned, having been forced to jump into the water instead of boarding the whale boat. They paid a high price for igniting the fire in such a way as to deny themselves access to their only means of safety.

Several days later, General Clinton summoned Tom. The General had been exercising with a body of troops. The work-out had been vigorous, as was evident from the sweat wetting his jersey top to bottom. His face was flushed and still moist, despite toweling.

"Well, what's your thinking? Did I tell you the *Phoenix* and *Rose* quit their stations two days after the encounter, returning south to rejoin the fleet?"

"We need to decide whether, if continued, and even ramped up, use of fire ships is a good idea. Hard to answer with the experience of only one encounter. Looking at August 16, we committed two fire ships, failed to damage either of the two enemy frigates that were our main targets, burned one tender and lost one captain and five crew. One way to look at it, and it's harsh, is to weigh our loss of two ships, one captain and five crew against the loss of one enemy tender and a large number of its passengers and crew."

"That's fair. But apparently General Heath has urged our Commander to follow up the August 16 affair with more of the same, aimed at the British fleet in New York Harbor." Smiling, General Clinton added, "Given the size of the fleet, it would be hard not to collide with some of them."

"The problem with fire ships is so much can go wrong. So much left to chance. In the dark, Captain Bass overshot both frigates to toss his grappling irons onto a tender. Being able to see is necessary, but to see is to be seen. The element of surprise is lost. And the targets can defend themselves with maneuvers and guns."

"I suppose it gets down to priorities. Do we have the strength to take on both the British Army and its huge naval armada? General Washington's call. But, if you were he, what would you do?"

"If I get it straight, the British have some 150 ships in their fleet, including many transports and merchants. The bulk of them are reported to be in New York Harbor, milling about or at anchor. If their captains get wind of the encounter, and ponder the possibility of many fire ships moving swiftly with favorable wind and tide, all at once, on a dark night with the element of surprise intact, they could most reasonably fear panic among the fleet when the fire ships ignite, leading to great loss. The large size of the fleet works against them in escaping our fire ships. The experienced mind of a ship captain can easily become clogged with terror over the prospect of fire breaking out amidst many vessels at anchor in close quarters. My strategy would be to harass the British by making them constantly aware of this threat. Outfit five or six fire ships and place them up river within eye-sight of the British fleet. They would be decoys, undermanned with only a few men; not expected to be used."

"Ignite not our fire ships but the enemy's imagination. Ingenious. I will pass it along to the General. Now, we must turn all hands to the chain. The General is pressing us hard on obstructions. And understandably so, because if the chain works, the size of the armada is irrelevant."

* * * * *

The next day Tom received a letter from Cambridge. No name of sender or address on the envelope, but much to the amusement of the soldier who sorted and delivered the mail, the odor emanating from the envelope was strong, so strong, in fact, that, as the soldier, laughing, informed Tom, "it had infected the whole damn pile of today's mail. I swear, by Jesus, the mailroom smells like a bawdy house."

Tom recognized the perfume immediately. His heart quickened to a rate more fitting for a dog than a hardened Continental.

"Private, how do you know what a bawdy house smells like?"

"There's perfume on that letter, Sir. Women wear perfume. Women work in bawdy houses. That's my thinking. Never been in one." The Private was scared. He turned to go.

"Not so fast, Private. That nose of yours caused you to jump to conclusions. Did you know that not all women who wear perfume work in bawdy houses? And not all women who work in bawdy houses wear perfume? And, Private, did you consider why someone put perfume on a letter instead of the female body for which it was made? Couldn't it be a signal, a password, a label or a nametag? A spy's message? Think of that the next time you jump to sordid conclusions."

Tom's darts had penetrated the lad, who was squirming with embarrassment, face flushed and red, especially the nose.

"Dismissed," Tom intoned in a voice edged with laughter that, he hoped, went undetected.

Opening the letter, he looked first at the ending to find: "Missing you, Lisa." The letter was short, written in a beautiful hand obviously well-trained and applied, at least in this instance, with care.

My Dear Lieutenant Machin,

Within the month of September, I plan to arrive at Fort Montgomery for a visit, assuming base rules allow. At some point I need to return to Convivial Hall, as I've heard my father is ill and spoke with apparent eagerness in wanting to see me and erase my estrangement. My visit there will be brief, after which

I will return to your Fort. I've sent word to Father that I will oblige him.

Tom's heart, having regained normalcy, leapt again upon digesting Lisa's message. Hers was not to be a brief stop on the way to somewhere else. Rather, it appeared that she intended to remain at the Fort for an indefinite period. How like Lisa, Tom thought, remembering her style to maximize options. Or was this the imagination of a lover reading too much into his beloved's words?

9

FORT MONTGOMERY AND CONVIVIAL HALL

He met her at the landing. Lisa was pink of cheek, her hair gloriously wind-blown, her mien composed, confident and happy.

"Lieutenant Machin, what a swift crossing! Didn't even have time to learn more than Private Frances' name. I'd hoped to learn more, particularly about you. Looking up river and down, I bet this is your spot for the chain. But where is it?"

"Still in the planning stage. Here, give me your hand and step out carefully. That's it. Nicely done."

For an instant, catching Private Frances' watchful eye, Tom hesitated, refraining from embracing her. She showed no restraint, closing the gap between them to press her body against his and insist on a long kiss.

They retreated to Tom's quarters. The Private delivered her bags and left them alone.

"What plans for supper?" Lisa asked, removing her cape and plopping down on Tom's bed.

"General Clinton has invited us to dine privately with him. In about an hour and a half from now. You'll like James, as he is known."

"Come here. Ever since you left, I have been wanting you; it's a feeling that's grown as the distance to Fort Montgomery has shrunk." She smiled, expressing modest feminine warmth, but her eyes flashed hunger, a contrast Tom couldn't fail to notice. "We have time now. Think of it as an hors d'oeuvre."

Tom had planned on giving Lisa a tour of the Fort, and then, after dinner, renewing their bedroom pleasures. She's ahead of me again, he thought, and in so many ways beyond the bedroom.

"You're the guest. I'm at your command. I remember the drill."

* * * * *

General James Clinton was gracious in his welcoming. Over good claret, white bean soup, bread, cold ham, tongue, mutton and corn pudding, conversation turned to Convivial Hall and its remarkable reputation as 'neutral ground,' where British and Americans found entertainment, sometimes within the same 24-hour period. Having been cautioned by Tom, the General refrained from questions about Lisa's recent history, but he did learn that she would visit her father within the next few days. Tom described the saga of the fire ships. Lisa was paying close attention.

"So," she said, "do you think the encounter enough of a success to continue trying to torch more of the British fleet?"

James said, "I must say it pleases me to find a woman so interested in our work. I thank you for this, and say 'keep thinking,' for we need all the intelligence we can assemble. Now, about the fire ships. It was more of a draw than a victory. But we are inclined to continue a threatening gesture toward the King's fleet, in hopes of worrying them enough so they don't come up river in strength."

"You've heard the story. What would you do?" Tom asked Lisa.

"I can imagine plenty of risks to this sort of attack. But, if the goal is to scare them into not sailing north, your strategy seems wise. Perhaps, if I come across the British at Convivial Hall, I could add weight to the threat."

"Good thought. Of course, they might not believe you, since they will probably find out where you've been."

"Unless you can convince them you're a spy for the King," James said.

"Not possible. I left home in protest against the King, and everyone around there knows it."

"Here's another idea, building on Lisa's," Tom said. "Suppose we give Lisa a secret message for General James Heath from General James Clinton, informing him of a plan to vastly enlarge the fire ship weapon, and deploy it en masse to descend on the British fleet, cause confusion and destroy as many ships as possible. Heath is at Kingsbridge, so it's logical he would need to be informed of such a major undertaking. The message would be sealed. Lisa's job would be just to deliver it unopened, to General Health. With her guile, I'm sure she could contrive to have the message accidentally fall into the hands of the likes of Cornwallis or other British brass who might be taking in the seductive airs of Convivial Hall. Handled right, her 'tragic' loss could be our gain."

James nodded in agreement. "Bravo, Tom. Capital idea. What say you, Lisa?"

"With a little luck, I think it could work. Turns any message I might deliver from dubious to creditable. Don't see a downside. Let's try."

That night, having repaired to quarters, Tom cautioned Lisa not to get carried away with the seduction nonsense.

"My goodness, Tom, I believe you're jealous. Come now, you don't even know of whom you might be jealous. I'm more alarmed than flattered."

She kissed him on the forehead and gently pushed her hand through his hair.

"Lisa, have you ever had trouble lying?"

"Not at all. Having played the family game at Convivial, I'm accustomed to lying, which is a vital part of that game. But here's a point of pride. I have made it a rule not to lie to friends or family. I render unto Caesar what is Caesar's, but to my friends and family, only what's true. Does that sound right to you?"

"Oh yes, absolutely." Much later that night, marking the hours like a metronome, first slumbering and then awake and tossing, Tom tried to understand, even to get a grip on, what made him at age 32 continue to lie, and to do so with all comers, family and friends included. To continue despite so many painful experiences of being called out. Through the worlds of consciousness and dream, he relived his earliest lie, one with such painful consequences that most people would suppose it broke him of the habit.

When a famous troupe of actors announced they were coming to his town to perform, Tom, then ten, when told of this event by his closest friend in school, and the fact that he was going to attend, boasted that he had been to London, where he had seen the troupe in exactly the same play. "No big deal," Tom advised his friend. As he later learned to his chagrin, his friend had intended to invite Tom to join him and his parents at the performance but, because Tom had already seen it in London, his friend picked another boy instead. A painful result, yet not a lesson learned.

Why did he continue, again and again, to lie to others? By now he knew enough to realize the lies were always designed to aggrandize or ennoble himself. As a fragile kid, this might have been understandable. But he had become a grown-up, a somebody, with nothing to apologize for, no need to boast of imagined glories, every reason to accept his life as it had become, accomplished. And yet, he sensed in the night's restlessness that it would be hard, if not impossible, to shed a need that, logically, was no longer needed. How, he asked himself, could he outgrow it, cast it off like pants that no longer fit?

* * * * *

Lisa found the Hall unchanged, but her father much so. Phillip appeared to be knocking at death's door. Lisa, in Phillip's eyes the prodigal daughter returning in loving contrition, played the part. Soon after her arrival at his bedside, thinking he was dying, Phillip forgave her, and beckoning, whispered something in her ear.

That night, the Van Hornes, believing Phillip would not see the next day, honored his life with a feast of his favorite foods, and toasts appreciative of the joyous life he had enjoyed. The Hall echoed with lively conversation augmented by a clutch of British officers, who had stumbled in without knowing of Phillip's condition but nonetheless, at Phillip's insistence, were welcomed in the established tradition of the Hall.

Among the officers was Major John Andre, well-known and popular in Tory circles, especially among the ladies. Lisa quickly saw what others understood. She decided to target him to play the discoverer's role in her act. Introducing herself to him as one of the Van Horne hostesses, she invited him to join her at a window seat somewhat away from the main party of family and guests. "It's quieter here," she explained. Lisa then began an intense conversation about the Howe brothers and what she told Major Andre seemed to her and many others a reluctance to carry the fight to Washington. She unspooled several examples of their odd behavior.

"So you're a Tory, eh? I thought your family was neutral."

"Oh, we're a large family with lots of different opinions." Lisa smiled, recalling what her father had whispered in her ear: 'I'm a patriot; the rest is show. Remember me that way.'

"I see, it's only Convivial Hall, itself, that's neutral."

"Not right. The Van Hornes, themselves, are trusted by both sides. We keep secrets. We deliver messages. We honor the faith invested in us by officers of both camps."

"There's a strange reluctance in Billy's inactions, given the extraordinary difference in strength he commands compared to Washington. Without throwing firearms, clothing, food and supplies into the mix, all of which Washington's army lacks, the manpower advantage at 30,000 to 3,000 or so, that's ten to one, makes him too deep to fathom."

"Speaking frankly, the Howes harbor the idea that they can achieve a far better peace by the threat of overwhelming force than by using that force to cause bloodshed and hatred amongst the people whose renewed loyalty they seek. The campaign of '76, now ending, has shown, at Long Island, Manhattan, Forts Washington and Lee and at White Plains, what the King's forces can do. We expect over the winter that Washington's meager and, I might add, dwindling forces will quietly fold up their tents. The revolution will end by the coming of spring."

With unconcealed amazement, Lisa stared at the attractive man before her.

"Major Andre, with all due respect, Sir, that expectation is absurd. It's naïve. It suggests a kind of school yard game the Continentals are playing. It conveys deep misunderstanding of the passion for liberty that your King's policies have engendered here and the determined set of this country's collective chin to honor that passion. To serve it not just until weather becomes too cold to play outdoors; no, until the yoke of Britain is thrown off. For as long as that takes."

Impressed by this burst of passionate rhetoric, the Major smiled. "Isn't he your King too?"

Lisa flushed, fearing that her uncensored diatribe had blown the attempt to present herself as a Tory. She knew that when in a hole, it was best not to keep digging. She ignored the question.

"My dear Major, there's a theory at large, embraced both by those skilled in matters military and by those experienced in the ways of beautiful women, that General Howe is bewitched by a woman hailing from Long Island but seduced by her while a married woman in Boston. A ravishingly attractive woman named Elizabeth Lloyd Loring. Besotted, perhaps to the point where he dances first to her tune rather than the tune of *our* King and Parliament."

Lisa saw that her charge had angered the Major.

"This is utter nonsense," he said. She put index finger to lips while throwing the Major a censuring look. Lowering his voice to a whisper, the Major continued in a snarl.

"General Howe has an unimpeachable record for personal bravery and leadership, especially under fire. He earned appointment to his present post not through patronage but in recognition of his highly successful earlier commands. After his victory on Long Island, your King knighted him. You haven't a shred of evidence."

"My dear Major, your argument proves my claim. It's undeniable that on many occasions in these early days of the war he could have wiped out the Patriots simply by giving an aggressive order. The question is why didn't he? Was he too cautious or indolent or sympathetic with the Patriot cause? Given your litany of his talents, none of these explanations serve. That leaves, as the most plausible explanation, his submission to the wiles of Mrs. Loring. It's well-known that Billy is as morose as he is manly, that he rarely speaks and is often wrong when he does. Just the sort who could be manipulated by a smart woman."

"Lisa, you have a clever way about you. Is it possible you envy Mrs. Loring? Are you jealous of her?"

"She's the clever one. And, yes, I admit to a touch of envy. Not because of her charms, heavens no. Because of her power. But, has it occurred to you that Mrs. Loring might be a secret agent of General Washington?"

"In fact, it has, and not just to me. But she checks out. Tory roots run deep in her family and her husband's. But my dear, dear young thing, your analysis left one thing out. Both the General and his brother, the Admiral, undertook their commands with the goal of conciliation, to heal and restore, let's say, the wayward child to the bosom of his mother. They are pursuing the right combination of force and persuasion. Velvet glove covering just barely the mail fist."

"Surely you can't believe that," Lisa exclaimed, showing growing agitation. "I very much doubt the Howes know the first thing about breast-feeding. The British war machine makes few friends. Your Billy's men plunder indiscriminately, turning even the most committed loyalist into a supporter of the rebel cause. Peace won't spring forth from the muzzle of a musket, and General Howe is much too smart to think otherwise. No, nothing answers like Mrs. Loring."

They were sitting close together on the window seat. Lisa had a rather large purse. "I must fetch my handkerchief," Lisa exclaimed, reaching for her purse and knocking it to the floor. Out came an envelope addressed to General James Heath from General James Clinton, written in large bold letters with the caution "Secret: For Your Eyes Only" appearing under General Heath's name.

"Oh, bother," said Lisa.

Quick as a mongoose, the Major dropped to his knees beside the purse, pushed the envelope back inside and retrieved the handkerchief, handing it and the purse to Lisa.

Both were relieved to turn the conversation to the Major, his experiences in the military, his family and similar uncontroversial matters. After using the handkerchief a couple of times, Lisa announced she was rapidly becoming indisposed. "It's a pain in my stomach. I'm afraid it's getting worse, even as we sit here. Would you mind helping me to the kitchen. Father's nurse should be there and will take care of me. I've been known to handle food badly. Oh, my purse. Would you mind terribly taking it to the vestibule and storing it in the small closet? I like to leave it there, so I don't forget it when going out."

Lisa was bent over, moaning in apparent pain and using her hands to rub her stomach. Taking one of her hands in his and holding the purse in the other, Major Andre guided Lisa to the kitchen, where the nurse was stationed. Leaving her in the nurse's care, he expressed hopes for her complete recovery overnight and disappeared.

Lisa underwent a miraculous cure overnight. Seeing the Major at breakfast, she thanked him again, apologizing for interrupting an interesting exchange. He said he must return to New York City forthwith and bade Lisa goodbye.

"My loss, Major. I had understood you'd be staying another night. Why the change, if I may be so bold?"

"Yes, that was my plan. But, you know better than many, that life in the military is as unpredictable as the weather."

"So I've heard. Even more so than a woman."

Finding her purse in the closet, she swiftly retrieved the letter, which retained the silage of tuberose. She examined its seal. The letters JC had been impressed in the wax. They were still there, but a subtle change in their alignment with the letter's edge informed Lisa that the letter had been opened.

Miraculously, Phillip had not only survived the night but was found in the morning to be much improved. In the days that followed, with good care and nourishment, his health was restored. He began to feel normal.

When Lisa returned to Fort Montgomery in mid-October, Tom was occupied in directing both the construction of Fort Clinton, on the south side of Popolopen Creek, well within shouting and musket range of Fort Montgomery, and the construction of the chain, which now was the chief obstruction planned to prevent the British from taking command of the Hudson.

Shortly after her return, word reached Fort Montgomery that an earlier effort at obstruction near Fort Washington had failed. Upon receiving the news, General Clinton asked for Tom Machin.

"The *Chevaux-de-Frise* and sunken ships we had installed across the river from Fort Washington to Fort Lee failed utterly of their purpose. This installation had been kept a secret, even among many of our own officers. I was the only one here who learned of the effort. On the 9th of the month, the *Roebuck* and *Phoenix,* each of 44 guns, and the Tartar, a frigate of 20 guns, ran through these obstructions, unfazed by them or by our batteries at both Forts."

"Ouch! Where are those warships now?"

"It puts stress on our project for the chain, and, ultimately, on you."

Tom nodded. "The warships?" he asked again. "Might they have troops on board? Might they be aiming to surprise our Fort? Does their passage mean Lisa's work with Major Andre failed?"

General Clinton seemed to abandon his command presence to give Tom the look of one lost in the woods. "Our best guess is they're anchored in Tappan Zee. But we're blind. No solid intelligence on their location, purpose or cargo. We do have some intelligence, and it's all bad. The Westchester Militia have become unreliable. Indeed, many have shifted loyalties to the enemy. We are in a weakened state. And we grow weaker by the day."

"I don't know when the 600 militia levied from upstate will arrive, but without nails we won't have the three barracks built to house them. In Britain, we never lacked for nails. And, oddly, much of the iron for them came from here. Try holding boards together without them. To an engineer, they're assumed, like mother's milk to the newborn."

Alarmed by Tom's tone, General Clinton seemed to remember his position.

"Now Tom, don't you start to despair. We feed off your optimism. Any turn to the darker side will spread like a virus through the Fort. As I see it, as long as General Washington is in command, we will survive. Have faith. And get to work on that chain." The General put his arm around Tom's shoulders, then gently shoved him towards the door. Their joint recital of despair was over.

But once outside, Tom sprang around to hold the General's arm. "Wait a minute. Given the date those warships sailed past our obstructions, Andre couldn't have reported to Howe about your letter. He hadn't even arrived at the Hall by the 9th. So Lisa's hook may still be in place and have effect down the road."

That night, hearing of the *Chevaux-de-Frise* disaster, Lisa peppered Tom with questions. "Let's face it, the enemy controls the river and can do as it likes. At 400 men, aren't these Forts undermanned? The mountains west and south could offer British troops concealed access right up to firing range."

"Your insights surprise me. You'd be even more pleased if you knew the Commanding General, in repeated correspondence to General Clinton, has been emphatic on the point of guarding those routes against surprise attack. We know what needs doing. We're sorely short-handed."

"Speaking of needs, Tom, even my military mind needs other sorts of nourishment now and then. I had a provocative dream last night. Can't remember the details. Only the feeling remains. It's been there all day. Put your concerns aside and come to me in bed. You have a free night. And I have a plan."

* * * * *

The Secret Committee was in overall charge of blocking the Hudson. Tom began direct communication with that group in July and quickly discovered that it did not contemplate leaving the engineering of obstructions to him. At his first meeting with the Committee, held at Fort Montgomery, Robert Yates, one of five members and apparently the spokesman, got right to the point.

"We know you're an engineer, and a favored one at that. What you need to know is that the predecessor to this Committee, drawn from the Provincial Congress, had assigned to it by the Commander an engineer named Bernard Romans. Like you, he was trained in England. Romans was given broad discretion, a decision our predecessor committee soon came to regret. For he proved to be both aggrandizing and egotistical and vastly over-confident of his abilities and judgment. In short, a difficult man to work with, so difficult in so many ways, that he was fired by the committee. That experience has led us to be cautious in approaching the matter of delegation where an engineer is involved."

Tom was dumbfounded. He knew of Romans' folly at Fort Constitution. But to allow him to taint the entire profession was unfair. Worse, it was downright stupid.

"With respect, Robert, not all engineers are the same. Just as not all Generals are the same. One rotten apple can spoil the barrel, yes. But engineers don't all come from the same barrel. To taint the profession with the sins of one of its members is wrong."

"We will work with you on this project. We simply must—and I say this for many reasons including how time sensitive it is—we don't have time to mess it up and start again—keep all those involved on a very short leash. As the decision-making is ours, so too is ultimate responsibility. You won't be blamed if things go awry."

"I understand. And I will work with you, tethered to a short leash. Not a new experience, by the way. So, what specifically do you have in mind?"

"Well," said Robert, "we are not of one mind. John Jay wants to try to block the river by tumbling huge boulders from Anthony's Nose down into it. He would leave depth enough only for an Albany sloop."

"Interesting idea. Who would do the tumbling?"

John Jay responded, "We'd need some eight to ten thousand Continentals up there with levers." At first, Tom couldn't believe Jay was serious. But, a second glance at his intense expression was convincing.

"I must disappoint you. The river is over 150 feet deep where the rocks would fall. It would take years to fill that depth, and half the Nose."

Like the sun's rays suddenly appearing through dark cloud cover, relief flashed across every committeeman's face save one.

"They all told me the idea was far-fetched, but most great ideas are rejected out-of-hand when first brought forth. But, here, I must accept your point, not having appreciated the depth."

"Other ideas?"

Robert pulled a sketch out of his leather case, inviting Tom to have a look. The day had become hot and humid, the air close and sticky. The unpleasant odor of human sweat became ineluctable.

"We actually have another plan, one even John accepts. We dropped the idea of stretching a chain across the river, preferring a boom. It would be a connected series of rafts using pine logs 50 feet long, spaced 10 feet apart and framed together by three cross pieces. The rafts would be placed 15 feet apart across the river from the Fort to Anthony's Nose. They would be connected by strong iron chains. The rafts would be anchored so as to have the logs facing up and down the river, their ends sharpened and sheathed in iron. We also considered adding another row of logs, similarly designed, downstream of the boom, to act as a first line of defense and, if broken through, to lessen the shock of the vessels against the boom."

Tom listened with care. "Have you been able to reckon whether this obstacle will hold against a ship like the *Phoenix,* which I understand is about 860 tons? With a favoring wind and tide, its speed could reach 11 knots. If the boom holds, the logs should penetrate the ship's bow; if not, the logs will be pushed aside."

"I'm afraid it's all a gamble. Of course, seeing the boom, the Royal Navy might decide not to risk a ship. But we can't count on that, and in the case you set out, we just don't know."

"Do you have experience to draw on?"

"We know Alexander replaced rope anchor lines with metal cables to prevent having his ships set adrift in the dark by underwater swimmers. Caesar did the same. And emperors of Byzantium stretched chained booms across the Bosphorus. But evidence of success is hard to find. Nothing that gives any assurance for our conditions. I fear it's a 'pig in a poke.'"

"My concern is with your choice of boom instead of chain. The rafts are chained together. The weakest point will be the connection between each raft and the chain used to connect it to the next raft. I doubt that the connection can be made as strong as the connection of one iron link to another in a chain stretching across the river and well-anchored. It's iron to wood against iron to iron. Well made, iron to iron wins every time."

A heavy iron-link chain worried the Committee on several counts: the long delivery time that they imagined, and the difficulty of installing a chain of iron that doesn't float compared to a boom of wood that does. What turned them, however, was the dismaying report of the woodsman present that enough 50-foot pine logs to build the boom were going to be hard, verging on impossible, to find along the Hudson south of Albany.

"With speed, we can probably scrounge up enough logs to build the smaller rafts needed to support a chain, but the boom you have in mind is another matter entirely. It would take much more time, and there is a good chance we fall short in footage."

With little further discussion, they opted for the chain and took up Tom's advice to order the links from Ancram, New York's first ironworks, owned by the Livingstons and located on their East Hudson manor.

"Gentlemen," Tom said, Ancram's iron is smelted from reddish brown hematite, brought from Salisbury, Connecticut on mules and horses. The Livingstons hold a large interest in the Salisbury mines, assuring the supply we need."

"Are we sure of quality from Ancram?" John Jay woodenly inquired, adding, to everyone's chagrin, as they had suffered many times before by indulging this knave's literary pretensions, "as you might know, a chain is only as good as its weakest link."

"My goodness, yes," Tom replied. "The Salibury ore contains much manganese, imparting unusual strength."

Soon after meeting with Tom Machin, the Committee met with Robert Livingston, who informed those gentlemen that, in May, Ancram iron had been hammered into chain links on order of General Lee, whose idea was to stretch a chain across the Richelieu River near the town of Sorel on the south bank of the St. Lawrence River, to block Canadian war galleys from working their way up the Richelieu into Lake Champlain.

"Splendid idea," Livingston said. "But our invasion of Canada fell to smallpox and lack of success in the field. When the patriots evacuated Sorel, the chain went to Fort Ticonderoga. I urge you to commandeer it for the Hudson."

Since the span from Fort Montgomery to Anthony's Nose was much wider than the Richelieu, some 1600 or more feet across, more links would be needed. To meet that need, Robert Livingston stood ready to order his forges to run both day and night.

The Committee had to work through General Phillip Schuyler, commander of the Northern Department, to try to obtain the chain. Without explaining himself, Schuyler wasn't encouraging. Meanwhile, a source for pine logs to start building the boom had been found.

The Committee returned to Fort Montgomery. They were in a quandary as to how to proceed. Robert Yates confessed to Tom that the Committee was inclined now, with materials in hand to install the boom, and uncertainty still existing about whether they could commandeer the chain at Fort Ticonderoga, to proceed with the boom.

Tom urged them to follow both routes. He reminded them of his strong opinion that a well-made chain would be far superior to the boom in repelling British warships. "Delay would likely serve if in the end a chain could be installed. The risk is mainly an attack on Forts Montgomery and Clinton by land, and we are getting ourselves prepared."

Robert Yates said, "We hear your men are indifferently supplied with arms. Both muskets and artillery. You want for ammunition, and even for nails needed for construction. Your barracks suffer. And we understand you are woefully undermanned in trying to defend these forts, each of them being dangerously exposed to the hills that lie to the west and tower over them. At any time now, the enemy could land a force on the west shore, at Stony Point, for example, and by forced march through the hills, surprise both forts."

"Not likely as we have sentinels posted in those hills, both day and night. In theory, a very large force could subdue us in our present state, but in truth, I believe the reports, from you and others, that the British forces are now fully occupied in New York.

"As for our fortifications, they are a work in progress. General Washington is aware of our condition. We must count on him. We do so with confidence. As you would, too. My point is simply that, if I am right about the relative strength, and therefore effectiveness of the two solutions, and I lack no confidence in asserting a vast difference favoring the chain, then it will make sense to marshall all efforts toward completion of the chain, while holding in reserve, without abandoning, the boom. And, in any case, the logs will be more than sufficient to build the smaller rafts needed to support the chain.

The Committee warmed to Tom's appeal. He had argued this wasn't a case of relatively equal solutions on offer, making it easy just to take the first one available. In his informed opinion, as an engineer, the chain stood a far better chance of achieving the objective. Thus, when news arrived that General Gates had released the Richelieu links for use on the Hudson, the Committee ordered Lieutenant Machin to move forward on the chain "without delay, using every possible diligence."

The blacksmiths Theophilus Anthony, Isaac van Dusen, James Odell and George Smart, all from Poughkeepsie, would be prepared to take the dumbbell-shaped iron bars cast by Ancram and forge them into the necessary chain links. The Committee directed Lieutenant Machin to contact Livingston and arrange the order.

Tom covered the short distance to Salisbury in several hours. Livingston greeted Tom with a boisterous smile and slap on the back, seeming for all the world to be greeting a long-departed friend. Guessing at Tom's mission, this shrewd and avaricious Scot smelled money. He was well aware of the threat posed by British warships, whose presence on the river could split the Continentals north from south, cutting lines of supply and communications necessary to sustain the war. A patriot to the cause of freedom who often boasted of his devotion, Tom discovered Livingston to be first, foremost and forever a businessman serving the cause of profit. His fortune already was immense as were his estates. He was aware that loss of the war would go poorly for patriots, particularly those of great wealth. And, yet, avarice was in his bones. He would squeeze the hard-pressed Americans on price.

"Your order is for 1600 feet of bar iron, two inches square, delivered as soon as possible. Our price will be 30 pounds per ton, and, depending on how it goes, that price may be increased. Since hostilities began, my workmen have found the cost of supporting their families has doubled and more, especially for linens and certain foodstuffs. I've had to increase their wages, and that more than once. I'm sure you understand."

"Mr. Livingston, that price is not fair. We know you charge only 17 pounds per ton to merchants. At first blush, this might look like an effort to swindle. But that could not be. You, a gentleman and a patriot. Surely, there's some mistake."

"No mistake here. Thirty pounds is the price of this gentleman and patriot. For iron of Ancram quality, it's the best on offer, that I can assure you."

Tom saw no alternative but to commit the New York Convention, which was responsible for costs in this war theater. Soon thereafter, iron bars began arriving for the blacksmiths in Poughkeepsie. But before half the order was supplied, ironmaster Livingston demanded 45 pounds per ton for the balance. Denying any attempt to squeeze a desperately worried commander-in-chief, Livingston blamed the unusual summer drought that had required the digging of a new feeder sluice to maintain the water level necessary to operate his iron works. But, as Tom, exploding in rage upon receipt of Livingston's message, said to General Clinton, in the unmistakable voice of the ironmaster, "What's a little extra cost for sluice diggers when I can profiteer from the growing British Naval threat at two times and more my normal price for merchant sales."

What Clinton knew, and now recounted to Tom, were the outlines of General Washington's disaster on Long Island and Brooklyn in late August. Howe's army had inflicted a crushing defeat on the Continentals. With minimal losses, estimated at around 400 of Howe's army killed, wounded and missing, with doleful mien and tears welling up in his deep-set eyes, Clinton said, "We lost at least 1,000 and probably many more, with three generals, Sullivan, Stirling and Nathaniel Woodhull taken prisoner."

"The silver lining, if one can so name it, was the commander's quick decision to abandon Brooklyn, cross the East River and escape through Manhattan rather than fight what would surely have been a climactic battle against long odds. A three-day northeastern storm, Tom, one you will recall bothering our progress on Fort Clinton. It proved a God-send, blocking Lord Howe from sailing up the East River to cut off the only route of escape. That, and General Howe's inexplicable failure to follow up his victory with hot pursuit, choosing instead to dig trenches and throw up embankments.

"Robert Yates reports that the New York Convention's Treasury is so low in funds that Livingston's outstanding bills for iron received cannot be paid. He wrote Livingston to inform him a week ago."

A light went on in Tom's brain. "That explains it! Iron shipments to us have dropped drastically. When asked, the shippers mumbled something about a slowdown on account of money issues. They refused to elaborate. Does this behavior by our gentleman and patriot surprise you? From the start we knew his loyalty was first and always to Mammon."

"We must look to Robert Erskine for what's needed. You should be pleased with your foresight in contacting him after Livingston raised his price to 45 pounds. Take a ride over to Ringwood and get them cracking."

Since Ringwood was in northern New Jersey, not far from Convivial Hall, itself located eight miles northwest of New Brunswick overlooking the Raritan, Tom suggested Lisa join him. Here was a chance for another spying project.

He told her he believed the feint she had enabled was working. Although he didn't want to disclose to others at the Forts Lisa's caper with Major Andre, and had no solid proof, the fact was no British warship had sailed up the river since the *Roebuck*, *Phoenix* and *Tartar* came on October 9.

Tom prepared for the trip to Ringwood, some 32 miles southwest, packing at Lisa's insistence, food and a bottle of claret to enjoy on the way. The day broke clear and clothed in autumn colors, the leaves turning but not yet released to drop earthward, despite being shaken by southwest breezes too strong to call gentle. Tom led the horse he intended for her. Looking at his choice, she scowled and shook her head.

"That one's not for me. I'll go to the stable and pick one that suits."

"This is Thistle. One of our best mares. Gentle as a lamb. Please, give her a try before you rampage around the stalls."

Like most athletic girls to the manor born, Lisa knew riding and loved it. At an early age she became proficient. Being competitive, she grew more proficient than those around her. And with proficiency, she developed horse-knowledge and a hawk-eye for the details of horse flesh that corresponded to excellent prospects in the saddle. In the Van Horne family, she had a reputation for being outlandishly particular about the horses she was willing to ride. She tested them in many ways, but the ultimate test was how well she fitted the horse when riding bare-back, eyes closed.

"Not a chance. Thistle is too old and tired for me. I see age in her eyes, and look at these teeth, all worn out. Come, now, my lover, do better than a thistle for your woman."

"But Lisa, no one has ever complained of her before."

"Ok, here's my proposition. Either you trade horses with me, or I rampage around the stable."

Lisa could tire him. And exasperate him. But seldom did she make him angry. With this horse business, she crossed the line. Tom's face flushed.

"Given that choice, I'll come with you to the stable and watch the rampage. And ride Thistle."

He found her process of selection way beyond his ken. Finally, she emerged with Ginger, a two-year-old filly full of energy and barely past the hackamore stage.

"I'm pretty sure that's a horse I wouldn't be crazy enough to try. I wish you luck."

"She's perky. I'm perky. She's raven black and so am I. It took us less than a minute to bond."

By noon they had covered more than half the distance, trotting except for the several hundred yards of cantering and galloping that

Lisa allowed Ginger, who signaled with growing urgency a need to run. Lisa freed the reins. Speaking to the horse, but more for Tom's amusement, she cried "Ok, Ginger, I understand, now show us some speed."

Ginger leapt forward, quickly reaching what Lisa thought her top speed. Tom followed as best he could, but catching Ginger was beyond Thistle's reach. When Ginger showed signs of having enough, Lisa brought her to the trot, and continued at that gait until Tom caught up.

"Now, Tom, my plan is to find a pastoral setting for lunch, the claret and then some passionate exercises in dappled sunshine. Don't tell me you're not in the mood, because you know I can change your mood in minutes. Nor are we duty-bound to press on. We are more than halfway there, the day is yet young and the weather divine for what I have in mind."

Tom patted the neck of his sweaty mount and wiped his equally sweaty forehead while listening to Lisa's plan.

"Does riding put all women in the mood?" Tom asked. "And did it all begin with the end of side-saddle?"

"Yes, but I can only speak for myself. As for when it began, I haven't any idea."

"If, instead of sybaritic pursuits, you applied your commanding presence to running an army, it would sweep the field."

"I've never had command of more than one man at a time. It suffices."

"I've never met a woman more consumed with sex than you. How do you account for this—this excessive devotion to the physical?"

"You know something, Tom. I've never met anyone who worries about sex as much as you do, or has as big a problem with just enjoying it while you can. In time, and it will seem like the blink of an eye looking back, you will be too old to partake. And, then, if honest with yourself, you might regret all the opportunities missed."

"As long as you're around, missing them seems impossible."

With little trouble, they found a grassy patch of level ground beside a brook, now almost bone-dry, shaded by a mighty Sycamore. Saddles removed and horses tethered with a trough of water nearby and rope enough to let them graze, Tom and Lisa spread a blanket, consuming chicken, bread, carrots and wine.

With one last sip, Lisa put down the empty bottle and turned to Tom, fire in her eyes.

"Now, Tom, I want you to lie down on your back, looking up, through green leaves to the blue and white above. I'm going to first undress you and then undress myself. I am going to bestride you, and while you recline in this garden of earthly delights, I will undertake to earn your love."

"You're an over-the-top romantic, Lisa. That's why you won't become the commander of an army. But isn't there danger that all these commands will squeeze out the romance?"

"Just you wait. I conjure you: wait and see!"

"Ok, ok. And what, pray tell, do you have in mind for me to deliver to you?" Despite himself, Tom was starting to anticipate in his groin the results of Lisa's plan.

"As I said, just you wait. Who knows, perhaps we'll switch positions. Perhaps, some effulgent foreplay. But, please, one thing at a time."

The sun had sunk to within four fingers from the horizon when they resumed their trip to Ringwood.

"Lisa, the time has slipped away. You had your way with me, as always, and now we're behind schedule."

"Oh, la, la Tom. We'll be at Ringwood in no time. Trust me."

Tom muttered something too soft to be heard.

"What was that?" she said.

"I said I've trusted you more than I should have."

She brought Ginger nose to nose with Thistle.

"And precisely what does that mean?"

The horses seemed unhappy being so close together.

"It means we are so different, you and I, that sometimes I feel like we need more space. The way Thistle feels just now."

On arrival, Tom and Lisa met with ironmaster Robert Erskine. The order was confirmed. 270 links to be fashioned from two-inch square iron bars and the necessary number of clips and bolts for fastening the chain to its supporting rafts. Delivery would be achieved by teamsters hauling the links on wagons drawn by yoked oxen to Brewster's Forge near New Windsor. There, Tom would assemble the chain, mount it on log floats and raft it down to Fort Montgomery.

Lisa innocently asked what risk there was of the rafts not bearing up under the weight of the chain.

In surprise, Tom looked at Lisa and then at Robert, to assure himself that the field was open for him to reply. At last, a chance to show off his knowledge, not just before the ironmaster but the woman who so often dominated him.

"Good question, Lisa. The answer to the buoyancy problem depends on many factors. One is the type of wood we use. Different woods have different specific gravities."

"Hey, cut the fancy words where you know I don't have a clue."

"Ok. Ok. Just trying to show off a tiny bit. Specific gravity means the ratio of the weight of a piece of wood to the weight of an equal volume of water. Hickory has an SP of 0.8, while white pine has an SP of 0.5. Of course we know as kids that, whether hickory or pine, logs float. But white pine logs have a much better carrying capacity than hickory logs. What an SP of 0.5 tells us is that, without sinking, a pine log can carry an object, say, an iron link, whose weight is equal to the log. If we construct a pine log raft of, say, five two-foot thick logs eight feet long and figure that raft's weight, we will know the raft's carrying capacity. It's that simple."

"Who figured that out?" Lisa said. "My father always claimed physics to be beautiful, but I never got what he meant. I begin to see. That concept is elegant."

"It's called the Archimedes principle. Here's how he stated his rule: Any object, wholly or partially immersed in a fluid, is buoyed up by a force equal to the weight of the fluid displaced by the object."

"Very tidy; very neat. You're a genius, my love!" Lisa gathered Tom in her arms and squeezed him tight, laughing in delight as Tom, seeing Robert staring in surprise, flushed red.

* * * * *

Arriving at Convivial Hall, they were greeted warmly by the family but cautioned about a group of the King's officers who were expected for the evening. After watering and feeding Thistle, Tom gave Lisa some final suggestions and headed back to the Hudson, where he was now needed to supervise raft construction at New Windsor, followed by the floating operation to get the chain to Fort Montgomery.

Lisa knew and quickly found among her family those open to the Patriot cause and knowledgeable about the British officers soon to arrive. Among them was Captain Duncan Drummond, aide to Sir Henry Clinton, who with two other Major Generals, William Howe and John Burgoyne, had been dispatched to Boston last Spring. Drummond was well-placed to know General Howe's plans. And possibly, given the rivalry between Howe and Clinton, open to complaining of Howe. Observing him taking refreshments soon after arrival at the Hall, she knew his type, which he wore on his sleeve: a prince among Captains, born to the purple and taught entitlement, a brain modestly endowed but fashioned by himself and those around him as superior, a mind hosting limited worldly knowledge and unawareness of those limitations. He was self-confident to the point of careless arrogance, imbued with the capacity to charm and to take delight in doing so, often until he lost perspective and sometimes even judgment.

Wearing more make-up than was her wont, and less bodice than usually covered her bosom, Lisa went to work.

Seated in her favorite alcove off the family's plush library, the same spot she used to enrage and trick Major Andre, Lisa became the target of those charms that Captain Drummond thought women of taste found irresistible.

"So you are one of the Convivial Hall family. How many of you make up this bevy of beautiful young women?"

"Do you hunt, Captain? I've only heard that word applied to quail. And that, we are not."

The Captain, back-footed and blushing, admitted to having hunted quail, but insisted he had no such thing in mind.

"We are a family of five girls, and our cousins number another three. When all together, we lean toward jollity."

"And are the others as beautiful as you, Lisa?"

"Ah, that's a matter of opinion, and very much in the eye of the beholder. But beauty to an officer long engaged at war is of a different order than to one not so tasked. It's often only skin-deep. May I pour you another glass of our family's diminishing store of claret?"

"I won't object. But tell me how you came to be a Loyalist?"

"I try to avoid such simplistic characterizations. Deep down, I'm a pragmatist. I'm astonished that the war continues. Knowing the towering strength of the British Army and Navy, I was sure the war would end in Boston. And then, if not there, on Long Island, or Staten Island, or for sure in New York City. But no. Your Commanding General, "Sir Billy" as some call him, or "the great chucklehead" or "Silly Billy" as do others, since taking the City, has remained quiet for 26 days, giving Washington time to regroup and gain reinforcements. Isn't this surpassingly strange?"

"Your knowledge impresses me."

Behind Lisa's appreciative smile was the certainty that he was considering more than just her mind.

"My leader, General Clinton, has strenuously objected to Howe's decision, ridiculing his claim to lack offensive strength. To no avail. We have sought to use Lord Howe's fleet to cut Washington off between the Harlem and Hudson. We thought such a move could pin down Washington's Army and end the war. The enemy moved too fast, while we dithered. But why am I telling you these things, for goodness' sake."

"Allow me to explain. It's the venue. This Hall has a reputation for inducing candor, allowing guests to vent, let off steam, whatever might serve, with confidence that secrets disclosed here will be kept within our walls. It's a reputation hard won and, frankly, well deserved. You may trust this family, as many others have. I see dregs in your glass. Allow me to pour you more claret in a clean glass. And while I do, ask you a question. Rumors abound in Convivial Hall. Among them is the notion that Mrs. Joshua Loring, Jr. is to blame for Howe's failure to crush the Patriots. That she is playing Cleopatra to Billy's Mark Antony."

Drummond drained his glass, then moved forward to take Lisa's hand, which she gave freely. Lowering his voice, he acknowledged the possibility.

"The General's affair is no overnight thing. It endures, as virtually the entire army has become aware. For Major General Clinton and other senior officers, this situation is alarming, increasingly so each day it continues."

"Is there suspicion that Jane Loring could be an agent of General Washington, a Delilah sapping the strength of her Samson?"

Duncan showed not a trace of surprise. For, in fact, he had discussed this possibility with Henry Clinton. "You're as suspicious as you're smart. Of course we have. Often. But we see no way to explore that question, without getting our Commanding General badly out of sorts. He won't abide anyone speaking of his affair, which he considers his private and privileged turf. Of course, everyone speaks of it, almost all the time, but never to him. We do all we can to check her out. If she communicates with your Commanding General, it's in mysterious ways we can't detect."

"Howe's obviously one of those middle-aged pleasure seekers, constantly aware that his days of indulgence are numbered. I've heard he's condemned games of chance in orders to his troops, while being seriously addicted to gambling himself. And they say he's prone to dissipation, whether in the arms of Mrs. Loring or not. Isn't he ripe for the attractions of Convivial Hall? I wonder if you could possibly lure him and Mistress Jane here for a couple of frolicking days of rest and recreation. It could offer many opportunities."

"Brilliant idea! Handled well, we might get to the bottom of what drives her. If only we could conjure him to do it. I'll speak to General Clinton. Who knows?" Under cover of this exciting idea, Duncan leaned forward to the edge of his chair, put his free arm around Lisa's neck and, anticipating resistance, aggressively kissed her. An onlooker would have marveled that Lisa, taken by surprise, showed not the slightest resistance.

"Duncan, if I may be allowed so to address you, please sit back now and listen. I wish to know more of the needs of your forces. What is lodged in my imagination is the chance that I might be of service. Teach me how."

"You came from the Hudson, I believe. Where exactly?"

"I'm with an officer stationed at Fort Montgomery. He's responsible for defenses there and across the creek at Fort Clinton."

"Interesting. A warm relationship, I imagine. And how good are those defenses?"

"Well, I'm sure I'm not telling you anything you don't already know about Washington's strategy, but from the outset it has been, at all costs, to control the Hudson Valley. Enormous energy, enterprise and manpower have been applied to the task, including construction of frigates, multiple installations of artillery and various designs for river obstruction. I've been surprised at the thoroughness of the Patriot effort and the dangers it poses for the King's forces."

Lisa filled Duncan's glass again, aware of his flushed face and ever so slight slurring of words. "Obstructions you shay. We've heard something about a chain."

"Oh my, you are well-informed, Captain. Yes, a most formidable obstacle I'm told, especially due to powerful cannon positioned on both sides to do heavy execution against ships arrested by it. Of course, I'm no military expert—can't you tell—but I fear for the British fleet if it tries to sail much above Kingsbridge."

Just then a bell rang, summoning all to dinner. Lisa entertained Duncan throughout a feast that became rambunctious. Conversations grew in volume as wine flowed generously to wash down roast duck and lamb, smothered in the many root vegetables of the season. And, then, immediately after devouring an apple crisp with whipped cream, Lisa rose from her chair with surprising swiftness and, taking Duncan's hand in hers, gave it a soft kiss visible to all and excused herself with steely conviction. Still seated, the Captain was paralyzed by indecision as she made a brilliant escape from whatever activity he had planned for her later in the evening.

10

THE FORT MONTGOMERY CHAIN

It was the evening of the day when, departing Convivial Hall before sunrise so as to avoid any reasonable chance of encountering Duncan Drummond, Lisa rode into Fort Montgomery in early afternoon. Tom didn't return from New Windsor until later, and had already eaten when Lisa greeted him in their quarters.

"My God, you're a fine sight for sore, worn-out eyes. Deeply tanned from the ride back. May I say you look gorgeous."

"Of course. And all washed and rinsed too, after a day of leisure. Time for you, my friend, to bathe. You're dirty. And did I say smelly. Your sweaty body betrays not leisure but a hot day's work. Put those clothes in the hamper."

"The rafts are progressing well, Lisa. What's tidy about this project is that the rafts will serve not only to float the chain from New Windsor here, but once here will serve to support the chain from the Fort to Anthony's Nose. If we plan carefully, the links won't need to be rearranged on the rafts once they arrive."

He began running a bath, then stripped off his clothes and stood proudly naked, facing her.

"Tom, I've admired you from this angle many times. Your hair's so thick and fair it would make a forest proud. But where's the subtlety? Why such a boast to an old-timer?"

"It wasn't always that way. No one's put that question to me before. Yes, I admit to pride in my pubic parts. And no embarrassment that my chest and back lack hair. And I know the source of my parading proudly about although I've never admitted it before, even to myself. You do have a way about you, conscious or not, of causing me to search myself and, one might say, mentally disrobe." He sat on their bed, looking kindly at his provocative companion.

"Well?" she said, insistent. He was suddenly embarrassed.

Head bowed to avoid eye contact, finally he spoke.

"In adolescence, I was extremely late to reach puberty. Pubic hairs refused to sprout. On close inspection, which I did more than once a day, no sign of them. I didn't like Church but was forced to go as part of my school's regime. I found the Jesus story hard to swallow, that is until it occurred to me that Jesus might be my passage to maturity if I prayed to him for pubic hair. And so I gladly went to Church and accepted Jesus. I thought we had an understanding: prayer for hair. It took two years of hope, of belief and prayer, to realize Jesus was letting me down. In school, we were forced to nakedness in the room where boys bathed. I looked different from all the others. Something missing. And there was no place to hide."

"What a painful tale. Here, let me give you a giant hug." She moved to the bed, wrapping her arm around Tom and trying to snuggle, despite the rank man-smell of a long day's-worth of clinging sweat. She sensed the need, once he had started down this painful path, to continue.

"But there's more. My classmates were cruel. Some unrelentingly so. They pointed. They squealed in delight until tears came. They predicted it would take years, if ever. They mocked my suffering, claiming I was more girl than boy. Humiliation stung. Became absolute. I wanted to strike back at them, to get even. But there was nothing I could imagine doing. Too many. Going to the authorities would have been even more of a humiliation. I just had to take it, day after day, when school was in session."

"There must have been some who were sympathetic and kind."

"I had the same thought. And searched. Even begged. I recall at the height of one day's misery, when a group was laughing at me and

I was feeling despised, I grew desperate enough to risk even more ridicule by shouting out: 'Isn't there anyone here to show a little kindness?' No one came forth. I now understand better the ways of kids in crowds. The bullies tend to lead. The shy are intimidated. And those inclined to sympathy are found among the shy. Breaking ranks can be hard anywhere. Among kids in a school, virtually impossible."

"Tom, your bath's ready. I'm going to follow you in because I have one more question. Later on did you forgive God and return to his bosom?"

"You mean after I got hair and other accoutrements of puberty? Hell, no. When at last they came, so easily, I blamed Jesus all the more. If he could fail in such a simple assignment, one most of my classmates were achieving without his help, why should I trust him for the next big uncertainty in my life. And, then, as I gained more knowledge of history and more perspective on the world and the impact Christianity had asserted over the ages, I grew firm, even proud, in my disbelief. In what I finally accepted as atheism."

"Tom, it's clear to me you've put a lot of distance between these painful events and now. I mean in terms of emotion. You seem both accepting and analytical."

"Perhaps." Tom sank into the bath. But I'm still unable to tell others I'm an atheist. And when I think about it sometimes, I think I'm pathetic."

Lisa took a scrub brush and began to exercise it across his back. She felt closer to him than she'd ever been.

"Thanks, Tom, for sharing that chapter. By the way, I've never liked those swarthy types with black hair front and back. But, now, let's turn the page."

* * * * *

Without mishap, the log floats arrived at Fort Montgomery bearing sections of the chain. Tom ordered the floats connected in a line along the west side of the river and tied with ropes to prevent the changing tides from sweeping them out into the current. Capstans were installed on either side of the river to which the ends of the chain would be connected and the chain made taut. On November 1, the final delivery by Ringwood Furnace of 37 links to New Windsor was effected. Log floats were ready to carry them down to Fort Montgomery, there to be connected to the floats already waiting in line.

When all these preliminaries had been done, Tom reported to General Clinton. "Sir, our chain is connected, all 1,650 feet of it, and ready to be strung across the river. The capstan on the west has the end of the chain wrapped around it with the final link anchored tight to bedrock. The capstan on the east is manned and awaits the other end of the chain. And I await only your approval and the next slack water."

The General was pleased. Pressure to get this job done had been building for weeks.

"Approval granted. And God's speed."

Tom saluted smartly and turned to leave.

"And, by the way, I've been meaning to mention—of course it's late to be worrying—but are we sure the chain is strong enough to survive through the winter months, with all that ice flow?"

Tom looked at the General in surprise. "My goodness, no. The chain couldn't survive the ice, just as the British ships couldn't survive it, and so we plan on hauling the chain onto land to be stored through the winter months. In fact, there's little time left before ice forms. I think of this installation as short-term, just a dress rehearsal."

General Clinton turned away from Tom, picked up his telescope and looked out the open door to the river, trying desperately to block Tom's view of the blushing face of this proud officer.

"I know, General, it may seem a little crazy to be installing it now, at the corner of the year, with ice coming soon, and no hint that the British Navy intends to move upriver before winter. All that plus the need to take it down so soon. But a test is vital. There may be flaws in our design or in the chain itself. We need to uncover them now, so that in the spring we can install the chain swiftly and with confidence that it will serve."

The General put down the telescope and, turning to face Tom, nodded.

When the tidal thrust of water subsided, Tom and his crew were ready. Positioned on both sides of the river, some on rafts supporting the chain, others in four double-ended bateaux carrying anchors to use to help hold the chain and rafts in place, the crew was bursting with collective excitement. Using the slackening flow upstream to assist them, they hauled the floats out into the current with lines stretched across the river. Oxen had been positioned to help in the effort, the line on the east side being fed through a pulley lashed to a large sycamore near water's edge, so the oxen could be driven on a path parallel to the river, with the line attached to the beasts' harnesses. Remarkably, the process was quickly completed, with the line wrapped around the capstan, wound up until the end of the chain was pulled in enough to replace the line on the capstan and then with the crew winding the final links of the chain, with the help of the oxen's pull, until the floats were lined up taut and in a slight curve across the now slack water.

Tom was at once thrilled and a bit surprised at the accuracy of his measurements. Of course, luck may have played a role, as Lisa was quick to point out when Tom basked in the praise that began flowing in, even to the point of pretending his measurements had been perfect.

A loud cheer from both Forts echoed across the river to Anthony's Nose and back when the chain was made secure at both ends. Surrounded by soldiers and a handful of the Fort's women, including Lisa, General Clinton proclaimed it a gorgeous sight. A cannon was fired and the General waxed eloquent in praise. "Make no mistake. What we see below is a triumph of man's will, ingenuity and organization over the forces of nature. But it's more. It's another mark of our irrepressible drive for liberty."

Crowds at both Forts stayed put to watch the bateaux, one towing a barge, pick up the crews and oxen on the eastern side and then retrieve the men standing on the two center-most floats. With all safely ashore at the landing below Fort Montgomery, the crowds

CHAINS ACROSS THE RIVER

dispersed. Lisa lingered with the General to look at the chain floating easily on log rafts sitting almost still in the slack water.

At its peak, some 65 million gallons or more of water flowed every minute toward New York Harbor and the ocean beyond, rushing through the 26-fathom channel between Anthony's Nose and Fort Montgomery. The floats offered blunt obstacles to the rapidly accelerating current. Tom, who couldn't stop watching his installation as it responded to the growing tidal pressure, sat on a perch far above the river, making nervous conversation with Lisa. As swiftly as the current's speed grew, so did Tom's self-confidence decline. "This ebb tide will be the test. We rushed the installation, and the quality of the material varied, coming from three different sources. Look at those waters lapping at the logs."

"You sound vexed, Tom. Don't be. You've done it well. The installation went brilliantly. I have total confidence in you, even if you don't."

"You're the best there is. A master manipulator of men, and I mean that in every good way. But I'm worried."

He watched the river with a hawk's attention to detail, noticing the swift-flowing water rise up higher and higher against the upstream sides of the rafts, at first just splashing water over them, but soon covering the logs with rushing waters.

In less than two hours after the celebratory cannonade, the chain broke apart in the middle of the river, separating the rafts. The two halves of the chain, still aboard the rafts, arced downstream to come to rest along both banks of the river.

"It's busted," Tom cried, loud enough for many in the Fort to hear. "Why did I rush the installation. Why remove the crews? Stupid, stupid me. Overconfidence. Always a mistake."

Lisa's efforts to console her mate were ill-timed and futile. Tom moved swiftly to the water's edge with his crew to determine the cause, fix the failure, check for others and, at the next slack water, reinstall the chain. Driven by both urgency and embarrassment, all this he and his crews accomplished with surprising speed. The cause, they discovered, was a defective weld of a swivel connecting the links.

But again, when the current next flowed hard and fast, another connector, fashioned from the same foundry as the one that broke first, gave way. This time Tom's confidence, briefly restored, gave way to gloom.

Given the lateness of the year, and the need for the New York Convention and the Continental Congress and the Commanding General to come to terms with the successive failures, their cause, alternative schemes, and ultimately, whether to drop the whole idea of chaining the Hudson, it would not be sensible, or with ice flows in the offing, even possible, to try a third installation until spring.

They would wait. After weeks of self-doubt building on top of the frustration he and his men were having in locating the source of the second break, they identified its cause—a defective weld in one of the clevises. Tom's confidence was, to a degree, restored, since both breaks appeared to have been caused by human error, not the overwhelming power of nature. He grew steadfast in asserting that, with alterations, he could make the chain sound and re-install it at Fort Montgomery in the spring to achieve the intended purpose. Debate among the revolutionary leaders over what steps to take ensued at Fishkill and Philadelphia, always with vigor and often with insult and acrimony. The charged atmosphere grew even more fraught when word came of the Patriots' loss of Fort Washington, giving the enemy absolute control of the river below and opening the watery way to the Highlands, unopposed.

General Schuyler started lobbying for abandonment of the log float scheme central to Tom's design. He imagined supporting the chain from the river's bottom. Of course, given the depth of the Hudson at Fort Montgomery, or for that matter, at West Point or other imaginable sites for a chain, supports reaching to the Hudson's bottom were simply impossible. This fact didn't stop the General, whose argument some interpreted as an indirect way of saying the chain idea should be abandoned. Tom's crew had towed the rafts, still bearing the two halves of the chain, into Popolopen Creek, where they could remain until a decision was made as to future deployment.

The New York Convention appointed a four-man military commission to examine the chain and determine exactly what had caused the two failures. General James Clinton headed this commission. The others were Captain Abraham Swartwout, Captain James Rosencrans and Lieutenant Daniel Lawrence. With the exception of General Clinton, whose close involvement with Tom caused him to place not a scintilla of blame on the engineer for the breaks, but rather continue with confidence to rely on his expertise and judgment, the others on the commission were open to all kinds of questions, fueled by the general sentiment of the Convention to re-examine all assumptions. Many had expressed doubt that, given the speed and weight of the Hudson's flows, any chain could survive. And, even if it could withstand the river, it could never withstand both the river's flow and a British ship of the line. Others thought the site too straight and open to those flows, arguing for the site at West Point because the sharp bend in the river there would, necessarily, slow the river's onslaught against the chain and, some added, the onslaught of enemy warships. And others, naturally enough, put the blame on Tom and all those engaged in fashioning the chain and installing it. Indeed, even before examination of the chain's points of failure, on order of the Convention, the Secret Committee refused payment to the blacksmiths engaged in its final assembly.

Clinton insisted that Tom work with the commission in its examination. He knew Tom had already identified the causes of both breaks. Tom chose not to get ahead of the commission. He would simply lead them to the source of the problems, and in that way speed up the process. And so it was. They quickly found that the first rupture came from a broken swivel, fashioned in Ticonderoga, and poorly welded, and the second from a broken clevis made in Poughkeepsie. The remainder of the chain was judged sound. The commission rendered its report on December 12. The Convention immediately ordered the blacksmiths paid according to their agreement, a swift step that relieved Tom, whose confidence in that group had remained high, despite the breaks.

"We're going to need them again and again," he wrote to the Convention, urging payment.

The Convention, not thinking too clearly, upon receiving the commission's report, insisted on re-installation immediately. Almost as an afterthought, the commission had brought Lieutenant Machin along when it delivered the report, since he was the only engineer on site and possessed of detailed intimacy with both river and chain. With the recent calamities from Brooklyn to Forts Lee and Washington top of mind for every Convention member, and rumors of a dwindling of Washington's army to a mere three thousand as it limped through New Jersey, a panic had swept the room, leading to the mindless demand for immediate re-installation. General Clinton suggested the Convention hear Tom's thoughts.

"Gentlemen, in wake of recent events, I fully understand the urgency of your interest in denying British traffic on the Hudson. But, if you will, allow me to acquaint you with certain facts that support my conclusion, and the one unanimously expressed by your appointed commission, that we should await the arrival of spring to install the chain again. First, ice has begun to form in the Hudson. Soon it will be frozen across. While designed to deter passage of the British fleet, and with shore batteries, to perhaps destroy the enemy's vessels, the chain is no match for winter's ice. We have always assumed it would be taken down for the season, to be re-installed when the ice was gone in the spring, before British vessels could seek passage past the Scylla of Fort Montgomery and the Charybdis of Anthony's Nose.

"Second, the British fleet would not be foolhardy enough to attempt an up-river passage at this time of year. These ships are as vulnerable as our chain. The danger of being frozen for several months in the ice, exposed to our troops and cannon on both sides of the river, and exposed as well to the crushing pressures of ice against the ships' hulls, is real and, without doubt, understood by the enemy.

"Exposing the chain to winter weather and loss serves no useful purpose. There is another angle to this matter. As some have pointed out, the West Point location has one advantage over Fort Montgomery, in that the water's flows at their peak would strike a chain sited there with less force, due to the river's bends, than at Fort

Montgomery. We now will have time to study the siting question more fully. My opinion remains that the present site is superior, but I welcome the chance to explore that conclusion with others, especially with the disturbing history of two breaks to inform us."

In fact, Tom was much less confident of his conclusion that the chain could withstand the flows at Fort Montgomery than he was willing to let on. Had he revealed his doubts, he might have gained some immunization from blame if the chain failed again, but the price for candor he feared was two-fold: loss of confidence in his expertise and judgment by those dependent on it, and immobility. He imagined the decision-makers, without a confident guide, being unable to decide, or deciding through weakening compromises, all with dangerous consequences come spring.

Tom had restored reason to the Convention, all of whose members were impressed with his self-assurance and expertise. They found themselves nodding approval as he found his seat with commission members. What remained was for the Commander-in-Chief to be satisfied as to where to locate the chain in the spring. He directed his Chief Engineer, Colonel Rufus Putnam, to examine the question and report. Putnam requested from Tom a sketch of the Hudson through the Highlands, marking feasible sites for the chain.

Overcoming his own doubts about the Fort Montgomery site, in the strong belief that it was necessary to avoid a muddle of indecision that could last into spring, Tom accompanied the sketch with a note expressing his arguments for using the existing site rather than West Point. His most compelling point was the existence of fortifications at Forts Montgomery and Clinton, and the lack of anything approaching them at West Point. When Putnam met with Washington at his headquarters in Morristown, Tom's arguments carried the day, despite Washington's lingering doubts over the adequacy of the defenses bestriding Popolopen Creek. He was instructed to use the Fort Montgomery site come spring.

Over the winter, when the often brutal weather permitted, blacksmiths and carpenters poured over chain links and fittings and the log rafts, repairing and replacing as necessary to have the installation in sound condition ready to span the river the instant that ice broke up in late March. To create less resistance to the river's flow, Tom had the rafts altered in two respects. First, he created a six-inch gap between the logs to reduce drag. Second, he sharpened both ends of each log to a point, at an angle that very gradually reached the full width of the log. Again, to reduce drag. Notwithstanding these promising alterations, Tom's anxieties continued, on and off, through the winter. He knew even a second-best decision, firmly made and executed, was far better than indecisive execution of the best decision. And he still thought the decision made was not second-best, all factors considered.

January 7, however, was an "off" day for anxiety. In ebullient mood, Tom returned to the quarters he shared with Lisa. "Guess what happened today."

"You're positively glowing, my man. I know. The Brits called it quits."

"Noble idea. If only! No, something much more pedestrian and local than that. My provisional commission as an artillery Captain Lieutenant came through."

Her smile broadened, wrinkling her face, seeming to push up the tip of her nose. "How wonderful. Worthy of a celebration."

She returned to her central idea. The subject, in the infinite ways of thinking about it, responding to it, submitting to it, dominated her mind and body. Tom was finally understanding this. For him, it was an utterly unique characteristic of the woman with whom he shared his bed.

"I'm beginning to realize you are obsessed with sex. It's always the first thing that comes into your head when an opportunity to engage arises. And you search for those opportunities like a hound on the trail of a rabbit. Remarkable."

"And you, I'm beginning to realize, have a problem with sex."

"Lisa, my love, we've had this discussion before. Look, I have no problem. Not one at all. I like smoking my pipe. But I take it out of my mouth on occasion. If you smoked, you'd starve to death. Speaking of food, I'm famished."

* * * * *

In January, Tom received a summons to appear on the 29th at Washington's headquarters in Morristown, New Jersey. The Commanding General wanted a first-hand report on the chain. General Clinton delivered the message, his face set against any possible signal. Tom was, at turns, delighted and concerned. James refused to support either emotion, saying with candor, as Tom twisted and turned with the news, that he just didn't know what the Commander-in-Chief had in mind.

"We've reported regularly, and since the General's decision to re-install here, those reports have all contained news of progress."

"Ok, but just make a guess, if you will be so kind."

Tom was squirming around, like a snake with someone's foot on its head.

"Look. General Washington, more than once, has stressed the river's importance. Knowing that, at the end of the day, you're his man on obstruction, he wants to sit face to face. To hear, learn and, yes, to evaluate. You'll do fine, Captain. And relax. After all, it's something special to be important enough to be summoned to Headquarters. Don't take my word for it, ask Lisa. She's got a military mind."

Retreating, Tom left General Clinton smiling. "It all sounds good. The General doesn't have a carpet on the floor, does he?"

* * * * *

Tom's anxieties returned as he approached the General's headquarters. The unknown breeds fear. No one really knew why he had been summoned, and the platitudinous assurances had, on reflection, worked in reverse. Might some new engineer have been found to take charge, perhaps one with a foreign accent and gift for self-promotion? The sad experience with Bernard Romans rolled around in Tom's head, causing him to ponder the possibility of a recurrence.

"Come right in, Captain Machin. Welcome to my sparse quarters. I've arranged tea, if you will join me. And have some passable New Jersey muffins, said to be a tasty specialty of the state.

"Now, to business. I asked you here to learn, first-hand, the condition of the chain, your thoughts on why it broke twice, your opinion on my decision to re-install at Fort Montgomery and, finally, the prospects you foresee for the chain to serve as intended come spring."

Tom was about to respond when the General resumed, pulling his chair toward Tom and leaning forward to within two feet of Tom's face, from which perch he looked down, for he was a tall man, burrowing deep into Tom's eyes with an intense, wise and altogether commanding presence. Yet one, Tom imagined, was tinged at the edges with kindness and even friendship.

"Perhaps I should add a point or two that inform my keenness in this Machin chain, as I've begun to call it. Controlling the Hudson is vital. It flows the length of New York. It's the only passage by which the enemy from New York, or any other part of our coast, can ever hope to cooperate with an army from Canada. Possession of it is essential to preserve our lines of communication between the eastern, middle and southern states. And in great measure upon its security depend our chief supplies of flour for our forces, whether in the eastern or northern departments. But, of course, you know all of that. Please excuse the repetition. I confess the Hudson River is an obsession."

Tom nodded.

"So, that's point one. Point two—and I'd like this to be just between us—is to deprecate the previous attempts to block the lower Hudson. We tried to do this where the channel is very wide and deep. Our labor and expense were thrown away. In October, with ease, the *Roebuck, Phoenix* and an accompanying frigate ran through our *Chevaux-de-Frise* and shore batteries. We received humiliating reports of much merriment aboard these vessels as they plowed the river north.

"And so, we come to the Machin chain. Fail, it must not."

The General had moved Captain Machin to tears, which he proved man enough not to hide. Highly motivated before, his ambition to make the obstruction serve picked up speed to soar, high among the clouds. He experienced up close how the man facing him led his troops, inspiring them to carry on despite one set-back after another. Although it felt like magic, what the General was radiating to this tiny audience of one was a summons to trust and believe in his courage, durability and leadership and to draw forth one's commitment, by all means within one's power, to do his bidding. The summons was irresistible. And Tom was not the only Patriot to find it so. Washington was an alchemist, trafficking in human beliefs instead of base metals. He turned hope into determination, chance into certainty. The meeting was a grand experience for Tom, one he would dine over for a lifetime.

Tom's report cheered the General, despite being told by Tom of his private uncertainties as to the adequacy of the chain's strength and its siting. In fact, the General took encouragement from Tom's admissions as to the spacing of the logs and his failure to sharpen the ends, both causes of more drag than necessary. The General said, as they parted, "Captain, your candor reinforces my conviction that you're the right man for this job. I also have the instinct that you carry luck on your back. We need all of that we can get. Now, before you go, give me your assessment of the Forts. There is little room left for me to doubt the Enemy's designs are up the North River. On that account I fear the imperfect state of fortifications at Forts Montgomery and Clinton. Danger lurks in the many passes through the mountains, in the many approaches to the Forts and in the heights that overshadow them."

"It sounds like you are sure Howe is no longer looking south to Philadelphia."

The General knitted his brow.

"The truth is we just don't know. From the least beginnings, rumors take flight and are blown abroad. For example, we have a report that General Carlton is on the Lakes, pushing down to Ticonderoga. If true, then surely General Howe would not go to Philadelphia but endeavor to cooperate with Carlton and secure the river. But we don't know. What's sorely needed immediately is a way to find out the Enemy's designs. I know this job is not your line of work, but...."

Tom was tempted to offer Lisa's talents and connections. Afraid to claim too much, he simply said, "Let me think on this project. I might have something to offer."

"Tom, I like your attitude. Now, let me have your assessment."

"I heard it said an army fights on its stomach. Our forces are weakened daily by lack of rations. Peas are now in season, but we have none. Too expensive, we are told. Other vegetables are scarce, pulse too. Meat, less than a week's supply. These problems are serious, a product of avarice on the part of suppliers and, alas, incompetence on the part of commissary.

"The Provincial Congress entered into a contract with Abraham Livingston to victual our troops last year. I know the rations were adequate, both in quantity and type. That arrangement should have been extended. I will check on the status. Your report is disturbing."

"The chain will hold, I predict, and will obstruct Enemy traffic if the shore batteries, with force from both sides of the river, can play upon the vessels as they approach the obstruction. Of course, it would enhance the defense if we had frigates positioned just above the chain, capable of offering frontal fire. There remains the danger of attack by land, through the many passes, which offer the element of surprise. I believe the Highlands can be adequately guarded and the Forts defended with a force of some 4,000 troops. At present we can boast of but 800, a serious shortcoming. And there is the matter of discipline. Our forces lack that essential quality of a well-trained army, and discipline imposed with the cat seems less successful with us than with the British."

"Too many conditions undermine your confidence. I take these cautions with the seriousness they deserve. We Americans, I've discovered in this job, are an independent and exceedingly free people. A people unused to restraint must be led; they will not be driven. We have much to do. Most of it from here. Carry on, Captain. I have appreciated your briefing."

As Tom began the ride back to Fort Montgomery, Washington sat down to write a personal letter to Brigadier General Henry Knox, commending the Captain to Knox's continued attention. "I cannot help reminding you of him, as he appears from observation, and information, to be a person of merit. He has also mentioned something to me respecting his pay, which you will cause to be enquired into—he has received none, he says, since the month of May."

The Commanding General's soft touch with Henry Knox was more than adequate to achieve the desired result, which came to Tom in the form of a warm letter from General Knox, confirming his promotion to Captain Lieutenant, effective January first, and enclosing all past-due pay, including the raise that accompanied Tom's promotion. General Knox added his expectation of coming with his wife, Lucy, to Fort Montgomery in May for an inspection of its defenses, as ordered by the Commanding General, whose anxiety over losing control of the river was now a fact well-known to all.

By mid-March, temperatures had warmed enough to begin the break-up of ice, pieces of which began to move with the currents as they melted away.

On March 30th, Tom directed his team through a dress rehearsal of the installation. At the suggestion of one of the team's members whose mechanical skills and insights Tom and others had grown to know and admire, the positioning of the chain's end on the west side was moved upstream about 50 yards, thereby sharpening the angle of chain from the current's flow between Fort Montgomery and Anthony's Nose. This change was expected both to strengthen the chain against the currents and deflect oncoming vessels towards the Fort's cannon.

On the following day, at slack tide, the team completed the installation in four hours. The chain measured 1,650 feet, comprised 850 links in all, weighed some 35 tons and was supported by over four hundred logs, each two feet in diameter, sixteen feet in length, pencil-sharpened at both ends and lashed together, with six inches of space between each log, to form 52 floats of eight logs each.

As the next flood tide reached its full force, early in a cloud-free morning, Tom and Lisa joined General Clinton to watch the rushing waters break against the floats. The sun, still arcing to the south, peaked around the southern profile of Anthony's Nose as the General and his companions, together with as many of the Fort's occupants who could free themselves of duties for a spell, were transfixed by the drama below them, man against nature, given a third bite at the apple to demonstrate his ability to learn from mistakes and adapt, the ultimate survival kit.

Unlike Tom, who couldn't take his eyes off his handiwork, Lisa's attention wandered. Her eyes moved from chain to beams of sunlight backlighting the hemlock and oak forest that covered the southern shoulder of that Nose of Anthony, clinging to pockets of soil from the mountain's top to its bottom. Lisa found the beauty of that scene irresistible, dissolving war-time concerns with the river's obstruction in pools of radiant light.

"It's holding! The Machin chain is holding!" General Clinton exclaimed, beaming with near-childish pleasure as he slapped Tom on the shoulders.

"So far, so good, my General. But, remember it held for a time twice before."

General Clinton nodded.

* * * * *

Ten anxious days passed. The chain held through the ebbs and flows of strong current. Finally, Tom relaxed enough to divert his attention to the early unfolding of spring. He took Lisa on walks in the forest, on paths leading south to the tiny village of Doodletown and from there east through wetlands to Iona Island, still occupied by a local tribe of Indians. Buds the size of acorns dotted the still bare branches of the large black and chestnut oaks that dominated the forest. Except for the occasional hemlock or white pine obscuring the view, before them to some distance the forest seemed open to light, illuminating those gray branches that within the month would be clothed in pastel shades of leafy green. But for the attentive traveler, there was more.

"Look, Lisa, do you see that snowball of white through the oaks, about 200 yards away? It's glistening in the sunlight. Seems suspended above ground. What is it?"

"I wondered when you might notice that. It's a shadbush. They're all over this forest. Those blooms mark the beginning of spring. What's so thrilling about them is that they drape themselves in pure white before any sign of leaf appears, either on their branches or on the oaks and maples. They are, indeed, like giant snowballs, remnants of winter, lingering mysteriously in a forest pregnant with Spring."

"And their name? Connected to the fish?"

"You got it. Shad runs start in the Hudson about the time the shadbush blooms. Someone long ago must have connected the two. I don't know if the tree has other names."

Having found one shadbush, they quickly began to pick out others, sprinkled here and there through the forest. What seemed remarkable, after they had examined a handful of these trees up close was the fact they all seemed to grow on rocks, with roots extending into cracks, places where they would get no competition from other trees. But, given the conditions, growth must be slow and difficult.

"Amazing," Tom said. "Do they chose those locations or are they forced there by more powerful competitors?"

"Who knows?" Lisa said. "Someday I'll ask them."

While Lisa and Tom were enjoying their trek to Iona and back, Private John Slatterly, who had grown up in Doodletown and now was serving in the infantry at Fort Montgomery, was rowing with his mate, Private William Slutt, on the river, dragging a modest-sized net to catch some of the very fish the shadbush was named for. Slatterly strained at the oars, while Slutt tended the net, which was weighed down by four small cannon balls sewn along the bottom edge of the net. John had grown up fishing for shad, but for Bill the experience was new, although he was comfortable in small watercraft. Upon hauling in the net, they were delighted to find they had snagged three shad of three pounds or more each.

"Beautiful, that's what they are," John cried. "Careful, now, Bill my boy, lest they jump overboard."

Once ashore, John threaded a long stick with the stub of a branch at its end through the shads' gills and the men climbed up to the Fort from the water's edge. Before they had reached their barracks, they crossed paths with Tom and Lisa, who were returning from their trek.

"Private Slatterly, what have you got there?" Tom said.

"Fish, Lieutenant. Three shad to be factual. Ever had one?"

"As a matter of fact, no. But Miss Van Horne has and speaks very highly of shad."

"Yes, particularly the roe," Lisa said.

"Well, if Private Slutt here won't report me a brown-noser, I'll gladly turn over one of these shad to you, seeing how till now you've missed something special. I guess Miss Van Horne knows how to gut, clean and cook the fish. If not…."

"I can handle it, Private Slatterly, have no fear. I've even tried boning, the very devil to do, I know. We'll manage. And, Private, at the risk of darkening your nose, on behalf of us both, thanks for sharing your catch."

That night Lisa was rewarded for tending to lessons learned in her early teens from a father who loved shad and taught her to enjoy it in the ways of the Indian. After gutting and cleaning the fish and removing its backbone and the many other little bones it was famous for, she nailed the shad to a buttered board and roasted it by suspending the board over coals. She was practiced and skillful, talents Tom ingested as happily as he did the product of her labor. She cooked the roe separately, in a saucepan with butter. After partaking of both, it was the combination that delighted Tom the most.

* * * * *

Generals Nathaniel Greene and Henry Knox arrived at Fort Montgomery on May 12th, ordered there by the Commander-in-Chief to review all the posts under command of Brigadier General Alexander McDougall and to give him advice and assistance towards putting everything in the most defensible state possible. McDougall commanded the lower Hudson from a post in Peekskill. In a note to McDougall informing him of why Generals Greene and Knox were suddenly looking over his shoulder, Washington wrote "The vast importance of these posts, and the great probability that the Enemy will direct their operations against them make me anxious for their security, and suggest this step. I doubt not proper regard will be paid to the judgment of these Gentlemen."

Word of Washington's oversight, and General McDougall's understandable anger over the message's harsh explanation, which he felt bespoke distrust in him, crept out of the Peekskill command post to reach officers at Fort Montgomery, and once there, quite naturally spread among the men.

Tom and Lisa heard the news as they were preparing to join General Clinton in welcoming Generals Greene and Knox at dinner on their first evening at the Fort. The sun was still high in the western sky when they gathered in the commanding officer's mess.

General Clinton said, "Gentlemen, before we seat ourselves, allow me to show you the river directly below us. There you can see what we affectionately call the Machin Chain, holding fast and taut against the current."

"We admired it upon arrival. Impressive." Henry Knox said, emphatically.

"Hard to avoid with all those floats. The obstruction looks natural, like it belonged there," said Nathaniel Greene.

Lisa watched the milling Generals with the wry smile of a mischievous woman.

"James, I noticed you called our guests 'Gentlemen.' Like our Commander-in-Chief, you're giving them the benefit of the doubt, so I will too. Gentlemen, your reference to Anthony's Nose put me in mind of another nose, one that we hear has become disjointed since your arrival at our Fort. What do you say to that, if you please?"

Tom was shocked at Lisa's unexpected frivolity, which he thought bordered on the insulting. My God, he realized, she's never even met McDougall. With limited success, he struggled to conceal his feelings, which were mostly a fear of embarrassment. Beyond a raised eyebrow or two, the Gentlemen seemed unperturbed. But that's the way with Gentlemen, Tom thought, continuing to worry.

"We've heard of Alex McDougall's reaction to our assignment. Frankly, we think it understandable," Henry said. "General Washington's anxious about conditions on the river, not about Alex. But his message could easily be misread. It is to address that anxiety that we are here, and part of the job is to work with Alex in relieving it."

"Well said. When I was briefing the General at Morristown last month, that anxiety was clearly at the top of his mind. But so, too, is intelligence. What he wants desperately is intelligence on Howe's intentions. Whither his army: Philadelphia or the Hudson?

We haven't been creative enough—yet—to answer that question for him. But just in the last day or so we have conjured a plan that might lead to useful information. Lisa, since you're the central actor here, why don't you explain."

"My family, the Van Hornes, have for a generation or so made their home at a well-named estate in New Jersey called Convivial Hall. My parents love entertaining, and since the war began, have continued this custom in robust fashion, hosting both British and Continental officers, occasionally in combination. The Hall has a well-earned reputation as a neutral ground both felicitous and hospitable. The combatants get to feel each other's muscles, even see them flexed, without having to actually deploy them. My sisters and cousins, of whom there are quite a number, together with their female friends, are often on hand to engage with the guests. To tell the truth, it's all rather bizarre."

General Greene said, "It's more than a bit weird and almost unbelievable. But all along the Hudson, war tensions grow and norms are broken. From New York City to Albany, the divisions between Tories and Patriots are deep and dangerous."

"I have visited the Hall twice in recent months, each time finding modest opportunities to mislead the British guests. And it's a venue, too, for the flow of information. Servants keep me informed of forthcoming visits by enemy officers. Thus, I've just been informed that Henry Clinton, the most senior British officer here, second only to Silly Billy, will be visiting the Hall in two days, staying one night only. My plan was for Generals Greene and Knox to join Tom and me as Convivial Hall guests on the same night.

As Lisa finished, both Generals showed enthusiasm. Henry said: "A visit to your Hall would seem to offer all manner of unexpected opportunities and outcomes. I congratulate you. A capital idea."

Nathaniel nodded agreement, then added a note of caution. "The Hall might be compared to a chessboard, offering the customary risks and opportunities of the game. Henry, we shall have to be on our guard. General Clinton is probably the smartest of the enemy's generals, as witnessed by his reported disagreement with most of

Billy's tactics. There was even word that he was close to quitting the field."

Tom was curious about this General, who would be the one to lead an attack on the Forts, if anyone did.

"I'm sure you've been briefed on Clinton. What more do we know beyond his being 40?"

Henry said, "Competent, hard-working, reliable, no dissipated habits or sloth, a skillful soldier capable of striking hard, but without any flare for tactics. But here's his weakness, one perhaps we can play on. He is possessed by an *idee fixe* that Howe had slighted and wronged him—a conviction, some say, that almost unbalances him. If one of us can play Iago to his Othello, the game could get interesting."

"That you will be well protected at the Hall, Nathaniel, you can be sure of as long as Lisa is with you. She's a pro in her own house, a fact Tom and James will affirm."

Tom nodded. "In addition to Lisa, it's three of us to one enemy General. He may be smart, but we aren't too shabby in that area. Now, if we get to work, you should be able to finish your project for the General before we leave for the Hall."

A dinner of spring fare was served. Conversation was lively, stimulated by the prospect of engaging the enemy's brilliant general on neutral ground, with wits instead of arms. As a dessert of strawberries and cream was being served, with the remainder of General Clinton's stock of well-aged claret, a messenger arrived from Peekskill, dispatched by General McDougall to report on the enemy's expedition to Danbury, a successful venture of 1800 men led by Governor Tryon, a Major-General in the provincial troops fighting in support of the British. Before Patriot militia could be assembled, under the leadership of Generals Arnold and Silliman, Tryon's mission was accomplished. Devastating damage was inflicted on the village, precious stores were lost and four hundred casualties suffered, including the death of General Wooster, one of thirteen general officers appointed by Congress to serve under Washington.

When the militia reached Danbury, a smart action ensued, but General Arnold's forces were badly outnumbered by those of General

Tryon and quickly forced to retreat. The messenger reported that General Arnold had his horse shot under him when within ten yards of an enemy soldier advancing with fixed bayonet. With his horse staggering, Arnold drew his pistol and dropped the soldier with a shot to his body.

The report affixed an alarming coda to the evening.

* * * * *

On the night before he left for Convivial Hall, while eating supper, Tom turned to Lisa, a quizzical expression crossing his face. "Lisa, I have a question for you. There are plenty of Negroes around Convivial Hall, and I imagine they were there aplenty when you were growing up. As a race, do you find them lazy and idle? Needing to be driven to work, like oxen?"

"My lover, that's a strange question to ask me, just after I returned from having my hair arranged by the post groomer. To say you hardly noticed would be rank exaggeration."

"I've been distracted by an unusual assignment General James handed me this morning. He's hurt his right arm, you'll remember, from a fall. Can't write. So, impressed by my hand with numbers, he assumed I could do the same with letters and gave me the task of transcribing a letter to his wife. This morning he dictated and I wrote out what he said. Some of what he said has occupied my mind all day. So, back to my question."

She stood, came over to him at the dinner table, finding his shoulders hunched up. She kneaded his neck, using two hands with fingers more gentle and effective than his.

"The Negroes of Convivial were neither lazy nor idle. They showed every sign of liking the tasks they were assigned. I always thought they considered themselves part of the family. And that they took pride in their service. I could be wrong, but slaves they were not, and none ever behaved or thought as a slave. The family believed it treated them well, and if memory serves, we had good reason to believe that."

"Just as I had assumed, Lisa. But the picture painted by the General is very different. I can remember every word of what I wrote down. Here's what he said to his wife:

> I would be glad Egbert would do his endeavour while he can stay with you to prevent the Negroes from being entirely idle and that they may feed the creatures right and not give them too much hay at once but oftener and see that they get drink. Likewise let them cut down all the trees in the wheat field for rails and firewood, clean your flax and thrash the wheat. There is work enough to do they ought not to be idle. If they will not work I will not keep them there.

"Lisa, the message here is that Negroes are idle unless driven to work."

"I agree. But so much we don't know. Did he pay them? Housing? Food? And treatment. Assume idleness and, perhaps, that's what you get. Assume hard work, and show by example, and, perhaps, you get good results. Who knows? I don't see the need for that kind of message at Convivial."

11

CONVIVIAL HALL REVISITED

General Henry Clinton and his senior staff had already arrived at Convivial Hall when the three officers from Fort Montgomery dismounted. Lisa had set out much earlier in the day and was well settled before either group reached the Hall.

Phillip Van Horne handled the introductions, expressing on his family's behalf how honored they were to have the chance to entertain such a celebrated group of officers.

"Gentlemen, I speak for our family in saying how thoroughly we despise this conflict. Our hopes rest on your putting arms aside and through negotiation achieving an amicable settlement of differences. We are all branches of an ancient and beloved tree that bleeds from this conflict. We plead with you to end it soon, not through the defeat of one side but through an abiding peace that would represent victory for both sides."

Lisa admired her father's practiced hand at threading the needle. His illness hadn't impaired his mind one bit. The cover he furnished her was not lost on Tom and his companions.

No one expected peace, like the spring season then being enjoyed, to break forth before they sat down to dine. To a man, they recognized that conversation at dinner would be just another skirmish in the war. Forthwith, it surged with energy that flowed haphazardly around the table from one diner to another. For the Continental Generals it was fraught with dangers augmented by the Van Horne wine cellar and the immediate recognition, in Henry Clinton, of a chess-master in top form and fully aware of the game he was there to play.

"I believe your commanding general expects us to assert control of the Hudson, no?" General Clinton said, seeking advantage from the first move.

Having discussed how best to proceed, Henry and Nathaniel had decided on truth-telling as much as possible, believing that to be caught out in a lie would likely impair the intelligence-gathering purpose, and not knowing what the enemy knew heightened the dangers of being caught out.

"He would not be surprised at the attempt. Indeed, he has for months exhorted us to be prepared for just such a move, and we are now ready. Undoubtedly, you know we have obstructed the river in many ways, including a chain at Fort Montgomery. Tom's the source of design and installation. We call it the Machin Chain."

"Ah, yes, we know it's there, but not its name. And, we know it broke twice after installation just before winter closed the river. We expect it will break again, as repeated tidal assaults tend to weaken even the strongest man-made playthings. But, tell me, why doesn't your General worry about our interest in Philadelphia, what those living there call the gateway to the south? The launching place of your revolt. Surely you know, that town's filled with Tories eager to join our ranks."

Nathaniel took the mantle from Henry. "British Generals are too wise to divide their forces—a military choice contrary to doctrine. It will be north or south; not both. And to the north we hear that General Burgoyne is assembling forces to move south, stretch his supply lines and take on Fort Ticonderoga, an awesome endeavor. This means British forces are already divided, so further division would be to invite disaster. Surely, you agree?"

"Impressive insights. But well short they fall in understanding our strategy, which, I admit, is sometimes obscure, even for me. We have many egos to nourish, and the nourishment comes from

London—a long way in time and distance. Logic suggests we must go north in support of Burgoyne. The prize of controlling the river from New York Harbor to the Canadian border is, we all know, of inestimable value. That's why you have tried to mount strong defenses, of which we are familiar. There are many vulnerabilities for an army travelling through hostile territory by ship along the confines of a river."

"Indeed," said Henry, sensing that Clinton had adopted the truth-telling strategy as well. "Your forces might not reach Albany to join Burgoyne. He might not get past Ticonderoga. Strongly fortified, most military experts consider it invulnerable. From there to Albany only uninhabited wilderness prevails. Thick stands of oak, chestnut and pine would block an army at every turn. Close to ground small shrubs create impenetrable thickets. Uncertainties pile up. We are ready whatever you decide. Our forces swell with the coming of summer. Taking on the Americans in their homeland is going to be an endless chore. Your King will feel as condemned as Sisyphus felt after that stone he had to roll up the hill kept rolling back down.

"The time and distance to your home base are reason enough, although there are others. This country is far, far larger and wilder than Parliament can imagine. You will bleed. No doubt Washington's forces will wax and wane with the seasons and through inconclusive victories and defeats. But they will not go away because this land is their home. The war will continue until the British people have bled enough treasure to demand that Parliament call home what's left of your army. I'm sure you're familiar with Thucydides' account of the doomed Greek campaign against Sicily. That Greek tragedy is repeating itself right here."

"More bold boast than reasoned prediction, my friend. How can you foresee so far into the future when you don't even know whither General Howe's army is bound in the current campaign season? I will admit to General Burgoyne's pretensions in, among other things, referring to himself rather grandly as 'Lieutenant-General of his Majesty's forces in America' and the many other titles you are obviously familiar with, leaving barely room on the page for messaging. And I will acknowledge General Howe's tendency to blend frolicking with fighting." A smile best described as wicked shaped itself on his face, where, with conscious effort, it remained until he was sure the Patriots had seen it.

"Yes, often, in favor of the former." Henry couldn't resist, a wide smile breaking out across his face.

"I pass over that point. Gentlemen, make no mistake. Burgoyne's record on the field supports his pretensions. He is fully capable of bringing his army to Albany, unassisted. And Howe's attractions to the ladies belie a remarkable ambition to succeed on the field here in America as he has done repeatedly in Europe. As for me, I am at least as motivated to serve my Crown as they are. In short, we are here to restore peace to a thriving, contented colony. At the end of the day, whether this season we turn north or south will prove of no account. Success is not in question. The time it takes is the only uncertainty. And, a final point. The more drawn out this conflict becomes, the more this land and its people will suffer."

Nathaniel returned to the field of battle for one last thrust at their wily opponent.

"When this war started, the Tories in this country far outnumbered the Patriots. Parliament knew it and so did the small brotherhood of Patriots meeting in Philadelphia. Parliament bet a British show of force would shrink Patriot ranks to the vanishing point. It is proving to be a bad bet. With every passing day in this war, more Tories switch loyalties to become Patriots and join Washington's forces, or at least support them. I conjure you to accept this point, as the proof can be found in plain sight throughout the country."

"The loyalties of noncombatants sway like palm fronds in a breeze. Such is the experience of countless wars in Europe. The tendency, at day's end, is for them to turn toward the winning side."

On the ride back to Fort Montgomery, Tom and the Generals debated the meaning of what they had heard.

"Let's face it," Henry said sadly, "we learned precious little."

"Clinton is a clever old dog," Nathaniel said. "He played the same game we did, and perhaps he was better at it. Acknowledging the known weaknesses of Burgoyne and Howe before trying to impress us with their abilities on the field made those claims convincing. But through all he said there ran a subtle, unintended theme—at least so I sensed—a theme of disapproval, and, perhaps, jealousy of his colleagues. If true, it holds promise for rivalry and confusion, even misunderstandings and mistakes."

"That's sounds like wishful thinking, Nathaniel, but I get your point and agree with it. He said some surprising things, for example, the role that time and distance play in slowing down receipt of reports from here and orders from London."

Tom said "Yes, with so many would-be chiefs, potential for cock-ups runs deep. My reading of Clinton was the same as yours, Nathaniel."

Henry said, "If Howe goes south, can Burgoyne make it alone? Tom and I know what it's like hauling artillery through forests. No picnic. And we didn't have lobstercoats taking shots at us along the way. Our militia can be formidable snipers."

"And mostly invisible," Tom interjected, "bothering his army every step of the way."

Nathaniel said, "That depends on so many things, but especially the quality and quantity of forces we can throw against him. The commanding general may divert most of our forces to oppose Howe if he turns to Philadelphia."

"Distance and terrain are our allies," Tom argued. "The Sicily campaign all over again. My bet is Burgoyne will bite off more than he can chew. Frustration and pride will drive him to over-extend."

* * * * *

Generals Nathaniel Greene and Henry Knox joined with Generals George Clinton, Alexander McDougall and Anthony Wayne, as the Council of General Officers at Peekskill, in submitting to Commanding General Washington, by date of May 17, 1777, a report on obstructions in the Hudson River. It read as follows:

> We have examined the Obstructions in the North River, and beg leave to observe that the object is too important to be trusted to its present security. If those obstructions in the River can be rendered effectual, and the Passes into the Highlands be properly

guarded, which can be done with about four or five thousand Troops, the rest of the Army will be at liberty to operate elsewhere.

To render the obstruction at Fort Montgomery complete it will be necessary to have a Boom across the River, and one or two cables, in front of the chain, to break the force of the Shipping before they come up to it. The two Continental Ships should be immediately man'd and fix'd; and the Two Row-Gallies, to be stationed just above the obstructions, which will form a front fire equal to what the Enemy can bring against them. The fire from the Ships and Gallies in front, and the Batteries upon the flank, will render it impossible for the Shipping to operate there, if the obstructions in the River bring them up; which, with the additional strength proposed, we have great reason to expect.

The communication between the Eastern and Western States is so essential to the Continent & the advantages we shall have over the Enemy by the communication, and the great expense that will be saved in transportation of Stores, by having command of the River, warrants every expense to secure an object of such great magnitude. We are very confident if the obstructions in the River can be rendered effectual, the Enemy will not attempt to operate by Land, the passes through the Highlands are so exceedingly difficult. We are with the greatest respect and esteem, Your Excellency's most obedient servants.

Tom was intimately involved in the development of these observations and agreed with them all, save the need for further obstructions across the river. He was firm in his belief the chain would hold without more. However, he could hardly object to strengthening the chain by adding a boom and cables. All it would require was more trees and more work by his team and him. Lisa was dismayed.

"You might have resisted more firmly, Tom. You're the engineer. Your opinion's worth far more than a pile of those Generals' opinions. Laymen, all. They know it; and you know it. It's not as if you have nothing else to do."

"Don't challenge me on this one, Lisa. It's been a long day. I did what I could. What in the end I thought right. Say no more."

For weeks, Tom sought to carry forward the orders of the Council of General Officers, reporting on progress to Major-General Israel Putnam at his headquarters in Peekskill. General George Clinton, to whom Tom had expected to report on this project, was in Kingston, discharging his new duties as Governor of New York. General Putnam enjoyed a reputation for skill and judgment in the one place where it mattered most—the mind of the Commander-in-Chief, who in March of the previous year had given Putnam command of the City of New York as British land and naval forces were about to attempt entry.

Putnam was known to possess a sharp sense of humor wrapped in a rather laconic style. Tom's first report to him, delivered after a swift journey by boat in the shadow of Anthony's Nose, following close along the eastern shoreline to Peekskill Bay, described the many frustrations Tom was having in seeking heavy ropes of adequate length to stretch twice across the river and the timber necessary for the Boom, which was to consist of rafts fifteen feet apart and composed of five pine logs two feet in diameter and twenty feet long, placed three feet apart and framed together by three cross pieces, each log to be pointed at the end facing downstream and sheathed in iron. The rafts would be connected by chains and anchored in three or four places across the river.

Finding trees adequate to build the rafts supporting the chain had been so difficult and time-consuming that Tom considered the additional logs necessary for the boom impossible to obtain in time to serve during the current year.

"Old Put," as he was known, listened to Tom's tale of multiple frustrations, and then, without comment or apology, changed the subject.

"Tom, did you hear of the spy we found in camp last week?"

"News travels slowly east to west, General. We know nothing." Tom couldn't imagine how this story could relate to his project, and wondered if Old Put had heard him, or understood his perhaps too-subtle plea for help.

"Well, he was a chap named Nathan Palmer. Behaved like a sturgeon pulled from the Hudson. We grew suspicious. Arrested him. At trial, we found him to be a Lieutenant among new Tory levies. General Tryon, the British commander of these Tories, wrote me demanding that I turn Palmer over, threatening vengeance if he should be executed. Which was exactly what we did yesterday. Here's my letter to Tryon, about to be dispatched. Unless you object, Tom." Tom caught Old Put's sly dog wink. Quickly reading the missive, Tom chuckled in approval:

Sir: Nathan Palmer, a lieutenant in your king's service, was taken in my camp as a spy, --- he was tried as a spy, --- he was condemned as a spy, --- and you may rest assured, sir, that he shall be hanged as a spy.
I have the honor to be, &c. ISRAEL PUTNAM
P.S. Afternoon. He is hanged.

"Masterful response, General. Have you reckoned with that vengeance thing?" Tom's chuckle turned to a broad smile.

"We await it with high hopes. And, now, Tom, you should find your way back to the Fort. I must turn to the unfinished business of this camp. God's speed, and a dollop of good fortune in your quest. I'm glad I could be of service. If more ideas come to me, you shall have them."

How could this man be a Major-General? How attain Washington's confidence? What strange behavior, Tom thought as his men rowed him back to Fort Montgomery. One thing was clear. General Putnam wanted no responsibility for the obstructions. His refusal, through silence, to engage on the project was deafening. This, despite Washington's exhortations to "push matters and let no pains be spared" to install the recommended rope cables and boom, delivered repeatedly to General Putnam from the Commander-in-Chief's headquarters at Middle Brook, as Tom later learned.

On hearing the story that evening, Lisa said: "He's never seen the chain, but he's watched the surging flows up and down river. He's convinced the obstructions won't hold and wants as little to do with the project as possible. He knows getting involved at all is a slippery slope. There you have it. You may not be able to find enough rope to cross the river, but Old Put will see that you have enough to hang yourself."

"I'm sitting here still puzzled by this amazing encounter. Didn't even give me the 'Go forth, lad, I have full confidence in you,' etc. nonsense. He'd put an ocean between the chain and himself, if he could."

While Tom talked, Lisa watched the movements of his Adam's Apple. She thought of bagpipes, ocean waves, an exhausted dog on its side, a flopping fish on deck. His was an unusually large affair with sharp definition, especially when viewed in profile. He had hair covering the top half, which, in shaving, required both skill and patience. Accidents occurred, not often, but enough for Lisa to have noticed blood on the hand towel and the ooze of droplets where the Apple bulged. Fortunately, for the towels and Tom's neck, he was usually too impatient to put razor to work on his Adam's Apple.

Lisa's childish curiosity operated chiefly in the realm of words. At a young age she had discovered the origin of the term for that protuberance between chin and shoulder.

"We've talked enough about Old Put. I've been watching your Adam's Apple, the way it moves, like waves lapping at a pier. I bet you can't tell me its origin."

Though glad to escape from his recent miseries, Tom found Lisa's change of subject annoying. Hadn't she been listening? Didn't she care? Repressing these angry thoughts, he answered her.

"Something to do with the Adam and Eve story. Beyond that, haven't a clue."

"God forbids them from eating apples and Eve, tempted by the Serpent, picks an apple from the Tree of Knowledge of good and bad, eats some of it and gives the rest to Adam, who also eats it. In so doing, a piece of apple gets stuck in his throat, making a lump, thenceforth to be a constant reminder of what is called their sin—in Biblical terms, the original sin."

"Interesting. That's why men have bigger ones than women. Odd, since it was Eve who first disobeyed God. Do you believe any of this stuff?"

Lisa was about to respond but then hesitated, her face lighting up, her mouth opening, eyes widening.

Seconds passed, close to a minute, before she spoke.

"You know I'm a non-believer. But, your question has triggered a thought. In the story, Adam and Eve were naked in the Garden of Eden, but not ashamed of their nakedness. Upon eating the apple, their innocent eyes were opened to their nakedness, and they were ashamed and sewed fig leaves together to hide their sex. And God expels them from the Garden where they might have enjoyed eternal life. The story taints sex with this original sin. Instead of celebrating the sexual act as a joyful aspect of humanity, the Bible associates it with shame—the stain of Adam and Eve's sin in eating the apple. A totally needless connection between sex and the original sin, lacking in logic or understanding. I'd never thought of this before, but Genesis got us off on the wrong foot!"

"One certainly grows up being taught that God's attitude toward sex is that it's intrinsically sinful. Except when indulging to create offspring. And in that case merely tolerated. Hold your nose while performing the duty to multiply. Why else make Mary a virgin? And equate "purity" with being chaste. Demanding of priests and nuns lives of celibacy? How much better it would be without the taint. That wave of guilt that each of us must throw off to enjoy sex."

"Yes, but for some, like you Tom, not too big a wave."

"Ha! For you, Lisa, not even a ripple. Who taught you that sin can be fun?"

"Runs in the family. Generations of sinners, I'm told."

Tom laughed. Then, a chord of memory turned him serious again.

"About that expulsion and the Fall of Adam and Eve, I remember, as a youngster, being told by a Rabbi who taught at the orphanage that the original version of Genesis didn't have God expelling them as punishment for childish disobedience, but rather because, having eaten from the Tree of Knowledge, they knew good and bad and, if permitted to remain in the Garden, could enjoy immortality from the Tree of Life. I've always liked the idea of different versions. Helps to weaken truth eternal for any one of them. And, by the way, you'll like this; he also claimed the Hebrew words, properly understood, put Eve 'alongside' Adam, 'his equal.'"

"Ha! I'm sure the Pope and his retinue were quick to blot that one out—'nip it in the bud' as these Highlands apple growers say."

* * * * *

By mid-July, Tom had commandeered the anchor lines from the *Montgomery* and the *Congress* recently arrived at Fort Montgomery from Poughkeepsie, where they had been outfitted. They were the only lines that Tom could find to stretch across the river in front of the chain. With the consent of General Clinton, the boom he was directed to install was dropped in recognition of the impossibility of rounding up enough timber. Of course, Tom's quiet reminder that in his professional opinion, the Boom was a gilding of a lily not needing improvement, stuck in the General's head, lending support to his decision to drop the project. However, the strong recommendation of The Council of General Officers that two Continental frigates and two row galleys be outfitted, manned and stationed just above the obstructions, so as to match Enemy fire from approaching ships, was carried forward by Captain John Grinnell. Grinnell had little to do in arranging the frigates, for the *Montgomery* and the *Congress* were already in place, thanks to Tom's efforts in regard to the lines he had lifted from them, and needed only new lines and adequate crews, which the Captain, with no apparent success, was trying to procure.

The summer passed swiftly. The chain held. The mountain passes to the south and west of the Forts were becoming familiar terrain to the handful of troops who could be spared to try to guard them. One morning in September, General Clinton called Tom and the other officers stationed at the Forts to his office to take stock.

"Gentlemen, you find me in an anxious state. General Putnam has informed me that, should the enemy land at Peekskill, as he expects soon, given Burgoyne's progress from the north, he will require of us some 1200 troops, who, upon call, must be swiftly ferried across the river to Peekskill Bay. That would leave us with but 1200 on the west side, divided 400 at Fort Clinton and 800 here. My protests to 'Old Put' fell on deaf ears—and I mean that both figuratively and as a fact, for the General's hearing is fading faster than summer.

"Tom, speak up. His brains too, I think I heard you whisper. I'll ignore that, if you please, and strike it from the record. But of course, you're right. Old Put kept making the point that an enemy landing on the east meant there would be no landing on the west. Of feints he seems ignorant. And when pressed, highly skeptical. He claimed that all signs point to a landing on the east. Hadn't the enemy come in May to launch its attack on Danbury? Weren't the mountains to the north less difficult on the east side? He wouldn't listen—'couldn't listen' you say—yes, yes, alas, that's the case—but the ultimate point is he outranks me and was put in command here."

"I was re-reading the May report of General Greene and the other General Officers," Tom said. "Its confident tone on the success of our obstructions turned on various key assumptions. One was that the Enemy would not attempt to operate by land because the passes through the Highlands were so exceedingly difficult. Having marched through the passes, I've never understood the logic. At another point, somewhat inconsistently, the report rests its conclusion that the obstructions will succeed only if the Highlands are properly guarded to the west, which the Generals opine can be done with about four or five thousand troops. In other words, the Enemy may attempt an attack by land, but with enough troops, we can repulse them. The problem, of course, is that we have but 2400, half of whom are on call to General Putnam, who imagines attack through the mountains on the west too remote to plan for."

Artillery Colonel Lamb observed that both General Washington and General McDougall, on separate occasions in early summer, had expressed in strongest terms a fear that the Enemy would overcome our very weak post, in the case of McDougall, by sailing through the night to break the chain, and in the case of Washington, by landing below the Forts, marching on a route through the Highlands not expected or protected, and overwhelming our undermanned outposts.

Tom said, "You have good reason to be anxious, General. I share the feeling."

Lieutenant Colonel Livingston could usually be counted on to find space between the rain drops. "Come now, Gentlemen, there is much to celebrate."

"Yes, indeed," interjected Captain Fenno. "Over one week's provision of meat. Consider the benefits of fewer troops. More meat to go round."

"You're out of order with that sarcasm, Captain," said Colonel Livingston. "We have the chain, holding well; and the cables in front of it and the ships behind, almost ready to do service. What's called for is a thorough inspection of small arms and cannon. We need to prepare ourselves. Send forth patrol after patrol until we are 100% confident that every possible route the enemy might use is known to us and covered. We have troops enough to guard the routes, even though it leaves the Forts seriously undermanned, provided we have practiced signals to recall them swiftly if the enemy is detected. With preparation comes confidence. It will build morale. Always has. Always will. And, don't forget, or let the troops forget, we occupy the Forts. That advantage is huge."

General Clinton said, "Colonel Livingston, I'm much in your debt for this—what to call it—a passionate exhortation. You lift our spirits."

12

—

GENERAL HENRY CLINTON'S
AUDACITY

Toward the end of September, orders arrived for General Putnam from the Commander-in-Chief, who, having endured the Battle of Brandywine, saw looming danger in the reduced state of his Regiments. Seeing his continuing engagement with General Howe near Philadelphia as a priority, he summoned a substantial number of Continental soldiers stationed at Peekskill to march with urgent step south.

At the beginning of October, Old Put wrote Governor George Clinton "Unless a greater force is supplied, you must be sensible I cannot be answerable for the Defense of this post."

On receipt, Governor Clinton said to no one in particular among those aides surrounding him, "Old Put can always be trusted to declare weakness or defeat well before the enemy arrives. Undermanned as we are, he's already got a call on 1200 of our troops."

Dismayed but not surprised by the General's message, Tom said: "The weak link in our defenses is found not among the links of our chain. It's our inability to defend the chain's anchor to rock on each side of the river. Release one or the other and the chain's gone. The enemy knows this as well as we do. Sure as I'm Tom Machin, they'll try to blind us to which anchor they'll go for."

"You're right, Tom. And splitting our forces, already inadequate, only assures defeat. Old Put's bet on the east side, and his insistence on taking our troops because he knows he's right, is not without self-interest."

"Doesn't give a rat's ass about our Fort," said Captain Fenno.

Sir Henry Clinton, left by General Howe in charge of New York City, was an impulsive man, eager to take the field and unencumbered by the female distractions that were afflicting General Howe. When a body of recruits arrived in town from Europe at the end of September, he resolved to take possession of Forts Montgomery and Clinton. His purpose was not to create a diversion to help General Burgoyne's advance toward Albany, since he assumed that General needed no help. His goal was to clear river passage from New York City to Albany, thus opening communication with General Burgoyne upon his arrival in that small city. Despite the efforts of Henry, Nathaniel and Tom at Convivial Hall, Henry Clinton's intelligence informed him of the weak condition of the Forts, strained to dangerous levels by Washington's call for troops to march south. He knew it was an opportune time to strike, and he had always been the consummate opportunist.

He embarked a force of 3000 men on transports under command of Commodore Hotham, arriving in Tarrytown Bay on the 3rd of October, where this armada was joined by more ships of war and transports. Weighing anchor the next day, the armada arrived at daybreak on the 5th, at Verplanck's Point, the eastern terminus of King's Ferry, where Sir Henry landed a small body of men. The Point was about three miles downriver from Peekskill and about six miles below Fort Montgomery.

When Old Put finally learned of the enemy's arrival in Tarrytown Bay, Sir Henry's forces had reached Verplanck's Point. Old Put claimed his scouts reported a large force of some 1500, who had overrun the slight breastworks at the Point, sending the Continentals flying, having abandoned one of the two twelve-pounders mounted to defend the Point without firing a shot.

Convinced that Sir Henry intended to attack Peekskill and then march to take the passes to the north and cut the chain at

Anthony's Nose, Old Put sent an urgent summons to Governor George Clinton for the 1200 men held on call for him at Fort Montgomery and repaired with his forces to the northern heights overlooking Peekskill Bay. Convincing himself that he was vastly outnumbered, even after the 1200 had arrived, bringing his forces to close to 2000, he thought it too dangerous to leave the heights and attack Sir Henry's army. On the following morning, he and Brigadier General Parsons reconnoitered the enemy's position to the south of Peekskill, and even then, having seen but a small detachment of British troops through thick morning fog, concluded that he was vastly outnumbered, rendering an attack foolhardy. His men were deployed along a high ridge running east to west, directly overlooking a Bay bathed in fog that morning. Old Put needed no persuasion to stand his ground on the ridge until the sun burned through the fog, enabling him to see what the enemy was doing.

In fact, Sir Henry had been active after sending off his small landing party at the Point on the 5th. Leaving 900 men there, he prepared to land 2100 well-rested, fed and armed men at Stony Point, the western terminus of King's Ferry, at the crack of dawn on the 6th. Assisted by the Tory Colonel Beverly Robinson, who commanded 400 Loyal Americans, as his regiment was known, and who knew the Highlands geography in detail, and a local informer, Brom Springster, Sir Henry led his men three abreast up the steep side of Dunderberg Mountain and down through the narrow Timp trail to Doodletown, deep in a valley leading north to the Forts, which were some twelve miles from Stony Point. The march was brutal for the redcoats, each carrying 60 pounds on a day of intense heat encased in high humidity. Rations consisted of rum and hardtack, when what was urgently needed was water. No rain puddle was too muddy to pass untouched.

Fort Montgomery was alerted to the arrival at King's Ferry of Sir Henry's armada on the 5th, when Old Put's breathless messenger commandeered half Governor George Clinton's forces. The Governor summoned Major Logan of Colonel DuBois' regiment, a wise and alert officer intimately familiar with the forests to the south, west and north of the Forts and with the Dunderberg, the mountain over which an army approaching from Stony Point would have to come.

"Major, we remain blind, alas, to the enemy's whereabouts and intentions. General Putnam assures us that Sir Henry's forces are landing on the east, bent on taking Peekskill and marching through the Highlands to meet General Burgoyne and, incidentally, stopping at Anthony's Nose to cut our chain. I'm dubious. His activity at Verplanck's Point could be a feint. He could be planning to land in force at Stony Point. We must know. Take 80 men, travel light and swift. And quiet. Reconnoitre between the Forts and Stony Point. Return with intelligence. Go, and with God's help, restore our vision."

The Major was steeped in Greek history, which, combined with his knowledge of the rocky narrow pass leading through the thick forest that covered both sides of Dunderberg, led him to recall the similarly narrow pass at Thermopylae, where, in 480 BC, King Leonidas and his 300 Spartan hoplites lay down their lives in battling the overwhelming forces of Darius I of Persia to delay the Persian Army for a week. Some 20,000 Persian soldiers were killed in trying to breach a pass where numbers didn't count for much.

"General, if we discover the enemy is approaching over Dunderberg, we could mount a defense at the summit in the manner of Leonidas. I know this might sound a touch grand, but believe me when I say I've imagined being in his shoes more than once. I'd like to give it a go, instead of retreating."

"No, Major, not this time. I need your report. I'm not sure I know of the incident you describe. In any case, I can't afford to lose you and your men, as that Greek King you mentioned—what's his name— lost his, no matter if you can delay the advance. I admire your brave ambition, but not this time. Come back safe and informed."

At first light on the 6th, before sunrise, a scouting unit of Major Logan's party sent down from the top of Dunderberg to a rise close by the river could hear what sounded like the rowing of many boats on the east shore. With daybreak, the fog covering the river began to blow away. They were able to count at least 40 enemy boats on the east side, and then watch them cross the river opposite King's

Ferry and start landing men on the west shore, near Stony Point. The scouting unit soon rejoined the rest, reporting what they had seen. Before climbing the Dunderberg, the unit noted the enemy was preparing to follow someone familiar with the narrow trail up the mountain. Possibly a local. A guide. Exact numbers of enemy no one could determine.

As ordered, Major Logan's party returned to Fort Montgomery around 9 am on the 6th. They reeked of sweat, dirt, damp wool and forest, uniforms torn and soaked through. Reporting to the Governor with literary flourish, he warned that "the enemy was embarked on serious mischief."

An hour before the Major returned, the Governor had received a message from Old Put:

> By the inhabitants who live just by Fort Independence, I am informed that the enemy have landed betwixt Kings Ferry and Donderbarrack; if that is the case they mean to attack Fort Montgomery by Land (which when I am sure of) I shall immediately reinforce you.

The Governor, with Logan's report in hand, thought Old Put would "be sure" at least as soon as he was, and probably sooner. With belief in Old Put's common sense, and aware of the fear shared by all at the Forts, knowing how undermanned we were, the Governor announced that reinforcements from Peekskill would soon arrive, exhorting us to hang on."

Fast as lightning strikes, the word spread throughout the Forts.

"Good work, Major. I will dispatch Lieutenant Jackson with a small party to discover the enemy's movements. Now, get some rest, Major. Your work today is not over."

Major Logan rejoined his company with an empty feeling in his gut, and not just from lack of food. He was heart-sick over a glorious opportunity lost. Having just experienced the difficult pass on Dunderberg's height, he knew what he and his small company of 80 could have done to arrest the enemy's approach. With trees enough to protect them, his men could have poured fire at the British, bright targets of red against the greens and yellows of the forest. He'd hit them as they ascended, close to the summit, allowing his men to shoot down into what he knew would be an exhausted and breathless column of men unfamiliar with their surroundings. He would divide his men in squads of three, able to keep up continuous musket fire. They would create chaos.

With sadness he contemplated Lieutenant Jackson's role. Jackson would likely confront the enemy around Doodletown, where trails widen into roads, where fields replace thick forest, where numbers count. "We could have done it," he muttered to nobody in particular.

"Lieutenant Jackson, sir. Reporting for duty."

"Lieutenant, I suspect from Major Logan's report that we soon will be under attack. You grew up around here didn't you? Your reputation as one knowing the flora and fauna—even the botanical names—is notorious. Early this morning the enemy landed at Stony Point. Take thirty men and find them before they find you. Ambush if you can. Attack as your judgment dictates. Retreat when necessary. We need every one of you back. Much depends on that."

Lieutenant Jackson's party were raw recruits. The forest frightened most of them. It had poured rain the previous two days and nights. As they set out, clouds were giving way to sun, which grew in radiance, showering the rain-soaked over-story with sparkles. Delighting in the corner of the year, the dogwoods had for a week or so been exchanging the deep green of their summer raiment for red, crimson, bronze and burnt orange. Above their tops the giant black, chestnut and white oaks soared, their leaves still untouched by the changing seasons.

Lieutenant Jackson was enthralled by the scene beckoning to his party on the road to Haverstraw—in truth barely more than a trail. The forest was alive with the singular sounds of rushing water, which surrounded them on the march. Heard but not seen, water gurgled and splashed, growing louder as the party approached each cataract, racing stream, rivulet, rill, streamlet or brooklet as waters plummeted down from steep mountains over, under and around rocks of schist and granite worn smooth from centuries of these gravity-driven flows. Waters oozed down the flat faces of huge stones to pool beneath, causing the surface to sparkle in the sunlight. Giant boulders, or 'Erratics' in geologist-speak, completed the scene, having come to rest here and there along the trail. They had been rounded and smoothed over centuries as the glacier that dug deep to fashion the mighty Hudson River receded. A wonder of their own, they glistened in blotchy sunlight, wet with lichen, moss and an occasional hemlock seedling taking root in soil collected over time in deep rock fissures.

The Lieutenant hadn't fully absorbed the message of danger the Governor was trying to convey. Having never faced enemy fire, the grim reality of it was beyond his ken. Instead, triggered by the sounds of the water, he recalled an equally wet scene when he passed through this trail on a warm March day, and yet a scene very different in that the deciduous trees of the forest were still bare, enabling one to see as well as hear the waters that tumbled down. He knew his mind was easily distracted. Snapping back into the line of duty, he warned his men against talking or making any unnecessary noise as they moved along the trail. "Listen for the chirps of the crickets or katydids, whichever, I can never keep them straight. That should keep us from making a racket."

The soldier in front of Lieutenant Jackson whispered back: "I think you mean the male cicada, since it sounds off during the day, while those others mainly at night, Lieutenant."

This correction reminded Lieutenant Jackson that General Clinton placed too much confidence in his Indian-like skills in the forest, skills he knew, through no fault of his own, had been blown all out of proportion. He longed for a real Indian guide to lead them, to detect the enemy before it detected them. Just short of two miles from the Forts, they came to a glen covered with densely packed maiden-hair fern infused with yellow coming from a low canopy of blooming witch-hazel. More of this fern in one spot than Lieutenant Jackson had ever encountered. He was now at one with nature, concentrating on all he was experiencing, most immediately by the ferns' beauty, which like the rushing waters crowded out his sense of danger. So distracted was he, that the Lieutenant allowed his party to stumble into an ambush just shy of the tiny settlement of Doodletown.

The first round from British muskets was like thunder. So much smoke enveloped the leaves that the forest seemed on fire. Continentals fell to the ground, some never to rise again.

"Return fire, return fire, cover and retreat. Into the forest, before they reload," Lieutenant Jackson ordered, more hopeful than realistic.

Six of the party slipped into the forest, and were the first to find their way back to Fort Montgomery, where they met an anxious Governor Clinton and his brother James, awaiting the report. Hearing it was no cause to rejoice.

Jackson's estimate of enemy forces numbered more than one thousand. A Doodletown resident, who slipped away after seeing the enemy divide its forces, sending what seemed about half, certainly more than one thousand, around Bear Mountain, presumably to find and follow Popolopen Creek down past the Torne to attack Fort Montgomery from the rear, had reached Governor Clinton just ahead of Lieutenant Jackson. Exhausted from running and breathless with fear and excitement, he delivered his alarming news staccato, between gasps for air.

General James Clinton now ordered Colonel Jacobus Bruyn with 50 Continentals and Colonel James McLarey with 50 militia back along the Doodletown road to delay the enemy.

Tom was attached to Colonel John Lamb's artillery unit. The Governor's expectation of Old Put sending reinforcements failed to relieve the stress the men felt from knowing, in detail, how grossly unprepared they were for the coming attack.

John Lamb said, "What's to me so amazing, Tom, is the audacity of the British to imagine making the extremely difficult march through a narrow passage up and down Dunderberg to attack us. They have to pass through dense and unfamiliar forest. To reach Montgomery, they'll have to go around Bear Mountain for seven or eight extra miles to reach the Fort. We didn't think it possible, did we? And we assumed rational behavior. That they wouldn't attempt it."

Tom said, "We didn't imagine guides. Now, we are caught with our knickers down. We want for muskets, bayonets too, not to mention regulars fit to fight. Alas, Old Put's less than a slender reed to lean on."

The Generals Clinton were holding counsel.

"Brother," said James, "my diligence early this morning, in dispatching Captain Lee with his strong company of 50 across the river to Anthony's Nose, now seems a sad mistake."

"Brother, you were obeying Old Put's order. It allowed for no discretion. Blind to what the General knew, or as things look now, what he didn't know, you had no choice. Lee's there, we're here and that's the rub. Quick now, we have two Forts to defend. And by some magic, Clinton's forces seem to know the terrain."

Old Put's order had come to James Clinton after dark the previous night. Immediately James summoned Captain Thomas Lee from Colonel DuBois' Regiment, who commanded a company of 74, among whom only 50 were then fit and armed for fighting. Lee was a lean and wiry 30-year-old veteran of the war, of average height and unremarkable face except for his hair, which was deep red, thick as a Persian pile carpet and long, drawn back against his ears as if to hide them and tied there with a yellow ribbon. He enjoyed a natural command presence that earned him generous respect among the men. But it was his sardonic and often reckless sense of humor that could, at once, shock and endear him to the company.

Clinton read Old Put's order to Lee, withholding his opinion, lest Lee become discouraged with the assignment. "Alert your company, take two days' rations and embark by 6 AM. I've arranged for the scows. Be sure to carry a spyglass and a few mirrors to signal with. We'll try to keep sight of your progress."

To execute Old Put's order, Captain Lee mustered 50 of his company. He laid out the plan, then urged the men to get as much sleep as possible and, with cleaned muskets and ample ammunition, be at the scows by 5:30 AM. "Questions?"

"You said our task is to prevent the enemy from occupying Anthony's Nose. Why would they want to do that? Unless they're goats. You said we were to defend the pass through Anthony's Nose.

I grew up here. There is no pass over that mountain top. There's one a couple of miles to the east, but no one could confuse that pass with the Nose. The enemy is here to take the Forts and cut the chain. The Forts are west of the river; the Nose is east. And atop the Nose, crows and one or two lost frogs."

"Thanks, Private Slatterly, for the geography lesson. Look, I have no answers. Our orders come from General James Clinton. They directed us to guard the top of Anthony's Nose. That's what we will do. If you're right, and the Forts are attacked by land, we'll have a front row seat. I hope you're wrong. Would be a shame, after all this, to miss the fight."

Henry Pawling, First Lieutenant in Lee's company, said: "General Putnam must know what's up. Perhaps the enemy will be trying to sneak around the mountain at water's edge and cut the chain on the east side. Then its ships could attack the Forts from the water."

"If that's their plan," said Private Gideon Goodspeed, "we will have fight enough on the East, that's for sure."

"Enough speculation for one night. We all know from experience, don't we, 'the higher the rank, the smarter the man.'" Lee's face formed a mischievous smirk. "That question's not for answering. You're in good hands. Now, get some sleep."

When sleep evades summons, night passes slowly. And, when assaulted by the insistence of whip-poor-wills in love, it seems suspended in time. Captain Lee might not have slept anyway, given the combined weight of duty, danger and suspense pressing on his mind. But the song of the whip-poor-wills clinched it. Emerging from his tent, Lee shouted to the birds: "I conjure you cease and desist. In the name of liberty, fly to the enemy and serenade them." Without noticeable effect, his message was enveloped by the darkness.

Embarkation proved easy, once Captain Lee had issued orders on what platoons were assigned to what scows. Rowers, some still exhaling rum-laden breath, were ready. One by one the scows were loaded and pulled away from a still darkened shore in the direction of a dawn beginning to show signs of awakening. The trip was a mere 600 yards. Landing at the foot of Anthony's Nose, the men quickly found the trail to the steep incline and clambered up through scree, loose rock often hitting the heads of men below. Private John Slatterly was first up, having been ordered by Captain Lee to lead the company in the ascent. The Captain had overheard Slatterly boasting that he knew the mountain even better than he knew his private parts.

Lee assigned a detail of ten under command of 2nd Lieutenant English to remain at water's edge and keep watch for any enemy trying to approach from the south along the shore. Mirrors would serve to maintain contact.

Private Slatterly was heading toward the Nose when he called out to his buddies among the English detail, "Take care, friends, you'll have no neighbors but owls, hedgehogs and rattlesnakes that bite first, then rattle."

"That's quite enough crap from you, Private," Lieutenant English shouted. "The copperheads love the Nose and bite without a sound. Watch where you put your hand."

Near the summit, smooth-faced granite eased the footing. By 9 AM Lee's company had arrived at a point from which they could look down on both Forts, look up Popolopen Creek to the falls and beyond, look up at Bear Mountain and, just one finger's-width north, to the bald outcropping of the Torne. Turning south, they could see that heavy fog was starting to burn off to reveal Salisbury Island and the surrounding marsh in front of Doodletown, but beyond to the south on the river the fog continued thick and still, concealing all but the top of Dunderberg Mountain rising high above the pass leading to Hessian Lake, a rough redoubt at its edge and Fort Clinton beyond, all of which Captain Lee could well imagine without seeing. The fog still hugged the shoreline at King's Ferry, where they could barely discern some activity. Captain Lee heard gunfire and saw smoke coming from the forest at Doodletown. Signaling with mirrors to Lieutenant English below, he determined no sighting of enemy on the east. Without orders as to what, if any, circumstances, should bring his company back to the Forts, and aware of the possibility of an enemy attack from both sides of the river, Lee knew he must stay put.

"Men, today looks like another one of those 'hurry up and wait' days for which armies are famous. Anyone have an idea how to melt the fog?" Captain Lee wasn't an impatient man, but having gotten to the assigned spot, he couldn't avoid a sense of having already wasted much time with a lot more likely to be wasted before the sun would drop from sight behind Bear Mountain.

"Piss on it, Captain. That will melt it fast enough," Private Andrew Goodspeed said.

When the laughter died down, Captain Lee said "Goodspeed, you're an irreverent bastard. And sharp as a razor. How in this crazy world did you allow yourself to fall into Washington's Army?"

Goodspeed's grin swung to embarrassment.

"I can see, Private, my question causes discomfort. Were you released from gaol to serve?"

"No, Captain. Not jailed yet, despite some stupid barleycorn stuff."

"So, you volunteered. For the pay? Pushed by your parents? Following your friends? Nothing to be embarrassed over."

"None of those, Sir. I believe ordinary people—like my buddies here—can make sound judgments on the big questions of Government. We don't need monarchy to do what we can do ourselves. There is something absurd about having this great continent governed by a little island—by a King living on that far-away island. I believe in the wisdom of people, not kings."

The Captain and those around him listened to the Private's explanation in surprise, wondering how Goodspeed had developed these well-formed, rather sophisticated ideas.

"Goodspeed, can you read?"

Not one in a hundred of Washington's troops could read English. The Captain's question was shrewd. For Goodspeed, who kept his education a secret, the question was received as an accusation, outing him among his buddies.

"I can. And, as I think you now must know, I read *Common Sense*. My mother had gotten a copy and urged it upon me. I feared I'd be unable to digest such a high-flown thing, but Paine's ideas were simple and clear, powerful. I was moved by them. They drove me to enlist."

John Slatterly spoke up. "Nothing here to be embarrassed over. Wish I could read. Wish we all could. Those ideas make sense to me. Worth fighting for, eh mates?"

Loud cheers gave warm answer. Goodspeed ceased squirming.

Emboldened by this exchange, Private William Slutt said, "Captain, you haven't told us why you signed up."

"A fair question, Slutt. I'll fairly answer. I hail from Boston. My father was a merchant. He traded in the West Indies, for rum, sugar and molasses. When England imposed duties on these goods, my father turned to illicit importation, for the duties would have driven him to bankruptcy. Instead, they killed him. Custom-house officers boarded his ship; violence erupted. He was shot and died of his wound. My hatred of the British occupation, of the duties, the stamp tax and the duty on tea, all these measures of enslavement, atop the murder of my father, drove me into General Washington's arms. I went to Cambridge and volunteered."

"Did you meet our Commander?" said Private Thomas.

"Yes, briefly. I've never forgotten what he said to me.

'Do you realize we face the most formidable nation in the world, flourishing in arms and naval power that exceed any other. Our ambition is audacious beyond imagination, in defiance of human foresight and calculation.'

"I stood facing him, in awe. You see, I think he wanted to be sure of me, sure that I had my eyes wide open. And then, when I nodded assent, he said:

'Withal, we can win this war, because we fight for our land, our freedom, our independence, against those who would subdue us from afar. Remember this, believe in yourself and win we shall.'

"I left his presence feeling the Almighty had spoken."

*****

At Fort Montgomery, the Governor ordered Tom to command a party of 20 from Major Dubois' regiment and 70 militia. They marched out at 9:45 AM on the 6th along the so-called Furnace Road, a dirt carriage path leading west to the Forest of Dean mine.

They had one field piece, but limited ammunition for it and no inkling of the enemy's numbers.

"Tom, the goal is to slow the enemy's advance. Take axes to fell trees across the road, Do all you can, and then fall back to the redoubts when you can do no more and stay alive. To that end, Tom sought axes from the quartermaster. He had none.

The party marched uphill in heat for two miles along the high ridge above Popolopen Creek, which flowed parallel but far below to their left. On the right, looming above them was the Torne, a steep mountain weathered to a bald peak of granite. Given the thick forest on both its sides, they were pretty sure the enemy would have no choice but to descend towards the Fort on the Furnace Road.

"Men, we settle in here, just before that narrow defile, which should crowd the enemy, making our fire more deadly." Time slowed down as they waited, increasingly apprehensive, knowing nothing, listening intently, peering as deeply into the forest as they could, a few even expecting first to smell the rotten British scum.

"Captain, how do we know they're coming?"

"Private Days, the answer is we don't. War is like chess. All supposition, guessing the enemy's next move, until it happens. To attack our Fort, if not this route, where?"

Suddenly, without warning, a pair of bucks emerged from the north, trotting onto the road, where they paused to examine the Continentals. As one, the party flinched in surprise. Two came close to firing muskets.

"Steady, men. Steady."

The deer had exposed how sharply on edge the men were. Tom felt embarrassment enough for all.

The sounds of battle at Fort Clinton reached their ears, a growing throb of muskets and cannon. Tom began to imagine his placement on Furnace Road a fool's errand. Shouldn't we be back at the Forts, where we surely were needed? Just then, looking up from scraping the mud from his boots, he saw emerging from the forest on either side of the road, and overflowing into the road itself, a large body of Redcoats. The road was a blur of red, bulging with enemy troops moving silent and swift, bayonets fixed, holding their fire. There were rows of them, seemingly of endless depth. A foil to the dark green that dominated the forest, they pretended to blend with the bright orange of the occasional beech bending toward the road on either side. But, in truth, this moving mass of red was totally out of place as it sprang forward, seeking the unnatural embrace of battle.

The Governor had come out to inspect Tom's placements and had remained until this moment when, grasping the large number of advancing Redcoats, he returned to the Fort to prepare for what he knew would be an onslaught. Every man in the party saw immediately how badly outnumbered they were.

Tom's first reaction on seeing the enemy emerge from the forest was to look around to see who was in charge, who would give orders and tell him what to do. Seeing the Governor, striding towards him, he relaxed.

"Tom, I must leave this in your capable hands. I must return to the Fort. I'm sure you understand."

As swiftly as the Governor turned to depart the way he had just come, Tom's mind gave way to terror. Unthinking and raw. Then, the many imagined scenes of combat that all soldiers repeat in dreams and idle moments at rest imposed themselves like a sharp bugle call, awakening Tom to his duty, as precisely the one, the only one, in charge. On reflection, he knew he was not the first commanding officer to go through what must be a well-trodden thought process.

"Hold fire until the first row's 100 yards. Then commence fire, lads, officers first, if you please. Look for the shiny gorgets at their necks."

The artillery unit got off 8 or 9 rounds, opening holes in the advancing column. The holes swiftly filled without allowing a dent in the enemy advance. Tom's work with the artillery piece was so distracting, he didn't appreciate how close to them the red horde had gotten, how frightening to his men the thrusting triangular-haped bayonets affixed to their Brown Bess Muskets had become. In fact, it took one of his own, shouting 'Captain, they're surrounding us,' to awaken Tom to the danger.

He ordered the artillery piece spiked and a retreat to the Fort on the double. In less than zealous pursuit by an enemy exhausted

The road was
a blur of red,
bulging with
enemy troops
moving silent
and swift,
bayonets
fixed, holding
their fire.

from a long march through mountains, their leading elements nonetheless warmed us with musketry fire. Some of the men were captured, others killed or wounded in what turned into an unruly dash to the Fort.

Upon reaching its outer perimeter, the enemy paused for some time, presumably to recover from the march and strategize over how best to attack the Fort. But before long, the attack began.

In the beginning, the defenders, divided among the three redoubts facing west, in two ranks behind parapets, gave regular fire, each rank firing and then stepping back to reload while the other rank came forward to fire. They were exhorted by the officers assigned to each redoubt, Major Logan and Colonels Livingston and DuBois, and especially by the Governor, who ran from redoubt to redoubt, exposing himself to gunfire while inspiring the men to stay and fight. At first, they were able to repulse successive attacks by the enemy, that in wave upon wave marched in discipline against the Fort. But, with each assault, the numbers of defenders diminished, their fire more promiscuous.

By five in the afternoon, with evening shadows lengthening, a British soldier came forward with a white flag of truce. The Governor sent Lieutenant-Colonel Livingston and Captain Machin to meet the flag. The flag bearer, whose manner suggested he was the commanding officer, demanded surrender of the Fort within five minutes, so as to avoid further bloodshed. Colonel Livingston responded with vigor that the two Forts would be defended to the last extremity. With a brave flourish Tom envied—for it sat far beyond his reach—the Colonel added that, if the British would surrender forthwith, they had his promise of being well treated as prisoners of war. To the British officer, such an out-sized boast under the dire prospects for the defenders of the Fort might have seemed amusing. But he showed only angry impatience to get on with the task at hand.

Within ten minutes of their return to the Fort, the enemy launched a concentrated attack using bayonets alone. They stormed the redoubts with far superior forces. Although no order was given, as the defenders' lines were smashed, the men gave ground, turning their minds to an escape only made possible by encircling darkness.

Isaac Bell, one of the Fort's blacksmiths, hailed Tom with urgent cries, so instead of following the others in his unit, he went to Bell where he stood just outside the blacksmiths' shop.

"Captain Machin, Sir, here," beckoning him into the shop, where he found the blacksmith, Samuel Boyd, slumped over his anvil, a bullet hole in his forehead. "Boyd's dead, Isaac. Too late now for last rites. Let's get out of here."

Outside the shop, all was confusion. Foes blurred with friends. With Colonels Lamb and Livingston, Isaac Bell and Tom found the Governor and persuaded him to flee. He wanted to stay down to the last man, but they appealed to his importance beyond this battle, now so obviously lost. "Not the time for storybook bravery, Governor," said Colonel Lamb, shouting to be heard over the bedlam.

They followed the Governor's path east and down the steep embankment to the river. The last in line, Tom found himself blocked by an enemy soldier, who thrust his bayonet deep into Tom's chest. Tom was sure the end had come, shock clogging his brain way ahead of the pain to come later. Isaac Bell fired at the soldier, the bullet throwing him back and with him the musket, in effect neatly removing the bloody blade from Tom's body. Tom shouted out to the soldier "Why did you do that?" but he was now flat on the ground, too far gone to hear this imbecilic question. The blacksmith Bell, who had killed Tom's assailant, was himself killed by a musket ball to the head a moment later, falling against Tom, knocking him down and coming to rest on top of him, a dead weight. Unable to move the stolid Bell off, Tom's panic grew as, again, he thought he was going to die. He cried for help. A retreating Continental, passing him and the dead soldier atop his chest, paused a moment to examine the scene before disappearing down the slope. But not before meeting Tom's plea with a repost rooted in the reality of defeat:

"It's a damned good fellow who can help himself now."

And, then, Tom realized that Colonel Lamb had returned, and was dragging Bell off and lifting him to his feet, pulling his arm around his neck and proceeding to lead and as often drag Tom with him. Tom then went into shock, as he was uncertain, from that moment until far up-river, not too distant below Fort Constitution, what he actually remembered and what he knew only from being told by others.

To put it in a nutshell, the Colonels Lamb and Livingston found a boat, searched in the dark to find oars and took turns rowing to safety. They were well up-river when Tom emerged from the emotional and physical desert of shock. Just then flames from the Montgomery and two row galleys, captives sandwiched between the swift ebbing tide and the equally strong Machin Chain, became pyramids of fire, lighting the profile of Anthony's Nose on the east and the vanquished Forts on the west. This vision was quickly eclipsed by a giant explosion as flames reached the ship's magazine. Darkness was restored. On reflection, a week or so later, Tom had distance enough and insight to wonder how beautifully—how perversely— ironical was the final function served by his chain before being cut the next day by enemy artificers.

*****

"Captain Lee, the fog's lifted over King's Ferry." They turned to peer south. Lieutenant Pauley put the telescope to his eye. They now could discern many flat-bottomed boats empty and at rest with lines tied to shore. Counting the large number of boats, now visible through the telescope, the Lieutenant said "40. The enemy seems to have landed in force—possibly as many as 2000. Those reports suggest they've made it over the Dunderberg. Shouldn't we head back, Captain?"

"Just because we're in the dark doesn't mean everyone else is. General Clinton put us here for a reason. We're in his hands."

"Logical, Captain. Perfectly logical. But General Clinton was blind too. Acted on orders from Old Put. But you know that. This command chain is too long to expect orders to move along it swiftly or, for that matter, with accuracy."

"Enough, Lieutenant. Damn it. Don't let your anxieties show."

Captain Lee had sent scouting parties of two and three to the east and south against the possibility of enemy advances. They found the air stirring softly and the mountain quiet, the breeze gently moving the oaks' reddish brown leaves, the witch-hazel below, defiant against the season, yellow in full bloom with hardly a rustle.

Captain Lee summoned Private Slatterly. "Tell me Private, what's it like to the east?"

"The mountain ridge line runs east from here all the way to another mountain range running north, about three miles away. It drops down into a valley running north just east of that north range, and running south too, leading to Fort Independence and Peekskill. Below us to the north there is an east-west pass that leads to that valley. I can't imagine the enemy trying to surmount Anthony's Nose. To what purpose I ask you? To reach the river and the chain, they would either have to come around the Nose along the shore, where Lieutenant English awaits them, or reach the east-west pass just to our north, requiring them to first have passed through Fort Independence. Sound travels up. We'd hear reports either way."

As time passed, anxiety among the men rose. On this clear day, when they could see almost everything, the dense forest on the west side of the river, with leaf cover intact, blocked their vision of all that was important. But they couldn't avoid noticing a growing amount of movement at both Forts, foreboding an attack. Then, early in the afternoon, with the sun now low to the southwest, soon to be hidden behind Dunderberg, they saw a body of their own men, running north to take cover at a stone breastwork near Hessian Lake. It was immediately clear they were being pursued by a much larger body of Redcoats, advancing rank upon rank, muskets leveled, bayonets fixed.

"Look, Captain, the Redcoats lack artillery."

"Yes, Goodspeed, quite right, so far. But in bayonets they vastly outnumber us. But, see, Colonel Brown's men are making a stand."

"I think that's Colonel McClaghry and his men too. Amazing. How bold they stand against that oncoming red hoard. The Redcoats are holding their fire. Hundreds of them advancing, being mowed down by our men."

"If only there were more of us there. Even at four rounds a minute, too many Redcoats pouring out of the woods. God save 'em! What are they waiting for? To the Fort. Retreat!" Captain Lee was willing his comrades across the river to seek safety within the three redoubts of Fort Clinton. And, as if they heard him, they fell back, firing as they went, into what temporary safety the Fort offered.

Captain Lee and his company continued to agonize over a battle they vicariously fought while being forced at distance to watch it unfolding at Fort Clinton. Later that day, they were forced similarly to agonize over a battle at Fort Montgomery.

No word came redeploying them. They saw and heard the 15 or so cannon at Fort Clinton explode with fire, under the direction, Captain Lee assumed, of Captain Moody of Colonel Lamb's Regiment. Later, they heard cannon far beyond Fort Montgomery, the sound seeming to come from somewhere along the Furnace Road running west up the pass between the Creek and the Torne.

Captain Lee was anxious and despite his best efforts to conceal his deeply felt confusion, uncertainty, frustration and fear, the troops around him caught the fever. Private Slatterly, always short on tact, raised the alarm all were feeling by yelling out so all could hear, "Look, Captain, in the sky over the Forts. Vultures! Turkey vultures gathering. Not a good sign."

Lieutenant Pauley turned his telescope to the scene unfolding above the Forts. "Seven of them already, and more coming. Dear God, what can we do?"

The Lieutenant's question went unanswered. As darkness began slowly to cover daylight, cannon reports grew less frequent, and in front of Fort Montgomery, ceased altogether. Not one of the company supposed that silence at the Forts was a favorable omen. And what they most feared soon became manifest with loud shouts at both Forts as the enemy stormed the redoubts without firing a shot, bent on mopping up with bayonet alone. Darkness seemed to stay its progress to allow Captain Lee and his company to see, as well as hear, the mayhem that ensued at both Forts. Hand-to-hand combat, although barely discernable, was loud and clear.

Now, every man among his company shared the same vision of enemy bayonets glinting, pointing, thrusting forward to seek out and penetrate deep in chest or stomach of their companions, who, lacking bayonets and mad with fear, were throwing themselves here and there to escape the advancing steel.

Lee and his men were helpless to resist what their minds forced them to imagine was happening in the killing fields they had known as Forts Clinton and Montgomery.

Private Goodspeed said "Look, our men are breaking up, turning away, fleeing down the embankment to the river. Oh, God must save them; we are too far away to help!" Just then the shouting turned jubilant, the effulgent cry of hunters atop their prey, who were in the throes of dying, fleeing or throwing down their arms and raising their hands in surrender.

No one else spoke as the shock of the crushing defeat unfolding before their eyes sunk in. No one that is, except John Slatterly, who moved among the company to find James Thomas, William Slutt and Jeremiah Crullin. To each, he whispered "Now."

Earlier in the day, John and his companions had expressed their fears for the Forts and for Washington's Army, but mostly for themselves. John said "We are tiny gears in a machine that's running short of fuel. Defeat after defeat around the city. Now, defeat facing our Forts. What were we thinking to imagine we could defeat the British?"

"The most powerful Army and Navy in the world. We were crazy" said William Slutt.

Lowering his voice so the others had to lean in to hear him, James Thomas said, "If the Forts are taken, we should disappear. John, you know the way, and the Nose will gather us up before we are missed."

"You're right Jim. Fall of the Forts I'd take to be a sure sign the game is up. We'll be entitled to take our own lives in our hands again. Wouldn't the Governor want us to?"

"All right. I'll lead you if the Forts fall. For now, not a word."

And so it was that these four soldiers went "missing" on October 6 and were reported as such in the next muster report.

When sounds coming from the Forts grew faint, making it obvious that the enemy's victory was complete, Captain Lee led his men northeast off the summit of Anthony's Nose and through the pass leading to the road to Fort Independence and Peekskill, where they joined elements of Old Put's command and gave them the bird's eye view of the appalling defeat across the river.

Captain Lee took careful note of Old Put's reaction, reminding himself not to explode in anger over having been placed beyond the action by order of this General. Old Put's face showed surprise and a defensive expression of scorn at the news.

"And you kept your company there the whole day! What a shame to be watching instead of fighting."

It was clear to the Captain that this man would assume not one iota of blame for the humiliation. It took strenuous effort to avoid saying anything that carried the hint of challenge.

* * * * *

How many plays have we seen where the dagger or rapier plunged into a man's chest ends his life? And that swiftly? Think Macbeth or Hamlet. On stage none survive. In battle many do. Because there are places a blade can go that are not fatal. It's all a matter of luck. Luck was on Tom's side. He emerged from shock to experience serious pain. Earlier, before he knew what was happening, Colonel Lamb had pissed on a piece of his undershirt that he had torn off and then stuffed it in the oval-shaped hole in Tom's chest to staunch the bleeding and prevent certain infection.

The pain lasted through the night, accompanied by high fever and profuse sweating. Remarkably, by morning, Tom was feeling less pain, and the fever was subsiding as well. A local doctor appeared at Fort Constitution, examined the Captain and, impressed with the depth of the bayonet's penetration, which he could tell was very close to emerging from Tom's back, decided it would be best not to try to stitch up the wound but to keep fresh dressings covering it and allow it to heal from the inside out. Here again, Tom was lucky, for this Doctor's decision proved the right one, the only one to avoid infection.

Captain Gershom Mott, commanding Fort Constitution with small garrison when Tom was carried in, shockingly fired upon the bearer of a flag of truce who Commodore Hotham and Sir Henry Clinton had sent upstream, demanding surrender. Awkward business. The Captain then ordered the Fort abandoned. Confusion reigned. The British Navy threatened now, understandably mad as hornets at the Captain's breach of the most basic among the rules of war. Danger to the Fort was palpable to all.

Colonels Lamb and Livingston found a skiff and someone to row Tom upstream about ten miles to the Orange County home of Governor Clinton. There he rested for close to three months, until pretty much restored to his old self. At least that's how he began to feel. And eager to get back to work. Anyone trying to overcome a life-threatening wound could do worse than submit to the care of the Clintons.

Lisa rented a small house in New Windsor while Tom was recovering at the Clinton's home in Kingston, some 40 miles north on the river. New Windsor was a vibrant village, rapidly growing with Continentals and alive with revolutionary fervor, a place Lisa hoped might offer opportunities to serve the cause while, at the same time, helping to nurse Tom to recovery.

She failed as a nurse. The distance to Kingston made her visits too infrequent and brief to be useful in that way. Moreover, the Clinton staff delighted in furnishing all the care Tom needed, and often more. They got their feathers ruffled at any suggestion by Lisa that there was something left for her to do. Lisa's role was to report on the goings on in New Windsor and elsewhere, as well as providing cheerful encouragement.

In mid-December, during a visit, they were in their customary positions, he in a rumbled bed, she in a chair along-side. She had been reporting on movements of the Commanding General. And, then, shifting in the chair and lowering her voice, she said, "Tom, I know you're itching to be up and out. The Governor, no doubt, has plans for you. I beg you not to worry about including me in whatever you do next. I don't want to be some kind of anchor that restrains you."

"You've been free of me since early October. I know it's been liberating, free to beat around New Windsor as you wish. I imagine you'd like to continue, to be even more unencumbered."

"Tom, don't! Don't tell me how I feel, particularly about you. "

Tom bent forward, tossing blanket and sheet aside.

"But Lisa, you just finished telling me how *I* feel. What's going on?"

"Sauce for the goose, sauce for the gander." We're both right. Let's promise to stick to what we know, which if anything much, is our own feelings. And here's what I feel. We should put this relationship on hold for a while. Separate with no expectations, promises, deadlines and see how we feel after a spell of being free and out of each other's way. I'm going back to Convivial Hall. Father's been asking for me. The house I'm leasing in New Windsor is good for the next six months and has an option to renew for up to a year. Why not take it. As good a location as any for your work on the river."

Tom swung his legs off the bed and leaned toward Lisa, looking serious.

"I've sensed something changing in our lives, call it an unbraiding, but I couldn't until now find words to admit it, even to myself. You've always been a couple of steps ahead of me. With coaching, I can say I need a break, as you do. I'll take the house. Thanks for your candor. And for sharing the intuition."

* * * * *

After cutting the chain, Sir Henry Clinton sent his forces north as far as Kingston. Had he continued north, could he have saved the day for Burgoyne?

No one thought so except Clinton himself. By the 14th Burgoyne was defeated. He formally surrendered on the 16th. It was very doubtful Clinton could have gotten to Saratoga, some 25 miles north of Albany in time to do much. Almost certainly, given Gates' very large forces, and the militia that were joining in growing numbers daily, Clinton's forces would have been destroyed. Yet, Clinton, after the dust settled and he was again ensconced in New York City, claimed that Burgoyne, upon learning of Clinton's triumphs at Forts

Clinton and Montgomery and further up-stream to Kingston, should have attacked instead of capitulating, inspired by Clinton's success."

It was a flight of ego-charged fantasy.

But the odd truth is Burgoyne never learned of Clinton's triumphs before surrendering. Of course, Clinton was quick to send a message bugling his victory, but the messenger, one Lieutenant Daniel Taylor of the Ninth Regiment of Foot, was captured on the 9th by a patrol near Little Britain, just north of the Highlands. The message was enclosed in an oval silver ball about the size of a bullet and shut with a screw in the middle. As he was being brought before the Governor, Taylor took the ball out of his pocket and plunked it in his mouth, swallowing hard. Suspecting this maneuver, the Governor administered a strong emetic, intended to operate one way or the other. It brought the ball up and out. But, somehow, when not guarded, Taylor swallowed it again. This time, the Governor made up a story about having caught another spy, one Campbell, and learned all he needed to know. He then demanded of Taylor the ball, on pain of being hung up then and there, and cut open to find it. Taylor quickly responded by throwing up the ball a second time.

Henry Clinton's letter, a short one, written from Fort Montgomery, said:

> Nous y voici and nothing now between us but Gates. I sincerely hope this little success of ours may facilitate your operations.

Tom knew Clinton's missive by heart. One afternoon before their separation, when Lisa was visiting Tom at what she called the Clinton Infirmary, Tom quoted it to her.

"You know, Tom, I met Sir Henry once at the Hall. We hadn't been together for even a quarter of an hour when he let me know he had become 'Knight of the Bath' in honor of his record at Bunker Hill. I know his type. It leaps off the page of that letter. We know he thought his success far beyond 'little.' And, imagine, belittling Gates to the then beaten-down Burgoyne when he knows the size of Gates' Northern Army at that point. But, the capstone: he forthwith took his little force south to the safety of New York City, in retreat from Gates. What a fatuous, dimpled and jowly scoundrel."

"Good grief, Lisa. But what do you really think of him?"

13

BEVERLY ROBINSON'S HOME

When Lisa returned to Convivial Hall, she found her father fully recovered and, seemingly, infused with uncommon energy, its immediate expression upon seeing her being a fit of anger at not knowing where she was or when she would return home. His friend, Beverly Robinson, from across the River, had visited for a couple of nights and had most warmly extended an unusual invitation, directed either to Lisa or Cornelia. If acceptable, the decision of which daughter was up to the family.

The invitation was one Phillip was keen on having one of his daughters accept. Lisa's absence made choice impossible.

Lisa entered the Hall covered with a halo of fine, light snow through which she had ridden for almost the entire journey from New Windsor, a matter of half a day plus. Her father's initial feeling of anger melted almost as fast as the snow covering her hat and coat. Squeezing her between his long arms, and kissing her cold cheeks, Phillip gently edged her into the drawing room for debriefing. It was a routine she was familiar with, a process essential for one seeking to maintain neutrality, friendship and a steady flow of information from both sides of the war. He shouted for Cornelia to join them.

When Lisa's tale was told, it was Phillip's turn. "You know Colonel Beverly Robinson I'm sure. You don't? But surely you've heard of him. Why, Lisa, his home, 'Beverly' sits close to the Hudson, on the east side, within easy sight of the Forts. You must have passed it in your travels with the Captain. Beverly was here for a couple of nights last week. Very much in his cups and swollen with pride in having led the charge against Fort Montgomery just four months ago. It was he who led Sir Henry Clinton's troops over Dunderberg and past Doodletown to positions from which they could take the Forts by storm. He claimed they did so with bayonets, that, on his order, not a shot was fired. And that he was first to enter Fort Montgomery, that he spied Governor Clinton at a distance, that he slashed his way with sword to gain advantage over the Governor, who, alas, seemed to vanish in the battle's smoke before he could reach the spot where he had stood, commanding. It was a bold tale, boldly rehearsed. And often retold, I'm sure. Some of it might even be true."

"But Papa," Lisa said, looking at her father as she might a daughter of five. "Beverly Robinson is an American."

"Why of course he is. But to some, himself included, better than that. A *Loyal* American, as he proudly describes himself. He organized a Regiment of Loyal Americans, drawn mostly from those who labored on his wife's immense estate, known as the Phillipse Tract. He led this Regiment, along with British Regulars, in the attack on Fort Montgomery, after Major Campbell was killed."

"How odd that he fights for the Crown."

"'Tis odd. You're right. The fact is, when the Revolution began, Beverly publicly renounced dependence on Britain, giving up the use of imported merchandise. As he proudly told the world, he would henceforth clothe himself and family only in fabrics made here. He didn't see himself as a fighter, however, preferring to wait out the war as lord of his wife's manor."

"So, what changed him?"

"Well, that's the interesting question. In truth, I don't know. I'm sure by now you're aware that our state is first among the thirteen in Loyalists. Although I don't know Beverly's wife, Susannah, well, I hear she's a fervent Loyalist, even though it is a well-worn Highlands rumor that her siblings are Patriots. And, entre nous, I suspect it was she who turned him around. By reputation, a powerful woman who likes things her way. And that, if I may, brings me to the point. Beverly would like one of my daughters, Lisa, for example, to stay a fortnight or so with his wife, as a companion during his absence. Apparently, General Israel Putnam was living at Beverly until the loss of the Forts, when he decided on other arrangements. Susannah misses company. You'd be part-time only. No duties, really. Free to come and go as you wish."

Lisa was quick to say yes. "If I can't do better at entertaining Susannah than Old Put, there's something seriously wrong with me. Wonder what was going on between him and Susannah?"

"Not much, I reckon. Although among the Continentals, there were nasty rumors whispered about Old Put's friendship with the Robinsons. I believe he left their house after losing the Forts."

"How will Tom like your decision to live at the Robinsons, sister?"

"He's not for marriage, and neither am I. We were together, close together, for over a year, and until Tom came into my life, a week's affair was average, a month's beyond imagining. We both needed breathing room. I knew it and I felt sure he did too, although it was not his style to say so. The past year was one of surrender. Surrendering freedom for security; adventure for safety; change for constancy; selfish love for love that's more giving than getting. It was time to release the ties that bound me so tightly to Tom, and he to me. To take back what for a year I surrendered. As for whether I live here or at the Robinsons, it won't matter a bit to him."

"Lisa, I just needed to hear a 'yes.' The rest makes me a Polonius without the curtain. Not my intention. I hope this was not some defensive rant. Listening, I think I understand and approve. Who knows? Your love for Tom may wax in proportion to the distance you place yourself away from him."

"Tom's about to leave the Clinton infirmary. He's taking over my little house in the village. He'll enjoy New Windsor. It's filled with single men and women searching for pleasure, and taking what they can find for as long as it lasts, which in these uncertain times is brief. Of course, he's consumed with obstructing the river, so the village night life won't be his thing."

"So, Lisa, you accept Beverly's invitation."

"Wait a minute, Papa. I just thought of something. Surely the Robinsons know I've been living with a Patriot soldier and would believe that choice reflects the side I'm on in this war. How could they want me?"

Cornelia burst in on the conversation. "It's freezing in this huge 'museum.' Are you going to find some wood to feed that fire before it goes out, Papa, or will you force your wayward daughter to search the house. Your supply appears finished."

"Ha. Just the smell should be enough to warm you. Remember what your mother always told me, on those rare occasions when she used the arts of persuasion instead of command, 'he who builds the fire gets warm first.' But I'll handle this job," Phillip announced, feigning a martyr-like mien as he disappeared through a door to an enclosed outdoor porch and struggled back with a modest pile of logs.

"Now, Lisa, your question. These are confusing times. Loyalists and Patriots co-exist, especially in the disputed area along the Hudson. Even within one family, as, to take a relevant case, the Phillipses, where Sir Frederick, Lord of Phillipse Manor, spawned two Patriots, with his third, Susannah, being a Loyalist. Beyond that, there is my reputation, and that of our Hall. I'm sure the Robinsons consider you an apple that dropped close to our tree."

"A choice one, no doubt. I'm feeling jealous," said Cornelia.

"I didn't imagine you'd have much interest."

"You're right. Just kidding. I don't, at least after I push aside an unchosen sister's feelings. I don't relish babysitting a Loyalist wife, anxious over the prospect of becoming a widow, no matter how charming Susannah might be."

* * * * *

She moved in at the Beverly toward the end of January. Lisa's best friend there was not Susannah but her steadfast attendant and woman of the house, Hillary Knowles. From Hillary's warm greeting, when Lisa first appeared at the door, onward for a week, in ways big and small, Hillary seemed to go beyond the expected in service, finding ways to please this guest. It dawned on Lisa that Hillary wanted something from her.

"Hillary, might I have hot tea served in my room tonight. It brings sleep more swiftly."

Lisa had changed for bed when Hillary knocked on the door to deliver the tea. "Oh, my how I love that smell. Thank you, a thousand thank yous. Do you like tea?"

"Shall I pour? Never been a tea-drinker. From those Tea-Party days on, I felt it disloyal to take tea. Don't mean to criticize you, Madam, but for me that's how I've always felt after the Boston Harbor thing."

"So, you have Patriotic leanings," Lisa whispered. "So do I. Close the door, if you don't mind, and sit down."

"Leanings, yes, but better a passion for General Washington and his army. Are you faithful to the cause? I've been told so, but wanted to be sure, before...."

"Before what?" At that moment Lisa realized what it was that Hillary wanted. She wanted someone to trust with her secrets.

"Of course I'm faithful to the Revolution. You know that Tom Machin, my close friend, is a Captain in the Continentals. He installed the chain across the river at Fort Montgomery, the one cut by the enemy after capturing the Forts. You can trust me, Hillary. Come, sit on my bed and tell me your secrets."

Hillary obliged and, as she began to whisper, Lisa could see the nervous strain on her face melt away.

"There was danger when General Putnam stayed here. Mrs. Robinson attracted him. She was a comfort. Fed his thirst for the family's best claret. And tried to get him to talk about the war, about defenses, about all the weaknesses at the Forts that he was burdened with fixing."

"Surely he knew that her husband headed a Regiment of Loyal Americans?"

"Yes, I'm sure he knew about Mr. Robinson. But as to her, he didn't seem to care. He accepted her as his very fond hostess. Harmless in matters of war. Welcoming at home. Old Put, as everyone seems to call him, at least when he's not around, seemed eager, without thinking too much, just to absorb the warmth of her welcome and sink into the comforts she offered."

"I found ways to be within earshot when they were together. I began to understand their talk, and it scared me. I knew that Mrs. Robinson wrote to her husband daily. I had seen one letter, left open on her desk. It reported in detail on things the General had talked about the night before.

"I said 'Hillary, old girl, you are working not just for a hostess but for a spy! Someone bent on hurting our beloved General Washington. How do I know she's a spy,' I asked myself. 'Look, stupid girl, I said, look at how she plies Old Put with spirits, getting him to describe the fortifications at Independence, Clinton and Montgomery, and report all to her husband, the Loyalist.' The more spying I saw, the more desperate I became to do something, but I didn't know what. And then you came and I got an idea."

"Alas, Hillary, I came too late to help you save the Forts. And Putnam is gone. Still, I'd like to know if you think Mrs. Robinson's spying helped the enemy?"

"I do. The General had complained to Mrs. Robinson that General Washington had stripped the Forts of so many men that they were sorely in need of reinforcing. And he complained that the militias were not responding to his call. This was in September. Later that month, I heard the General tell Mrs. Robinson that a British fleet was headed north on the river. To my surprise, he then asked her if she knew which side of the river they would attack if they came as far up as Peekskill. She replied 'I don't have any idea, General, but if you want me to find out, I'll try.'"

"Oh, my God. What next?"

"Well, a few days later, I overheard her tell the General she was surprised he would ask, given his knowledge of terrain on the west side of the river. 'Don't you think those mountains make attack impossible?' she asked, more as assertion than question. 'If they come,' she said, 'they will assault Fort Independence, and then cut the chain from the eastern shore at Anthony's Nose, which lacks fortifications.' Then she added: 'But surely you must know the terrain better than I, General.'"

"Old Put was duped. Your story helps explain his refusal, throughout the attack on Forts Clinton and Montgomery, to send troops across the river. It's happenstance leading to tragedy. He preferred the fairy dust story of Mrs. Robinson to what his eyes and ears were telling him on October 6.

"Putnam wasn't disloyal. Just dim-witted. He believed that if a family was distinctly American, like the Robinsons, it followed that the family must be sympathetic to the Patriots' cause. He couldn't imagine that one could believe oneself an American and still think that remaining in the British Empire was the country's best option. Hillary, now that we know Mrs. Robinson's a spy, I hope you will continue your eavesdropping. It could be important. You're a great American Patriot, Hillary. I look forward to your reports."

"Thank you for that, Lisa. But, unless Mrs. Robinson can find someone else to spy on or Old Put returns, I'll not have much to report."

"Have no doubt on that score. Once hooked, it's hard to shake the habit. He'll be back."

Lisa's new-found knowledge of Susannah's activities enlivened her interest in developing the role of companion to this war-widow. She sought over many afternoon teas to draw Susannah out on the subject of obstructing the river. Determining the extent of her knowledge would, alone, be useful. And it might lead to uncovering her sources.

One blustery March day, they were huddled around a pot of tea, with Lisa recalling the fall of the Forts and the cutting of the Machin chain.

"A sad day for the Patriot cause," Lisa said.

"Of course, Lisa, I'm aware of your intimacy with Captain Machin, the genius who designed and installed the chain. A big Loyalist loss turned to Patriot gain."

Lisa studied Susannah for some clue to her meaning.

"I'm afraid I'm not following you."

"With most deserters, it's not much of a loss to the British Army; in Machin's case, a serious blow."

Lisa rose to her feet, upsetting her half-filled cup of tea, which emptied on the service.

"Tom was no deserter. He came here as an engineer. In 1772 I recall. Became a Patriot. Disguised himself as an Indian to toss tea into Boston Harbor. Fought the British at Breed's Hill. What you say can't be true."

Susannah's broad smile suggested nothing less than a cat pleased with the trap she had set for a now caged canary.

"Forgive me if I bear troubling news about your Captain. All I know is from General Putnam's first-hand account of the deserter's arrival at General Washington's headquarters in Cambridge. Apparently, his escape was the talk of the base for some time. According to General Putnam, he had been encouraged to desert by Henry Knox, who got to know him as Private Machin of the British Army, when Knox ran a bookstore in Boston. The General would have no reason to dissemble."

Lisa sat, trying to absorb the story. Slowly she processed it, coming to the conclusion that Tom had lied to her.

"Did the General ever mention the idea that Captain Machin came here before the war began, and was in the Boston Tea Party?"

"In fact, he did. He said the Captain had put that story out around the Forts, that he saw no purpose in undermining the Captain, given his importance to the cause. And, shame on me, he asked that I keep the conversation secret and here I've gone ahead and told you."

"Tom's a proud man, justifiably so, and I suppose, if what you claim is true, he didn't find it compatible with his self-image to recall the desertion, even to me. Who's to know where truth is buried. Especially in matters like this. I've had enough tea for this afternoon."

14

NEW WINDSOR

It was January. On his own in New Windsor, Tom ate more nights than not in Will Bedon's Alley, a local tavern. His wound was healed. Washington was urging the installation of another chain and fingering Tom to be in charge of this urgent undertaking. Governor Clinton was ratchetting up the pressure on him to commence, develop a plan and execute. But, as Tom kept saying to anyone who'd listen, we need to pick the location, a decision better made by an informed and expert group, where the risk of mistakes is lessened and the consequences of mistakes shared.

Tom didn't lack for companions, for word of his exploits at the Forts got around, making him a young man of interest to both the men and women of the village. Once having downed a brew or two, they came to his table unabashed. In this way Tom came swiftly to know many villagers, and they to know him, as he was always open to telling his stories and equally so to listening to those who joined his table. There were young women in abundance. In fact, abnormally so, he guessed. And he was right, for the village had evolved into a Continental military post and watering hole as well as a place to pause and rest for New York's state officials and others trekking north to Albany or south to New York City. Growing numbers of men in New Windsor were exerting a magnetic pull on the opposite sex.

One evening, with his table full with soldiers and young women, Tom drew on his schooling in science to advance a rule for New Windsor, or any other village or town along the Hudson: as the quantity of men expands, the quantity of women expands in equal measure.

"Look, it's a corollary to Sir Isaac Newton's Third Law, that for each action there is an equal and opposite reaction. In this case, equal but only opposite in the sense of gender. Or, if you prefer, call men nectar and women the worker bees. More nectar; more bees."

Caroline, a particularly verbal, and often acerbic, young woman of around 25, challenged Tom. "Of the Bard's Seven Ages, how many do you think could collect enough nectar to be worth a bee's trip from the hive?" Caroline had looks more interesting than beautiful. Her hair was of dish-water brown, with a sheen, her skin pale and unblemished, her eyes penetrating and blue but too deep-set to be sure, her nose aquiline, her mouth wide, her chin etched with determination and her teeth in place and sharp. Her speech was augmented through earnest and exaggerated facial expressions and use of her hands, which joined the thrust of her voice, holding nothing back in adding meaning and conviction to her words. To Tom, a commanding presence.

"Oh, Caroline, I'm not up on the Bard, the one we less literary types know as William Shakespeare. I don't even know what play that speech on the Seven Ages is from. But I get your point. Women seem to prefer young to old, even at the expense of cleverness, which grows with age. But I'm no expert. I wish they would make their preferences known." Caroline and her friend Marilyn drifted away. Tom feared he had bored them. They reminded him of bees who, having collected all the nectar on offer by one flower, move on to the next.

Two nights later, Tom returned to Will Bedon's Alley for supper. Nick, the bartender, called out to Tom as he opened the large, heavy oak door, "How now, Tom, I think you and Colonel Lamb have been fingered in rhyme by an admirer. Others among our male patrons didn't fare half so well on the point of Filippante's pen. There, see for yourself."

Tom moved to the posting board on the far side of the large dining room to which Nick had gestured. There he saw a poem without title signed "Filippante," a name he knew not. Reading quickly to get the gist, he saw it was a clever enumeration of qualities seen by the poet in a number of men who frequent the tavern. Most men would find the poetic lines addressed to them offensive, despite being expressed with creative flourish. But a few, including those for Tom and Colonel John Lamb, chose praise for their theme.

Here's what the poet wrote:

For Tom this:

"Last, Tom Machin's merit be my pleasing Theme.

My thoughts by Day, at night my constant Dream.

He's generous, gay and without satire smart,

Engaging, chatty, free from Vice or Art.

Genteel in manners of a noble soul

And born o'er female Bosoms to control."

And for John, this:

"John was the first whose mighty powers to please

Tell all our sex who know his grace and ease.

He'd mount a table by his Charmer's side

And Lord how prettily the Boy would ride."

Tom was intrigued. He had no idea who wielded a pen in the name of "Flippante." No idea beyond his conviction it was a woman. The sun was setting, and with equal regularity, the tavern was filling up. Finding the only empty table left, Tom sat down, still pondering the poem. The barmaid arrived just as Marilyn appeared in front of Tom to invite herself to take a seat.

"Two dark ales if you please," Tom said, confident Marilyn would not object.

"I'm delighted to see you, Marilyn. Perhaps you can explain that new poem on the posting board. It appears but a raw attempt to embarrass Colonel Lamb and me."

Marilyn was round of face, short, well-shaped and cute, with blond hair cut to fall well above the shoulders and be curled back under. She laughed a lot, although now, on hearing Tom's question, she just smiled.

"Oh, yes, I saw the poem. It's Filippante's work."

"That's not telling me a thing I couldn't read on the board. Who is this 'Filippante' and what's her angle, singling us out like that? I'm sure this muse is a female. They always are."

Tom was botching an attempt at anger. His pleasure in being fingered shone through the make-believe clouds that furrowed his brow.

"What are you smirking for? Yes, a female, your muse. Of that much I'm sure."

Colonel John Lamb appeared at the table, still bundled from the severe cold of a winter day in wraps of a long gray scarf and fleece hat with ear flaps.

"Why, greetings, Colonel. We were just talking about the poet who found you graceful, whether mounted or not. I noticed you reading the posting just now, as confused by it as we."

"Join us, John. I'm trying to get to the bottom of this business. Do you know Filippante? But first, warm yourself at the fire while I whistle up a brew for you. You bring signs of how frigid it's gotten."

"Temperature's plummeting. Snow on the way. Don't wander. I'll be back after adding a log or two to those embers."

"If you like, Tom, I can lead you to the poet, whose real name begins with C."

"I should have guessed. Caroline's just the type to obsessively analyze every man she meets. But I didn't think her superficial or frivolous. I've some things to talk over with the Colonel, but I'll come looking for you when we finish." Caroline appeared and, having moved within hearing range behind Tom, dropped into an empty chair and burst into the conversation.

"For goodness sakes, at your age, still splitting infinitives. Didn't the Brits teach you how offensive that can be to trained ears?"

"Too much training, my dear Caroline, puts you out of competition. But now, out with it. Why are you hiding behind that surly nom de plume? What you said about the Colonel and me is too perceptive to be intended just to amuse."

With hands warm, John returned.

"I heard you two wanted some privacy for 'soldier talk.' Come along, Marilyn, leave them to their tittle-tattle."

John sat as the girls rose. His ale had been served and he was now thawed out enough to enjoy it.

"What news, Tom? All I can tell you is our Commander-in-Chief is fed up to here with Old Put. Hamilton blasted him late last year, after reconnoitering in this very town for several days. Wished him recalled and replaced by the Governor. I think the axe is soon to fall. And, as you know better than I, pressure from the Commanding General is building for a new chain."

"Yes, pressure indeed. The Governor gave me a week to prepare a new map of the 23-mile stretch of river between Stony Point and Newburgh, with a view to making a definitive decision where to locate the chain. Just finished the map on the 4th. It should cast light on the potential sites, which we can count on one hand."

"Let me guess: Anthony's Nose again; Salisbury Island; and West Point."

"That's it. Nothing much has changed, except the chain at Anthony's Nose was cut, not because it failed but because Old Put failed—failed to adequately defend it—or as Caroline would have it, adequately to defend it. The choice remains difficult. Hard for just us Americans, but, thanks to Ben Franklin and Silas Deane, we now have to listen to a French engineering officer whom they recruited. At first blush, home-spun French arrogance worn on a laced sleeve for all to see. He's likely to cause trouble."

"Who that?" John was groaning.

"Colonel Louis Deshaix de la Radiere. His arrival threw Old Put into a tizzy. All accent, no judgment. With the speed of a bullet, with minimum analysis, he had decided the chain must again be installed at Fort Montgomery. His reasons were scandalously superficial. He showed but passing interest in my opinion, which didn't change when he was informed the role I had in design and installation of the first chain. 'But it failed' he kept repeating. Old Put asked the New York Convention to name someone to help in picking the site. They responded by naming five Fortifications Commissioners from

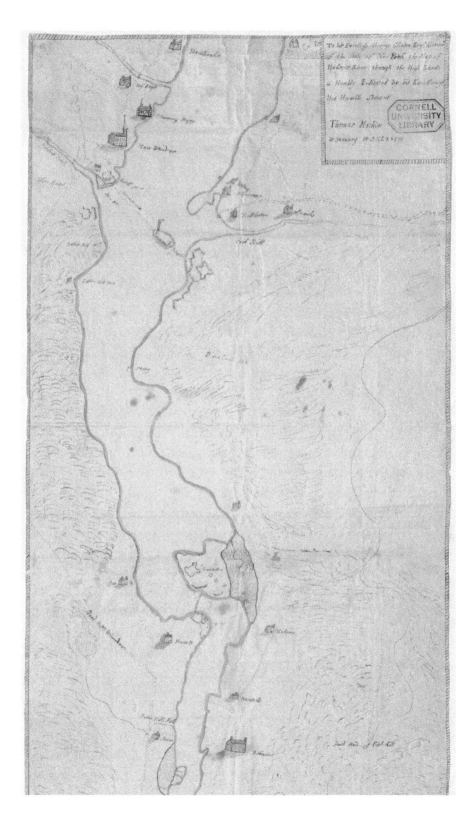

CORNELL
UNIVERSITY
LIBRARY

182

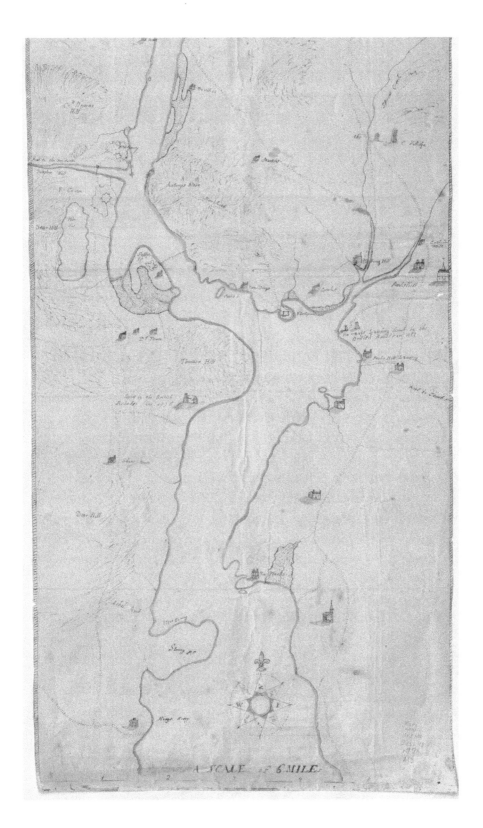

A SCALE of 6 MILE.

183

Poughkeepsie. We meet tomorrow to address the question. How would you respond, John?

"What's with our leader and his attraction to Europeans? How long did it take to get rid of that faux engineer from Netherlands?"

"Mistakes like weeds take root when given a chance and become hard to pull out. Always harder to fire than hire."

"Like to order supper? Hey, Nick, we'd like something to eat, if you please."

A waitress appeared, offering menus.

"What's in the lamb stew, aside from lamb?"

The waitress knew her stuff. "Onions, turnips, carrots and potatoes. Cloves and rosemary for spice, and plenty of garlic. You'll love it."

"About the chain. The Salisbury site has no obvious advantage over the Nose. Both are hard to defend from land attack. And both, unlike West Point, have long straight approaches to the chain, making it much harder to stop a well-armed ship favored by strong wind and tide. On the other hand, we know the chain works at the Nose because you installed it there and it endured until cut.

"You know, I've been giving some more thought to Henry Clinton's success against the Forts. We had assumed they could not be easily defeated by a land attack, given the dense forest and lack of roads or trails easy to find and navigate. Which seemed true from any spot they might land on the west shore. All those who knew those forests well said a foreign army wouldn't stand a snowball's chance in Hell finding its way and mounting an effective assault. Of course, this point is especially strong in the case of the part of Clinton's forces moving the five or so miles around Bear Mountain from Doodletown to attack Montgomery.

"A good point you make, John. The iron in the ground between Dunderberg and Fort Washington throws compasses off. And the forest is dense and confusing. I've never admitted this before, but I actually got lost once between Fort Clinton and Doodletown until I heard voices and moved to follow them.

"The fact is, Tom, I believe we were right in these assumptions. But, what we failed to foresee, and the wily fox Clinton figured out, was the role a Beverly Robinson could play. His intimate knowledge of the forest enabled the attack. Without him, if I invest Henry Clinton with a shred of common sense, there would not have been an unsuccessful attack, there would have been no attack at all. His luck or whatever it was in finding Robinson was our misfortune.

"Returning to your question, on balance, and with precious little thought, I'd probably opt for West Point, given the sharp bend in the river that almost brings ships to a stop right in front of the massive firepower we could mount high above. As surely you know by now, I pass my opinions through the mouth of a cannon."

The snow was now falling, thick and white. They ordered another round to embellish the stew, which had just arrived at table, steaming. Tom turned to the matter of Caroline. "What shall we do with this poet? She encroaches on my mind too much since I took in that poem."

"I'm keeping arm's length and more. Do you suppose she'd take to that French engineer known to be in the neighborhood? How about you, my friend? Lisa removed the leash, you told me. And you seem capable of giving as much as you get from Caroline."

"Worth shaving over once or twice. Right now, I've got to turn my mind to tomorrow's meeting. Lovely evening, John. Out into the wintry blast."

✶✶✶✶✶

When Tom reached Poughkeepsie and entered Town Hall, the meeting was just getting started. The five Commissioners were seated around a large table, fashioned of a rare type of sugar maple bearing prominent curls embedded in its surface.

John Sloss Hobart, Jr., a Justice of the New York Supreme Court, was acting as chair. In addition, there was Robert R. Livingston, Chancellor of the State, Zephaniah Platt, Chairman of the Poughkeepsie Committee of Safety, Henry Wisner, gunpowder manufacturer, and militia Colonel John Hathorn. Present, too, was Colonel Radiere, already red of face. Tom had no idea what had agitated him so quickly but could see bottled-up emotions likely soon to be uncapped.

"Welcome Tom. I believe you know everyone. And we know you, at least most of us do, as the genius who engineered, assembled and installed the only chain this river has ever known."

"Yes, Mr. Chairman, and it was one that held firm against the current," said Robert Livingston. "Such a pity it was never tested."

Colonel de la Radiere jumped to his feet.

"Your Honor, Mr. Justice Hobart, Sir, I wish the floor, if you will, so that this meeting can be 'tres court'—that is, a very brief affair. There is little here to debate. The Montgomery-Anthony's Nose site is by far superior to West Point. Pourquoi? Because, Gentlemen, we have an insurmountable object on the east side and two forts on the west which, through recent experience, we know all about. The strengths, which we can increase, and the weaknesses, which we can eliminate."

As he continued, the Commissioners couldn't avoid noting that his argument lacked serious analysis. Yet, when finished, he stood for a time, beaming self-approval and appearing to Tom and the others around the table as if he were expecting applause.

Robert Livingston endorsed the Colonel's opinion, reminding all of how woefully undermanned the Forts were to begin with and how big a failure of intelligence and vigor followed to deny the defenders any support. "In short, my friends, the Forts fell and the chain was cut not due to siting but to gross failure of leadership in Peekskill."

The Judge said "That's a matter, as you know, our Commanding General is having addressed by Court of Enquiry."

He turned to Tom.

"You know the site better than any of us. You were involved in its selection over West Point the first time. You fought in the battle. And, of course, you will bear ultimate responsibility for installing the new chain. Give us your thoughts."

Tom poured himself a glass of water from the big pitcher sitting in front of him.

"I've thought a lot about this. The arguments made by Robert and the Colonel are weighty ones. Most definitely, whatever site is picked, its success will depend on stationing an adequate force—say at least 2000 combat-ready men—to defend the chain from attack by land and handle the big guns necessary to punish approaching enemy ships.

"In terms of the chain, itself, I'm relatively indifferent, although one advantage to West Point is the fact that some 300 less feet of chain would be necessary.

"The big unknown in this project is one easy to forget. Will the chain hold to block Enemy ships? We just don't know. What we do know, however, is that a ship of the line may weigh some 850 tons and, if propelled by tide and wind, will present an awesome power slamming into the chain. So, for me, a siting decision must consider which offers the best topography to reduce the shock of impact.

"In this the Fort Montgomery site suffers in comparison with West Point, and for me, it is the decisive factor. A ship coming toward Montgomery with favorable tide and powerful wind has an almost straight line to travel from Peekskill Bay, some three or more miles. In contrast, at West Point the river bends 90 degrees west directly below the Point, and then bends another 90 degrees to follow the river north. This spot offers the strongest ebb tides and swiftest currents south of Albany. The air currents swirling over the waters are treacherous. The prospect of a ship becoming becalmed below the heights of the Point, and needing kedging to continue, is high, and the dangers from cannon fire from water batteries installed on the heights are even higher, even if the ship only loses some headway.

"Another difference is the lack of earth at Forts Montgomery and Clinton, necessitating the use of timber for construction of redoubts. Access to timber there is very difficult. In contrast, there is an ample supply of earth at West Point, and to the extent timber is needed, it can be hauled over roads offering relatively easy access to the Point.

"So, Gentlemen, these considerations tip the balance in favor of West Point."

"Well put, Tom. Cogent reasoning," said Judge Hobart.

Robust discussion ensued. It became clear to Tom that four Commissioners agreed with him. Commissioner Livingston must have had unexpressed reasons for favoring Fort Montgomery, since his expressed point of needing adequate forces applied equally to both sites. Colonel de la Radiere grew increasingly agitated as he caught the wind's direction. Finally, the vote was taken, with four in favor of West Point and only one favoring Montgomery. The Judge invited Tom to work with him on a report. And the Colonel exploded in rage.

"I come to this tiny village at the invitation of Commander-in-Chief George Washington to pick the site for the chain. The weather is abysmal, the food scandalous, yet I came. Mon Dieu! Do you imagine he lacked most excellent reasons for this appointment? Do you imagine he didn't know of my singular accomplishments in engineering? In fortifications? In design? I have done exactly what your Commander-in-Chief asked of me. I picked the site. And yet I am insulted and ignored. General Washington will learn of this, tout de suite, of that I can assure you. Au revoir."

Rising with all the hauteur of which the haut monde of Paris was capable, the Colonel stiffly vanished through the door, exciting both humor and alarm in the faces around the table.

Tom was asked to draw up specifications and, with Hugh Hughes, the 2nd Deputy Continental Army Quartermaster General, pick the foundry to execute the order. It was mid-January, meaning the river would be clear of ice and open to enemy ships inside of 12 weeks. They knew much rested on their choice.

Tom would not even consider for this job that difficult and less than patriotic foundry-man, Robert Livingston. Peter Townsend's Sterling Iron Works at Sterling Lake in the Ramapo Mountains was, for Tom, the best choice, and Hugh Hughes agreed. Tom wanted a chain twice as strong as the one untested at Fort Montgomery. His design would require 750 links of about 32 inches in length and 10 inches in width, fashioned from iron bars at least 2 inches thick, somewhat more than the thickness of the one at Fort Montgomery. He would need up to 8 swivels and about 80 clevises. With a view to assessing this foundry's interest and ability to complete such a demanding order by or before the time the river opened to traffic, Tom proposed an immediate visit to Peter Townsend at his home in Chester.

Dining at Will Bedon's Alley the night before riding to Chester, Tom hadn't sat at table for more than five minutes when Caroline allowed herself to join him.

"Tom, you look alone and distracted. I've arrived just in time to awaken you!"

"To what will you awaken me, Caroline, or do you prefer Filippante? Tell me in which sense do I slumber? And by all means feel free to join me."

"It is some 'nonsense' of thought that distracts you. I mean to awaken all five of your faculties to the joys of my company."

"Humm. Five? I can only think of four. Sound, sight, smell and taste."

Caroline reached across the table, taking Tom's hand in hers. "Ah, you forget 'touch,' perhaps the most important."

"Yes, if one is blind and deaf. Will I have your company for supper, or, bee-like, must you pollenate some other tables before returning to your hive."

"I'll sup here. Order for me. I'll return soon enough."

Tom placed two orders for turnip soup, beef stew and ale. While debating whether to trust her with the work then consuming him, she returned, saying excitedly as she sat, "I hear you're traveling to Chester tomorrow. I'm planning a trip myself in the same direction, through the Central Valley to Sloatsburg, and…"

"I get it. You're offering me your company. But how did you know my plans, which I just settled on yesterday?"

"Military secret. Word gets around fast in New Windsor. How about it? Perhaps, if I play a lady's hand and ask for protection from Claudius Smith and his notorious gang of Ramapo Cowboys, you'll find it harder to resist."

"No need to do what becomes you not. But you'll need a good horse to keep up. I will swing by your 'hive' at 7 AM if you'll tell me how to find it."

The waitress arrived with a full tray. "Captain Machin, sir, I've been watching and I do believe you're holding your own with Miss Caroline. Not many as can, and that's a fact."

"Lily, can't a patron get some privacy in this fishbowl? Mind your manners now and leave us in peace. The Captain has weighty matters atop his mind."

"After we eat, if you'll walk with me, I'll lead you to my hive."

The night was dark when they left the tavern. The temperature had plummeted to well below zero, turning every footstep in the two-day-old snow into a loud squeak, every breath into a cloud of moisture. Caroline's small house was but a ten-minute walk, closer by almost a mile than Tom's abode was to the tavern. She invited him in. They removed their coats. She moved close to him, wrapped her arms around his waist and bit off a button on his shirt. Putting her tongue on his chest, she announced "I intend that you experience that fifth sense in ways perhaps new to you."

Tom succumbed. It was not the first time a woman had successfully asserted control over his body by first controlling his mind. What was it, he wondered as he handed the reins over, that marked him as an easy target for women like Lisa and Caroline? Was he unusual within his gender or were they within theirs?

The trip to Chester was favored throughout with bright blue skies, windless cold and abundant sunshine. Caroline took to referring to him as her favorite drone and he reciprocated by naming her his not entirely gentle Queen. At Chester, they found Peter Townsend in obliging mood. He suggested Caroline stay for lunch before continuing her journey to Sloatsburg, where, she explained, her parents lived. "We can defer our business until you have resumed your trip, Caroline."

After lunch, upon hearing the project, Peter grew animated. He described himself as both a business man and a patriot.

"But first, a patriot. I've taken the Oath. What's more, I understand Washington's desire for his watch chain to be installed as soon as possible. Let's see what we can do."

Calculations followed. Tom recognized an ironmaster who knew his trade.

"Here's the big challenge I put to you, Peter, as master of all things iron. The chain must be strong enough to withstand not just the tidal flows, but the shock when a ship of the line crashes into it. At the same time, it can't be so heavy as to make handling or floatation impossible. By my reckoning, links should not be made from bars more than two inches square."

"I've considered the point. We can go to two and a quarter. Trust me."

"That's why I'm here, Peter. Let's go with it. I see you want this project, despite the challenges."

"No, Tom, because of them. Because I know we can do it. But my Artificers will need exemption from military duty. Here's why. To do the job by the first of April, I will need to work around the clock, with at least seven fires for forging and ten for welding, running continuously. I will need at least 60 artificers. They must be dedicated and capable. I can find them. But only if they are exempted from military duty not just to April but beyond for several months of rest to recover."

"I will get them. But, perhaps I interrupted you. There's something furrowing your brow. Is there more?"

"For two years we have been supplying the Continental service with iron for anchors, iron for various and sundry, and steel, all without payment. We cannot proceed without discharge of the arrearages."

For Tom, Sterling was the only viable choice. The fact was that the Long Mine used by Sterling contained black magnetite ore of 60% or more purity. It was the best in the country, equal and perhaps superior to Swedish iron. Tom knew this. He knew as well his friend General Henry Knox's insistence on Sterling ore for casting artillery pieces. And beyond this, there was Peter Townsend's commitment to the war. Tom believed if anyone could get this job done by the time the river opens to traffic, it was Peter. The arrearages must be paid or there would be no chain.

"We will cover the arrearages. Give me a week or two. I will return with Hugh Hughes to finalize terms and sign a contract. In the meantime, take what steps you can to prepare for a swift start."

Returning to New Windsor, Tom alternated in ruminating over why he seemed to attract aggressive women and why the Board of War or the New York Legislature couldn't pay its bills, at least to one, like Townsend, who was an honest and highly talented patriot and, beyond measure essential to the American war effort. No answers were forthcoming. But, when he stopped at Earl's Tavern several miles north of Monroe for food and drink, and was in the middle of consuming his order, he was amazed to see Caroline open the tavern door and peer around until her eyes met his. Tom surmised she must have seen his horse and decided to join him in returning to New Windsor.

"My goodness, Caroline, you surprise me. Do sit down. Thought you intended a longer visit with your folks down in Sloatsburg. No problems I hope."

"None at all. Just a little check in, to assure they were ok. Old age makes health unpredictable. But they're fine. And here I am, under my drone's care again."

"You know this is the heart of Cowboy country. We're near Smith's Clove, named for that villain Claudius Smith's father. There's a $1,200 Reward on that Cowboy's head."

"What's he done?"

Just then the bartender came over. "What's Claudius Smith done? Just murder, including Nathaniel Strong, a Continental Major. And robbery, burglary and repeated thefts of horse and ox, which he delivers to the British. And withal he's a spy. All his vile deeds are done, he claims, in service to the King. This tavern's in no man's land and survives through neutrality, but that doesn't mean its bartender can't keep his ear to the ground, or be a patriot."

"I hear Smith scorns meanness. That he's hospitable. Have you ever met him?"

Tom listened in amazement to Caroline's questions. He knew Smith to be a brute, smoldering with hatred for patriots and eager to wreck vengeance on them.

"Indeed I have lovey. He and his lawless Cowboy gang have been here. Seeing him seated, swallowing some ale and joking around with his gang, he seems normal, perhaps even hospitable as you say. At least he was to me. Thanked me for serving, handed me a generous tip. Someone like you, who don't know what he's done, could be fooled. But, believe me when I tell you his deeds are vile."

"But you kept the tip," Caroline said, a smirk covering her face. Flinching, the bartender retreated. Caroline moved around the table to snuggle close to Tom, asking for a full report on the Townsend meeting.

"You know how curious I am. And how well I can keep a secret."

He demurred, still pondering her unkind comment to the bartender; she grew respectfully insistent. When he continued to demur, she changed tactics.

"I bet he turned you down. 750 links delivered to New Windsor by summer? Impossible."

Slowly, bit by bit, through prod, challenge and appeal, all deployed with instinct and wile, Caroline wore him down. Rationalizing, he saw in her a supporter whose knowledge could in no way hurt the cause. Proud of his progress with Peter, he was inclined, when she challenged him, to boast. He responded naturally to her interest in his work, which seemed to confirm his belief in its importance. He warmed to her recognition of it being worthy of her understanding. By the time they left the tavern to resume the trek to New Windsor, Caroline had secured a rather complete picture of the negotiation.

"Am I right in assuming the chain will be shipped directly from Chester to West Point?"

"No, the wagons will bring the links to New Windsor, using the very road we are now on, up the Central Valley, through Highland Mills and Woodbury. Distance about 28 miles, the terrain rolling at worst. There will be finishing work and assembly to do before we float the chain down to the Point. In theory, the shorter route would be across the mountains standing between Chester and the Point. In fact, that way with heavy laden wagons would likely be impossible, but in any case would take longer and be far too risky."

* * * * *

After Caroline left Tom in Chester, she picked up the pace, riding hard to a trail on the outskirts of Sloatsburg. It was obscured by heavy growth, but she knew how to find it. Slowing to a walk, she moved along a trail crowded on either side with saplings, mountain laurel and other undergrowth that her horse had to brush against until, as the forest deepened, the heavy canopy of tall trees caused the undergrowth to disappear.

In about a mile she came to two caves among the huge granite and schist boulders that centuries ago must have tumbled down the high ridge line above. The upper cave was some ten feet high and extended over 30 feet in depth. The lower cave was smaller but deeper. By the number of horses sheltered there, Caroline supposed it served as a rough stable for stolen horses. Below the caves was a small cabin. There she was greeted by a gang of dirty, rough looking men. Even at distance, they smelled. One, a tall, bulky man of prideful strength, with an unkempt white beard, short hair and powder burns under his right eye, came forward.

"Claudius, I see you're still sporting that wide red sash."

"How welcome you are, Caroline. It seems an eternity since you were last with us. What news?"

"News of value, Claudius, if you handle it well with your British friends. Do they pay you as well for secrets as they do for horses?"

"That all depends on quality, just like the horses. Come along into my cabin. There's a fire needs tending. While I add some logs, you can tell me what you've got."

"There's a body needs washing too. Not just yours. All of them."

Claudius turned too quickly for Caroline to catch his expression, striding swiftly back to the cabin.

She followed him into the small cabin, which seemed to serve the Ramapo Gang's leader as office, kitchen and bedroom. It was neatly fashioned of Chestnut beams and posts, with roofing of cedar shingles and horizontal siding of hemlock boards ship lapped to avoid leakage. The rest of Smith's Gang lived in the cave itself, suffering the lack of conveniences enjoyed by their leader.

Caroline unreeled the story she had pried out of Tom. Smith was quick to grasp its value, particularly the schedule Tom expected to get Townsend to accept and the route the ox-drawn wagons would take to New Windsor. Smith saw money in both the intelligence and in what he might undertake in the way of damaging the Sterling furnaces, harassing the convoys and possibly stealing parts of the chain.

That night, Caroline supped with the gang and slept with its leader, activities she had undertaken before. To a man they had found time to apply soap and water to their bodies. As rare an occurrence, Caroline imagined, as pouring salt on a humming bird's tail.

Her reasons for servicing Claudius in this way were simple. Love for the monarchy, joy in the adventure of serving as a spy, pride in the ease with which she successfully duped the patriots and, finally, the rewards of sex with this lustful, hungry and inventive marauder who neither sought nor gave commitment beyond a long night of satisfaction.

The next morning Caroline began to retrace her path, hoping to meet Tom somewhere along the way. At Earl's Tavern, she got lucky.

*****

On January 22, Tom met with Quartermaster Hugh Hughes in Poughkeepsie to report on his trip. He saved the worst for last.

"Admirably done, Tom, all we could hope for. You covered all the points. I will report to Governor Clinton. No need to scowl. I'm sure he will swiftly approve our return to Chester to sign a contract. Townsend's confidence and enthusiasm for the work inspires. We must strike while the iron is hot, as he might say. Ha!"

"Actually, Hugh, there a couple of points yet to work out. One, the pricing. The other, the question of who delivers the chain here for assembly. But Peter offered reasonable approaches that we can work on with him. The issue looming over use of Sterling—the big issue, Hugh—is the fact that Peter is owed over 5,000 pounds for iron and steel, tons of it—anchors, carts, wagons, spindles and other material—furnished on credit over two years of war. Sterling won't undertake our work without first receiving the arrearage."

Hugh was stunned. "What did you tell him?"

"I said he was entitled; that we'd find the money and return to sign the contract. Didn't want him to doubt that the work would proceed. Of course, I had no basis for this. Do you?"

"We have no funds. The military treasury needs a loan, and not only to pay Sterling but many other bills as well. Come, sit with me to compose a letter to the Governor. He might be able to get a loan from the Legislature. We should urge him to appeal as well to General Gates and the War Board. I share your thought. There's no choice here. A chain that breaks is no chain at all. We need Sterling. I'm sure our Commanding General, whose sense of urgency is well-known, would agree. But I hope we needn't engage him on this. We go to Chester on the assumption Peter's bill will be paid. In two days' time."

Tom nodded. Having settled plans for the trip, Tom returned to New Windsor and stopped, as was his custom, at Bedon's Alley for supper. Colonel Lamb was there, as Tom had hoped, and they began exchanging news even before the bartender took their order for ale.

They hadn't exchanged more than a word or two when Caroline, posted out of sight at the far end of the bar, appeared at their table and, smiling in that all-knowing, flippant way she claimed title to, pulled out a chair and sat down.

"We should brief John on your successes with Peter Townsend. And on today's visit with the Quartermaster."

"My dear Caroline, I didn't know you were part of Tom's meeting in Chester."

"I didn't either," said Tom, forcing a laugh to cover his embarrassment. "We rode together to Chester. And she joined me on the return as well, after a quick visit with her parents in Sloatsburg. Have I got it right, Caroline?"

"Right as rain, Tom. When do you return to Chester? You know, to button things up with Sterling Forge? As someone once said, 'The sooner they start' on Washington's watch chain...."

"Hey, just a minute Caroline. I sat down to get a briefing from my Continental friend here, and you seem already to know what I came to hear. I don't mean to be rude, nor invite the posting of a sonnet of insults, but Tom and I have military matters to discuss in private. I invite you to take that ale you brought to table and allow us some privacy."

John knew it was difficult to rattle Caroline. Accepting his message in good grace, she took her glass, rose and, bowing to each of the men, departed.

"Tom, how did she know you spent the day with Hugh?"

"No idea. Was wondering that myself. Perhaps, on the ride back from Chester, I told her I'd be seeing him. She's told me before that secrets are restless in New Windsor. Calling our project Washington's watch chain was new to me until I heard Peter do the same thing."

"And to me. Her manner exudes an insider's perspective, as well as a kind of cynical humor. Are you sure she's a patriot?"

"Oh, yes. Most certainly. It's just her self-confidence. That, combined with an obsessive interest in the War's progress. Makes her unusual. But her politics she wears on her sleeve and it colors 'Patriot.' If she were a man she'd be a leader of the Skinners or a Continental Regiment."

Over a supper of over-cooked white beans and pork rind along with a dessert of ginger bread and apple sauce, Tom brought John up to snuff on negotiations with Peter Townsend as well as the arrearage problem.

"Aren't there other foundries?"

"Yes and no. Others, yes. But of the commitment and reliability of Sterling, doubtful and untested. Except for Livingston's Ancram foundry. But his patriotism easily gives way to greed. Went that route with the first chain. And, what's more, the ore available only to Sterling is far superior to any other. Magnetite of 60-70% purity. Remember, General Knox insists on it for your artillery."

"More ale?" the waiter said.

John nodded; Tom ordered two drafts. "Have you got any fresh bread to offer. Need something, if you please, to soak up this bean gravy."

A couple of days later, Hugh Hughes rode to New Windsor early in the morning, picking up Tom to continue through falling snow to Chester, where they remained for three days of negotiation with the hardheaded, ambitious and confident boss of Noble, Townsend & Company's Sterling iron-working complex. The cause being accepted as paramount by both sides, the exchanges were open, candid and friendly.

Hugh gave assurance that the arrearages would be paid. "Let us put that aside. The key for us is speed. We need to install the chain when the river clears for passage. Or before. The chain will serve us nothing if the British fleet can pass West Point before it's installed. We need delivery completed to New Windsor within two months."

At first, Peter seemed to flinch on hearing the expected schedule. But with coolness, he took pen to paper and swiftly began a reckoning with numbers. Except for the pen's pensive scratching, silence filled the room. Hugh and Tom could see Peter understood the urgency of speed and had called time out from negotiating to study the question, in terms of capacity, manpower needs and cost. Peter was quick and sure with figures. And he knew the business. He suggested Hugh and Tom have a look at his chickens in the barn, until summoned back.

"It won't be long, Gentlemen. But you put me to a challenge more severe than expected, and I need a few minutes to work things out."

Before the chicken odors grew ugly, Peter called them back. "I think we can do what you ask. But, putting first things first, the price will be steep."

The price Peter said he needed, was higher than Hugh or Tom imagined it could be: 4 shillings per finished pound of chain, several times as much as Robert Livingston or the Poughkeepsie blacksmiths were willing to accept for the Fort Montgomery chain.

"Look," Peter explained, "it's a combination of things, inflation, the time schedule you demand, which dictates many forges burning round the clock, immense amounts of charcoal, at least an acre of forest consumed per day of operation. And the manpower. Not just miners, blacksmiths and colliers. Lumbermen, teamsmen, quarriers, ore pounders, firemen and, of course, overseers. I expect half our crew will be deployed just to fell trees and cut them to make the charcoal. As for the Fort Montgomery chain, this one is twice the size, weight and strength."

On February 2, the contract was drawn up and signed by Hugh, on behalf of the United States, and Peter, on behalf of Nobel, Townsend & Company. Putting two bottles of his very good claret on the table, he said, "What our signing lacks in ceremony I trust can be made up with the best wine we can offer." Peter read the terms as Hugh and Tom followed the written words.

When they came to the "In witness whereof" ending, Tom had an emotional surge of patriotism. "Gentlemen, when, with the help of the Sterling chain, the war is won, history will treasure this document. I suggest adding after the date these words: 'in the second year of American Independence.'"

"What a noble idea, Tom. Why, I see you've shed a tear. Good for you. You're brought ceremony to the occasion. And I understand your emotions. I have only to forge the chain. You must assemble and install it, all before the British can push up the river."

Hugh said, "This contract records a moment fraught with exciting possibilities and much danger too. I raise my glass to your addition, Tom. You prove an engineer can be an historian too. Here's to many more years of independence."

The snow was falling hard and blowing out of the southwest when Peter set off for his foundry to get the project organized, to be followed in an hour or so by the two Army negotiators, who were asked by Peter to speak to his employees about the extraordinary assignment he had just committed them to.

"I need some inspirational talk from you," Peter shouted over the wind, as he rode off.

Tom deferred to Hugh as the motivator-in-chief, given his superior rank and a natural flamboyance that seemed to infect others with whatever enthusiasm he was peddling.

"Ok, Tom, I'll deliver the message if you jot down my thoughts. You're better than I am at inventing the right thoughts."

It took an hour for Tom to develop a talk and Hugh to master it for delivery. On the way to Sterling Lake, they discussed the Contract, at three pages a marvel of succinct sentences expressing the meeting of minds. They were so pleased they spent much of the journey picking out terms to congratulate each other about.

Finally, Hugh brought this silliness to an end. "It's said that the sure sign of a good contract is that both parties leave the negotiating table slightly disappointed. I worry about what it means when both parties leave the table thoroughly elated and tipsy."

The Contract specified completion, on or before April 1, of an iron chain 500 yards in length, made of "best Sterling iron" 2-1/4 inches square, each link to be about two feet long, together with dozens of Swivels and Clevises and at least 12 tons of Anchors.

The Company agreed to repair "all failures of their Work, whenever happening, whether at the Works or River, or in extending it across." And for fair consideration, the Company agreed to use its teams to transport the chain and anchors to New Windsor or elsewhere as requested. For its part, the United States agreed to procure for the 60 Artificers who would be steadily employed on the work an exemption from military duty for nine months from signing and to procure from the Army such hands as can be spared to keep seven fires at forging and ten at welding, both night and day.

Arriving at the east end of Sterling Lake, Tom and Hugh were greeted outside a large warehouse by Peter, who ushered them in and up to a rough-hewn lumber platform before a rowdy crowd of about 100. Peter had told them only that a huge undertaking had come their way, and should make them and their families very happy.

Without flourish, Peter introduced Tom and Hugh and sat down. Hugh rose. The crowd was standing, huddled together with looks on the faces of some suggestive of squirrels trapped by a couple of dogs and desperate to escape. The air was thick and chilled. Sight of the audience Hugh faced scared Tom. He knew he would fail at the assignment Hugh was about to undertake.

"General George Washington said in January 1776: 'Few people know the predicament we are in.' Today, with two years of war under our belts, the General's words remain true. We face the most powerful army and navy in the world. A military colossus driven by a popular King wallowing in glory amidst a court infected top to bottom by bribery, favoritism and corruption. And driven as well by misguided patriotism. You've all heard the song:

'God save Great George our King.

Send him victorious, happy and glorious,

long to reign o'er us.'

"King George will not withdraw from this battle. Nor will he settle for anything less than continuing enslavement of Americans forced to submit to his will and the will of Parliament.

"Peace will come, one way or another. But, our freedom depends on peace through victory, crushing victory against the British military, the villainous Parliament and the foolish, obstinate and unrelenting King. Short of that, no peace will serve. And victory must be achieved not only against these lobstercoats, damnable enemies of our independence, but against the Hessian mercenaries, hirelings directed by the King to use every means of distressing America. No settlement can assure our independence. Only capitulation.

"For distressing America is precisely what they are doing. Destruction of our homes, our crops, our ships, pillage of our property, rape of our women, and incitement of the Indians to follow their path. They seduce Americans to become Loyalists, and to fight against us. They ridicule our Continentals as 'peasantry,' 'ragamuffins' and 'rabble-in-arms.' And they torture soldiers they've captured with conditions assured to bring slow but certain death. They forget how our Sons of Liberty fought at Breed's Hill, at Trenton, at Princeton and Saratoga."

Someone yelled out, a loud boo from back of the room. Picked up by others, the boos rolled forward to the speaker, and there subsided.

"There is no middle path in this fight. Liberty or death. For two years, the odds have been long against us. And yet, under General Washington's leadership, his perseverance and spirit, we survive— we survive to fight another day. And, if Noble & Company succeeds in its undertaking, for many more days will we not only survive but begin to flourish, until victory is achieved.

"And what is Noble's undertaking? In truth your undertaking, each of you. To fashion and deliver to New Windsor, within eight weeks, a chain of some 750 links of 2-1/4 inch bar to stretch across the Hudson at West Point. It will be the greatest chain ever forged since the world began. And it will be remembered, and so too those who devoted many nights and days to fashioning it at Sterling's forges. A wonder, rivaling the pyramids.

"Without this chain, the British Navy enjoys free navigation of the river, cutting our country in half, stopping communication and blocking passage of men, material and supplies essential to victory. For example, in lands east of the river, there is no flour. To the west, no meat. But with this chain, enemy ships will be stopped, put in irons and destroyed by shore batteries.

"There are two urgencies we beg you to meet. One is timing. The chain must be in place when the ice clears. Hence the extraordinarily demanding schedule. The other is quality. At Fort Montgomery, the chain broke twice due to faulty work. You know the saying. In your chain—or Washington's watch chain as we will call it when the Commander is not around—there must be no weak link. Not one. On that our liberty depends. And so, to work, work that will make each of you proud. And a hero in the eyes of your neighbors. God's speed."

Tom watched Peter as Hugh spoke. His pleasure at Hugh's passionate and moving words spilled out from his face throughout the speech. Turning to the audience, Tom could see Hugh had struck precisely the right chord to wrap the men around the enterprise, inspire and motivate them and generate in each the personal commitment needed. Indeed, the prolonged applause attested to this reading.

* * * * *

In New Windsor, soon after Tom and Hugh returned, Caroline took up with Tom where she had left off. Around town they became known as a couple.

In Garrison, it took Lisa the space of less than an evening to conclude that Susannah's story of Tom was true. It took her a longer time to decide what to do about the lies Tom had told her. She wanted to confront him, to hear his excuses, to try to understand what could compel him to tell such blatant lies about his personal life—ones that could so easily be refuted. But she didn't want to reconnect with him over this issue alone. She knew she could paint the issue on a large canvas or small, and which she chose would make a huge difference in their future relationship. Meeting to explore the lies might convey an impression she'd later regret.

It was not long after Susannah's disclosure that Lisa heard of Tom's attachment to Caroline. After learning as much as she could from friends in New Windsor, she decided to write him about what he apparently was calling his 'romantic fling.' She would not raise the subject of lying, thinking there would be ample opportunity to do so down the road.

Much to Tom's surprise, Lisa was jealous, a fact he couldn't miss from the harsh tone of her letter. To reach this conclusion, he had to dismiss one paragraph as pure guile.

Reading this reaction to your behavior with Caroline might lead you to conclude I'm jealous. If that's what you think, you don't know me very well. I've never been jealous. This despite much more provocation than your fling presents. I'm not the jealous type. This letter reflects my concern for your welfare, and that alone. From inquiries, I know this woman is not good enough even to wait table for you. And, also, that she is known as an eager seductress with more on her selfish mind than her victim's enjoyment. So, Tom, I beg you, dwell not on my 'jealousy', which is simply a figment of your imagination. In reality, it does not exist.

'She doth protest too much" was Tom's first and final thought on the subject. Why had they separated if not to be free to do as they liked. Lisa, he realized, didn't think this one through. The childish effort at concealment was badly botched. In deep denial, she ignored the possibility that, like all human-kind, she was not immune.

15

CLAUDIUS SMITH

Lisa finally made a decision. She would visit New Windsor to bury Tom's fling, something she knew she could do. She would simply open his eyes. And, then, depending on how things went, she might address the lying. Before she could carry out this plan, however, her father sent word to her at Beverly, summoning her to Convivial Hall. The travel was difficult, due to a hard cold snap that followed the heavy snowfall the negotiators had encountered upon traveling to Sterling Lake. Lisa arrived as dessert was being served. Taking a small flagon of rum in hand, she fell into bed without more than a word or two for her father and the extended family surrounding him at table.

"This afternoon we entertain the Cowboys," Lisa's father announced to the family at breakfast. Their leader, Claudius Smith, is a friendly sort, and likes to come here for quiet meetings with the British. In service to our neutral reputation, we indulge the Cowboys. As we would the Skinners. Lisa, I wanted you here for this."

"In service to the intelligence we gain, Papa?" Lisa smiled knowingly, as did her father. "Are these the infamous Tory Cowboys of the Ramapos, Papa?"

"Indeed. This Smith fellow has broken out of more jails than I knew existed. They specialize in stealing horses and cattle and driving them over to the British."

The Cowboys arrived as expected, late in the afternoon. A boisterous group of seven. Claudius was conspicuous with his flowing white beard and short hair, pale complexion and powder burns under his right eye. He radiated open good-fellowship that failed fully to conceal a steely presence of command and resolve, as well as a capacity for cruelty, which one could easily imagine from his reputation.

Lisa noticed Smith's eyes taking in the whole room at a glance and then returning to examine her in a way that caused a momentary burn on the tips of her ears. Making his way to her, he bowed with faux formality and introduced himself as "Claudius Smith from the Ramapos."

"I'm Lisa. One of the Van Horne family. Mr. Smith, your reputation precedes you, and not only in this Hall but throughout the Valley. We know of your fame—leader of the Ramapo Cowboys. Why, you've become a legend! Here, let me fill your glass with our family's famed rum punch. Unless you don't favor the stuff."

"Not true, Lisa. Legends follow death, and I'm still very much alive." Claudius quaffed the punch with barroom zeal and positioned his glass to suggest a taste for more. Lisa obliged.

"I hear your family tends to loyalist persuasion while pretending to keep a neutral house. Must be hard to feign neutrality among the British officers you favor."

"We manage. Tell me, what's keeping you busy these days?"

"Mostly rounding up stray horses and cattle for the British."

"Do they pay well?" Lisa asked, again filling his empty glass to the brim. "By the way, our family is flattered by your appreciation of its punch. And I am impressed by how well you manage the strong concoction."

"Most tasty. Especially in my empty stomach. They pay well enough. But I'm here to engage them in a far bigger matter, for bigger stakes."

Here, Lisa sensed, was the beginnings of a boast, flung out by a tongue starting to loosen from Van Horne lubrication.

"That's fascinating, Claudius. Bigger than horses and cattle? What could it be, you sly white-bearded fox?" As she whispered this question, she moved closer to him on the couch where they were seated alone, in the much-used alcove just off the main living room. Taking the pitcher once again, and recalling the many occasions she had succeeded in exchanging drink for intelligence, she emptied it into his glass.

"Fox you say. I prefer 'wolf' if you please. The British officers I expect to meet with tonight want me to stop General Washington from putting a chain across the Hudson. It's something I can do, and will do, if they pay me enough."

"Claudius, aren't you confused? The chain at Fort Montgomery was destroyed by General Clinton last fall. There's no other chain to block."

"That's what you believe. But I know there's a chain being forged right now. At Sterling Lake."

"But how can that be?"

"It's true. By the Noble Townsend forge. And it's going to be put across the river at West Point. But first it will be delivered to New Windsor. In links. By teams of oxen."

Beside her, Lisa saw an intoxicated Cowboy, puffed up like a male grouse in mating season. "I'm impressed Claudius. How do you come by this news?"

He lowered his voice to a whisper. "I have a well-placed source. Totally reliable. And you know why? Because she sleeps with the engineer whose job is to install the chain. Ha!"

This tale cut through her like a knife, Lisa's face mapping the shock and distress. Claudius hadn't noticed.

Seconds passed. Finally, Lisa blurted out "Wow. Good for you. So where do you and your Cowboy gang come in?"

"Getting awfully nosy, aren't you? Can't you imagine where we come in? Suppose some of those chain links never reached New Windsor? Missing links, chain comes up short. This job's easier than shooting duck in water."

Just then the British officers burst gaily through the front door. Lisa had noticed Claudius beginning to slur his words just enough for the most curious to notice. Now, on rising from the couch and walking to greet the officers, she could detect a slight imbalance in his walk. The rum had done its work, she noted, packing a punch, even in the gut of this proud and rugged Cowboy. But had she overdone it?

As Claudius grew animated with the British officers, Lisa took leave of the gathering, retreating to her bedroom. The price of discovery can sometimes be high, and so it was for her intelligence gathering session with Claudius Smith. Her rage at the source of Smith's knowledge continued through the night. Her emotions were raw and blurred by competing stabs of pain and wild plots of what to do about Caroline and Tom. Again and again she denied her reaction had anything to do with jealousy or heartbreak. Her self-esteem, built up through childhood, had as it central building block the avoidance of commitment and its consequences. She prided herself on being unanchored, independent and free, as she liked to say, to be herself. Not until early morning did sleep subdue her throbbing brain.

By the time she reached the Robinson's, she had sorted things out in her still troubled head. Her rage had been conquered. In its place, the first priority would be to convince Tom that Caroline was a spy, and his dalliance a danger to himself and the country. She had wrapped herself in the cause of independence and it served to deflect personal feelings.

Afraid of what she might uncover if she came to Tom's door unannounced, Lisa wrote him advising of the day and time she expected to visit. The weather was bright and the temperature cold when she rode into New Windsor and found his home at 25 Chestnut Street. Tom greeted her warmly enough, clasping her close to him in a hug that he could, but chose not to, turn into a kiss.

"How about a cup of tea to warm you up? I have some buns in the oven. That must have been a cold trip this morning. We can sit in my small kitchen. So much catching up to do."

"Lovely." Lisa took a seat at the small kitchen table, allowing Tom to wait on her, a novel practice.

"You look slightly grim, Lisa. I felt there was an agenda behind this visit; I suspect it has something to do with my new friendship here in New Windsor."

"It's about Caroline. You're right about that. When we agreed to time out, we freed ourselves to develop other relationships, to explore, even troll, the waters to see what was swimming around and might bite. I know you imagine you were trolling and she took the bait. I am here to tell you the truth. It was Caroline who trolled and you who took the bait. She's a spy for the British."

Tom's face read like pages turned in a book. First, anger, then fear and finally acceptance of at least the possibility Lisa put forth, as she meticulously presented her case. He had wondered at the strange things Caroline knew, and her insistent curiosity about matters military, and particularly about the chain, but found it all more curiously odd than suspicious. He pinned it on her zealous patriotism. But it seemed to become clear as a mountain brook when the label "spy" was applied. But, still, he wasn't convinced, or at least fought against the conclusion, given the fool it would define him to have been.

"How do you know?"

"You mean 'how did I find out?' I heard all about her conquest, and the intelligence she gained through it, from the man on the receiving end. One Claudius Smith, renowned in the Ramapos as leader of the Cowboys. I was visiting family at Convivial; he appeared there to meet with his British clients. His roving eye fell on me. I rewarded his attentions with enough rum punch to drop the average lobsterback. For Claudius, it simply greased his tongue."

Tom was stunned. "He claimed to know Caroline?"

"Never mentioned her name. Just described his source as a woman who had seduced the officer in charge of ordering from Noble, Townsend, assembling at New Windsor and installing at West Point a chain of 750 links. From all his boasting, I gathered Caroline was a woman he had correspondence with in more ways than one."

Lisa knew in advance that her last thought was mean-spirited, hitting below the belt and wholly unnecessary. The impulse to hurt was too strong to resist.

Thoroughly crushed, Tom's face paled as he slumped in his chair, slowly stirring his tea, now stupidly cold and abandoned, which precisely matched the way he felt about himself.

Lisa waited for Tom to speak. One minute passed. Then, two. He appeared so beaten down that Lisa wondered if she'd have trouble detecting a pulse.

"Look, Tom. I knew this news would fall heavy upon you. But there's an upside to your knowing who she is without her knowing you know."

The idea seemed to revive him.

"Yes, there's scope for deception in the other direction. Will you help me plan?"

Wisely, Lisa knew this was no time to reveal what she had been told about his past.

* * * * *

Peter Townsend agreed with Tom to start delivery of links as soon as enough for a convoy was ready. Shortly after Lisa's visit, Tom went back to Chester to discuss details. For safety, he asked Peter to send sledges in groups of ten, each to carry over half a ton, consisting of nine or ten links (or equivalent in weight of swivels, clevises and anchors) and be drawn by two oxen. The trip to New Windsor would take two days. They would spend the night northeast of Monroe at the Woodbury Falls Tavern just over the Cornwall Township line.

General Washington had insisted there be as little known about Townsend's project as possible. He wanted the sledges covered with canvas, their contents kept secret. For reasons he kept to himself, Tom went further. In addition to the teamster, each sledge would carry a well-armed militiaman, concealed from easy notice by the high sideboards to be specially mounted to help conceal the contents as well as the soldier. He would have three muskets ready to fire. Each teamster would be trained in technique for rapid re-loading.

Tom's explanation for these precautions, though fuzzy, met no resistance from either Peter or the teamsters. After all, as Tom put it, Monroe was the location of Smith's Clove, named for Claudius' father, and now infested with Tories. Claudius' Cowboys inhabited the very area through which the sledges must pass. Aware that their reputation was well known throughout the Ramapos, he didn't dwell on their ruthless ways.

Colonel William Allison, commanding the Fourth Regiment of Orange County Militia, was assigned the duty of safe-guarding the chain's parts on their journey from Sterling Lake to Samuel Brewster's forge on the south edge of Murderer's Creek, a mile from the Hudson.

Tom continued his relationship with Caroline, leaving a bitter after-taste with each get-together. He found ways to reduce the frequency of their bedding, and when he was compelled to perform, it was only to exploit the relationship, physical release overcoming emotional disgust. Lisa had insisted, for the sake of the war, that he continue the deception. She pointed to the many women famed in history who seduced men they cared not a fig for, in order to achieve some other purpose.

"Tom, you must, quite literally, stand erect for independence." Smiling broadly at her little pun, she continued. "Consider," she said, "Delilah with Sampson, Judith with Holofernes, Julia Agrippina with Claudius, Cleopatra with Julius Caesar, Diane de Poitiers with King Henry II. From Adam's day, women have been using sex to deceive. But it's not a gender thing. If they can do it, so can you."

As the winter days passed, and the Sterling forges roared night and day, Caroline's curiosity about the state of play at Noble, Townsend grew intense.

"When will the first links be ready for shipment?"

They were supping, as usual, at Will Bedon's Tavern.

"As I've said before, Caroline, progress is swift. Any day now the first sledges should head off. But why need that concern you?"

"And I've responded before. Your concerns are mine. That's how love works. And I know from your restlessness in bed, and other signs, that you are anxious about your chain. There's no need. The way to us from Sterling Lake is easy. You know that as well as I. Will the teamsters be armed?"

"Not well armed. No need. Some will have pistols I suppose, but they expect more danger from ice and snow than enemy attack. The path leads through ground controlled by Continentals. Tories keep to themselves. Cowboys are neutered by Skinners. Oxen have been known to collapse, but that sort of thing can be quickly handled."

"Yes, if they have too heavy a load. How many links to a sledge? And how many sledges will travel together. Don't shake your head. These are matters you must consider. I can't do all the thinking for you."

"Heaven forbid, Caroline. But, of course, you're right. Peter and I've discussed those matters. The sledges will carry nine or ten links. And travel in pairs, as soon as filled. Safety in numbers, right?"

Caroline hurried through supper. Sensing this, Tom invited her to remain the night. As expected, she declined. When questioned the next day, one of her friends told Tom she had ridden out on the Central Valley road at dawn.

* * * * *

At Brewster's Forge on the south side of Murderer's Creek, less than a mile from where it flowed into the Hudson, in late January Tom had assembled two large crews, one of lumberjacks to cut and haul the trees; the other of artificers to fashion those trees into rafts.

Looking over the crowd, Tom said: "I hope you're as strong, tough and committed to our cause as you appear. We have a big job to do, and only a month or so in which to complete it. Here's what I need. Logs. logs, and more logs. We need them so the artificers among you can fashion them into rafts to support the world's largest chain, which, as you know, we will install across the river at West Point. Logs for the chain must average two feet in diameter over their 16 foot lengths. Their ends must be tapered to a point to reduce drag from the river's flow. We must drench them in pitch. We will use four in each raft, two feet apart and connected by two cross beams of at least one foot in diameter. Any questions so far?"

"What kind of trees? And how far between rafts?"

"We must have conifers. Preferably White Pine, because it has the best floatation. The links will weigh about 114 pounds each. As for distance between rafts, we are figuring on six feet, and since the distance between West Point and Constitution Island has measured out at 1500 feet, we reckon the number of rafts at 75."

One of the artificers raised his hand. "Do we wait till all the links are delivered to start?"

"The links are going to be hauled by oxen as soon as they are completed; we must keep pace in making the rafts, so we start as soon as you lumberjacks bring us the trees. By the way, we expect you to use your adzes to cut away the bark on these trees, cut them to length and sharpen the ends to reduce drag. The artificers will see to drying and applying the pitch necessary for waterproofing."

The scope of work was beginning to seep in. Tom's math had revealed that each raft would require logs totaling 92 linear feet.

"And get this. By the time you're finished, you will have delivered to this Creek logs that, end to end, would stretch almost a mile."

Some of the lumberjacks were alarmed, others thrilled; but all were dumbfounded by the project's scope and ambition.

Someone asked Tom about the boom at Fort Montgomery.

"That boom was mostly built but never installed. I hear it might be used at West Point."

"You heard right. The boom is our first line of defense. It will be strung across downstream of the chain, to absorb the initial shock of an enemy ship. The idea is to use as much of the Montgomery boom as possible, with the shortfall being supplied by you. I was coming to this. Logs for the boom should be two feet in diameter and 21 feet long. Perhaps as many as half of the 250 or so logs we will need are already in hand."

"How will the logs be connected? Could someone walk across?"

"Yes, but only by jumping. Logs will be connected by chains of three links each, 1-1/2 inches square and 18 inches long, attached to clips bolted and stapled to the ends of the logs. So, the distance between logs will be close to four feet. After you lumberjacks have stripped the logs of bark, I will ask you to use your adzes to change the middle of each log from a round shape to an octagonal one. This will give anyone seeking to cross on the boom good footing as he jumps from log to log.

"Men, count yourselves lucky to be part of these crews. In future days, your achievement will be compared favorably to the pyramids and other wonders of history. We've contracted with the Noble, Townsend foundry to forge and deliver 750 chain links, as well as sufficient swivels, clevises and anchors, in less than two months. They use ore that compares favorably with the ore used by the Swedes to forge their superior swords. They will operate around the clock seven forging fires and ten for welding. A mammoth undertaking. But no more so than what we expect of you in the coming days. You are enabling the biggest, strongest chain ever to span any river anywhere in the whole world, and by so doing, you are assuring victory for these United States. I'm dead serious in saying this project is outsized, beyond human scale, beyond measure. I'm already feeling very proud of what you're about to accomplish. You will feel that way too, and for a lifetime. God's speed."

* * * * *

Caroline reached Smith's caves at dusk. Claudius greeted her with the usual hug, followed by an eager kiss, wet and prolonged enough for her to understand what she was expected to do for him that night, after matters of business were complete.

They sat down in his small cabin, alone except for Joy, the cook who was preparing a meal of wild duck with grape jelly, parsnips dug from a garden covered with a foot and more of snow and potatoes taken from the dug root cellar and almost too soft to eat. On setting this supper before them, Joy had two comments.

"The parsnips, you'll find, are unusually sweet. These low temperatures concentrate the sugar. Enjoy them; the last I could find to dig. As for the duck, take care you don't break a tooth chomping down on buckshot. Bound to be some."

Claudius offered rum, the only alcohol left in the cabin. He drank while she passed on exactly the intelligence he needed to defeat Machin's chain.

"If you can spot them when they start off, this will be like shooting fish in a barrel."

"My dear Caroline, you amaze me with your ignorance. Taking possession of a sledge full of links, I agree, will be easy. But then what? These heavy links aren't like horses we capture and can drive swiftly to British lines. Links don't move on their own. Nor are they easy to destroy. Word of our little intervention is likely to spread swiftly, bringing strong forces against us."

Claudius dug into the duck, forgetting Joy's caution until he felt the buckshot.

"Damn! God Damn it to Hell. I just broke a tooth."

"Dear Claudius. Here, take some rum, make the tooth swim in it. Pain will go bye bye even before you start to feel it."

"Doesn't help much." He winced in pain trying to swallow the rinse of rum.

"Be careful. It could happen to you. I'll stick to parsnips and potatoes. Where were we?"

Just then, Joy appeared, a fistful of cloves in her hand.

"You old fool. Here's some cloves for the pain. Suck on them. Don't eat them."

"So, back to our plan. Dust to dust, as the Bible teaches. I have to get the links to a furnace where they can be restored to their molten condition. There's a small furnace in Monroe, tucked out of sight in the forest, whose owner has Tory sympathies. He's promised help. With warning, he'll have the furnace blazing hot when we arrive. We will seize the two sledges as they enter Monroe and drive them to the Monroe Works. With nine links each, we will have destroyed 18. Should cause enough delay to allow the Navy to seize control at West Point and further up-river."

"And the teamsters?"

"Tie them up tight and leave in the snow. Uncomfortable, but alive. In time, to be rescued."

The next morning, Caroline took leave of Claudius to ride back to New Windsor.

On mounting her large bay, she blew Claudius a kiss.

"Oh, dear. One thing before I go. It bothered my sleep. How will you know when the sledges head north?"

"I have that well in hand. The owner of the oxen is straight down the line neutral. Cares chiefly for money. We've already paid him to let us know."

The first shipment was ready to travel on March first. It was separated into two units, the first of four sledges and the second, leaving 30 minutes after the first, the remaining six, each with a saddled horse tied behind. Colonel Allison was in the first sledge and Lieutenant Isaiah Houton the second. Two Corporals, picked for their skill in musketry, rode in the other two sledges of the first unit.

Six more of Allison's Militia traveled in the sledges of the second unit.

Well briefed, the teamsters and their escorts expected trouble at some spot along the route. When or where it would come, they knew not, setting up a tension that grew as they moved up the Central Valley.

Oxen are hard to get going. Raisers urge the animals to lean into the yoke, to snort and moan, to crinkle their tails, and finally set themselves and their load in motion. They used no whips. Voice commands are supplemented with a goad, a sharp brad fixed in the tip, long enough to draw the ox's attention without drawing blood. Once underway, it was wise not to stop oxen unless absolutely necessary.

One of Colonel Allison's men asked the teamsters why they didn't use horses. Peter Townsend, hearing the question, observed it was like asking a breeder of dogs why he didn't prefer cats.

Happily, and with a loud guffaw, the teamster replied. "The reasons are as fish in the sea. Oxen are stronger, less apt to get scared, less inclined to flounder in snow and mud, not given to sickness, less expensive to buy and keep, and, of course, better to eat! I could go on my friend, but you must, by now, get the notion."

Trouble came as the first unit entered Monroe. Claudius rode just ahead of his band of six Cowboys. They came at a gallop from the northwest out of dense forest along a timbering road. Surprised to see four instead of two sledges, Claudius was unfazed.

"Look, men. Four to take. Double the fun."

He and his men formed a semi-circle in front of the first sledge. They held pistols and wore cutlasses. They looked ugly, mean, all business.

"All you teamsters, get down on the ground, belly to the snow. Be quick about it. We don't want to kill anyone." Claudius was calm and determined, a voice of authority.

On seeing the Cowboys, the teamsters had spaced the sledges enough so that, when ordered to the ground, they were almost side by side. On a loud whistle from the Colonel, he and his men stood up with muskets aimed at Claudius and three of his band.

"Drop your weapons and dismount," Colonel Allison commanded.

For what seemed to some an eternity, the two sides stared at each other, awaiting orders.

"We don't want to hurt anyone," Claudius said, his voice still determined but now on edge. "We want the sledges. Turn them over and you can go free. Don't be stupid. We outnumber you."

"Won't do that, Smith. At this distance, muskets trump pistols. And each of us has three, primed and ready to fire. Even a Cowboy can count. I repeat, drop your weapons and dismount. By the count of three."

All you teamsters, get down on the ground, belly
to the snow. Be quick about it. We don't want to kill anyone.

Noting the two musket barrels leaning against the sideboard next to the Colonel, Claudius decided to abandon the heist. Caroline was wrong about those fish in a barrel.

"I've changed my mind. We'll leave you alone. Come on boys." Claudius began to turn his horse. "Stay put, or you're a dead Cowboy, Smith."

Whether out of anger or frustration or by mistake, one of the Cowboys discharged his pistol, hitting the front of the first sledge. The Militia responded, firing with deadly accuracy, dropping three from their saddles, dead, and wounding Claudius in the arm. Before the soldiers could raise their second muskets to aim and fire, Claudius and the three remaining Cowboys had turned their horses and were galloping back towards the forest. The three he left behind were Eduard Roblin, a long-time member of the band, and Claudius' two sons, James and Richard.

"Hold your fire," the Colonel yelled. "We've done enough killing. From here on, I believe the chain will be safe."

Consistent with General Washington's intense interest in keeping quiet anything having to do with the chain until it was in place, news of Colonel Allison's success against the Ramapo Cowboys was suppressed. Tom didn't learn of it until the ten sledges arrived at Murderer's Creek. And Caroline knew nothing until, a few weeks after Claudius had returned to his caves to allow his wound to heal, she paid him a visit.

It didn't take Claudius long to turn on Caroline. Angry words tumbled out, describing what had happened and then placing on Caroline the full brunt of blame.

"Two sledges, driven by unarmed teamsters. Fish in a barrel. Some fish. Some barrel. You are either an agent for the Americans or a duped fool. Which is it?"

Caroline suddenly understood.

Tears ran down her face. "He must have found out. He must have known I was a spy. But how? No one in New Windsor knew. You're entitled to be very angry with me. But not for disloyalty. For being duped, yes. For telling anyone what I was up to, no, no, no. Never. Who knew, besides you? I'm sure you never told my secret."

"Of course not. However he found out, it doesn't much matter, since your spying days are finished."

Returning to New Windsor, Caroline knew her nights with Claudius were over too. It had been an arrangement she enjoyed for its adventure, and for the way it enabled her in spying for the Crown, something that made her feel useful. But not an arrangement she'd miss.

16

—

ACONITUM

Caroline stayed away from Tom. He was so busy with raft-building, and finishing work on the chain as the links were delivered, that avoiding him wasn't hard. She was confused over her feelings. A heap of embarrassment and shame. Shame over being caught spying, shame over faking love, and shame over having been manipulated. Quite enough to keep out of Tom's sight.

Lisa heard about Colonel Allison's success when she came to town to check up on Tom and Caroline. Hearing the news, she realized Caroline was of no further use to the war effort. Her suppressed rage at this interloper sprung back to life, energizing her to deal with Caroline, and do so not just as a spy. After all, she thought, hadn't he been in love with her before he knew she was using him? Would Tom handle Caroline according to the rules of war. To be tried, convicted and hung as a spy? She doubted it. Nor would legal process satisfy her. Still unwilling to acknowledge the fact, she was jealous, deep down. She could feel the ache in her bones. From early childhood, she had learned her father's philosophy. "Don't get mad, get even." Could, in fact, she master the theory? The anger burned in her head.

Lisa had admired the Robinson's well-tended garden and mastered its contents out of a consuming interest, developed as a child with tutoring by her father, of labeling nature's bounty, whether it be birds, animals, trees or flowers. Her father taught her mushrooms, and how to distinguish the poisonous from the delectable. He taught her herbs and their uses in cooking and medicine. Her horticultural journey of discovery led to a particular interest in flora housing poisons. For example, Aconitum, the tall perennial with dark purple flowers shaped like the cowl of a monk. She read of its use by Indians to poison arrows used to kill wild animals. Of how deadly it was to humans, causing nausea, vomiting, diarrhea and then, with amazing speed, death by paralysis of the heart. She learned that the flower, stem and root all contained the poison. Lisa also was schooled in Roman history. The uses of poison after the Republic was replaced by a string of Emperors was familiar ground, as was the fact this weapon was deployed by women as well as men.

Lisa knew the bed in which the Robinson's Aconitum rested. Armed with a shovel, she removed the layer of snow that had kept the soil from freezing solid and was able to dig up some roots, cut them up like one does with garlic cloves and boiled them until most of the water had evaporated. She put the remaining liquid in a vial and returned to Tom's house.

He had no time for her, given the shipment of links that had just arrived. But he needn't have worried, because Lisa was in town to see Caroline, whom she found in Bedon's Tavern that evening. The bartender pointed her out, sitting alone at a table in a dark corner of the room, lighted by a slender candle. "Are you a friend?" the bartender asked. "I think she needs some support. Not her joyous self these days. But why should I be telling you these things. I see you're not a friend. I talk too much. Forget what I said, if you will be so kind. A drink?"

Lisa laughed at this outburst. Banter to a bartender, she remembered, was as breathing is to the rest of us. "Give me an ale."

Glass in hand, she went over to Caroline's table, pulled out the unused chair and sat down.

"You are Caroline I believe. My name is Lisa Van Horne. I know Tom Machin, as you do. I want to talk to you about him."

Caroline was confused by this uninvited intrusion.

"There's nothing to say. I broke it off. We don't see each other anymore."

"Do you think he still loves you? After the chain incident?"

Caroline flinched. She reached for her glass and took a gulp. In the darkness, she couldn't read Lisa's expression.

"What chain incident? I don't know what you're talking about. As for his love, that's none of your business. Now, perhaps you will leave my table."

"You're a spy, Caroline, a spy for the British, a spy who was uncovered by Tom. What you don't know is how Tom came upon this knowledge. I thought you might like to discuss that."

Caroline was known among friends as a cool bird, hard to throw off balance. Lisa was testing this reputation, pushing Caroline's composure to the limit. And beyond.

"You're a living nightmare, come to haunt me. A very bad dream. Yes, yes, I'm desperate to learn how I was uncovered. Not knowing afflicts me. It weakens me. All right. What do you have to say?"

Caroline leaned forward, trying to read Lisa's face, as if needing to make sure she was not just a trick of imagination.

"I can tell you a lot. But first, the bathroom. Don't go away."

Lisa was gone but a few minutes. When she returned, Caroline rose to go to the same place. "Be right back."

Lisa took out the vial of Aconitum concentrate and, with shaking hand, emptied it in the half empty glass of Caroline's beer. What she had started out imagining as a remote possibility, a dream really of what she'd like to do was now a reality. The deed was done, and she knew there was now no way to turn things around. When she returned, Lisa came directly to the point.

"Your friend Claudius Smith was the one who disclosed your game. He came to my home in New Jersey to meet British officers. He came on to me. He drank. He boasted. About a spy who had seduced the officer responsible for installing the chain. He didn't mention your name. Nor Tom's. But knowing Tom, and the fact he had taken up with a woman in New Windsor, I could add two plus two. Smith gave me all I needed to finger you as the spy."

"I see. A tragedy for Claudius. Drinking and loose tongue caused his heist to fail. And boasting. Worse, he doesn't even realize he was sole cause of his undoing."

Lisa took a deep drink of her ale. Prompted, Caroline did likewise. And then she took another. She smiled awkwardly at Lisa and then vomited.

"How stupid to do that. I'm sorry. Something funny's going on."

In minutes Caroline collapsed in her chair and slumped to the floor.

Lisa summoned the bartender, suggesting Caroline had just had a heart attack. The bartender examined her where she lay, taking her wrist in his hand. No pulse. He pronounced her dead. In the confusion that followed, Lisa knocked Caroline's glass off the table, shattering it and splashing its contents on the floor.

"Get a mop," the bartender yelled out to someone watching from the kitchen. 'How do you think this happened?" the bartender asked Lisa.

"Probably a jolt she hadn't expected. She was a British spy. I had just uncovered her. Must have stressed her heart."

Friends of Caroline were contacted. She seemed to have no family that anyone was aware of. Lisa and the bartender briefed her friends, who then took over the task of arranging for burial.

Lisa returned to Tom's house, finding him rummaging around the kitchen for something to eat. He was dirty and reeked of dried sweat.

"Hey Lisa, you're just in time to help me with supper. Raft-building day. Pooped. What you been up to?"

"I met Caroline at Bedon's. Told her I knew she was a spy. And how I found out. She had a heart attack. It finished her. Her friends took charge of the body."

"Oh, my God. Did you just bump into her or what? I can hardly believe it."

Lisa studied him.

"Does it make you sad? You were taken *by* her at the beginning. Before you were taken in."

"Lisa, that's not funny. Were you jealous? I'm sad I can't bring her to justice. It would deter others. But being taken by her, as you put it, hardly. A little fling, that's all. A salve for loneliness. But look. You might have been the cause of her death. Does anyone suspect you?"

Lisa flinched, quickly covering her face to recover the confident mien she had promised herself to maintain.

"Cause, perhaps. Murder, no. I told the bartender about her being a spy, about my uncovering her over an ale, how the shock of discovery might have triggered the attack."

When Tom went off to the bath, Lisa stayed in the kitchen, where she rinsed out the vial, wrapped it in newsprint, smashed it on the stone floor and put the broken glass with the trash that would be picked up by the village and taken to the dump. Then she threw up, involuntarily covering the glass with the contents of her highly agitated stomach. I'm many things, Lisa thought, but not, until now, a murderer.

* * * * *

Lisa felt pulled in different directions. The drive that propelled her to doom Caroline, and its results, now frightened her. The point of fighting in a war is to kill the enemy. Yet this analogy, she knew, wouldn't serve. She thought of returning to the warmth and safety of Convivial Hall. She was still drawn to her position at Robinson's, furthering her sense of purpose in the battle for independence. And then there was Tom, with whom she had unfinished business. To avoid him at this moment began to feel almost cowardly, and she kept reminding herself that she was no coward.

When Lisa finally reached the decision to move in with Tom, she never doubted he would have her. She would ease his loneliness, making further flings, little or big, unnecessary and, by her presence, impossible. And, at the right moment, she would confront the lies.

It was early March. Tom accepted her decision, but not because of loneliness, which he now associated chiefly with the months of December and January, when he was recovering from his wounds.

Once on his feet again, he had become a dynamo, attending to several projects all at once. He was supervising raft-building, connecting the chain links with swivels every hundred feet to permit twisting in the turbulent currents, and stapling the links to rafts lined up at the mouth of Murderer's Creek. In addition, he was supervising the boom to be placed down-stream of the chain and given some slack, in hopes it would absorb the blow of a warship like a pillow absorbs a fist. The logs from the boom intended for Fort Montgomery were about 15 feet in length and one foot in diameter. The additional logs needed to string the boom across would be 21 feet long, 2 feet in diameter and dressed by adz in the center in the shape of an octagon four or five feet long and finished at both ends with iron straps joined by three chain links 1-1/2 inches square and 18 inches long connecting the logs. The gap between them would be about four feet. The flat surfaces of the octagon would facilitate foot passage across the boom from one edge of the river to the other, at least for those nimble enough to spring across the distance separating the logs.

Beyond all this, he was making time to finish installing the *Chevaux-de-Frise* between Pollopel's Island and the west shore of the Hudson near New Windsor, and to direct the raising of the Galley Washington, which the Continentals had sunk to avoid loss to the British when Henry Clinton's forces advanced as far as Esopus with a ten-warship fleet after destroying Forts Montgomery and Clinton.

"I must warn you, Lisa, I am way over my head in projects where, frankly, I feel like the only officer in charge, with none to consult. I'm not going to be great company, at least until after the ice breaks up and installation is complete. Won't be around much and when I am, I'll carry the stink I know you've learned to hate."

"Come on, Tom. No one to consult? You like it that way. Other engineers come and go. I know you despised having Bernard Romans imposed on you, and then the magnificent Colonel de la Radiere. You loathed their presumptions of superiority. You told me you would never consult with them, unless directly ordered. Now, they're gone and these projects are yours alone to manage. Don't pretend you don't glory in having them to yourself."

"I suppose you're right. The two things I despise most among so-called experts are first, a refusal to imagine you could be wrong, even on a difficult matter of judgment, and second, in the face of crushing evidence that you are wrong, a refusal to admit it. Those engineers you mention, heroes in their own heads, suffered from these bugaboos. I recall some wise man saying the spirit of liberty is the spirit which is not too sure it's right."

"Have you ever found yourself guilty of those things you hate?"

"Yes, to tell the truth, both of them. As a young engineer just finished training. The faculty and fellow students scorched me for vaulting arrogance. The details I must have erased."

"But it's likely your experience then is why you despise them in others now."

Tom had removed his filthy clothes. Asking Lisa to see about some food, he headed for a hot bath. As he emerged, dripping and clean, Lisa greeted him in the bedroom with clippers in hand.

"Sit down on the bed, Tom. I'm going to do your fingers and toes."

"What? I thought, alas, the days when you tended to such matters were over. I've missed your attentions and, not incidentally, our banter from toe to toe."

"Your nails, my friend, have grown long in my absence. What manner of woman would I be not to address the problem? Come, sit beside me, and tell, if please, your favorite lines from Shakespeare."

"That's an easy one. The Agincourt speech of Henry the Fifth, a brute of a man whose shrewdness and eloquence inspired his troops to triumph over the French. We had to recite it in school. I can still recall most of the lines.

"We few, we happy few, we band of brothers,
For he to-day that sheds his blood with me
Shall be my brother, be he ne'er so vile
This day shall gentle his condition:
And gentlemen in England, now a-bed,
Shall think themselves accurs'd they were not here,
And hold their manhoods cheap whiles any speaks
That fought with us upon Saint Crispin's day."

"Lovely, Tom. I imagine you see a parallel to our current war with the British. But, of course, I've never thought Henry believed a word of his speech. Common soldiers turned into gentlemen back home! Not likely."

"Let's hope our outcome measures up to Henry's. Now, it's your turn. What's your favorite Shakespeare?"

"That's it for the hands. Now, for the toes. And Shakespeare. My favorite role will not surprise you. Rosalind. She's got feminine curiosity freed of feminine dignity. She makes love to the man, instead of waiting for the man to make love to her. Her wit and wisdom are boundless. Reading *As You Like It* makes me yearn to be Rosalind. So there, my secret is out."

"Not surprised one bit. There's a Rosalind-like directness about you. I admired it from the start. But you didn't mention your desire, or better, your need, to control. I think you share that trait too with Rosalind."

"Welcome words, Tom. Particularly, since I am now going to be direct, uncomfortably so. I have learned that the stories you told me about coming here, acting the Indian in the Tea Party, fighting the British on Breed's Hill and the rest are just that—stories made up by one who joined the Continentals after deserting. Why did you lie to me?"

Color drained from Tom's face. He struggled to mount a response.

Finally, he said slowly, "Who claimed I was a deserter?"

Lisa explained her conversation with Susannah, emphasizing the eye-witness account by Old Put of Tom's bedraggled arrival at General Washington's headquarters in Cambridge.

"How could you mislead me? It was wrong."

Tom bowed his head, covered his eyes, as if to prevent Lisa from seeing him, and wept. The pain of lying as a boy, the humiliation of being caught lying about his intimacy with Thomas Paine, these deeply buried wounds of self-infliction surfaced to wet his face for many minutes.

Lisa wrapped her arms around him -- awkwardly because, having no place to sit beside him, she was forced to bend over. She felt his body shaking in her arms, which she held tight until the shaking ceased.

"Do you know why, Tom? We all lie now and then, but why such a big lie? Why to me?"

Tom stood up, looked at Lisa and hugged her.

He said, "I don't understand the 'why' of it. Wish fulfillment? Deeds imagined fathering integrity lost? Blind confidence that secrets already known would remain concealed? I've thought of Claudius' downfall, from boasting a truth. Mine is worse—boasting a lie. As an intellectual matter, I have long known this habit was insane. And yet, at some other level, it's continued, seemingly irresistible."

"What's odd is the act of desertion in the cause of liberty, to become a Patriot, to join the Continentals and fight the British, all that is a record to be proud of, one that makes me proud to know you. Claiming to have tossed some tea didn't attract me as much as the truth does. So, here's my message. These lies are forgettable. What I ask of you in the future is to take pride in who you are, in all you are accomplishing. Enjoy the fruits of all this, including my love for you, and foreswear lies, even embellishments."

Tom nodded, closing his eyes as if shutting the door to these past failings.

* * * * *

A few days later, when Tom returned as the sun was setting, Lisa proposed inviting John Lamb over for supper.

"I bumped into him in the village today. He asked how you were bearing up. Seemed aware of your various projects. He's going to stop by to say hello. We can have him dine with us, if that suits."

"Sure. Do you have a menu?"

"Of course. Turnips, potatoes and loin of pork, studded with cloves; already in the oven. Get cleaned up. You reek of something nasty. He'll be here any time now."

John Lamb arrived at 7. Tom emerged from the bedroom to greet him, his hair still wet. He looked scrubbed and clean in fresh clothes. And for the first time in weeks, he looked happy. Being alone registered as loneliness for him, although he didn't know that was the problem. He found it hard to admit a craving for company. In fact, he fought it.

The chemistry between the Colonel and the Captain remained strong. Bonds forged in battle resist erosion. So it was with these veterans of Clinton and Montgomery. Over a bottle of Madeira consumed even before supper reached the table, they relived the day's dangers and the battles lost, bathed in the special friendship and warmth of survivors.

"If you weren't such a sure friend who, I know, won't take offense, Tom, I wouldn't dare to ask. But I must: the smell of pitch almost overwhelms."

"Oh, damn it. I can bathe, and scrub and change my clothes, but still the smell of the day's work lingers. We're putting tar on the logs we will use to make the rafts supporting the chain and also the logs for the boom we plan to stretch across the river below the chain. Messy job, it is. Smell as hard to remove as garlic from one's breath. Sorry about that. Don't get too close."

"You might not want to kiss him either, John. Who knows how much garlic he had at lunch."

When supper was served, John turned to more current matters. "There's much to discuss. Lisa, tell me about the poet's death. I hear you were with her at Bedon's when she fell off her chair."

Lisa had steeled herself for John's question.

"Caroline gave poetry a bad name. But as a spy? There she excelled. Tom can testify to that. But you know the story. As for her death, it must have been the shock and shame of being fingered. A weak heart, perhaps. We'll never know."

"As the one, it could be said, who knew her best, Tom, what thoughts?" John was smiling broadly. As he put the question, John noticed Lisa's face turning dour.

"Her death baffles me. She was a strong, energetic woman giving every appearance of good health. She had no time to take her own life. Only plausible explanation is Lisa's. Lisa charmed that Cowboy into talking too much. In ending Caroline's career as a spy, Lisa ended her life as well."

Lisa flinched. As the back of her ears began to redden and burn, she looked across the table and was relieved that neither of the men seemed to notice. She feared these involuntary exhibits of guilt, like this one, produced simply by Tom's unknowing, accidental comment. The mind can control speech yet lose control of the other ways a body communicates. She knew she'd faint if they really believed her a murderer. Or empty her stomach again.

"And, incidentally, Lisa, you brought his dalliance with this spy to an end, re-establishing yourself, it would appear, as the woman of the house. And making of you, Tom, an honest man. If we weren't out of wine, I'd drink a toast to Lisa's splendid work," said John.

The color in Lisa's face drained away. The men were too attentive to one another to take note. She feared losing control, blurting out the confession these sorts of comment brought to mind.

"Not so. Allow me a minute to open another bottle, and we can both raise a glass to Lisa."

The cork pulled, the men toasted Lisa most generously. She had time enough to recover, and even could flash a cunning smile. Raising her glass in thanks, she ended her little toast with the words "To accidents favoring our revolution."

John quickly added "And guided by the hand of God."

"I've known you a long time, John, without realizing you were a believer. Do you really think there's a God watching over our struggle, helping us defeat the British?"

"Yes, indeed. Consider Washington's successes at Trenton and Princeton. Miracles, both. God lent a hand."

"Did God slumber while we lost Brooklyn and New York City, and then at White Plains and Forts Washington and Lee? Did he sleep while Sir Henry Clinton wiped us out at Forts Clinton and Montgomery? Snoring when they cut the chain?"

"He works his will in ways unfathomable to us. But, whether fast or slow, he moves mankind to a better place. For us that means a place of independence."

Lisa observed "Better for mankind here, far worse for mankind in England. So, you must conclude, God favors us more than the British."

"Good point, Lisa. And John, consider this: our Commander-in-Chief is, I believe, of my persuasion on divinity rather than yours. I have never heard that he prays for victory. He accepts Providence, not God, but without believing he can summon it in support. I think he considers Providence as remote and haphazard. I was present on Dorchester Heights when that violent storm turned back Howe's attack, deeply disappointing Washington, who saw great victory in the offing. I'll not forget his words: 'I do not lament or repine at any act of Providence.'"

Lisa laughed. "I've heard Tom on the subject of God before. He's quite open to having God on our side, but, regardless, he insists we must have the chain."

"She's right. God's optional. Chain's mandatory."

"So, when will all the links be delivered? And installed?"

"Delivery should be complete by the end of this month. Before breakup of ice. The heavy guard detail for the teamsters has seen no action since that first ox-train was attacked. Smith and his gang must have returned to stealing horses."

"Smooth sledding, to put a point on it."

"Hush, Lisa. I'm trying to answer John's question. We should be able to float the chain down to West Point and get it installed by the beginning of May. But our amazing General must make two personnel changes, now. The French frog, Colonel de la Radiere, must be sent packing. His opposition to siting the chain at West Point has continued since the decision was made -- unanimously. He argues with anyone who listens. Especially Thad Kosciuszko, the young, talented and wholly agreeable engineer from Poland. Radiere's jealousies rampage. His foot-dragging throws sand in our gears.

The second is Old Put. He must be replaced. Enfin! You were supposed to be working on that, John. I'm not sure you've heard the latest story about Put's failure to respond to Clinton's attack last fall. Lisa can tell you."

"Well, John, you know I've been living with Beverley Robinson's wife in their home near Fort Montgomery. She's as staunch a Tory as her husband, who is still away from home leading his Loyalist militia. Mostly, I hear, he sits around like a dry sponge, soaking up praise for his success at the Forts.

"Their maid, I discovered, is a keen patriot. I found her willing to talk about what she saw and heard. She told me Put was infatuated with Beverley's wife, who generously fed the infatuation to gain intelligence. On the day of Clinton's attack, she apparently kept him at a game of chess until it was too late in the day to aid the Forts. Incredible. Yet, on reflection, the story becomes believable. I think it should be passed on to General Washington."

"I'm in touch with the General concerning Old Put. I will let him know. I'll also pass along your ideas on personnel. You know, don't you, how much stock he puts in your judgment."

"If so, John, please tell him this, the chain must have the support of batteries on both sides of the river, well-armed and manned by trained forces. Nothing like this exists today, and as long as responsibility stays in Old Put's hands, it won't get done."

"The General well remembers the weak link that lost us the first chain: grossly undermanned forts."

Lisa poured out the remaining Madeira, equal parts in the three empty glasses. "Another bottle?" she asked in a voice slightly slurred.

The men shook their heads.

John said "Let's hold that idea. I want to get a bit technical with Tom on his chain, before he turns tipsy on me. So, Tom, how do you plan on allowing our ships to pass the chain? There's Continental traffic up and down river. The chain must not stand in the way."

"Yes, and that goes for the boom too. I found a way at Fort Montgomery. It worked. We will do the same at West Point. We will install for both chain and boom capstans on Martelaer's Rock. They will reel in the chain and boom and make them fast. Taking the chain first, on the west shore, the end will be fixed to a large wooden crate filled with stone seated just at water's edge and secured more fully by chains linking it to two similarly loaded crates planted behind. Then, the first three rafts extending east will be heavily anchored to similar crates sunk beneath the chain. Between each of the these rafts the chain will be connected by a clevis, permitting it to be parted. Passage of our ships will be done at slack tide, between ebb and flow. The capstan will pay out enough chain to allow one of the clevises to be opened, and space sufficient between two of the rafts to permit a ship's passage. It will take time. With practice, the process will speed up. But one hopes for limited traffic. The boom will work in the same way."

"Ingenious, Tom. I knew you had solved this problem at Fort Montgomery, but never got down to shoreline to see how. Except when I escaped in the dark, with no inclination to linger. Sure it will work?"

"As sure as you are that God is on our side."

"That's good enough for me. And you Lisa?"

Lisa nodded, tilting her head and jutting out her jaw just enough to show some impatience.

"Let's be done with chain talk. John, what women in your life? Speak of your loves, lest ours grow stale."

Tom felt the heat of Lisa's question, which she had neatly turned into a well-aimed taunt.

"I've fallen again. Her name's Chloris. Met her, naturally, at our favorite tavern."

"You fall often, John, but as often pick yourself up without getting hurt. Wasn't your previous tumble with Chloe, and before that Clara? You seem bent on exhausting the C's." Tom laughed, pleased with his jest.

"Tom and I have talked about you, yes, we have, behind your back. Because we love you enough to want to see you happily involved. Even married. How does it happen, this migration from one woman to another?"

"I'm not sure. But here, right or wrong, is my recent discovery: I am a serial philanderer. Never admitted that before. Your Madeira encourages self-discovery, loosening the tongue and inhibitions. I fall into love too easily. And, then, when my affections are returned, often with interest, I start to feel uncomfortable, and then some fear creeps in. What do I fear? Being confined, tied down, restrained in my freedom. It's odd. To suddenly become afraid of having accomplished precisely what one set out to do. I can't make the commitment, and that leads to my being tossed off. I'm left by one after another, each wounded through love put at risk and unrewarded. A vicious circle. And what's pathetic? I know each step of the way but can't break out."

Tom recognized some similarity in John's dilemma to his long struggle with lying.

While they had been enjoying supper, snow had been accumulating outside, like a stalking cat. The flakes were fine and dry, like desert sand, and were blowing into emerging drifts that would grow swiftly in size if the heavy fall continued. Given the turn in conversation, he chose not to report to the others.

"So, what is love?" Tom put the question rhetorically, with intent to answer. For of late he had given the matter much thought.

"I speak of love that survives the romantic beginnings, for that, like sap from a wound, bleeds away, weakening its source. The love I speak of is lasting. The secret that sustains it is dependency. Reciprocal dependency between a man and a woman. Without the weft, the woof can't fashion a flat-weave rug. A one-sided arch won't stand. A one-handed clap won't sound. Without pectin, grape juice won't jell. You get the idea."

Lisa admired Tom when he talked this way. Silently she listed the ways they pleased and helped each other, and the many ways he needed her. Missing from the lists, of course, were the ways she needed him, for she denied any existed.

"I'm beginning to catch on. You're right, of course. I not only haven't been dependent on these women, I've been aware and proud of not being one iota dependent. The root of my problem. You put your finger on it."

Lisa said "Were your parents a happy couple?"

"Not in the least. My father left home when I was nine. I never learned why. If mother knew, she didn't want to tell. Embarrassed, perhaps, if another woman the cause. Mother supported herself as a singer. Sometimes doing housework. Spent time with men but never re-married. I didn't know either of them well."

"How about older brothers or sisters?"

"None younger or older. Only child. Raised mostly in school, by teachers and peers. One advantage out of this mess: I could pick my mentors."

Tom and Lisa were searching for the same thing: the key to understanding the Colonel's success. For his repeated break-ups with women were but peccadillos in the sweep of John's brilliance as an artillery officer, and his awesome skills in rising to military prominence through merit alone.

"John," Tom said, "there's plenty of common sense about you, and that's found beyond the rainbow, who knows where. You must have been born with it. And how well it's served you. The cornerstone to a foundation of good judgment.

"My success in the Artillery was not a birth-right. It came through belief in God. That, and practically being adopted by your friend, General Knox. I've always believed we became such close friends by dint of our both being protégés of the General."

"Speaking of Henry Knox, I meant to tell you I had a letter from him, saying he was in Valley Forge or headed that way after some time off in Boston with the two Lucys, and was expecting his wife and daughter to join him there in early May. He proposed coming up to West Point to meet them. He would escort them down to Valley Forge after staying a few days with us in New Windsor. He even mentioned the chain, hoping it might be strung by the time of this rendezvous. I hope the plan works out, and that you are around to enjoy a reunion."

"Yes. I will count on it."

The fire was reduced to embers. The room was growing cold. After throwing another log on, Tom went to the front door, opening it wide enough to see how much snow had fallen. And to allow the others to see too.

"That's a lot of snow, Tom, and it's still falling fast. I best be getting home."

"Indeed, John," Lisa said, "before this uninvited act of God swallows you up in a snowdrift. I think we all have a lot to ponder in the remarkable life of Colonel Lamb. We look forward to continuing the discussion over another supper—soon."

17

—

COURT OF ENQUIRY

By Resolution of November 28, 1777, the Continental Congress directed General Washington "to cause an enquiry to be made into the loss of Forts Montgomery and Clinton… and into the conduct of the principal Officers commanding those Forts."

Thereupon, the Commander-in-Chief, on March 17, 1778, issued a Warrant to Hold a Court of Enquiry into the Loss of Forts Montgomery and Clinton, appointing Generals Alexander McDougall and Jedediah Huntington and Colonel Edward Wigglesworth as Members of the Court, and summoning them to Fishkill to commence the Enquiry on March 30th.

The Warrant set forth ten specific questions to be investigated, as well as an eleventh question embracing such additional matters as the Members may judge necessary to understand the causes of the loss of these two Forts.

At the speed of rolling thunder that so often traveled the length of the Highlands, news of General Washington's Warrant became known from Haverstraw to New Windsor. Tom heard the news from Governor George Clinton, who informed him that they were both expected in Fishkill to testify at the Enquiry.

"Tom, I know how busy you are with the West Point chain project, what with the raft-building at Murderer's Creek and the arrival of chain links. But the Enquiry is a command performance. You must be there."

When Lisa heard of the Enquiry and Tom's attendance, she said "I'm coming with you!"

"Lisa, my dear friend. Your enthusiasm impresses. But it's not contagious. This is not a public hearing. No one will be in the room beyond Members and witnesses. Here's my promise. I will attend as much as I can. And take notes. And, when it's finished, I will report on the proceedings. I will promise to omit nothing that an historian might find important, quirky or intriguing."

From West Point, where he had gone to pick the sites on either side of the river for attaching the chain, Tom travelled to New Windsor on the 28th, stopping at Smith's Tavern the night before, but not alone to pick up gossip and local news, for which that tavern had earned a far-flung and well-deserved reputation. Colonel Lamb was going to be staying the night at Smith's Tavern, on his way to testify at Fishkill, and had sent word to Tom to consider joining him there.

John Lamb sat alone in the Tavern's pub, cradling a brew when Tom entered. The morose expression on his face vanished on recognition of his fellow survivor, the "Artillery Engineer," as the Colonel was prone to call him, replaced by an uncommonly warm smile of recognition.

"Tom! You managed. What a pleasure. Here, dust off that coat and take a seat. What will it be: mulled cider or Smith's brew?"

"You look well, John. I'll warm up with the cider. We must speak of the Enquiry, but, of course, there's more ground we could cover on that subject than hours in the night."

The pub was simply a bar occupying a corner of the Tavern's ground floor, with stools and some tables salted in a semi-circle around a high, open and notably shallow fireplace, which defeated the risk of smoke drifting into the room with an impressive draft powered by a chimney extending far above roofline. The only light came from a bright flame of oak logs. Their frequent flickering would have lent a conspiratorial feeling to the scene, but for the loud buzz of boisterous talk by patrons, punctuated by frequent bursts of laughter. Every seat was taken.

"I know you're still heavily engaged with the new chain. But no smell of tar tonight. I keep forgetting your first try never got a fair test. Do you think it would have held?"

"In truth, I have no idea. The point was to avoid the test of a fleet crashing into it under full sail with strong tide and following wind. Shore batteries and our ships were always expected to play the role of slowing, and perhaps stopping, the onrushing ships before they hit the chain. Clinton's attacks changed everything. Washington, you know, warned repeatedly that an attack by land could defeat the whole plan. But, what am I telling you. All of this you know well."

"Our General was right. And now we assemble to cast blame. A sticky business."

"This pub's getting crowded. We should lower our voices."

"Better yet, let's move to that small table near the bar. The noise there will drown us out."

When seated, Tom said, "You know something, in fact the chain did serve its purpose. And here begins the irony. The chain worked. It deterred the Royal Navy from attack by water. But it drove them to boldness by land. One given to the perverse in our struggles could conclude the chain caused the Forts' defeat."

John said, "Stop searching for ways to blame yourself. The historians will decide such things."

"I hear Washington appointed McDougall to take command of the North River Department, replacing Old Put. It looks to me like he already knows the answer the Enquiry will come up with and decided to act on it swiftly. It's close to a miracle that we still control the river, given the problems of leadership in the Highlands, and the continuing difficulties those in charge have had in picking the site for the new chain."

"Or appear to, as long as Howe refrains from sending his forces north. McDougall has some fascinating insights on our dilemma. We dined here last spring. At the time he was fixated on the question whether Howe would turn north or south. I know his fixation continues. He points out the extreme difficulty of penetrating the Enemy's design when he has command of the water. If Howe were for Philadelphia, wouldn't he post ships at King's Ferry, to interrupt our passage of troops south? Does his not doing so support the idea of a northern push to take control of the Hudson, since the more we move forces south, where they do no harm, the better. McDougall rejects this theory, arguing Howe would know we would see the posting as a beacon, illuminating his decision to take Philadelphia."

"Amazing these uncertainties persist, even after victory at Saratoga. But did McDougall reach a conclusion?"

"Yes, and I found it persuasive. He pointed to Hannibal. In waging war with the Romans, he didn't try to conquer the whole country. He went to Rome. McDougall believes Howe recognizes conquest of America is impossible. He intends for Rome, in hopes of creating panic and forcing negotiations."

They ordered dinner, and another round of drinks.

"So, McDougall sees Howe abandoning the established theory shared by both sides: British control of the Hudson could assure not just some negotiated settlement but outright victory. The Battles of Clinton and Montgomery point in one direction; Saratoga the other. Washington's urgency for defense of the river is greater now than before these battles. Perhaps, he doesn't share McDougall's reasoning."

"The Commander believes in paradox. Only by projecting mighty defenses along the river can he deter the Enemy from testing them, turning him south instead, to Philadelphia and beyond."

"Tell me about the Enquiry. For me, a new experience, one I don't look to with joy."

"First thing to remember, this investigation casts a questioning light only on the principal officers commanding the Forts. The second thing is simply to speak the truth, letting the chips fall where they may. No harm comes from honesty before a Court of Enquiry. Dishonesty, on the other hand, is risky business."

"I see a big difference between speaking truthfully of the facts and drawing conclusions from those facts. For myself, unless pressed hard, I suppose I will refrain from conclusions. I intend to point out that, from the end of July, when General Clinton left for Albany and his duties as Governor, nothing material was done at the Forts for their defense. That's a fact. And important. But, I do not intend to state my conclusion as to that fact."

"Understood. But, please, state it for me."

"Old Put let the Forts down badly. They were his to command. His responsibility to protect. Even more so with the Governor summoned away. He did nothing beyond making calls upon the woefully inadequate forces at the Forts to support his arms at Peekskill from imaginary threats. We probably won't hear it at the Enquiry, but disgust among survivors is widespread. Now, tell me, John, what you intend to say."

"Put's behavior in this Battle was a scandal, and I intend to convey that opinion to the Members, consequences be damned. Here's the truth. By 8 AM the Governor had a letter from Putnam, advising of intelligence to the effect that the Enemy had landed in force on the west side of the river. Advising, further, that he supposed they intended to attack the Forts and that, as soon as he was certain, he would send reinforcement."

"As soon as he was certain? What did that mean?"

"This sentence is incomprehensible. Lt. Inglis commanded the scouts sent out from Major Logan's party to watch the river below Dunderberg. I have spoken to him and also to Captain Rosicrans, who was part of the Logan party. Both say that, between dawn and sunrise on the 6th, they at first heard and later saw across the river at Verplanck's Point 40 boats full of men. The boats moved some two to three hundred yards along the shore and then came across the river to land at Stony Point. Obviously, if these men, from the west side of the river, could count the boats and see them full of troops on the east side, the fog must have begun to lift. Old Put and his men should have seen them too. And removed any uncertainty."

"The whole thing is inexplicably tragic."

"Indeed. The whole day passed before steps were taken, and of course, they were very modest steps that, in any case, came too late. Some said Putnam spent most of the day 'reconnoitering' at King's Ferry instead of preparing his troops to reinforce the Forts. Others have charged that he remained at the Robinson house in the morning hours. Whatever the facts are, he knew how weak were the forces at the Forts. And yet, and I bet you don't know this, on the day before the attack, Putnam ordered 50 men from the Forts to climb Anthony's Nose to prevent its possession by the Enemy!

"Putnam knew, or should have known, that the Peekskill post could not possibly be held if the Forts fell. Defending them was his chief, surpassing duty. He ignored that duty. If Lisa's story gleaned from her stay at Beverly is true, his failure was gross. Of course, what's really interesting, as you mentioned earlier, is Washington's jumping the gun on this Enquiry by putting McDougall in charge. Super-human eyes and ears.

"By the way, I'm not suggesting Old Put was traitorous. Just not the brightest candle in the room. Unsuspecting and highly susceptible, especially to women."

* * * * *

The Court of Enquiry began in Fishkill at Colonel Direck Brinkerhoff's office on March 30th, with all members present. Tom was the fifth to testify. When finished, he travelled to Murderer's Creek, returning on the fourth and final day of testimony, April 4th, when General Putnam submitted his version of the facts. Listening to Old Put, Tom couldn't avoid the impression that, after General Washington commandeered a significant portion of troops under Old Put's command in Peekskill, Old Put willed the defeat of the Forts and behaved in line with his worst fears. His letter of September 29th to John Hancock, President of the Congress, makes the point. With apparent pride in his misguided foresight, he read the letter at the outset of his testimony.

> The Post is of as much Importance as any upon the Continent and I will exert myself to the utmost, for its defense, weakened as it is. But permit me to tell you Sir, that I will not be answerable for its Safety, with the strength left me against the force, I am sensible the enemy can and I believe will, speedily send against it.

The most condemning part of Old Put's testimony was his dismissal of the warnings he received early on the morning of the

6th, to the effect that the enemy had landed on the west side of the river near Dunderberg. He claimed he doubted the account because the source was a Tory and the morning so foggy it would be hard to see boats on the river. This testimony was directly contradicted by Old Put himself in the letter he had written to Governor Clinton early enough that morning for the Governor to receive it at Fort Montgomery by 8 AM. That's the one where he acknowledged the enemy's true intentions and promised reinforcements.

My God, Tom thought, recalling this was the letter John Lamb had mentioned over dinner. Tom listened, as Old Put continued, claiming the enemy had some 5500 at Verplanck's Point and on board ships and boats, and yet, in reconnoitering the morning of the 6th, there was no sign of them on the east side of the river, and he had been told they had gone over to the west near Dunderberg. If he didn't believe these sources, where did he imagine the enemy had gone? What did he imagine they had come up-river to do? Might it make sense to venture onto the river to find out? Tom tried to sympathize with Old Put, reminding himself of the forces Washington pried away from him. At the end of the proceedings, however, he felt deep disappointment in the Court, whose members seemed to be giving Old Put a pass. Again and again, they missed the easy chance to ask the hard question.

* * * * *

In mid-April, Tom and John Lamb were heading out for supper, when they got word from one of his staff that General McDougall was in town and hoping to catch them both for supper. They met in Bedon's. The General had chaired the three-person Court of Enquiry into the loss of Forts Clinton and Montgomery. His purpose in meeting with Tom and John, as he put it, was to discuss the evidence adduced at the Enquiry.

After ordering the night's special of black bean soup, corn beef and cabbage, and a strange aspic the chef had concocted from oranges, the General put aside small talk. He seemed in a hurry. First, he explained why, when the Court's Report was submitted to General Washington on April 5, 1778, he didn't join the others in signing. Pressing duties had prevented him from studying all the evidence. He knew then he had much to add to the Report, but was in no position to do all that he wanted.

"My colleagues were open to signing a second draft, if I would prepare one, but much time passed before I could do the proper task of research. Now I have, and am looking for time to write out my thoughts. In the meantime, knowing you both were actually there, in the battle, and admiring your probity, I wanted to test my conclusions against your better judgments. And, let me start by saying I now intend to sign the report submitted to his Excellency, but observe that it is woefully incomplete."

John said, "we welcome this surprise, a most pleasant one. Both of us were deeply distressed by the Enquiry's outcome. We look forward to your thoughts."

"So, I have a rather long list of what I call findings. Allow me to read them. And, by all means, stop me at any time.

1. Putnam received advice from Parsons on 9/25 of Clinton's intention to come up in force to attack the Forts.
2. Notwithstanding this advice, no council of war held till after loss of Forts, no Cannon-firing signal or smoke relays established to warn of enemy advance.
3. Detachments in other posts not called in to succor Forts.
4. Public stores not removed from Continental Village on the 6th.
5. The enemy made no advance from Verplanck's Point to Peekskill on or before 10/6 nor did it make any demonstration on the afternoon of 10/6 to land at Peekskill or other place on east side.
6. A landing at Peekskill or further north was more likely for enemy if bent on gaining the Highlands from the east side, or to destroy stores at Continental Village, because it was a shorter route by six miles than from Verplanck's Point.
7. Enemy ships aiding the enemy attack on the Forts must have passed Peekskill early in afternoon of 10/6 and could not have done so unobserved if any lookout had been established.

8. The firing at Doodletown, Fort Clinton and on the Furnace Road between noon and 2 PM must have been heard in Peekskill and Continental Village.

9. At least by 2 PM on 10/6, and probably earlier, the known and knowable actions of the enemy determined his object to be the Forts."

That's my current list. It's likely to get longer."

Tom stared at the General. "I don't think either of us would quarrel with any of these findings. For Old Put, they are as devastating as they are true. It is very misleading for our leaders to conclude, as I fear to be the case, that the Forts were lost not from any fault, misconduct or negligence of the commanding officers, but solely through the want of adequate force."

"I agree with that. I think my findings point the finger of fault at Old Put. Let it be. I see the duty I owe to the Country to require their submission into the record."

John said, "I've been hearing many things about Old Put of late. Perhaps knives are coming out to get even with him for old insults. But all I hear is bad. In Boston, he was described by one militiaman who watched him riding back and forth along our lines, shock of white hair flowing, as being unfit for anything but fighting. After the Breed's Hill battle, John Stark called him a poltroon. Now we know these early soundings were on to something."

They finished their meals well before the extensive discussion of the General's findings ended. The General took his leave.

"Gentlemen, thank you for putting up with this one-sided talk. Your thoughts were valuable, and reinforcing. I know you both are engaged at the moment, and you, Tom, in particular, working night and day to chain West Point. I apologize for monopolizing our evening together. I can be a listener. In time I promise to return for an evening devoted to your projects."

18

FROM NEW WINDSOR TO WEST POINT

The last ox-train to deliver parts of the chain left Sterling Lake before dawn on March 20, a cold and cloudless day promising sunshine and warming conditions throughout. It consisted of six sledges, each drawn by two yoked oxen and carrying about half a ton of iron, consisting of the last links, clevises, pins and swivels on order. With each teamster was a militiaman well-armed but noticeably less on edge than those accompanying the first shipment.

Peter Townsend saw the draymen and their guards off with champagne and toasts all around. The pump having been primed by the boss, it took the draymen little imagination to conjure a visit to one of the taverns along the well-travelled central valley, now covered with a foot or so of corn snow. Progress was good—so good, in fact, that there ensued an over-night stay at Smith's Tavern and from there, on the 21st, like bees on a binge in springtime, the men had moved from Galloway's to June's to Earl's, collecting ale as workers gather pollen until, so weighted down with the stuff, they could stomach not another drop. By the time the train reached its destination at Murderer's Creek, both draymen and militia were high as the turkey buzzards soaring above. Only the sober, clear-thinking oxen, being so familiar with every inch of the route that they could have traversed it without human guidance, saved the trip from turns missed or drays overturned at the many dangerous spots along the way.

So delighted was Tom Machin with the arrival, at first he failed to notice the mass intoxication. This condition became obvious when the men began to dismount the drays. Some fell, others, having put foot to ground, staggered as if walking were new to them, stumbling off to pee behind the nearest tree.

Tom had planned a celebration with fresh donuts and hot mulled cider. When word came of the train's approach, he had the refreshments nicely arranged on an outdoor table. The lumberjacks and artificers joined in loud cheers to greet the arrivals. Sadly for Tom, the response to this exuberant welcome was strangely subdued for men having completed the last of close to one hundred trips lugging chain parts from Sterling Forge to New Windsor. But not strange to anyone following their last exuberant journey.

When, finally, Tom grasped the men's woeful condition, he ordered the cooks swiftly to add hot coffee to the table's fare. It was a case of too little too late, and he knew it.

About half of the men turned away from the table, wobbling insecurely to their bunkbeds inside a large barn. The others, perhaps having been less indulgent at the taverns, or because they had greater tolerance, ravaged the offerings with gusto, filling their mouths with one donut after another and washing them down with the hard cider Tom had insisted upon, a decision he now privately lamented. Then, this contingent staggered off to sleep somewhere in the barn, but not before peeing or puking (or both) in the snow-covered weeds along the way. The celebration was over almost before it started.

* * * * *

Raft assembly at Murderer's Creek consumed the lumberjacks and artificers for the whole of March. Tom had searched everywhere for the obvious tools of the trade to handle the trees and then the logs they would become, both on land and during their trip down river to West Point. Axes, of course, they had, each one belonging to a particular woodsman, with its hickory handle hung right for its owner. And where there was an axe, there too could always be found an oilstone. But he needed other tools in quantity. Locating them was a challenge. From hand-hook, to pike-pole, from cant-hook to hoading hooks, whipsaw and adze, many of each were necessary to get the work done.

As the sun's presence increased and the temperature warmed, the ice began to melt. Tom felt the days slipping away toward spring. He got the crews to start with the break of day. More important, he sought to capture their minds. To get them all to share with him, but really, as he put it, "with our Commanding General's whole army and all the patriots of this country," the urgency of getting the chain down to West Point and installed before the river became navigable.

"The enemy is itching to sail up river, as they did last October, after cutting the Montgomery chain. You remember the plunder and destruction the enemy fleet caused all the way up to Esopus and Kingston. Ten warships and a thousand troops they sent. All that restrains them from doing it again, with even more ships and men, is the ice. And it will soon enough melt away. We must be ready with boom and chain to stop them. If we fail, it will be far worse for us than swimming nude in parade before our commanding general when the tide goes out."

Throughout the winter months, and even into the early days of March, the bone chilling cold registered with anyone within ear-shot, for the sound of expanding ice cracking echoed from the Highlands on both sides of the river day and night. Tom's camp at Brewster's Forge on Murderer's Creek was well within range of the oft-heard booms, the absence of which was the direct cause of his alarm. Mid-way through the month, the unmistakable sound of expanding ice ceased. It foretold of ice melting.

On the 22nd of March, Colonel Lamb went to Brewster's to find Tom and deliver some news.

"He's done it, Tom. As you wished. Just last week, your Commander-in-Chief informed Old Put that he was relieved of command. General McDougall is taking over. Ever reluctant to remove officers from command, especially when their misconduct is grounded in want of capacity, as he believed, our leader pinned the decision on 'prejudice of the people,' who, he opined, would no longer support Old Put. He suggested the General's time might be better applied to preparing for the court of enquiry."

"Better news I could not imagine. We, I suppose, are prominent among those 'people' with 'prejudice.' Especially me. On the engineer question, alas, things will probably get worse before, with McDougall in charge, they get better. De la Radiere has returned, with Washington's urging, and has begun fighting with Kosciuszko again. He's an ever-growing menace. General Parsons called me down to West Point to work with Kos on various construction and defense projects that are woefully behind schedule. However, the good news is that, in proceeding with the chain, I ignore him and he ignores me. So far, this mutual turning of backs is working."

"Here's another bit of hard to believe gossip. Some say so thick is the wool de la Radiere has pulled down over our supreme leader's eyes that he passed on to Congress the Frenchman's claim that 'his honour and the Public Interest' had been impugned by Putnam and Kosciuszko."

Tom threw down the cant-hook he had in his hand, crying out in despair: "Oh God, spare us. Radiere wouldn't recognize the public interest if it stood an inch away from him in bright sunlight."

"But fear not, Tom. McDougall is empowered. A man of action who knows a hawk from a handsaw. The Frenchie's days at the Point are numbered."

By mid-March, the ice began to break up where Murderer's Creek empties into the Hudson, near to where Tom's rafts were being built. Across the river, the ice was starting to break and move with the tide. The huge work of assembling the boom, the rafts and the chain and stapling the chain to the rafts in readiness to be floated down to West Point had been finished in the first week of April. The weather had turned warm by March 20th, and continued, spring-like, into April, advancing break-up in the river to the point where Tom deemed it possible, on April 7th, to take down the newly fashioned parts of the boom. The parts made for Fort Montgomery and never used were already waiting assembly at West Point. Getting the logs down would be far easier than the rafts and chain, but, still, moving 250 or more logs was not child's play.

Looking at the assembled boom, Tom was shocked by the immense scale of the long, thick logs connected by links of chain at either end. Shocked, despite having been the one to create the specifications. Yes, he now was sure, they would absorb all that a ship of the line could deliver. He had gathered a 40-man team consisting mostly of riverhogs, all rugged men with weathered faces covered in hair, and wearing the riverman's uniform of gray pantaloons, red flannel shirts, long boots and woolen covering for their heads. The remainder of this crew consisted of somewhat more than a handful of lumberjacks and artificers claiming water skills and evidencing an overpowering enthusiasm to be involved in the climax to months of brutally demanding work. They met to discuss the project on April 5th.

Before Tom could begin, one of the hogs shouted out, "Boom or chain, which first? For me, the boom, just to test the waters. Ha! Ha!"

"You're right there. Boom it is. For that reason and another. The boom will be below the chain, and so we must string the boom first. Now, we have ten oared bateaux. Each should be manned by two of you. The others will ride the logs, well-spaced. We will rope some of the logs together in clusters of ten, allowing each of those traveling by log to have a ten-foot wide platform from which to help steer the boom and keep it well behaved. You should divide yourselves up to fill these different posts."

"Do you have paddles for those on the logs?"

"We have swept the villages for paddles and, now, have enough, together with the long oars some of you scullers will be using."

"How long will the trip take, do you reckon?"

"The distance is somewhere between four and five miles. We must fit into the tidal pattern. We will have to move the boom to river's edge and tie it fast each time the tide turns against us. That's every six hours. And we're not going to try to move in the dark. I expect the trip will take up to three days. Be rested and ready for early departure day after tomorrow, with johnny cake enough and other provisions to keep you going through the day. And sleeping gear packed. Other meals will be handled by our kitchen staff, if they can find us along the way."

A hog in the back of the crowd yelled, "A not so easy task with that huge mountain between us and West Point."

"A joke. Have no fear. We should think of this trip as a landmark in our war for independence. The hinge that opens the way to victory. Yours is a river trip to stop the British. To win the war by blocking their mighty armada. It's easy to lose the thread that binds us all together. Never forget the high purpose to which you have committed yourself.

"The effort expended in the past two months by our lumberjacks—those bushrangers and timber cruisers, as they call themselves, was immense. To get us to this point. An achievement beyond measure to describe. In contrast, this trip with the boom should feel like a frolic."

"Not just a frolic, a boon!" someone shouted, triggering laughter all around.

"Yes, you put a fine point on it. But now it's your turn, all you river hogs."

One of the hogs interrupted Tom. "Good rivermen are born, not made. By what right do these woodsmen and artificers join our playground?"

"They have proved themselves in the forests and at river's edge. They will do so again on the river. They have the balance, judgment and quickness you want. Tree sense and river sense are two peas from the same pod. Mark my words, you will need them and be happy they are with you. And fear not, when it's over there will be enough praise to swell every heart.

"Now, we will bivouac each night and our cooks will fill us up with pork, beef, cabbage and turnips, with rum enough to wash it down. And shad too if they've started their run upriver. And maybe sturgeon, and even roe. Those not on this trip will dearly wish they had been. You're the lucky ones. The chosen."

As the loggers sculled the logs out into the Hudson, on a sunlit morning in April, the river-scape to the south invoked awe even in the thickest head among the jaded river hogs herding the convoy to West Point. The river seemed to drop from sight through giant portals on either side, more like the backs of welcoming elephants facing away from the waters than the threatening Scylla and Charybdis that Odysseus faced. Along both shorelines, the pastel greens of Spring caught every eye, the unfolding of countless leaves, from birch and dogwood in the understory to towering oak, maple, tulip and sycamore above. The sun, now two fingers above the mountain on the east, subdued the colors beneath while polishing the ones below the mountain on the west.

Tom experienced this scene with an upward spiritual tug beyond the often emotional response to music he could recognize even before it started to wash his eyes, as often it did, whether in sadness or joy or just in recognition of beauty. Now, he considered the war— his purpose for being on the river— and the contrast between it, a purely man-made thing, and the scene set out before him, so pure a thing of Nature. This river and the mountains through which it ran had been there long, long before the war began and would be there long after the war concluded. To him, this moment bracketed two sides of eternity. Did these thoughts diminish the war's importance? Was it, at best, a triviality in the larger scheme of things? As tears washed his face and dried, he could not answer this question except to hope it was not so.

It took four days to reach West Point, where in a cove beneath Fort Clinton that immediately became known as Chain Battery Cove, they parked the boom, stretching it out along the river's edge. Large rock cribs had already been built and filled with stone in readiness to become the land "anchors" for the chain and boom on both sides of the river.

They arrived with a favorable tide about noon. Impatiently, they awaited the downstream flow to abate. Sensing the collective frustration with even a minute's delay, having worked so hard for so long to reach this moment, at the edge of success, Tom urged one final bout of patience.

When the tide slacked, they pulled the boom across the river. On the west side, they had fixed it by clevis to a long chain which had clevises spaced between the links to allow a temporary opening for friendly ships to pass. It was attached both to the rock crib and a capstan on shore. This great spool fashioned of a single large log revolved around a central shaft and was pierced around its top by eight capstan bars, enabling eight strong men to tighten the boom. There was an identical capstan installed on the east side, which eight men turned to bring the boom to the curve across the water Tom had drawn for them on a flat rock, to guide their eye. When finished, the men burst forth with loud huzzas. With lungs filled with prideful exuberance, they chased one another, wildly racing across the boom to West Point and a celebration Tom, with cautious optimism, had previously set in motion. Leaving the capstan, Tom followed, picking his way with caution, mindful of the work still to be done and lacking the log-sense so deftly displayed by his riverhogs. Moving from log to log, he appreciated their octagonal shape and thrilled at the sight of the boom in full, imagining it an elegant necklace spanning the river, east to west. He was in awe of its immensity, of how fitting its placement, proportionate with the majesty of river and highlands.

The river hogs stayed overnight at the Point, amid layers of praise from the garrison over the achievement. The scene at mess was boisterous. Tom and his 40 stalwarts, dubbed by commanding General Parsons as 'Machin's Log Riders,' were toasted repeatedly. Strong spirits flowed freely from sources thoughtfully spaced around the cavernous hall in which they had gathered for supper.

Course after course followed. As General Parsons explained, the arrival of the boom, the expectancy of the chain and the prospect within days of having these obstacles to river traffic in place had ignited a blaze of excitement throughout the garrison, giving excuse to mount as great a feast as could have endowed any festival known to the galley staff. The feast offered quail, hare, venison, pork, chicken and beef as well as fresh fish from the Hudson, including striped bass, sturgeon and, by accident of timing, the much loved shad and its coveted roe. Freshly baked breads with olives or garlic appeared, with plates of butter. Other plates were piled high with pickles, aspic and diverse jellies. There were turnips, parsnips and early lettuce and green peas as well as normal out of season fare such

With lungs filled with prideful exuberance, they chased one another, wildly racing across the boom to West Point and a celebration Tom, with cautious optimism, had previously set in motion."

as white and black beans, cabbage from cold storage and sauerkraut from jars, and tomatoes put up last fall in the same way. And, for dessert, apple sauce and ginger bread with whipped cream in bowls for topping.

Back in New Windsor, Tom found Lisa waiting to welcome him with less pomp but beckoning expectation.

"You're the boss on the river. The town's awash in a loud whispers of your glorious trip. I want the story, in detail. But first to the tub. I'm the boss of the bedroom. You need a wash. Tub's full. Strip off those ugly rags and jump in. I'll follow, just to see to things."

He did as he was told, not even pretending to dislike being ordered about by the woman who shared this home. With speed, she undressed to follow him into the bath, sitting comfortably on his stomach, legs bent, feet neatly curled around his shoulders. She took a brush to his chest, the bristles tugging tenderly at his black hair, massaging his skin, propelling ripples of feeling to course through his body until they reached the soul. How much he loved being pampered.

Lisa knew her business. Before she met Tom, bath time with other men had become a practiced skill involving more than washing. When she felt the sign, a gentle nudge at the base of her spine, she was ready, hands on the sides of the tub to lift her up, her feet ready to push her back and, then, her own weight more than adequate to bring him inside her, where she intended to keep him until kingdom come—a period long and slow while tiny waves lapped, lapping gently against the sides of the tub.

Still wet, they threw themselves down on the bed. Lisa pressed Tom for his story, knowing he was better at looking forward than back, and that, only though her commanding presence had she been able to restrain him from using bath time to plan the next, and final, journey south with the tide.

"You know I have to be off early tomorrow. Let's have a bite while I talk. And then to bed. Oh, and by the way, did I say I love you. How short you'd fall in trying to imagine how much I love you for forcing me to accept your plan instead of mine. When wills collide, yours emerges victorious. Every time. Weaker sex? Don't try that one on me."

By sunrise, Tom was dressed, fed and nursing the dregs of his second cup of coffee.

"So, Lisa, final days in this long trek. I expect to see you at West Point within the week, enjoying the spectacle of 'Washington's Watch Chain.'"

"I only hear it called Captain Machin's chain. And so to me it shall be, always. Any farewell words?"

"Well, these river hogs, whom I learned to love, have a bunch of expressions, some even repeatable among lady-folk. So, they say 'we'll get the chain to West Point, *Come Hell or High Water.*' And '*It'll be As Easy As Falling Off A Log.*' I love them all. Really I do."

With that, Tom was off to Murderer's Creek and the shores of the Hudson River. With the boom, the scullers had been a key to maintaining direction. But the limited number of long oars proved a problem. Tom had ordered more oars made for the next voyage, with more scullers to wield them. With luck, they would keep the rafts aligned with the river and free to flow with the current. The other idea he had adopted from an old river hog, who had grown impatient with the tidal delays between downstream movement with the boom. It was at dusk each night to have the bushrangers build bonfires along the banks of the Hudson, on both sides, to cast light on the water sufficient to continue the trip when the tide cooperated, even at nighttime.

Using more experience and intuition than engineering skill, Tom decided to bring the rafts downstream in five units of 15 rafts each. Each raft had chain links loaded and pinned down in place. Peter Townsend had made five clevises with pins to connect the five separate parts of chain when time came to string the chain across the river, and a number of extra ones to use as needed to connect the chain ends to the cables used on the capstans. Tom assigned ten rivermen to each unit, equipped with long oars, pike-poles, toggle chains if needed to hold any wayward logs in place, and plenty of bread, cheese, johnny cake and water. Of course, many brought their own libation, mainly strong-bodied rum, and therein lay a danger. Even with spiked boots and years of experience, a riverman with rum in his tummy could lose enough judgment, balance and quickness to turn triumph into disaster. Tom had urged the crews to put the alcohol aside until they arrived at West Point, but experience with the first trip, before which he made the same speech, suggested his words would again be ignored.

The river hogs blessed his suggestion that 15 rafts spanning up to 300 feet could be managed. Trying for more would be dangerous not just to the rivermen but the whole enterprise. There were no spare links.

Tom picked among his team what he believed the ten best hogs to show the way on the first string of rafts. Perhaps they were the best, but, like all river hogs, they thought they were, and with confirmation from the Captain, they allowed their imagined skills to overtake reality.

Although Tom had planned an early morning departure, one hold-up after another caused the day, April 16, 1778, to pass close to dusk before the tide was again flowing downstream, enabling the first string of rafts to pole away from the river's edge.

The rest shoved off at 20-minute intervals. Tom was aboard the last to leave. As darkness slowly descended over the river, bonfires appeared on both sides, building in size to cast shadows that flickered as if giant crowds of fireflies had gathered on the shores.

The winning scullers selected for the first string of rafts were ebullient finally to be out on the river, moving in the swift current. Aided by a following wind from the northwest, they were speeding along at 3 miles per hour. The wind was cold. In defense, they turned to their stashes of rum. Feeling happy from head to foot, they began to splash their crewmates, the water shockingly cold. Such fun were these now tipsy heroes having that no one noticed the three pointed logs sheathed with iron beaks sticking a foot or so out of the water as the rafts drew near Pollepel Island, wayward reminders of the *Chevaux-de-Frise* that Captain Machin had installed much earlier in the year. The logs were supposed to be slightly submerged and pointing at a forty-five degree angle downstream, but these three, lodged in a sunken frame of 40-foot logs filled with stones, had somehow moved with the tides to become visible and unexpectedly to be leaning upstream, despite the flow.

A raft near the middle of the string hit two of the iron beaks hard, jarring the whole string and its occupants. The raft came apart as the beaks held for seconds before giving way to the powerful force of the tide-driven string and submerge, now pointing downstream. A cry was heard as an unlucky sculler lost his footing and fell on top of the third iron beak, which was passing between rafts, untouched by them or the chain.

Flickers from the flames on either side of the river cast imperfect light on the scene, but enough for the sculler's mates to see the gruesome accident and realize there was nothing to be done. Twisting to escape, he succeeded only in driving the beak further into his body, his cries loud and urgent at first, then slowly dropping in volume until only moans of resignation could be heard. Then silence.

On shore, some of the lumberjacks heard and saw the same scene. Using the double-ended bateau they had tied up near the bonfire they were tending, and would use to move downstream building fires as they went, four of them rowed out to the impaled sculler. Too late to save him, they were able to tie up to the log below the sculler's body. The iron beak now protruded several inches beyond the sculler's stomach. They lifted him up to clear the beak and placed him gently, as if he were still alive, on the bottom of the bateau. At one of the men's suggestion, a white cloth was tied onto the iron beak.

"It looked like a frigging crucifixion," the hog whispered.

They had just finished their appalling work when the second string of rafts appeared. The story quickly told, the lumberjacks returned to shore, where, as custom dictated, they removed the sculler's spiked boots and hung them on the lowest branch of a large black oak, where they would remain visible to boat traffic for many moons to come.

The tide turned against Tom's rafts about 2 AM. The strings gathered on the west side, using toggle chains to hold the five together for the next six hours. Word of the sculler's end traveled like lightning through the crews, now beyond sober in imagining

*Twisting to
escape, he
succeeded only
in driving the
beak further
into his body...*

257

a death outside the realms of nightmare. Each one of them knew what happened to Alonzo Weyant June, a natural-born river man accomplished at sculling, could have happened to him.

There were no other accidents. The raft broken from impact was repaired. The remainder of the trip took a bit more than two days. The first string of rafts reached the shoreline at Chain Battery Cove around noon on April 30, 1778. Using cables tied on shore the men undertook to slow and then control the rafts, which were propelled by strong tide and heavy weight toward New York City. The objective was to nestle them along the shoreline awaiting the other strings and the ebb tide needed to assemble and install the chain.

"Stopping the rafts is the hardest thing we've ever done. Can't believe it," shouted the crewman on shore who was trying to stop a cable wrapped around the truck of a large oak from slipping. "Like reining in a racehorse," another of the crew exclaimed, coming to help hold the cable. And then Ephraim Vaughn, who was more scientifically schooled than the others and found no shame in displaying that fact, explained, as Tom had done too many times, Newton's First Law of Motion. Before he could finish saying "Newton," a cry rose from the rest of the men. One shouted "Heard it before." Another, "Go bugger yourself, Ephie."

Exhausted, the crew members were a happy lot. Splayed out on shore or rafts, they awaited the arrival of the other strings and, aboard the fifth, their leader, Captain Machin. As string followed string, excitement among the men grew. Within 90 minutes, all rafts were accounted for, each string lashed to another, the whole reminding Tom of a hive full of honey. Just as the hive is the product of skill, dedication and work beyond reckoning by numberless worker bees, so too the rafts and the trees used to fashion them, the chain links and the foundries, ore and charcoal used to forge them, the sledges and oxen used to transport them, and the numberless men of high skill and dedication, who toiled over nine frantic weeks to bring into being the weapon of defense now held fast at Chain Battery Cove—this 'hive' Tom admired with a rough blend of astonishment and pride.

Anticipation along the west side of the river continued to build, abetted by the Continentals stationed at West Point, who to a man had come to witness what all sensed was a big moment for the United States, one that could change the course of the war, one for the books of history yet to be written.

The tide continued hard downstream. The hogs grew increasingly restless. The arrival on shore of the lumberjacks responsible for the bonfires only added fuel to the emotional fires and many of the woodsmen joined their river colleagues on the rafts, determined to be among those who would complete the job.

Tom addressed the men.

"Looking out among you, and at the wonder of these 75 rafts and their precious cargo of iron links, I feel awed at all that you have done. And I understand your eagerness to finish the job. I know how impatient you are, for so too am I. But, while there are many aspects of nature we can control, the tides are not among them. Not yet. So we must wait for our moment of glory, just as we did with the boom. It won't be long in coming, for the tides are regular, and this one will be spent within the next 30 minutes.

"Here's how I handle my impatience. Perhaps it will serve to divert yours too. This uncommon moment is one to dwell on for a lifetime. It ought to be stretched out, prolonged, devoured in slow motion, minute by minute, so that today's memories remain in our brains, stuck there like glue for a lifetime."

In preparation for the arrival of slack tide, the portions of chain on each of the five strings of rafts had been connected by the clevises, their pins driven home with sledge hammers.

Finally, the downstream flow ended. Tom marked the moment with a cry.

"Now's the moment. Not a minute to waste. Take her across."

Using long oars and every bateau available, the men moved the 1500-foot string of rafts across the river, west to east, from the huge stone crib between Horn Point and Love Rock to the equally large crib on Constitution Island. A capstan on each side was turned by eight of Tom's tough lumberjacks, shirtless in proud display of their impressive physiques, tightening the chain, and the rafts with it, which, notwithstanding the weight of the chain, were still just buoyant enough to allow waters to slosh over them without causing them to sink. The chain arched just upstream of the boom, appearing to Tom like a second necklace, adorning the beautiful dark waters of the Hudson as two sparkling diamond necklaces might adorn the beautiful white neck of a patriotic lady.

When the sledge-driven pin of the clevis connecting the final link to the cable wrapped around the capstan on Constitution Island was finally seated, a cheer began as the capstans turned and grew in volume as the chain tightened. When Tom signaled the job was done, the cheer turned to shouts from the water's edge and the heights of West Point far above. Although the rafts were separated by six feet, the river hogs on Constitution Island began running from raft to raft, stepping on the chain links sitting in the waters between rafts just long enough to leap forward onto the next link and then the next raft. Hoops of laughter accompanied the rivermen, none of whom fell. The lumberjacks, no less bold but lacking the honed balance of river hogs, attempted the crossing too and, to a man, accomplished it, but not without many slips, falls and splashes along the route, providing fodder to amuse those watching from the West Point shore.

Tom rowed back in a bateau containing the remaining members of his crew, those who were exhibiting prudence, exhaustion, injury or who knows what. Tom congratulated them. "For your wisdom in joining me, rest assured wise ones, I will tolerate no effort to tease or shame."

Celebrations were planned for the evening, built around a feast comparable to the one offered when the boom was strung across the river, and would include music, dancing and spirited beverages. At Tom's insistence, the celebration was preceded by a burial service for Alonzo Weyant June. On his orders, a grave had been dug by garrison personnel while the chain was being strung, and just before supper, a large gathering of Tom's crew and almost all of the Continentals stationed at West Point gathered at the grave, sited beneath a large Chestnut Oak somewhat removed from the parade ground but, by dint of being closer to the river, having a view of the chain, something Tom had included in his directions for picking the site.

Tom's eulogy was brief.

"We started this mission of delivery with a crew of 40. Thirty-nine remain, gathered here to pay tribute to the only man lost to the effort, Alonzo Weyant June, an accomplished river man of many years' experience, a man dedicated to his craft and skilled at it, a man of honor and humor, a man beloved by his colleagues, one who will be sorely missed by all who knew him. He gave his life in service to the cause of freedom and independence. A cause we all serve. A cause we willingly would follow to the grave as Alonzo did."

While having purged from his mind the stories of Jesus' resurrection and all its trappings as if they were baby teeth to be ejected from his mouth, Tom remained appreciative of the Bible for its human values. For example, he saw no need for the existence of God for humans to advance and live by the Golden Rule. And, so, surprising as it was for a non-believer, Tom summoned forth a selection from the Bible he had been required to memorize as a child:

"'In the sweat of thy face shalt thou eat bread, till thou return unto the ground; for out of it wast thou taken: for dust thou art, and unto dust shalt thou return.' Alonzo, may you rest in peace.

"And for those standing here, as you celebrate the mighty accomplishment of this day—by which you have denied the enemy's navy access to the Hudson and most assuredly established a major turning point in our battle for freedom—please remember Alonzo and his contributions. May the luck that ran out for him, for you continue apace far into the future."

* * * * *

On the first of May, after the excitement of installation and celebration had tapered off, Tom and Lisa returned to New Windsor. But not before Tom gave the chain and boom a final check to be sure all was well. He had watched closely when the current was at its peak, flowing first south and then north. The waters were washing over, through and around the rafts with little apparent drag. Neither chain nor boom appeared under enormous strain.

Returning from his last inspection, he gave Lisa a "thumbs up."

"My friend, you have much to feel proud of."

At home in New Windsor, they found a letter from Henry Knox, advising that he expected to arrive on May 10th, with his wife and daughter arriving from Boston on the 11th. He promised a grand reunion before leaving with his family on the 14th. Time enough, he hoped, to see the chain. Almost as an afterthought, he added some startling news:

"I suppose you've heard by now of our treaty with France recognizing the independence of these United States. We paraded here amidst much rejoicing. I was ordered by our Commander-in-Chief to fire 13 big guns. We expect the French to bring us ships and troops to supplement the arms they've been sending. Dined with the Commander that evening. He showed great happiness, even unbending enough to tell a couple of jokes at table and to play cricket with our junior officers after supper. It's a new day!"

"Indeed it is," said Tom, upon reading Henry's final paragraph. "News travels slowly, if at all, in this backwater. If France follows through, the war's won."

"But will they? Haven't we been disappointed by promises unkept?"

"Yes, but now, with recognition, their role is out in the open and can be pursued with vigor. Their reputation's on the line. Very hopeful."

Lisa sent word to John Lamb, telling the news and inviting him to dinner on the 12th.

Tom and Lisa were witnesses to the joyous reunion of the Knox family, when on the 11th, Lucy Flucker Knox and her daughter, Lucy, arrived by carriage. Henry and Lucy corresponded constantly when apart, but that loving connection through words was no substitute for the hugs and kisses that followed hard on the opening of the door, through which little Lucy raced ahead of her mother to be swept up in the large arms of her father and almost crushed against his enormous chest and protruding paunch.

Henry entered Washington's forces as a man large in all respects. As the war continued, he grew not only in his Commanding General's estimation but in weight as well, adding pounds to his body as the war added months to its duration. Lucy put it well when they were last together, in Boston, "About this war and your weight. They can't continue in tandem. Something's got to give."

Henry was given to excesses in the letters he penned to Lucy, trying to make up for his absence, and overcome, if possible, the anxieties Lucy lived with daily in imagining the dangers of battle. He begged her "to believe me to love you as much as is possible for a Mortal to do."

After putting his daughter down beside him, he greeted his wife without words but with unabashed emotion, demanding her lips and holding them in a lusty kiss that to his rapt audience seemed to have no end. Until it did. Only then would he allow Tom and Lisa to welcome the two Lucys. "Most certainly an appealing man who hasn't lost his large appetites," Lisa whispered to Tom after showing the Knox family their room.

John Lamb arrived early for dinner, eager, it seemed, to have as much time as possible with his esteemed friend Henry Knox. He found the General sitting in the small living room, on a loveseat with his wife, whose hand he was holding like one clutching a life preserver. Nearby was Tom, playing "trot, trot to Boston" with little Lucy, who bounced up and down in pleasure, astride his knees. He looked more captivated than she.

"Here's a most happy scene. And not only because the French are with us," John said, obviously having found the news a splendid surprise.

Lisa said, "We're serving claret, if you find that acceptable. Make yourself comfortable. I'm putting the finishing touches on supper."

"How fortunes change," Henry said. "Six weeks ago, in Boston, I received a letter from Nate Greene, reporting on desperate conditions at Valley Forge. Troops almost naked, without meat for seven days and without bread for several more. Despite some relief, he said the patience and moderation of the troops had run out. They came before their officers to state, in humility, that they were starving and could continue in camp no longer. At that moment, some relief came, averting disbandment. But starving they were. And the horses too, hundreds having already starved to death. He had written for advice on taking the post of Quartermaster, an assignment being urged upon him by Congress and the Commander-in-Chief."

"How did you respond?" Lisa asked.

"Accept. The post needed someone with his set of skills. But I drifted away from my point. With the speed of summer lightning, fortunes change. France recognizes us, sends ships, men and material. The sinews of war. And with that news, the morale of even starving troops at Valley Forge can be restored; and with it the will to survive and fight another day. The blessings of our Father, who art in Heaven, have turned this war on its head."

"Emphatically, I concur," said John.

Tom said, "After Trenton and Saratoga, I never doubted we'd defeat the British. How long it would take, that was unknowable. And still is. But now, perhaps, the day of victory is closer at hand."

"But not as close as Supper, which is on the table. Please come. I've rigged a sort of high chair for young Lucy, who insists on sitting next to Tom. Something's going on there. Tom looks smitten, and not by me."

During supper, for the first time in his life, Tom considered marriage and the creation of a family for himself. Of course, he had often thought about these natural events, but only as they occurred to others. Looking around the room, Tom considered Henry's marriage to Lucy and little Lucy, the radiant product of that union, as often he had done before when they were together. But as applied to himself, never until this moment. That was, he thought, something for later. It was little Lucy who turned him inward. Tom knew he was of an age when the tide starts to flow out. If ever he were to have a family, it suddenly dawned on him, it should be soon because time wasn't on his side or that of the woman who would bear him an offspring. For that woman, he then knew, watching her at the other end of the table, would be Lisa, and she was close in age to him.

Once embarked on this train of thought, it filled his mind for as long as the Knox family rested in New Windsor. As swiftly as the fortunes of Washington's army turned with French recognition, so did Tom's approach to marriage and family change. The more he thought about it, the more urgency he felt. Fears of missing out or failing filled his mind. He became obsessed, resolving to broach the matter with Lisa as soon as the Knox family left for Valley Forge.

On the 13th, Tom, Lisa and John escorted the Knox family to West Point, where they happened to arrive to examine the obstacles just as an ebbing tide reached its peak velocity.

"We are in luck, Henry. We can watch the chain under maximum strain. Watch how the waters assault the rafts, which, I'm relieved to see, are standing their ground."

Henry noticed the pointed ends of the logs.

"Good detail, Tom, to sharpen the logs like giant pencils. The water lacks much drag as it speeds toward New York, passing easily over, through and around."

"That alone could make the difference. Who knows? But the boom's holding well from the looks of it. You'll notice we gave it plenty of scope, thinking it might give way like a half-filled balloon when hit by an enemy ship, absorbing its energy and wasting it while at the same time putting the vessel in irons, to be bombarded by shore batteries."

"Gentlemen, do you recall that the Montgomery chain broke twice before, with the third try, after Tom applied some fairy dust, it held? This chain is a success from the start. So I ask, don't you wish for an enemy attack?"

Lisa wore a mischievous grin.

"I mean, how else will your theories get tested?"

John joined the argument. "You look fetching, Lisa, but I won't be sucked in. The enemy has been unsure about the river from the beginning. With Saratoga, less so. Now, with this double jeweled necklace that Tom has fashioned adorning the river, and word of that fact carried by spies to the city, who are known to exaggerate their reports to inflate their importance, I bet the true value of Machin's obstructions will be in discouraging the enemy from even attempting a break through."

Henry nodded. Tom looked disappointed and so did Lisa. Both yearned to know if it worked. But victory could come in two ways.

Returning exhausted to New Windsor, John went to his home and the others ate a small supper and went directly to bed. The Knox family made an early departure the next morning. Little Lucy had tears for Tom as he hugged her. Tears continued, washing her face and his as he lifted her into the coach. Goodbyes all around, before the pair of horses put the coach in motion.

Tom knew the time had come. Finding Lisa cleaning up in the kitchen, he asked her to sit with him to talk over an idea. It was unlike him to have planned a discussion ahead of time. Surprised and curious, she had no hint of his agenda.

"What's going on? You look more anxious than when the first chain broke."

"Let's finish off the coffee," he said, half-filling two cups and carrying them to the dining room table.

Once seated, Lisa said, "So, out with it."

Tom was gripping his cup with both hands, as if to stop it from flying away. He leaned over to her, put one hand on the back of her head and, with a gentle kiss on the cheek, said, "I'm asking you to marry me."

He pulled out from the chair next to him an impressive bouquet of cherry blossoms, cut from the tree in his back yard, and offered them to her, accompanied by these few words:

"With these blossoms, I do intend thee to wed, as soon as arrangements can be made."

She took the bouquet from him and put it on the table between them.

"How lovely. Have you lost your mind?"

He thought it possible she'd want to ponder the idea, that they'd talk it over before, inevitably, she'd accept. But never a response so harsh. He recoiled in pain.

They stared at each other, searching for clues.

Recovering, he answered.

"We have been together through good times and hard. We are a team, a good one that loves and works together very well. We can, and should, expand that team with offspring, and that entails marriage. I can't imagine you don't share these thoughts. I should have remembered that, often, the first things out of your mouth aren't really the things you mean to say. Upon reflection."

"Oh, my dear Captain Machin. We have a serious misunderstanding. Since you spoke directly, allow me to do so too. Speaking bluntly, but true to myself and consistent over many years, I loathe the institution of marriage. And equally motherhood, the idea of bearing children, yours or someone else's. These views might seem strange to you, although they shouldn't, for you had signals aplenty since we met that I hated being tied down, whether by my father, the magnetic pull of Convivial Hall, my family, or the men in my life who have come and gone. Just as we are fighting for independence from England, I have always fought for freedom from institutional entanglements, whether coming at me from the Church, the family or others. When they close in, as you've just done, I am driven to escape. I look for the door. I fear having my neck thrust into a yoke. For life. I know, it sounds crazy. But there's no right or wrong about it. It's just the way I am."

He saw his concrete plans turn into dreams that Lisa blew away like dust. Given his hopes for building a family, which grew firmer with her rejection of them, he knew they were going to part, this time for good. Forlorn, he would grieve over what might have been. He would question the path he had traveled, ignoring the pleasures that path had offered to dwell only on the final outcome. He would resolve to look elsewhere to achieve his new plan. And much later he would accept the idea that life is separated into chapters, each of which must be lived fully, taking the bad with the good, the pain with the pleasure, and savored to the end, for better or worse.

And Lisa? What would happen to her? He put the question.

"You might find this odd, but I actually have a plan. I just hadn't seen the right moment to tell you. You see, I wanted to be with you until the chain was successfully strung, but after that, I thought the time had come for us to go our separate ways. I am going to travel abroad, to France, a country I have never visited. With the French joining us in the war, I see a successful outcome just a matter of time. So my ambition to help is really not needed, if ever it was. I won't be writing or sharing my address. Better to just cut things off than linger. At least that's not my way.

He sat subdued, looking at her with respect.

"You are a great Patriot, Tom Machin. You have preserved the Hudson for Americans. No small feat. I know you will go on to more triumphs until the war ends. And I'm sure you will succeed famously in landing a wife and siring a family. Now, give me some help in planning my escapade to France. For starters, with Howe in New York, from what port do I depart?"

* * * * *

In a letter of October 2, 1778, from Fishkill, New York, General Washington wrote Governor Clinton about Tom Machin: "Captain Machin has been employed since the year 1776 in the engineering Branch, without ever coming to any regular settlement for his Services. He does not choose to fix any price himself, and I am really ignorant of what is just and proper. You have been a witness of a good deal of his work, and he is willing to submit the matter to your decision."

By letter of October 3, 1778, from Poughkeepsie, Governor Clinton replied to General Washington:

"While I had the Command at the Works when Captain Machin was employed as Engineer, he was in that Capacity exposed to uncommon personal Labor and Fatigue, particularly in fixing the Chain and sinking the Frizes and frequently endangered his Health by working in the Water when it was floating with Ice."

What price to put on the twice-successful task of chaining the Hudson to block the Enemy fleet? Records fail to disclose. The chain at Fort Montgomery was never tested before it was removed by the British from land after capturing Forts Montgomery and Clinton on October 7, 1777. The chain and boom at West Point were never tested either, and their presence may very well have deterred the British from even attempting to gain control of the Hudson. To the extent the British believed the chain and boom were capable of restraining a 850-ton British warship under full sail, they served to deter attack whether they would have survived the warship's strike or not. Spies who reported on the installation couldn't have avoided being impressed by the enormous scale of the obstacles and aware of their potential for repulsing the enemy.

At the time both British and Continental military planners were convinced that control of the Hudson would lead to victory. East of the river there was no flour. West of the river there was no meat. And the two areas needed to be free to communicate, to move forces and to move back and forth with foodstuffs, munitions, horses, tents, and other things essential for an army. Those military planners were right. Control of the Hudson was maintained by the Patriots. And control did, indeed, lead to victory. In this sense, one might fairly conclude that Captain Thomas Machin's contribution to American victory was so large as to extend beyond measure.

ABOUT THE AUTHOR

BEVIS LONGSTRETH is the author of four historical novels: *Spindle and Bow*, *Return of the Shade*, *Boats Against the Current*, and *Chains Across the River*. He is a retired partner of the international law firm, Debevoise & Plimpton, where he practiced for his entire legal career, except for Government service in Washington as a Commissioner of the Securities and Exchange Commission from 1981-84. He authored *Modern Portfolio Management and the Prudent Man Rule* (Oxford University Press 1987), a book arguing for interpretative change in the legal standard of care exercisable by fiduciaries responsible for other people's money to reflect current developments in finance economics. He lives in Manhattan, New York with his wife, Clara, and their dog, McKenzie. They have three children and nine grandchildren.

See *bevislongstreth.com* for further information about the author and his writings.

ACKNOWLEDGMENTS

In writing an essentially fictional account of Captain Thomas Machin, an actual figure of importance to the American Revolution, I attempted at all times to surround the fictional parts of this novel with the most accurate historical facts that research could reveal. To accomplish this goal, libraries were essential and the professional librarians who facilitated my access to their treasures were extraordinary in being generous with their time and enthusiastic in their encouragement and support. Temples, I believe them to be, where knowledge and truth can be found.

The libraries that rewarded my time include the New York Public Library, the New-York Historical Society, the Fort Montgomery Museum, the Sterling Forest Visitors Center at Sterling Forest State Park, Washington's Headquarters State Historic Site and Hasbrouck House in Newburgh, New York, the Putnam History Museum in Cold Spring, New York, the Historical Society of the Town of Warwick, New York, and Cornell University's Krock Rare Books Library (for Machin's map). I am grateful to them all. A special tip of the hat goes to Grant Miller, Executive Director of Fort Montgomery Museum, whose interest in my project and readiness to assist in exploiting the historical records he maintains was amazing and deeply appreciated. And to Don N. Hagist, Managing Editor of the distinguished publication, *The Journal of the American Revolution*, who led the way in my research to uncover Machin's desertion from the British Foot, and cast his critical eye and deep knowledge over the essay I submitted on the subject of the chains for publication in that journal.

As with my three previous scribblings, Karen Shepard, Professor at Williams College and author of several highly regarded novels, gave me wise insights and suggestions for improvement in the drafts she reviewed. And my wife, Clara, read the next to last draft and gave me valuable reactions which I have tried to reflect.

I also wish here to acknowledge with appreciation the art work of Noah Saterstrom, a highly talented artist from Nashville, and the layout work of Tony Bonds, who operates under the intriguing business handle "Golden Ratio Book Design."

Finally, I want to pay tribute to the inspiration behind my imagining, for the first time, around 2002, the possibility of writing an historical novel. It was my friend and mentor Walter Lord, now long deceased, whose dedication to research and immense skill in story-telling, produced many acclaimed books of history, including the unforgettable *Night to Remember*. I miss him often and regret that he never knew what an inspiration to my writing efforts he was and remains.